The Best Short Stories 2025

The Best Short Stories 2025

The O. Henry Prize Winners

Guest Editor:
Edward P. Jones

Series Editor:
Jenny Minton Quigley

Vintage Books
A Division of Penguin Random House LLC
New York

A VINTAGE BOOKS ORIGINAL 2025

*Copyright © 2025 by Vintage Books,
a division of Penguin Random House LLC
Foreword copyright © 2025 by Jenny Minton Quigley
Introduction copyright © 2025 by Edward P. Jones*

Penguin Random House values and supports copyright. Copyright fuels creativity, encourages diverse voices, promotes free speech, and creates a vibrant culture. Thank you for buying an authorized edition of this book and for complying with copyright laws by not reproducing, scanning, or distributing any part of it in any form without permission. You are supporting writers and allowing Penguin Random House to continue to publish books for every reader. Please note that no part of this book may be used or reproduced in any manner for the purpose of training artificial intelligence technologies or systems.

Published by Vintage Books, a division of Penguin Random House LLC, 1745 Broadway, New York, NY 10019.

Vintage Books and colophon are registered trademarks of Penguin Random House LLC.

Permissions credits appear at the end of the book.

Vintage Books Trade Paperback ISBN: 978-0-593-68960-8
eBook ISBN: 978-0-593-68963-9

penguinrandomhouse.com | vintagebooks.com

Printed in the United States of America
1st Printing

The authorized representative in the EU for product safety and compliance is Penguin Random House Ireland, Morrison Chambers, 32 Nassau Street, Dublin D02 YH68, Ireland, https://eu-contact.penguin.ie.

*For the memory of my mother,
Jeanette M. Jones, my first teacher*
—Edward P. Jones

Contents

Foreword • xi
   Jenny Minton Quigley

Introduction • xv
   Edward P. Jones

The Stackpole Legend • 3
   Wendell Berry, *The Threepenny Review*

The Arrow • 13
   Gina Chung, *One Story*

That Girl • 30
   Addie Citchens, *The New Yorker*

The Pleasure of a Working Life • 54
   Michael Deagler, *Harper's Magazine*

Blackbirds • 76
   Lindsey Drager, *Colorado Review*

Hearing Aids • 90
   Clyde Edgerton, *Oxford American*

Sanrevelle • 95
   Dave Eggers, *The Georgia Review*

Stump of the World • 120
   Madeline ffitch, *The Paris Review*

Shotgun Calypso • 137
   Indya Finch, *A Public Space*

City Girl • 154
   Alice Hoffman, *Harvard Review*

Sickled • 162
   Jane Kalu, *American Short Fiction*

The Spit of Him • **188**
   Thomas Korsgaard, translated from the Danish by Martin Aitken, *The New Yorker*

Winner • 204
   Ling Ma, *The Yale Review*

Countdown • 220
   Anthony Marra, *Zoetrope*

Just Another Family • 236
   Lori Ostlund, *New England Review*

Mornings at the Ministry • 281
   Ehsaneh Sadr, *Ploughshares*

Rosaura at Dawn • 301
  Daniel Saldaña París, translated from the Spanish by
  Christina MacSweeney, *The Yale Review*

Three Niles • 308
  Zak Salih, *The Kenyon Review*

Strange Fruit • 328
  Yah Yah Scholfield, *Southern Humanities Review*

Miracle in Lagos Traffic • 333
  Chika Unigwe, *Michigan Quarterly Review*

The O. Henry Prize Winners 2025:
  The Writers on Their Work • 343
Publisher's Note: A Brief History of the O. Henry Prize • 363
How the Stories Are Chosen • 367
Acknowledgments • 369
Publications Submitted • 371
Permissions • 393

Foreword

Last summer, as our guest editor was reading through a hefty box of stories to select his 2025 O. Henry Prize winners, *The New York Times* announced their list of the one hundred best books of the twenty-first century. Can you guess whose work was voted the best work of fiction by an American writer in the 2000s? Of course, the answer is our guest editor Edward P. Jones, who appears on the list twice: first with his Pulitzer Prize–winning novel, *The Known World* (2003), listed at number 4, and again with his story collection *All Aunt Hagar's Children* (2006) at number 70.

To highlight his prestigious showing on the list, renowned *New York Times* critic A. O. Scott traveled to Washington, D.C., for an interview with Jones. A quarter of the way into our current century, a writer like Jones, who is not on social media or regularly out promoting himself, might seem to occupy a more distant place in the literary firmament than showier and more recently arisen stars. The headline of Scott's piece is "Visiting an Elusive Writer, and Revisiting His Masterpiece." A historical novel, *The Known World* revolves around a Black slave owner in nineteenth-century Virginia, and Scott assumed it had been heavily researched. But while listening to Jones, Scott suddenly understood: "My mistake had been assuming that the novel, which feels absolutely true on every page, was in some way an empirical achievement, rather than a triumph of imagination. Repeatedly in our conversation, Jones asserted the fiction-writer's freedom—his delight and also his duty—to make things up."

Marveling at the ways writers make things up is on Edward P. Jones's mind these days. Throughout this delightful year spent observing him at work selecting the 2025 O. Henry Prize winners, it's been clear to me his objective is to find the kinds of truth that only that "fiction-writer's freedom" to invent, shape, communicate, and testify can yield. The stories he's chosen are indeed triumphs of imagination that ring truer in our hearts and minds than any thin facsimiles of reality we've come to accept as substitutes for the real thing in an age saturated with cheap information.

Jones has won two O. Henry Prizes for stories published in *The New Yorker* and included in *All Aunt Hagar's Children*. Small miracles of the imagination appear throughout his collection. Describing Jones's writing won't do it justice, so I will include just a few examples. From the opening story, "In the Blink of God's Eye": "They stood there for a long time, time enough for the moon to hop from one tree across the road to another. The moon shone silver through all the trees . . . most generous with the silver where it fell, and even the places where it had not shone had a grayness pleasant and almost anticipatory, as if the moon were saying, I'll be over to you as soon as I can." Really you can open to any page. From "Old Boys, Old Girls": "He was not insane, but he was three doors from it, which was how an old girlfriend, Yvonne Miller, would now and again playfully refer to his behavior." Even out of context, these lines soar, and what they do in context—well, you can imagine.

Reading Edward P. Jones while corresponding with him this year has been a thrill. He has a strong yet modest voice and an observant, accepting sense of humor. When I wrote to him about

"In the Blink of God's Eye," he responded, "Once I knew the story I wanted to tell, it became somewhat fun. I didn't know anyone who was in D.C. in 1901, so I just had to go with what I knew the country had at that time—like little gas lights at the end of corners and people relying on horses for travel. And at the center I could see in my mind that this young woman loved that guy and was happy to go across the Potomac to a foreign country to be with him. The phrase 'You can't make that stuff up' is simply not true." Jones is an illuminator. To use his own phrase, he is "generous with the silver." When we notified the winners, it was remarkable how many said they were inspired by his writing.

Separated by a century, Edward P. Jones and O. Henry share a desire to expose the truth by turning phoniness inside out and shaking out its contents. In O. Henry's story "One Dollar's Worth," a counterfeit coin made of lead is used to save the day. In "Old Boys, Old Girls," Jones conjures new life from old relics. "The girl had once seen her aunt juggle six coins. . . . It had been quite a show. The aunt had shown the six pieces to the girl—they had been old and heavy one-dollar silver coins, huge monster things, which nobody made anymore."

Are we making real magic anymore? Last summer was also when I discovered artificial intelligence in service of celebratory toast-making. A grandson gave a sweet tribute to his grandmother at her birthday party. Later his mother told me that ChatGPT wrote it. The next month several of us plugged details about a friend into ChatGPT to churn out a sentimental toast for her wedding. The program strings together coined phrases like "in hindsight," "in all seriousness," and "May your love continue to shine brightly" to sweeten its sauce. But it's full of clichés and as light as confetti. It can't be true. Perhaps the future of creative writing is what AI cannot overhear, as it has yet to be spoken. In the "Writers on Their Work" section at the back of this book, so many of this year's winners describe their imaginations at play in the writing process, in ways that no chatbot could imitate.

What lies in the pages ahead are not brilliant writers showing off what they know or what they have overheard, but true stories they have dreamed up out of nothing and turned into weighty silver dollars, coins that shine under Jones's moon as it hops from story to story, "as if the moon were saying, I'll be over to you as soon as I can."

Jenny Minton Quigley
November 2024

Introduction

There were small reasons, there were large reasons that I was reluctant to be the guest editor for *The Best Short Stories 2025: The O. Henry Prize Winners*. I had not been keeping up with the world of published short stories and felt incapable of judging what was now being created and shared in the magazines not only in the United States but in other countries as well. Now and again, I had come across work that I did not care for, that I thought might be representative of what was currently popular—extremely short pieces, in some cases, works catering to societies of folks too busy to take in substantive structures, works that were just Snapchats, works that were, as William Faulkner said, "not of the heart but of the glands." There was, for example, a "story" about a woman sitting in a Starbucks-like shop watching people come and go as they bought sweetened swill—line after line of bland descriptions of people buying. Then, as if the writer had grown tired, the piece ended after two pages. That was it.

And I feared "stories" like the one read by an author who once participated with me at a festival. To explain what he had written and to help the audience see the grandness of his work, this guy relied on a giant screen on which various images were projected. I kept wondering what he would do if he read in a place where there was no electricity. Would the audience understand what he was saying? Can there be light in darkness when all you have is your voice and the hope that your characters, your people, are living and loving and dying for that audience?

I shuddered to think I would have to read things like that, stories of glands and pitiful magic, to plow through such things to find jewels. I was most fortunate, however, to work with the O. Henry series editor, Jenny Minton Quigley, who knew far more about what was being published and wanted to share much of it with me. We are not always the best judges of what is out there in our world; sometimes it helps to have a guide who goes out far beyond the front door.

So I have come with these twenty stories, and rightful and legitimate stories they are. Travel for a while in a canoe with the paralegal Hop in Dave Eggers's "Sanrevelle." Hop, who lives and works in a nearly empty forty-story office building, is rowing out in the waters around the Golden Gate Bridge. It is dark. It is Christmastime. Boats of festive people all around. Without a light in the canoe, Hop, though he may not fully understand it himself, is rowing not only to find the no-nonsense Sanrevelle, but to discover something, inaccessible until now, within himself. Hop may not know it, but we, his reader-passengers, do.

This journey without the heart fully understanding its ultimate mission is perhaps a part of all these twenty stories. The narrator, a young woman, in Jane Kalu's "Sickled," lives with her sister weighed down by sickle cell anemia, a weight that ironically lifts her ever to life, something that the narrator, living in their house of "dread," does not always see. And bear witness to a different kind of dread in Lindsey Drager's "Blackbirds," a wondrous portrait of an asthmatic eight-year-old girl forced to care for her baby brother in a house where their mother has abandoned all duties and their father is away. The house she lives in is an eerie one, mostly because the girl cannot be a child and has had to morph into something far beyond her capabilities.

Children not allowed childhood is also part of Addie Citchens's "That Girl," whose precious Shirlee reminded me of the girl Linda in the movie *Days of Heaven*—a child whose life is about to fall into a sad horror. She has learned to carve out a little place for herself in her topsy-turvy world, but that place has not much of a foundation, and Citchens does not flinch when showing us what that foundation is made of. And like "That Girl," Thomas Korsgaard's "The Spit of Him" reminded me of another child in another work of art—James Joyce's story "Araby." Korsgaard's Danish Kevin sets out on a rainy evening to sell "stickers" to help Save the Children and discovers something new and unfortunate about his father, and that something is a thing he cannot yet grasp at that moment in his life. Kevin, making his way in a world of cold rain, is as confused as Joyce's narrator standing in a nearly empty Dublin bazaar. Those boys are cousins to the one in Zak Salih's "Three Niles," as well as to the sisters in "Shotgun Calypso" by Indya Finch, who take a mad trip with Ma from one sketchy world to another one, just as sketchy in its own way.

There were some stories that I reacted to in a primarily emotional, visceral way... Like Chika Unigwe's "Miracle in Lagos Traffic," with a grieving mother doing something she knows rationally she should not, but in her new world the rules have changed... Like Ling Ma's "Winner," with a young woman who perhaps learns that the only way to know the new her is to visit the place of the old her... Like Daniel Saldaña París's "Rosaura at Dawn," with another woman out to find peace... Like Ehsaneh Sadr's "Mornings at the Ministry," with a man not easy to like, but certainly a man one can understand. And like the haunting "Strange Fruit" by Yah Yah Scholfield; the story is no doubt inspired by the poem and song written by Abel Meeropol, a song sung heartbreakingly by Billie Holiday, about Southern lynchings.

Many of the writers in this volume I, unfortunately, had never read before, but there are three I knew fairly well—Wendell Berry, Alice Hoffman, and Clyde Edgerton. Berry, with "The Stackpole

Legend," gives us the well-built, old-fashioned storytelling that teaches us all over again about Faulkner's "old verities and truths of the heart," and those things are eternal. The story, in its way, is simple enough, but the people are solid and they are made all the more so because Berry's language is poetry ("Stump's father passed from the light and air down into his grave"), and truthful poetry puts echoes in our heads.

All of these twenty stories are, in one way or another, about families, even Edgerton's "Hearing Aids," in which Forrest looks over his life to try to find someone to bequeath his aids to. "The Arrow" by Gina Chung has a mother and her twenty-something daughter coming together at a most difficult time for the daughter, proving that stern mothers can love and teach without offering a bunch of empty words. That surprising element appears with "Stump of the World" by Madeline ffitch in a crazy relationship between a struggling mother and her thieving son; watch him take his mother's hand and lead her "to the center of the earth." And settle into Hoffman's "City Girl," with a stepfather who is just what a girl needs in a New York City that is sometimes ready to pounce and devour.

In the 1990s, I read an article about bombs going off daily in Beirut. The article reported on the horrors people were suffering, to be sure, but there was a paragraph about how bombs shredded the leaves and limbs of trees. The death of trees was probably something considered. I felt something similar with Anthony Marra's "Countdown." We know perhaps a good deal about the Russian invasion of Ukraine and what it means for the people, but Marra's heartbreaking story looks at the Russians who want no part of what the government is doing.

That "oh wow" factor also happens with Gary Minihan in "The Pleasure of a Working Life" by Michael Deagler. Gary has worked for thirty-five years for the Postal Service. Yep, that place. Gary is the best evidence that the most profound characters can come out of the simplest places.

By far, the longest story in this volume is Lori Ostlund's "Just Another Family." It is lush storytelling, even down to the "minor" characters who are onstage for just a few moments, and when you have finished it, there is the feeling that you have read a novel, so vast is the landscape and so many are the characters. An entire place in Minnesota created in a short space appealed to a man who collects Japanese netsukes and American stamps—those tiny things offer whole worlds. Ostlund's story, like the other nineteen stories in this volume, is what I call fiction that is true, offering solid portraits of human endeavor, with all its ups and downs. The fiction that is false, untrue, is that bland stuff created from the glands, created by people who were taught that all one needs to write is a dictionary and a thesaurus.

These twenty stories do not require something fancy like a projector and a big screen. These twenty show what happens when writers fish in the rivers of their own imagination.

Edward P. Jones
Washington, D.C.
November 2024

The Best Short Stories 2025

Wendell Berry
The Stackpole Legend

Once in time, as Art Rowanberry would put it, a boy, the only child of a couple advanced in years, entered the world in the neighborhood of Port William, to be distinguished after his second day by the name of Delinthus Stackpole.

His name did him no harm until he started to school, when some of his fellow boys took too much pleasure in repeating it while pointing at him with their forefingers, but the harm of that he overlooked. For teasing to be effective, the teasee must recognize that he is being teased. The young Delinthus Stackpole recognized no such thing. He went his way, not noticing, smiling evidently at something farther on. He was not teased.

His peers then, of course, undertook to molest him physically, which brought forth another revelation: he was not pushed. He was a mild, good-humored boy, big for his age. He was not overtall but not short, not fat but wide and thick. The bulk of him may have suggested that he was soft, therefore pushable. But when his peers put their hands on him, they found him to be solid. He had a way of entirely filling up his clothes, sometimes overfilling them, for he grew fast. When the pushers pushed him, and he remained standing on his big feet exactly where he was when they started, only smiling upon them as if bestowing a kind interest in their activities, they permanently shortened his name to Stump.

At the age of fourteen, when he finished the eighth grade and emerged at last from school into the unobstructed world, he was as full-grown as he was going to get, and there was a lot of him.

From a time shortly after he learned to walk, he had served his father as a hand—a third hand, you might say, and sometimes as two extra feet. By the time he was out of school, his father, as he freely confessed, could not get along without him. He could do any of the work his father could do and, by then, more of it. For this was yet another revelation. His peers, who thought because he was so bulky he would be slow at work, were obliged to notice from somewhere behind him that he was fast, and remarkably nimble for one so large. He was not outworked, just as he was not teased and not pushed.

You might say that he was gifted in body, but as if to make up for that he was markedly deficient in speech. He was not mute or tongue-tied, but seemed perhaps constitutionally to be at a loss for words. He struggled to speak. Since he was by nature a person of good will, it was both natural and reasonable that when at all possible he spoke by smiling.

Or perhaps he simply was in the habit of not speaking. He was an only child, longed for and late come. Though he learned to talk eventually, mostly he did not need to, for his mother anticipated his needs and wants often before he knew he had them. When he accompanied and then helped his father at work, his father did the necessary talking, and the boy, being a person of good will and bodily gifted, learned to anticipate his father's instructions. And the Stackpoles were somewhat isolated, for the long lane up Owl Hollow ended at their farm. Though his parents maintained the customary relations with their neighbors, until he started to school the young Delinthus lived most of his life in a society of three. And so when he came at last into the schoolroom to face one question after another asked directly of him, he may well have been astonished into speechlessness. At any rate, to say something, he had to begin by saying nothing.

As a boy among the other boys, once he gained their respect and became Stump, he got along very well. The rough games the boys played at recess and walking home after school required, really, nothing in the way of speech, and in the freedom of their play the other boys said so much, and at such volume, that the silence of only one of them was not noticeable. But several years had passed before the Stackpole boy said anything, if even as little as possible, to a girl.

After Stump began farming all day every day with his father, their relationship slowly altered in the way of nature. At first Stump worked for his father, and at last his father worked for him. This immemorial change was accomplished without any particular attention needing to be paid to it. Their farm's business at the Independent Farmers Bank of Port William had long been conducted under the single name of Stackpole. Though by Stump's time the Stackpole family was old in Port William, it had never been numerous. The male line in fact had stayed so thin that a Stackpole man had rarely needed a first name. Stump had needed to be Delinthus only to give him a sort of normality in the eyes of Professor Skelton, monarch of the school, who otherwise identified the boys by the length of the switch he needed for their instruction. And so when he came of age, Stump inscribed "Stackpole" on a piece of paper for Mr. Fawker, monarch of the Independent Farmers Bank of Port William, who looked upon him with favor, for Stackpole deposited more frequently than he withdrew.

In the way of nature, Stump's father passed from the light and air down into his grave in the Stackpole plot on the hill at Port William. And then Stump and his mother were a society of two. In the way of immemorial tradition, Stump's mother kept the house and Stump kept the farm, with passages back and forth as help was needed. As things had gone a while ago with Stump and his father, his mother eventually began to do less of the housekeeping and Stump more of it, until at last he was doing all of it. The old lady had gone for the last time to bed. And then for a while, with help from a neighbor's dutiful boy, Winky Hample, and now and again the neighbors, Stump kept the farm, kept the house, and nursed his mother until she occupied her place beside his father on the hill at Port William.

And so Stump was left to make his way somewhat deliberately to appreciation of the present world's first piece of good advice: "It is not good that the man should be alone." Stump could boil and he could fry. He could wash thoroughly and iron approximately. He could, within five to fifteen minutes, thread a needle. Hittingly and missingly he could sew on a button. Only scandalously could he stitch or patch. He could not darn. Using, like his mother, the bunched and bound tail feathers of a tom turkey, he kept exposed surfaces free of dust. He did not mind dirt too much as long as it stayed on the floor.

It came to him at first from time to time, and then more often, that he needed a woman, a wife, a helpmeet for him. And of course he looked upon his need with dread and bewilderment, for he knew the ways of the world. To get a wife, he would have to look about, find a young woman more or less his own age, offer his attention to her, in various ways make himself agreeable to her, with the hope that she would consent to be his wife. But for that he knew himself to be a man far too shutmouthed. For far too long he had talked only when he had to. Now suddenly, for the first time in his life, he wanted to.

He saw he would have to practice. And so he began. When he was at work and knew himself to be safely alone, he began, speaking aloud, to tell himself what he was doing. Since he liked his work and knew what he was talking about, he found that the words soon began to come to him fairly freely, as if by their own will. He found himself listening to himself attentively, with an unaffected interest in what he had to say.

One day when he was plowing his tobacco with a rastus plow and the good mule he called Bud, he was so absorbed in his work and his ongoing commentary that he did not see his friend and sometime helper, Winky Hample, until Winky spoke. "Who you talking to, Stump?"

"Whoa!" Stump said.

He said, "Wellsir, Winky, I was talking to old Bud here. He misses old Buck. He gets lonesome working out here by himself. So I talk to him to kindly keep him company."

And so there was some risk in the practice by which he was converting himself into a man who had something to say. But when he was caught, almost always by Winky Hample, he was surprised by how readily he improvised his excuses. "Why," he said to himself, "you're turning into a regular jaybird for conversation."

That year went along and went along, and his confidence grew. At church on Sunday mornings he looked about him like the good stockman he was, sizing up the several still-available women of about his age and somewhat younger. He did not stare. His gaze went over them passingly, comparing them and taking sharp note of their qualities and attributes.

He owned a very presentable, everyday sort of saddle horse, old Bill, broke to harness and fit to draw a buggy. But when he cast his eye over the buggy that had served his parents, he saw that it would not do. It was visibly worn out, cracked and sagging, and speckled with sparrow droppings. So one morning he saddled Bill, rode him down to Hargrave, and drove him home in a new set of harness, hitched to a new buggy. Remembering his mother's care for such things, he looked at his best clothes hanging in the closet, and he flinched somewhat before shutting the door. On his next trip to Hargrave he bought himself a new Sunday suit, black of course, and a black tie and a white shirt. He was getting ready, you see, looking ahead, looking around, foreseeing problems, anticipating needs. When he wondered how he and his old house might look to a young woman, he found the going hard. He asked himself a lot of questions beginning "How do you reckon . . ."

At church his eye fixed upon a young woman somewhat, in fact a good deal, younger than he was, whose last name he pronounced with great favor and perhaps with envy. Jones. She was Kizzie Jones, not bad looking at all. She looked alert. She carried her head not high, but up. She appeared to be good-humored, for he often saw her smiling or laughing. She had size. She looked strong. She had about her the glow of exuberant health that stockmen call "bloom." But there was something else too, something he did not see, but felt. He felt it strongly. When he was feeling it, he felt his heart clinch like a fist, and it ached. He was as innocent of illness as a freshly laid egg. Nothing so far had prepared him for such an internal event. Several times he wondered if it could kill a man.

As I recall this story of Stump Stackpole out of the story of old Port William, which was told off and on a few sentences at a time in Port William's unstopping conversation about itself, I am wondering how a young woman who was clearly such a prize had so far escaped the claim of a man more usual than Stump. Rather than speculate, I will tell what I know: that Kizzie was precisely the middle child in a generation of Joneses that, besides her, consisted of eight brothers, the older of whom had done at least their share in raising her, the younger of whom she had done more than her share in raising. The eight Jones brothers, by now down to the youngest, were not small or backward, were known as pretty good old boys but also as somewhat dangerous to mess with. The man who might have reached out his hand for Kizzie might have become overly fond of his hand.

Stump's advantage, simply, was that it did not occur to him either to mess with the Jones brothers or to fear them. It was nonetheless with some agitation that he made his first direct approach to Kizzie. He wrote out his opening speech, memorized it, and put the piece of paper in his pocket in case of need.

On Sunday morning when church was over, he caught Kizzie's

attention by means of a little bow, which stopped her and caused her to look straight at him. He said, "Miss Kizzie, could I ask you, if you please, if I could come get you this afternoon and take you for a ride in my buggy?"

For a moment he felt himself pushed backward by the force of his question, but he held his ground. He received from Kizzie then, as it seemed to him, a very pretty smile.

She said, "Yes. Ask me."

It took him a while to compose his next speech. "If I was to, would you?"

"Yes," she said.

And so in about the middle of that afternoon, Stump drove old Bill and the new buggy up to the Joneses' front gate. He tied Bill to a gate post, which was only a formality, for Bill, who was always willing to go, was always willing to stop. Stump shook himself, walked to the front door, and knocked.

When Mrs. Jones came to the door, she smiled at Stump and then called over her shoulder into the house, "Kizzie? Here he is."

As he escorted Kizzie across the yard to the buggy, having decided not to take hold of her elbow, Stump tried to walk in a manner that was both deferential and protective. He knew however that, as a gentleman, he was expected to help the lady into the buggy, and he did then take hold of her arm just above the elbow. Fearing to grip too tightly, and perhaps also too eager to help, he caused his hand to slide up her arm until he felt with the backs of his fingers a fullness and softness from which he quickly slid his hand back down. "Scuse me," he said. "I didn't mean nothing by it."

And Kizzie said, "I didn't think you did."

When Stump had untied Bill and come to his side of the buggy to get in, he was pleased to see that Kizzie had picked up the lines and so put herself in charge, to assure his safety as he was climbing in. When he was seated, she handed the lines to him, and he thanked her.

They drove upriver along the river road. The road then was only a pair of wagon tracks that forded the creeks and skirted the slues, passing through the fields of the broad bottomlands and now and again through patches of woodland. In the wintertime the road would be interrupted by mudholes and seasonal swamps. But by this time in the late spring the ground had solidified, and Bill drew the buggy easily and soundlessly along.

For a while Stump kept silent, allowing Kizzie the opportunity to be first to speak. This she declined. She seemed perfectly comfortable in riding along in silence, looking about at the country slowly revealing itself as they passed into it. Finally Stump thought somebody ought to be talking. Since it was left to him, he took up conversation as he had practiced it when he was by himself.

In a way perhaps charming, he told Kizzie about his crops and how they were faring. And then he told her about his cattle and his flock of sheep and his ways of caring for them. And then he told her about the twin calves born in early spring, both of whom had lived and were thriving. And then he told her about his foxhounds, going on at some length about the master hound he called old Cap. She listened, nodding and smiling, and her smiles, it seemed to him, were at times accompanied by too many teeth. At times he thought he could see jawteeth. Perhaps because of her interest in hearing more, she did not interrupt. He carried on bravely, conducting the conversation the best he could by himself, grateful to be sustained by his curiosity as to what he might say.

He did, however, wish that she would say something. His defense against the encroaching silence came to be afflicted with uneasiness as he enlarged his description of his farm and its contents, of his work, its results, and its prospects—thereby giving his listener a far better description of himself than he would have dared to offer her on purpose. But he began to be afraid that if he stopped talking nobody would talk. And so he talked, pursued by his fear of silence.

For some time the pressure he was feeling exteriorly had been accompanied by a pressure growing inwardly. Presently he was aware that the pressure within him was increasing faster than the pressure closing around him. It occurred to him that the trouble in his inwards might have been the result of the stress, entirely new to him, that had befallen him with his love for Kizzie Jones, or it might have been something he ate. As a stockman, anyhow, he readily identified his affliction as bloat or wind, and he knew it to be portentous of the worst sort of damage. And there was no use in speculating about the cause when the effect had become urgent.

He was dumbfounded at last. He began to sweat. The mere moisture became drops that ran down his face. He wiped them off his forehead with the back of his hand. He blew them off his upper lip and the end of his nose. He had never imagined that such a thing could happen to him and so of course he had never imagined anything that might be done about it. No doubt only desperation could have made him think of his pistol.

Among the several disciplines of his trade, he was a sheepman, a shepherd, ever mindful that his tender flock was at the mercy of an ignorant dog or a dog gone wrong. And so he was never far from a firearm of some kind, often his father's forty-four-caliber revolver, a mighty weapon, which he happened to have brought along on that day's fateful ride.

At the final, the ultimate, clinch of his crisis, he got out the pistol from under the seat, aimed it at the sky, drew back the hammer, pulled the trigger, and it misfired. After the puny snap of its hammer, the pistol's silence partook of the silence of the morning before creation. But a great blast nevertheless had come forth, a rippit that, to Stump's ear, seemed to tear the silence like a bolt of lightning—except that it did not have the rapidity of lightning. Grown exquisitely sensitive, he suffered its reverberation among the surrounding hills. He continued to stare, transfixed, at the place in the sky at which he was still aiming the pistol. Old Bill drew the buggy onward, and Stump rocked with its motion as rigidly as if cast in bronze.

And then he heard from somewhere nearby a most beautiful sound. It was the sound of a young woman freely laughing. He turned his head then and looked. He looked out through the glow of his face that was as hot and red as a stewed tomato. Still holding the pistol at arm's length, pointing at the sky, he saw that Kizzie Jones was still there, looking back at him. She was the young woman who was laughing. She said, "Mr. Stackpole, what is the matter with your pistol?"

Stump heard from his own throat then a sound that he did not recognize, a sob perhaps, or maybe a strangle. But the next sound he heard was that of himself laughing.

After that, they were acquainted. After that, Nature and then the preacher laid the way clearly before them. The story of Stump and Kizzie Stackpole continued a long time on their good farm at the head of Owl Hollow and in the conversation of old Port William. They brought into the world a daughter and four sons, as healthy and hardy as themselves. They taught their children to work in support of their family and their farm. When the time came, by hard work and hard thrift, feeling that they could do no less, they sent their children away to school. The boys, owing to their homemade discipline and their schooling, found ready employment, for good money, in the city. Not waiting for success to find them at home, they went in search of it, and found it, to their satisfaction, in the world of the future, a long way from the old life they had lived as children. Only the daughter, Anna Lee, came home; married, I believe, one of the forefathers of Grover Gibbs; and cared for her parents to the end of their days.

It has been many a year since anybody in the country around Port William has answered to the name of Stackpole.

Gina Chung
The Arrow

It starts like this: you, staring at the stick balanced precariously on the edge of your bathroom sink and praying, *Please, God, I'll do anything*, but you can't think of what to say after that, what to offer that might be a fair trade for not being pregnant. When the pink cross appears, it feels like a confirmation of what you've known all along—that God, if he exists, does not give a shit.

But once your initial panic subsides and you've managed to catch your breath, you begin to feel tender toward it, this unasked-for clump of new cells that seems so determined to live. You find that you sleep better at night, comforted by the presence taking root in your body, unfurling itself one piece of genetic information at a time. You buy yourself fresh fruit and vegetables at the market. You take vitamins. You hold yourself more carefully on the subway.

This is ridiculous, you think, but instead of making a decision, you go looking for signs. You decide you'll start believing in anything, just to get some kind of guidance on what to do about the baby. You pay an astrologer in Bushwick $200 to squint at a computer printout that has your date, time, and place of birth stamped on it in smeared ink, even though your time of birth is just a guess you hazarded because you didn't want to call and ask your mother, who raised you all by herself in your father's absence and has never let you forget it. The astrologer, a girl a few years younger than you who has one pierced eyebrow and goes by Citrine, tells you that you have a strong propensity toward self-sabotage. That your fire moon and water sun are conspiring against each other. When you ask her about babies, she says that motherhood won't come naturally to you but that you're destined to raise three strong boys at some point in your future, which sounds depressing and inaccurate.

You go to an ayahuasca ceremony with your friend Melissa at someone's apartment in Gowanus, a huge one-bedroom with bumpy white walls and flickering candles everywhere, and at the last minute, decide not to drink the tea offered to you. You sit back and watch, feeling embarrassed when Melissa starts to channel a spirit that makes her sob and call out for her mother. On the subway ride back home, you see an old Asian woman wearing plastic bags on her feet asleep on the seat across from you, her purse agape. Before you get off the train, you tuck a ten-dollar bill inside her purse and zip its mouth closed. She does not really look like your mother, but these days, any Asian woman over the age of sixty looks like your mother to you.

You go to church for the first time in years. You avoid making eye contact with anyone who nods or smiles in your direction and practically flee at the conclusion of the service. You come back, not during the afternoon service for twenty-to-forty–somethings, but to the sparsely attended early morning service where it's mostly older people. You screw your eyes shut and try to picture God as the warm, healing ball of divine light and energy that Melissa told you she saw once during an acid trip out in the Arizona desert, not as the bearded white man in the clouds that you imagined scowling at your pee stick just before it went positive. But all you see is bursts of color in the dark behind your eyelids.

You remember how, as a child, you used to mash the heels of your hands into your closed eyelids to make colors appear in that dark. How, whenever your mother hit you with the back of her hand, you could close your eyes and conjure those blossoms of light in your mind, like fireworks seen through a dirty window, or anemones in dark water.

When you open your eyes, all you see is the backs of old people's heads, nodding in their separate pews, and the spit flecks flying from the pastor's mouth.

Here are the facts: you are not in any way ready to have a baby, living paycheck to paycheck in an apartment you cannot afford, in a city that feels increasingly unfamiliar to you.

But everywhere you turn, the world seems ready to convince you otherwise. The neighbors who move into the unit across from yours, a small family—a wife, a husband, and their two children, all four of them red-cheeked and thick-limbed and smiley—make your teeth ache with loneliness. You listen to the patter of the children's footsteps and the babble of their high baby voices and wonder if they are happy. The father is friendly and the mother avoids you, her eyes rarely meeting yours when you stop to hold the door open for her and the multiple tote bags she is perpetually carrying. She always seems tired, and her fatigue feels like a rebuke to yours, you who have so few responsibilities or obligations to anyone and fulfill them so badly.

Here are some more facts: you are pregnant, and you do not know exactly who the father is because, in the span of one bad week, you slept with your ex, a chef whose late hours you still haven't unlearned; your married coworker who says he and his wife are experimenting with ethical non-monogamy; and a tattoo artist you met in a cheesy bar in Williamsburg. This all took place in the days after you called home for the first time in a year to wish your mother a happy birthday and she hung up on you.

Sleeping with your ex was easy enough, like climbing back onto a bike after falling off. After you finished most of a bottle of peach-flavored soju, doing plasticky shots alone in your dusty kitchen, you called him at two in the morning when you knew he'd be buzzed on cognac and cigarettes and just getting off work. He came over with a Styrofoam container of miso and honey chili-brined chicken wings and you licked the sweet-salty glaze off each other's fingers and gnawed all the bones clean. He always liked that you were an eater, didn't care if your stomach protruded after a good meal or that the upper sections of your arms had grown soft and fleshy in the months since you'd left one another. Afterward, he fucked you on your secondhand couch. The floorboards creaked and the couch springs screamed, and you worried that the family next door might hear, until you did not care anymore. In the morning he was gone, without leaving so much as a stray hair on the couch cushions, and then you threw up peach-flavored chunks in the bathroom until your body felt as light and hollow as the discarded chicken bones at the bottom of your trash can.

Your coworker you fucked in the women's bathroom at work, long after everyone else had gone home. He made small, grateful sounds as he moved in and out of you, which made you feel so generous you let him finish inside you, telling him that you were on the pill, even though you are negligent about taking your doses at the same time each day. "Megan hasn't let me do that in ages," he said, his damp mouth pressed to your neck, and you wanted to shake him off, annoyed at the mention of his wife, a woman you've met once or twice at office holiday parties. You remember her being tall, pink-skinned, and honey-haired, with freckles and an athletic glow about her. You wonder if he has ever tried to count all the freckles on her face and shoulders, or played connect the dots on them with his tongue. You don't want to feel guilty about Megan, but you do.

You went home with the tattoo artist after he let you win at darts at a bar, and because he had an appealingly crooked smile, one gold tooth flashing in the back of his mouth like a star. In his dimly lit apartment, the walls washed with red neon from the gas station sign outside, you traced the lines of his tattoos with your fingers, the teeth and talons and feathers and leaves inked all over his arms and chest, and he told you how much each one hurt; how the pain eventually starts feeling so intense you can get high from it; how afterward, for a few hours, colors seem brighter and everything is louder. Before you left, he said you should call him if you ever wanted to get the tattoo you'd told him you were thinking about, a slim arrow pointing down the length of your forearm.

"Where is it supposed to be pointing?" he asked, and you hesitated before answering.

For much of your life, you have been driven toward success because that was the only surefire way to get out from under your mother. In school you learned that sharks die if they don't keep moving, and you followed the same principle, applying for scholarship after scholarship and working as many side jobs as you could fit into your schedule, all in the name of leaving your tiny, smog-choked Southern California town behind. You thought of your fear as a golden arrow that pointed outward from the dark surrounding your mother's house, a beam that led you away from orange smoke and bumper-to-bumper traffic on the freeway and endless sunshine and rotting fruit on sidewalks, toward a future where you were no one's daughter, where the only dreams and desires you had to follow were your own.

Whenever you call home, your mother berates you for leaving her, for not coming to visit, in the same breath that she starts accusing you of stealing from her—her money, her youth, her life. She tells you that God is watching you, that he knows what you are up to. When you hang up, your hands shake and you have to stay drunk for several days.

But this is all too much to tell a one-time hookup, and so you lie and tell him that the arrow represents your zodiac sign, and he tells you that he has the same one, isn't that funny?

You wonder what sign this baby will be born under. If it is born. You do the math in your head, decide it'll be an early spring baby. "Summer is the worst time to have a child," your mother always said, as though you yourself were not born in the middle of July.

This is what your friends say: that you are crazy for even thinking about having it. All of them make more money than you, their arrows pointing them toward bigger and better and more expensive futures than yours. Diana and her girlfriend are saving up for in vitro. Sujin wants to have two kids and move to Long Island but is waiting to make partner at her law firm before she starts trying with Andy. Melissa is engaged to a software engineer who goes to Burning Man with her every year.

You are sure that all of them talk about you behind your back in hushed, pitying tones—your primarily administrative job at a glorified online content farm that, despite your hopes that it would turn into an editing position, has remained a dead end; your bad taste in men; your tendency to drink just a little too much. Their voices practically vibrate with pleasurable anticipation at brunch or happy hour when they ask you to tell them about your latest escapades. "We're living vicariously through you," they sigh. "We're such old ladies these days."

The thing no one tells you about living in New York City is that it's all fun and free shots at 3 P.M. and parties at someone's boyfriend's loft in Tribeca at 10 P.M. and sloppy slices of pizza at 2 A.M. and cab rides home at 4 A.M. until it is not, and then the engagements and promotions and movings-away start and the music stops and you are the only one left without a chair. *When did parties start ending so early,* you wonder while climbing into and out of the gray train of your life. Even the rats that scurry along the subway tracks look tired. Maybe they, too, dream of life in an easier town, with a yard and a house and a better public school system.

Sometimes you dream of picking up and moving to another place entirely, a remote desert town or a cabin in the woods, without telling anyone. Because you're beginning to worry that you will never change, that you'll continue sleeping with the wrong people and drinking too much, until your mistakes outgrow the lessons you've tried to glean from them and you become exactly what your mother always said you were—a mistake. A failure.

You are both alarmed by and resentful of the passage of time, the years that have come and gone without making you into a better, more successful person, a kinder, more forgiving daughter. There is a part of you that wants to have this baby because you think becoming a mother will pull you toward that imagined version of yourself, will make your arrow burn gold again.

The internet tells you that at this stage, the baby is the size of a raspberry. You toy with the idea of making an appointment at a clinic you happen to pass every day on the way to work, but you cannot bring yourself to pick up the phone and call.

You linger by the baby clothes in Target. You hold a pair of impossibly tiny pink sneakers in the palm of your hand, touch lavender and yellow tulle skirts. For some reason, you feel absolutely certain that the baby is a girl.

A clerk smiles at you and asks how far along you are. "Two months," you say, startled.

"I can always tell," the woman says. "Congratulations."

You want to ask her what she thinks you should do, but you just smile back, pretending that you are a woman whose pregnancy has been planned, who is safe and loved.

You finally break down and call your mother, your Korean even clunkier than usual. There is a silence, and for a moment you think she's hung up, and then she asks you to repeat yourself.

"I'm pregnant, Umma," you say. You are so terrified that all thirty-five years of your life flash before your eyes. You brace yourself for screaming, for the sound of her smashing the phone into the wall, the way she did when you told her you were dropping out of law school years ago.

But instead, your mother just asks you how far along you are. If you are eating well. And then, hesitantly, who the father is.

"He's married," you say. A half-truth, or at least one-third of it. "He doesn't know."

"Are you going to tell him?" she asks.

"I don't know," you say, and she sighs, not in the way of a mother exasperated or angry with her child, but in the way of a woman who knows how these things work, because she went through the same thing with your father, when she had you.

When she calls the next day to tell you that she is flying out to New York, you are relieved that you will no longer be alone in all this, until the fear sets in.

At the airport, she is thinner than you remember her being. She is dressed in a performance fleece and wrinkled pants with a floral print. Her hair has been dyed a brassy red-brown that makes her face look even paler than usual. When you were growing up, she hated how dark your skin got in the summertime—"Just like your father," she'd say—and would chase you around with long-sleeved shirts and wide-brimmed plastic visors. At fifteen, you learned to eschew sunblock at the beach in an effort to achieve a golden tan just like your best friend Mimi Kang's, whose parents could afford to send her to tennis camp in the summer, but you succeeded only in getting your first sunburn. To this day, when you slather on SPF in the morning, you can hear your mother bemoaning your stupidity, the premature wrinkles she predicted would follow your repeated exposures to the sun.

You pull her into a stiff hug, noticing how terribly light she feels in your arms. She is full of complaints about the flight, the weather, the other passengers, how dirty New York is. She has brought only one carry-on item with her, a suitcase with a half-broken handle and a squeaky wheel that you end up pulling through the terminal.

She hates your apartment, is horrified by what she calls "the state of it," even though you've been cleaning for days. But you realize this is a good thing, because it gives her something to fuss about. Within an hour of her arrival, she is on her hands and knees scrubbing your kitchen floor with a vigor that you would not expect of a sixty-four-year-old. You squint at the rubber gloves she is wearing, which you are almost 100 percent sure you do not own. Could she have brought them with her?

"I didn't raise you to be dirty like this," she says as she scours your stovetop, which is crusted with grease streaks and blackened crumbs. You don't have the heart to tell her that the apartment was like this when you moved in, that you barely cook anyway. Instead, you go to your room and lie down to sleep—you've been so tired recently—and when you wake up, nearly two hours later, the whole apartment smells like seaweed soup. Your mother spoons a mound of white rice onto a plate and pushes a bowl of soup at you. Golden pools of oil gleam on its surface. "It's good for the baby," she says.

In the mornings, your mother wakes up before you do and makes barley tea. She sends you off to work with a thermos of it. "No coffee," she says. "It's bad for the baby." Beyond this—and the fact that she buys you prenatal vitamins along with clusters of citrus fruits that she insists are good for the baby—you and your mother do not discuss your pregnancy much. You study the fruit piled on your kitchen table. When the morning light filters through your windows, the orange and yellow globes smell sun-warmed and ripe, like a small orchard is growing in your apartment.

There is no question in your mind, now that she is here, that you will keep this baby. Because your mother, no matter how you feel about her, is a reminder that what you want—to have this baby and raise it on your own—is possible.

Your married coworker texts you during the workday, asking if you'd like to go out sometime this week, on what he calls "a proper date." He says Megan is cool with it. You feel a great weariness sandbag your bones. You tell him a version of the truth, that you are not feeling well and that your mother is staying with you for a few weeks. He expresses his sympathy before asking you to send him a dirty pic. You oblige, because who knows when you will be desired again. You go into the bathroom and contort yourself over the toilet bowl to get the shot, in the stall next to the one you fucked him in.

You wonder how long you will be able to keep your pregnancy hidden at work. If you'll need to, eventually, get some kind of paternity test.

Your friends do not understand any of this. "I thought you and your mom didn't speak," they say. "You told us she was awful to you growing up." You don't deny this, the times she locked you out of the house for talking back or coming home from school with liquor on your breath—although you never got in trouble for your grades; you never let those slip, no matter how much you wanted to die on a day-to-day basis.

Once you unfolded a paper clip and etched line after line of red down your forearms, just to feel something. When your mother saw the cuts, the jagged borders where you had dug into your skin again and again, all she said was, "If you're going to do it, do it right. And kill me too, while you're at it."

Later, you told yourself that this was her way of trying to get you to stop. That she was a scared single mother working two jobs to support you and herself and didn't have the slightest clue of what to do with you, her angry, unruly teenage daughter. That she was using reverse psychology, Jedi mind tricking you, in the way of all Korean mothers. And it had worked, because the pit of chalky despair you felt in your stomach every morning turned into an ironclad resignation to keep on living, just to spite her.

But how can you explain to your friends that this mother, the one in your apartment now, seems to be a distant cousin of the one you remember from childhood? That while she is still as sharp-tongued as ever, she has grown softer around the edges? During the day when you are at work, sending fake-chipper emails and avoiding your married coworker's cubicle, your mother has apparently taken to walking in the park. She does a full loop, she tells you proudly, and while she remains disgusted with the general grime of the city and disapproves of the fact that Americans do not pick up thoroughly after their too-large dogs, she likes the park, its graceful trees and rolling hills and winding pathways.

At dinner, over the dishes of your childhood, she tells you about little things she saw that day. A bouquet of yellow roses, abandoned on a curb. A single swan, floating on the green surface of a pond in the park. A kite shaped like an octopus, with eight legs streaming behind its bulbous painted head, and a child in a red jacket attached to it, laughing whenever the wind blew the octopus farther upward. Her voice is soft and wistful, and you recall that before the smog of Los Angeles, before the glittering skyline of Seoul, where she met your father while working as an office girl at his company, she had grown up in a village to the north, in the mountains, where pine trees grew tall and mornings were blue and misty.

The image of the kite reminds you of your father, whom you saw rarely throughout your childhood and felt in awe of. He was a tall, dignified man, handsome, you suppose, judging by the one photo you have of him. He was married when he met your mother, and he is still married to his wife ("that woman," your mother calls her). Your mother had been your father's mistress, which was why he did not live with you, why he came to see you only on certain days of the year, and why your presents from him were always expensive and slightly wrong, as if they had been purchased for another child. Like the heavy wooden chess set you never learned how to play, or the set of leather-bound encyclopedias you were too embarrassed to tell him no one used anymore in the age of the internet.

Only once did he ever bring you a present you loved. It was

a stuffed plush octopus that could also be worn as a hat, with Velcro attached to its legs. You named her Olivia and carried her around everywhere, until her pink plush turned a dull gray. When your father stopped visiting and answering your mother's calls, she threw out the presents he had given you, including the encyclopedias—all except for Olivia, whom you wedged into a hidden spot between your mattress and bed frame, although you eventually lost track of her, too.

At three months, you show your mother the ultrasound, and the two of you admire the dark shimmer of the baby's heartbeat, tiny but strong. Your mother's eyes swim. She takes the ultrasound from you, sits with it. "Your father didn't go with me to my appointments after I found out you'd be a girl," she said. "I always thought if you had been a son, he would have stayed in the end."

Even though it's what you've always suspected—that your mother hated you for not being enough to keep your father around—it still hurts to hear her say it. "Maybe not," you say. "Maybe he was just an asshole."

You learn that the baby is now the size of a plum, that she is growing fingernails and that a fine layer of hair covers her, like a carpet. How clever the engine of the human body is, you think to yourself as you stare at the emerging bump, the rise and slope of your stomach.

A few weeks later, you tell your ex, your married coworker, the tattoo artist. One by one, they panic, pace, and finally calm down when you reassure them that you don't expect anything of them, that this is your decision and that you will be doing this on your own. Your ex says, "Shit," and opens a bottle of whiskey. Your married coworker cries. The tattoo artist asks if he can touch your stomach, and you say no.

You realize that you are living the plot of a romantic comedy, except that no one is laughing and that the only romance here is the one developing between your mother and the baby. Even though you've read online that it's still too early to feel the baby's movements, you can't help but think you feel them—joyful and quick, like those of a sea otter cavorting in the waves. She seems particularly active whenever she hears your mother's voice, as though she, too, wants to participate in the conversation.

Pregnancy makes your dreams vivid, eerie. You dream that your body has turned to water, that the baby has somehow floated out of you in your sleep and is lying, nestled and flippered, in the twin rivers of your arms. She has slippery skin like a dolphin's, but she is perfect. You dream that you are standing in a dark field and a golden star spills from the sky, its tail a fiery stream that fans out into the shape of an arrow. You follow it until you wake up.

Your mother has started referring to the two of you as one entity, "the baby." As in, "The baby needs to eat," or "And how is the baby feeling today?" She is happier than you've ever known her, singing hymns in the morning when you wake up and making elaborate meals for the three of you. If you had known that all it would take was getting pregnant to get your mother to love you, you would have done it ages ago, you think.

Your hair, which has been pin-straight for most of your life, starts to go wavy. Your *chanmori,* baby hairs, get caught in the static electricity generated by the friction of your wool scarf against your cheek. "It's hormones," your mother says. "When I was pregnant with you, my left foot grew half a shoe size. I still can't wear heels." You feel as though you should apologize for this, but you don't, because for once it doesn't sound like your mother is blaming you for ruining her life. In fact, she sounds almost dreamy, nostalgic.

You take your mother shopping for a winter coat, because she has never had occasion to buy one, after more than thirty years in Southern California. Together, you linger in brightly lit aisles murmuring over merchandise. You hold up coats to her thin frame in the mirrors, like she used to do to you at the Salvation Army where you got all your clothes as a child.

She selects a purple coat with gray faux-fur trim, a far cry from the sober navy or practical black coats you thought she might choose. "I didn't know you liked purple," you say.

"There's a lot of things you don't know about me," she says.

Outside, the city is dressed in red and green. A small, light-up Christmas tree in a store window shudders colorful sparks. Your mother wears her coat out of the store and links arms with you. You realize that a stranger pausing to observe the two of you would think you were any ordinary mother and daughter, rather than two people who just happen to be related to one another, women linked by their carelessness with men, the loneliness of their lives made legible in the way they lean on one another but do not speak or laugh or even turn to look at each other. The baby dances inside you, performing a quick shuffle, and you zip up your coat against the knife's edge of the wind. *Things will be different for you,* you tell her.

A neon rose blinks in a window. AURA READINGS, a sign says. You pull your mother inside, emboldened by the success of the coat. "I've read about this place online," you tell her.

Inside, you take turns sitting in front of a large black camera. A bored-looking man in a tan blazer explains the process to you, and you translate for your mother. The camera takes a long exposure of the subject, he says, while tiny rainbow crystals inside the device, activated by light, can determine, via photo capture, what color a person's aura is.

Your aura is a soft cloud of yellow and green. "Yellow is good," the man says. "It means confidence. Green means renewal and energy. You carry within you a strength and resolve for the future."

"That's the baby," your mother says proudly.

Your mother's aura is bluish, a moody billow of violet and

indigo. "Purple signifies compassion," the young man says. "Blue means awareness. Sadness, mixed with wisdom and maturity."

Your mother nods slowly when you explain this to her, as though sadness is her birthright. You study her large eyes and high cheekbones, which you did not inherit, her large ears and thin eyebrows, which you did. The small mole at the corner of her mouth, which you used to stare at as a kid in order to avoid crying whenever she yelled at you, because crying would only make the yelling worse. "You think you've done something good?" she would say at the first sign of tears. "You think you deserve to cry?"

"What?" your mother says.

"I was just thinking about how much we don't look alike," you say.

"Nonsense," your mother says, looking at your two aura pictures side by side. She taps the image of your face. "Maybe when you were little. But now you look just like me," she says. You bend over the photos to see what she sees, and maybe it's just a trick of the light or because you want it to be so, but it turns out there is more than a passing similarity between your faces, in the way you both lift your eyes to the camera's gaze and your chins come to a determined point.

Here is how it ends: one morning you wake up and everything is wrong. It feels like a hand has reached inside you to wring your womb dry. You rush to the bathroom and it is as you suspected; more blood than you ever thought possible crimsons your underwear, your pajamas. You close your eyes, wait to wake up, to feel the sea otter flutter inside you that will let you know all is right. But it doesn't come, and you let out an animal wail that scares even you, as your mother bursts into the bathroom, her eyes round and wild with fear.

You call in sick, stay in bed for what seems like years. Your baby, the magical fish that swam inside the bowl of you for over twelve weeks, is gone, like a balloon that has been released into the sky. From far away, you see your mother hover over you, urging you to eat. She pushes a bowl of rice at you, like you are a sick dog, and you push it away. Your arms ache. Your breasts ache. You collapse into yourself, until you turn into a story that's been told so many times it's no longer recognizable. She tells you that you have to go to the doctor, but you refuse.

"Go away," you tell her, in a fever of hate. "Go home. I don't need you here anymore." She retreats, for once, her face a dim moon above the rising tide of your rage, her mouth so downturned it's almost comical, like a parody of sadness.

One morning you wake up so early that it is still dark outside. You feel empty, like an eggshell that's lost the slip of its yolk. The apartment is silent, and you realize that for the first time in a long while, you are alone. That your mother has finally left and that perhaps this was God's way of answering your prayers after all, because hadn't you prayed to not be pregnant, in the beginning?

But when you stumble into your kitchen, your mother is there, standing over the stove and muttering to herself over a pot of juk, with just the stove light on for company.

"Finally, you're awake. You have to eat," she says.

You sit down, too weak to argue. A bowl of juk, topped with soy sauce and sesame oil and scallions, materializes in front of you. The handful of times your mother let you stay home sick from school while you were growing up, she would make this porridge for you. Someday, she'd say, I'll teach you how to make it for your own children.

She doesn't say anything, just sits down next to you and squeezes your left hand as you spoon juk into your mouth, crying all the while, until you can't eat anymore. Afterward, she smooths back the still-curly baby hairs from your face, with a tenderness you have never known.

"I've booked my return ticket," she tells you, and you nod.

"Thank you," you say. "For staying."

She does not tell you that she loves you, nor does she tell you that everything is going to be okay, because both of you are past believing things like that. And as the sun climbs over the lip of the sky, and the two of you watch its ascent, gold filling the corners of your apartment, you begin to understand that there is only this moment, and then the next, and then the next, and that the only thing to do in the meantime is to keep on living.

Addie Citchens
That Girl

Underneath the huge, old, rusty awning, it was three shades darker and ten degrees cooler than in the street. Theo had been sitting on the porch rocker watching Shirlee go back and forth. It was strange to see a girl walking alone, but Shirlee was always out and about by herself. She always looked the same, too: once-upon-a-time-white canvas shoes, T-shirt tied above her belly button, jeans pulled up into her crotch. With one hand on her hip and the other shading her eyes, she stepped into the yard.

"Do a dude name Melvin stay on this street?"

The girl's hair was scraped up into a short peacock, styled with gelled baby hairs and curlicues. Her lips shined like she had just eaten chicken. Theo wanted to bust out laughing, but she knew that would be the absolute wrong thing to do. Shirlee had stopped short of climbing the porch steps.

"I don't know no Melvin."

"Oh, he owe me some money," Shirlee said, squinting at Theo's lap. "I know it ain't the summertime and you up there reading a book?"

Theo rolled her eyes and her neck. "S-so? And?"

"What's it about?" Shirlee said, suddenly softening her voice.

"I just started."

"Your mama and daddy in the house?"

"Nah, my big cousin."

"Read me some."

"R-r-read you some?"

"That's what I said, didn't it?"

"I can read good in my head but not out loud," Theo said.

Shirlee clambered up onto the porch and dropped down beside her. "I don't mind if you be stuttering. See, I'm the opposite—when I'm reading, it seem like my brain stutter, but I can count them dollars."

"What grade you in?" Theo asked.

"Going to the ninth but supposed to be in the eleventh. Teacher at Treadwell act like she couldn't give me one damn point, but I don't want to talk about that. Read the story."

"Well, this takes place in England during the First World War," Theo said. "And I'm going to the ninth grade."

"Okay, that's cool," Shirlee said around the fingers in her mouth. She sucked the two by the thumb and was moving the rocker with her foot. "All we need is one of them hanging things."

"What hanging things?"

"Like what people in Hawaii lay down in—uh, they hang it in the middle of two trees."

"Oh, a hammock."

"Yeah," Shirlee said. "We need a hammock."

The miraculous thing was that, unlike in school, Theo's voice got clearer and sturdier as she read. She didn't ever want to stop reading. Or to be away from the soft puff of Shirlee's breathing. She didn't want an end to the pressure of Shirlee's foot hooked around her shin, or to cease hearing the determined sound of Shirlee sucking her fingers. She also didn't want her mama to pull up and act crazy. Jane didn't like strangers at her house.

"My mama'll be home in a minute," Theo said.

"I feel you," Shirlee said.

She stood and stretched her long arms, revealing a narrow, muscly belly as her shirt crept up. She raked the back of her hair with her fingers, worked her lip gloss out of her pocket, and smeared it on.

"Well, it's been real, girl," she said, and bounced down the stairs.

Theo was tired of being friendless and lonely, of having no one who could understand her. She jumped up to follow Shirlee.

"You can come back," she said. "Just only between the hours of nine and three. If you see a white Buick in the driveway, pass on by—oh, and never on the weekends."

"Okay. You like Kool-Aid and pickles?"

"Who don't?"

Shirlee threw up her middle finger and switched off. Jane would not approve. She, of all people, had seen fit to grow judgmental. Maybe it was because her third husband was a good man. He went to church, worked at the post office, and had got a big settlement check a few years ago. Sighing, Theo went into the house to tell Keita she was going to ride her bike, but Keita was still locked up in the guest room with Freddy Pettis. They were gonna have to break it up soon.

"On my bike," she called as she continued out the back door.

She unchained her bike and skidded from the driveway into the street. She'd just make a few blocks and come back, take some time for herself before the adults got home.

"He's a good man," Jane must have said a thousand times about Roger, after previously saying you couldn't melt and pour another man on her.

Theo had to admit that, in the two years since Roger had come along, Jane barely hollered or whipped her anymore. She was too busy in Roger's lap, picking in his hair or rubbing his feet. Another thing was that he kept Jane out a lot. Roger spun Southern-soul records at the Classic Hitz club on the weekends, and Jane always went with him. His DJ name was Roger That. It tickled Theo when he sauntered through the house singing in his beautiful voice and practicing his routine. He cupped a hand over his mouth, making it sound like a CB radio: "You better Roger That and keep on dancing." No, Roger wasn't so bad.

After several blocks, Theo spun her bike back into her yard. She could hear his system thumping. Every evening, he came in turning on music. Bobby "Blue" Bland, Aretha Franklin, Millie Jackson, the Eagles, the Doors—anything could be playing. At the moment, he was blasting "Atomic Dog," and Theo could hear him singing before she opened the door. Jane was dancing in her socks while Roger checked a pan on the stove. He spotted Theo, looked her sincerely in the eye, and began barking like a rabid dog. She didn't want to laugh, but she couldn't help it. That was the difference between him and the last man: Roger didn't mind looking stupid.

"Girl, get ready for some macaroni salad, Italian sausage in a potato bun, and baked beans," Roger said. "And look down there at that monster melon I picked up."

He was also a much better cook than Jane.

As soon as Jane left the next day, Theo parked her rear on the porch swing to wait for Shirlee. Keita came out to investigate. "I'm waiting on my friend," Theo said.

"Okay," Keita said. "Boyfriend or girlfriend?"

"Girl, duh," Theo said.

She stayed by the house all day, but Shirlee didn't show. If Keita remembered, she didn't mention it. Theo was not only ashamed but stunned, though that didn't keep her from going back and forth to the porch the next day, too, until Keita shouted at her to quit going in and out. Theo chose to stay out, and by two o'clock she figured it didn't make no sense for Shirlee to come then. She got on her bike to clear her head.

At dinner, Roger said, "The girl sure is quiet tonight."

Jane set her fork down. "Something wrong, Pooh? You and Keita getting along all right?"

Theo nodded.

"You probably tired from riding that bike in the high noon," Jane said. "Gone mess around and be black as a field hand. I remember . . ."

Jane forked the potato salad but didn't eat it, nor did she continue her train of thought. She had gained weight since she quit smoking and started eating all of Roger's good cooking. One night, Theo had caught her standing in front of the sink, shoveling a hunk of pound cake into her mouth. She'd frozen like a burglar.

"What were you saying?" Roger asked.

"I forgot," Jane said.

"You all right, doll?" he asked Theo.

"Right as rain," she lied.

Around noon that Friday, Shirlee finally switched up the street carrying a large paper bag. She wore jeans well ventilated with holes and a small doughnut on the side of her head, tied with red yarn ribbon.

"Took you long enough," Theo called out.

"You must've missed me," Shirlee said.

Theo rolled her eyes but was curious about the contents of the bag.

"Whew—can we go inside? It's hot as hell out here," Shirlee said.

"Lemme check," Theo said.

Theo was sure Keita wouldn't mind, but she didn't want to chance it, so she stepped into the house, and, finding the front room cool and empty, she motioned for Shirlee. They tiptoed into Theo's bedroom.

"Girl, you so lucky—got your own room. I don't even got my own bed sometimes."

Shirlee unloaded Vitner's hot-and-sour chips, two pouches of sour pickles, Kool-Aid packets, and peach Faygo onto Theo's vanity. It was as if she either liked everything Theo liked or had somehow read her appetite.

"Mind if I help myself to these chips?"

"Go 'head, girl," Shirlee said. She had got on her knees in the closet and seemed more interested in exploring Theo's stuff than in eating. "All these shoes—ugh—you oughta give me some. What size you wear?"

"Six," Theo said, but Shirlee was already trying to work her feet into a pair of low red heels that Roger's grown daughter, Natasha, had sent her.

"Damn," Shirlee said. "Li'l-ass feet. I wear an eight—my daddy got big feet. I'm like, how I'm so skinny and my feet so damn long? At least I could have a big booty to balance it off."

Theo started on one of the pickles. "You still got time to grow one," she said to encourage her.

"Thank you, friend."

"I'm your friend?"

Shirlee nodded, sat very close. Theo's neck was getting hot. For some stupid, embarrassing reason, her eyes filled with water that ran down her face. Shirlee kissed her forehead, her cheeks, then her lips; Theo could double taste her tears. They kissed, then said "Um" before kissing some more. Finally, Shirlee drew back.

"You want me to leave?"

"Not unless you want to," Theo said.

"You be having bad dreams?"

"Yeah," Theo said. "Sometimes."

"Me, too, friend."

"I got a good book for us," Theo said the next time she saw Shirlee. She wore a low-rise denim skirt and had a paper bag clenched in her hand.

"Cool. I brought you something."

Shirlee sat beside Theo on the swing and dropped the package in her lap—lip gloss, bubblegum, chips, Zebra Cakes, mini candy bars, and a hot-pink bottle of bubbles. Theo took the bubbles and shoved the bag back into Shirlee's hands.

"Friend, I can't take all this stuff."

"Yes, you can, friend. I got it for you."

Theo fished the wand from the bottle and slowly blew a long stream of bubbles up toward the awning. Together and quietly, they watched them fly around and die.

"How 'bout I do something to that head of yours?" Shirlee said. "All that hair and you got them ponytails like a baby."

Theo nodded, and in a moment they were in her room. Shirlee was sitting on the chair, and Theo on the floor between Shirlee's knees.

"Whew," Shirlee said, stretching a piece of hair down past Theo's bra.

"My cousin's goes to her waist, plus it don't nap up like mine do," Theo said.

Shirlee stopped in the middle of brushing and leaned to one side.

"Girl, you wouldn't be able to tell me absolutely nothing if my hair went all the way down to my waist. I'd be too busy shaking it."

"Like this?" Theo said, tossing her head.

Shirlee yanked a scarf from Theo's dresser and hung it around her own head. "More like this," she said, and began to whip it from side to side, lifting her leg to make her butt jump. They laughed so hard. Finally, Shirlee picked the brush up again, but she didn't go back to work on Theo's hair. Instead, she stared into Theo's mirror.

"Can I tell you something?"

"Okay," Theo said.

"It's something that happened to me last year. Now, do you really want to hear this?"

"Girl, if you don't hurry up," Theo said, hoisting herself from the floor.

"So Mrs. Tyler sent me to the office because she said my shorts was too little, and Mr. Barnes checked them all right. I walked in the office, and he stopped what he was doing and frowned at me. He said, 'Come here, child. Come round the desk.'

"I went over there, and just like that he stuck his hand between my legs. My breath went out of me. You just don't expect no man like that to do that to you. But seemed like I blinked and his hand was gone. His face had been regular and everything. He was like, 'You don't want to be walking around with this on. You'll have them nasty tail boys thinking all kinds of things about you. Now, go ask Mrs. McCaskill to let you call your grandmama, and don't wear them shorts back.'"

"You didn't say nothing to nobody?" Theo said.

"Who gone believe *me*? Sometimes I think I made it up 'cause it happened so quick. Other people felt on me before, but they did it with their fingers or wanted me to touch on them. He just touched me like he was checking my temperature down there or something. Do you think that count?"

Theo didn't know what to say, so she didn't answer. Shirlee was still gazing at herself. Theo gazed at the reflection but couldn't call Shirlee's expression. She couldn't call her appearance, either. Shirlee had very good things about her, like her dewy, yellow skin and her pillowy lips, and very bad things, like her hairy sideburns and teeth troubled by a lifetime of finger-sucking. Maybe she, too, was conflicted by her face.

"I must be too damn touchable," she said to the mirror. "What's the book?"

"Dun-dun-dunnn," Theo said, getting it off the nightstand. "It's *Dead W-w-wrong: A Look at Some of America's Most Heinous Killers*."

She had highlighted and written all over the pages, even though it was from the library.

"What do *heinous* mean?" Shirlee said.

"'Evil,'" Theo said evilly.

She plopped down on her back, and Shirlee lay beside her. Theo read about Joe Ray McDonald, a Wisconsin drifter who strangled and bludgeoned his prostitute victims, then dug his initials into their stomachs. Shirlee every so often butted in with a "Damn, that's fucked up." As she sucked her fingers, she played with Theo's earlobe, and Theo finally had to set the book aside for lack of concentration. She wondered if Shirlee was a dyke, if they were both dykes.

"Men always killing women," Shirlee said. "We should go around killing *them* for a change."

"Yeah, girl, you right. Jane's husbands used to beat her and everything."

"This how we gone do it. We'll hang around at the pool hall and whatnot, and when we see one of them looking at us we gone go up to them and say, 'I got a yo-yo for you to play with.' That'll drive them wild, and they gone come running."

Theo giggled and practiced: "I got a yo-yo you can play with."

Deep inside, she trembled with fear, and power, and the fear of power. She had not stuttered any of those words. Some nondescript man slithered toward them, trying to trick them into his car. So intent was he to get down that he either ignored or didn't notice the ice pick she had raised above his head. It went into the skin and muscle of his back with a nasty crack. She described the process in great, bloody detail. Beside her, Shirlee had firefly legs.

Shirlee's house was a shadowy place choked with listless bodies, a roaring TV, and bold roaches. Upstairs, a fight was happening, composed of what sounded like an army of boys. Shirlee's grandmother hobbled down the hall without looking up, humming a church song.

Shirlee was primping in the bathroom mirror, working patiently with her baby hairs, swirling a dollop of Ampro gel with Vaseline so that the gel wouldn't crust up. Then, an eternity of cherry roller ball for her lips; eyeliner to make her eyes look tiny, mean, and sexy; and a beauty mark beside her mouth. Theo couldn't understand how Shirlee could be so calm and cool in there: the room smelled strongly of piss, and the watery light from the bulb made Theo's eyes ache. Hard-dragging footsteps were getting nearer, and the door of the bathroom swung open, causing the girls to turn. Shirlee's mother came in with a low *umph,* staring them up and down.

"You think you cute? You ain't cute, bitch."

When the woman left, Shirlee threw her head back so tears wouldn't mess up the fresh eyeliner. "Come on, girl. Let's dip."

Theo grabbed her hand and squeezed it briefly. They walked through the hall and out the front door.

The sunshine was a shock after the dim house.

"We gone get some green," she said.

Theo stopped in her tracks, heart thump-thumping. "I ain't never smoked no weed before."

"Trust me. It's all good. We gone fly high, li'l mama."

But Theo became more and more uncertain as they went. It was getting hot, and Shirlee was walking too damn fast and too damn far; no wonder she was so skinny. Finally, they came to a brick house with green grass and a flower bed in front of a bay window. When Shirlee knocked, a big bear of a man opened the door.

"Uh-uh," Theo said, "I ain't going in there."

"One second, Lane," Shirlee said, sounding like she was trying to stay collected. She pulled Theo over to the side of the house. "I been knowing this nigga. He give me tat for tit."

"I ain't doing that."

"You ain't got to do it. I'm gone do it," Shirlee laughed. "You staying up front."

"Girl, that's a grown man in there."

"That boy ain't but seventeen. Now, do you want some weed or what?"

"Not if you gotta get it like that," Theo said.

"I don't have to get it like that. I want to get it like that. That's the difference."

Shirlee disappeared into the house; Theo sat on the couch with her legs pinched together. "This Is How We Do It" was on the stereo. After it had played four times, Theo decided that Shirlee had been gone an unreasonably long while. She began to suspect that, somewhere in that house, bear boy was showing Shirlee's young body no slack. When Shirlee returned, Theo would remind her about the Wisconsin drifter and the danger of this kind of lifestyle. She hadn't heard screaming or a thump or anything like that, though, so she figured that whatever was happening was welcome.

She decided to leave, but as soon as she'd locked herself outside she regretted it. The heat was suffocating. Her tongue felt like dough in the stove of her mouth. Each step seemed like her last; she fought the urge to give up and lie down in the street. Finally, her house shimmered before her like a mirage. Miraculously, she was under the awning, and her key was turning in the lock. She stumbled onto the couch. Some time passed; she could hear Keita's voice cutting through to her consciousness.

"I hope to God you're not pregnant."

"I might be a dyke," Theo mumbled.

The next morning, her back hurt. She felt not only like an old woman but like she had been born an old woman. The sounds in the house were unfamiliar, quieter. Her bedside clock claimed it was ten. That couldn't be right; she never slept this late. She got out of bed and was surprised to see Jane in the hall. Jane never missed work.

"I'm playing hooky to take care of my baby," she said. "Anything you want to talk about, Pooh?"

Theo shook her head.

"'Cause you know you can talk to me about anything . . ."

Since when?

"You sure you and Keita getting along okay?"

Theo nodded.

"You not gone say nothing?"

She shook her head.

"Rog made you blueberry waffles. Make your bed while I throw you one on the waffle iron."

Theo jumped to it. She had discovered the word *delectable* while looking up synonyms for *delicious*. As she straightened her sheets, she envisioned Roger quitting his job and opening a restaurant called Delectables where he sang the menu. People would come from far and wide, and Hollywood would hear about it and give him his own cooking show, *Delectables with Roger,* and he would sing and kiss his fingertips because the food was so good. At the end of each episode, he would cup his hand over his imaginary radio and say, "You better Roger That and keep on cooking."

By the time Theo got into the kitchen, Jane was working the waffle out of the iron. Her arm fat shook, and dimples were pushing through the fabric of her shorts.

"You look different, Ma," Theo blurted.

Jane set the plate in front of her—one egg sunny-side up, a waffle, and a sausage, perfectly circular and evenly brown, not charred the way she had made them before Roger. Jane's hands went to her hips.

"Different how?"

"Never mind," Theo said.

Jane emptied the coffeepot into her mug and dumped in sugar. "Some girl came by for you earlier this morning."

That fool! Shirlee knew not to come by when Jane's car was in the driveway.

"I hope you don't be having folks in my house, Theodara Robinson. You nor Keita. I better call and talk to her real good."

Theo was just happy Jane hadn't said anything bad about

Shirlee. She would've gladly slung a few choice words if Jane talked bad about her.

Shirlee sat cross-legged in the middle of her bedroom floor, between the bunk beds, rolling them something to smoke. Theo wasn't about to sit on that floor with all them roaches marching, so she perched on the edge of Shirlee's bunk. To keep from staring at Shirlee's smooth, yellow skin and open legs, Theo focused on the part in her friend's hair. Shirlee looked up and caught her gaze. She smiled, took a bite out of her Kool-Aid pickle (which she ate without sugar), and scooted over to give Theo sour, bitter kisses.

"Guess what?" Shirlee said.

"What?"

"You oughta let me spend the night with you."

"Huh?" Theo said.

"You heard me," Shirlee said, rolling her neck.

Theo had heard her. The *huh* was for not understanding why she would say such a thing.

"Shirlee, you know you can't spend the night over my house."

"Yes, I could. I could just dart in the back door and into your bedroom and just dart out before anybody get up."

Theo smiled at the simplicity of the plan, and then a terrible coldness poured over her heart at the thought of Jane catching them. She must have frowned.

"I ain't scared of your mama," Shirlee said.

"You ain't got to live with her, and, besides, I see you almost every day."

"But not on the weekends, and night is different. People sweeter at night. You probably smell like a baby, probably make little noises. And it's things you can only do at night."

"Like what?"

"I don't know—secret, sweet stuff," Shirlee said.

Theo was melting at the idea. It would have to be on a black night with no stars. She would leave the back door unlocked with the hope that a serial killer wouldn't discover it before Shirlee did. Once Shirlee was in the bedroom, every stitch of her clothing would come off as if by magic. Her nipples would be like erasers on her chest, her shoulders pulled back like a gymnast's. A small light shone in the spot where the principal had once cupped her, the light of the world. It winked as Shirlee walked toward Theo's bed. She would smell like Juicy Fruit and pilfered Cool Water and, faintly, of pickles.

"Let's go to Mr. Campbell's. My sister wants some pink bobby socks," Shirlee said when they got into the street.

Stepping inside the Sophisticated Lady Shop gave Theo a frantic, welcoming rush. There were a zillion things for sale or snatch, too much for any shopkeeper to inventory: plastic music-class recorders, debutante gloves, lace doilies, powder puffs with powder that smelled like fairy feet, Don't-B-Bald serum, Valentine's Day body stockings, fake hair hanging off tracks—Mr. Campbell charged by width, so some women came just to buy bangs—and anything else that could make a woman's insides and outsides pleasant. His anti-theft precautions were two big mirrors angled from the ceiling and his old mother on a stool at the back.

Theo's right hand fingered the mascaras, colored blue and purple, but she put those back. Cherry roller-ball gloss, Blue Nile roller-ball fragrance, and a unicorn-head key chain went into her bra. Shirlee liked to browse, but Theo went up all the aisles just once, preferring to get in and out. On her way out, she grabbed a bag of Skittles and a rusty half-off pair of hoop earrings to pay for in order to seem legitimate. Surely Mr. Campbell could hear her heart going *thup-thup-thup* as he rang up her purchases, but he smiled at her, gave her change, and put her things in a bag. Theo felt awful when he smiled.

Still jittery, she walked off a bit from the store and lit a cigarette as she waited for Shirlee.

"Take your fast ass home, Robinson," a woman shouted.

Theo took off running.

"Mind your mothafuckin' business," she heard Shirlee yell behind her.

It took Shirlee a minute to catch up.

"Scary ass," she said, skidding to a stop.

Theo wanted to slap the taste out of her mouth. Shirlee had Theo hanging around the hood like a vagabond; Theo was bound to get caught up.

"I gotta go," she mumbled.

"Bye, scary Mary."

Shirlee stomped off. Theo was relieved to walk home alone; sometimes Shirlee was just too much. She locked her bedroom door and soothed herself by examining her new possessions, one by one. Keita knocked, causing Theo to jump.

"Your mama here."

Theo shoved the things into her pillowcase and got to the front door, panting. Keita was coming up the walk with grocery bags. Theo went to see if there were more and carried some to the kitchen table. Much to her disappointment, Jane had started getting pots and pans out of the cabinets.

"Roger not cooking tonight?"

"Nah," Jane said.

Theo's insides frowned; she hoped her mother wouldn't be trying something with a high degree of difficulty. Jane was staring into the refrigerator but came out with twitchy eyes and no food. She ground her knuckles into her eye sockets.

"What am I supposed to be doing?"

"Cooking," Theo said, trying to get in to hug her mother.

"Please," Jane said, pushing her off.

Theo went to her room to lie down. After a while, the radio came on, which meant that Roger had arrived. J. Blackfoot commanded a taxi to take him to the other side of town. Soon Jane was calling her to eat. Theo counted to thirty and went. Jane's meat loaf looked grumpy and tasted grumpy, even after Theo microwaved a coat of cheese on top. No one was eating it; as a matter of fact, no one was eating at all. They were looking Theo in the face.

"Huh," she said.

"What a word to say to your mama," Jane said.

Roger spoke. "What you be doing here in the daytime, Theo?"

"Reading, riding my bike. Keita be doing her schoolwork. I w-watch TV sometimes. Jerry Springer."

"Oh, no," Roger said.

"It's funny." Theo forced herself to giggle.

"I love you, you know that?" Jane said.

The words came out hard, hard enough for both Theo and Roger to look at Jane funny. Her eyes resembled a baby seal's.

Theo couldn't sleep that night. Her thoughts were feverish, wondering if Shirlee was mad at her and then picturing her buttery legs in her shorts. The more she thought about her friend, the more she thought Shirlee should be able to spend the night. Other people's friends spent the night at their houses. Jane was too unreasonable. While Jane was in the tub, Theo phoned Shirlee and asked if she still wanted to come over.

The third time, they were too bold. Shirlee came earlier, around nine, so she could stay longer. Not an hour later, Jane was shaking the knob.

"Who you talking to, girl? Unlock this damn door."

Before Theo could get to her feet, Jane had shouldered it open. Shirlee ran out the back of the house while Theo lit out for the living room with Jane on her heels swinging an extension cord. It landed on Theo's thighs, her shoulder, her cheek. Why did she have to be in only her drawers? Why had they been greedy?

"What's going on?" Roger said.

"Don't come out here, Roger," Jane growled.

Fuck this shit, Theo wanted to shout. In the seconds of

distraction caused by Roger, she snatched the knobby end of the cord and wrapped it around her wrist.

"If you don't let go of this damn cord."

"No!" Theo said.

Jane wrapped her end around her wrist as well. Theo pulled herself to her feet, body sparkling with pain. Jane gave the cord a yank, and Theo yanked back. Theo saw Jane preparing for the jerk of all jerks, and she let go of the cord, sending her mother tumbling to the floor, looking more stunned than hurt. She went to stand over Jane, wanted to mash her foot in her mother's face.

"Get from over me," Jane snapped. What the fuck was Jane mad about? She wasn't the one who had been assaulted. Theo's welts tightened and released, but the pain was interesting, not overwhelming. The worst was on her shoulder, where the skin was raw. She noticed Total's "Kissin' You" super low and still on repeat on the CD player. Just a few minutes ago, the song had her feeling like a goddess, but now she felt like a kicked dog. Jane was off the floor, looking for something. Theo flinched when she came near her. Jerkily, Jane laced Theo's arms into a robe and tied the waist. Theo didn't make a move. If she got into a fight in school, she couldn't say, "I learned it by watching you," the way the boy on the anti-drugs commercial had said to his daddy. A row with Jane made her feel a thousand times worse than a school fight. When she turned sixteen, she would move out.

"I should've followed my first mind and made you talk to me. Maybe it wouldn't have come to this," Jane said. "You need to understand that I'm your mama, and I am the only person you got in this world. I'm responsible for everything. And you cannot be a bulldagger."

At least they couldn't have no out-of-wedlock children, Theo thought, as she watched her mother vacantly.

"The mere fact that that girl is out all times of night like this should tell you something. She headed for the pipe and the needle and will have you headed there, too."

Theo wanted to tell Jane that she was her own person, but she knew it would do no good. Jane was worried about the wrong damn thing; what she should be worried about was how she had just ripped Theo's skin open with an electrical cord. She could tell Jane was going off to cry, even though she didn't have any reason or right to.

Theo woke to the sound of fiddling and scraping in her room but didn't take the blanket from over her head.

"Your mama told me to come get the TV," she heard Roger say.

The electric screwdriver whined, stopped, and whined again. After a while, it stopped for good, and she heard a huge commotion. She could tell Roger was looking at her.

"You want something to eat, girl?"

Theo said nothing.

"Your mama just want the best for you."

Roger was new here and didn't know any better, so there would be no point in trying to set him straight. When she peered from under the blanket, she saw that he had taken her door off. He returned and put a tray on her nightstand. She didn't touch the food, but she read the note from Jane.

THEO'S NEW SUMMER SCHEDULE:

Mon–Fri—Magnolia Day Services w/ Aunt Trina
Tuesday—Adults on Fire for Christ Bible Class
Wednesday—Youth on Fire for Christ Bible Class
Thursday—Usher Board meeting
Friday—Upper Room Counsel w/ Mother Buchanon
Saturday—Youth Choir practice
Sunday—Upper Room Counsel w/ Rev. Tod

Theo was embarrassed to see how Jane had put everybody in her business. Spending all that time in church was bad enough, but going to Magnolia Day with Aunt Trina was going to be the worst. For one, it was with Aunt Trina, and, two, it was an adult day-care center for special people to get out of the house. Three weeks of it would kill her or turn her into one of them. She didn't know how she'd make it through.

"How was your day?"

"Great," Theo said, returning the smirk her mother gave her.

But, really, the day hadn't been too bad at all. It had been like watching a real-life TV show with very peculiar characters. She'd learned all sorts of things, like when Aunt Trina said you could put disorder on a schedule as long as you kept it busy with quality activities. She'd also learned plenty of new vocabulary words listening to her aunt talk in her bill-payer voice. Like how Ishmael and Poppy were verbal and high-functioning. Donald was nonverbal but could sign what he wanted. A tower of a man, he walked on his tiptoes and kept his fingers flapping by his ears, as if as long as he heard them they were still there. Or maybe they were telling him delectable secrets. Only one student, Nadine, really disturbed Theo. She rocked side to side and repeated a single syllable in varying lengths and volumes—*lub, lub, luuub*. All the other students looked a little different, but Nadine could've been on TV. Her skin was clear, her wavy auburn hair in a long braid, and she had seafoam-green eyes. Right before lunch, Theo had spotted her all alone and went up to her. She tried to focus Nadine's lovely eyes by holding the woman's shoulders steady, looking her straight on, and saying with her mind, If you keep your eyes still, it will change your life.

"Lub," Nadine said.

"Theodara, leave Nadine alone," Aunt Trina said.

Aunt Trina, who had a lot in common with her sister Jane, had been the biggest surprise, sweet and gentle to the people she worked alongside and sweeter and gentler to the special people. But she was still the same old Aunt Trina to Theo. They were having lunch together in Aunt Trina's office when she started up with the questions.

"Theodara Robinson, you weren't really doing what Jane said?"

Theo rolled her eyes.

"The old folk used to say that stuff will make you weak as water," her aunt said, laughing.

But it wasn't funny to Theo. Her mother was such a traitor, and she talked too damn much. Theo had never told anybody about the time she'd caught Jane and a man who looked like Olive Oyl hunching on the kitchen floor when Jane was between husbands.

Devotional duty was supposed to be rotated among the Youth on Fire, but they knew better than to ask Theo. Keith Jackson, however, marched right up to the front like Bobby Jones. Keith was in eighth grade and looked like a pear; in spite of that, he was smooth on the microphone.

"Good evening, saints," he said. "It was on my spirit to do something a little different tonight. I hope don't nobody mind. Brother Dobbs, can you come up here and help me? You, too, Cecelia."

That left only Theo and Rodney Anderson for the audience. As Keith and the others began to sing, Theo carefully considered the lyrics: "I want two wings to veil my face. I want two wings to fly away." Though a many-winged creature would surely be an awesome sight, Theo decided she needed only the two wings it would take to get away. When the song was over, Keith prayed. Theo's attention went to a rickety card table, which held juice and cookies for the end of class. After a triple amen, Keith squeezed in beside her, spilling a portion of his thigh over into her seat. Now she wouldn't even be able to read the Harlequin romance she'd brought to pass the time. Jane would pay for this. As soon as Jane turned sixty, Theo was going to put her in a nursing home where they neglected their residents.

Up front, Brother Dobbs was telling everyone to turn to Revelation. He stumbled through a reading, something about Jesus having a wedding—not at *a* church, but to *the* Church.

Cecelia Tod was another star student. "The whole point of this scripture is that the Church needs to make ready for Jesus to come like a bride would for her wedding," she said.

"You're on fire tonight, Li'l Sister Tod. What does it look like for the Church to get ready?"

Duh, Theo thought, the Church has to douche and shop for a dress. Theo pictured Jesus on his wedding night, gently removing his robe. His hair blew continuously and without wind. His holy rod trembled with desire, and he bit his lip, trying to hold back the emotion. Theo covered her laugh with a cough and kept coughing until Brother Dobbs told her to go see about herself. She darted out of her chair and into the hall, where she noticed that Reverend Tod's study door was ajar. She cut through the gloom and sat behind his desk. She slid her feet out of her shoes and tugged the shaggy carpet with her toes. The room's dimness and the air-conditioning raised up hairs all over her skin. Making fun of Jesus, freaking with Shirlee, stealing—Theo should soak up this good air since she was probably going to roast like a weenie in the hottest fire of hell.

Maybe hell was inescapable. Some people had hell on earth, like the flat-headed kids in Romanian orphanages or Sojourner Truth. Some people had hell of the mind, like the students at Magnolia Day. And Theo, probably. Doing all this thinking, she was leaving fingerprints all over the pastor's glass desk. In the hall, the pale, red glow of the exit sign beckoned, so she crept toward it. The door opened with an enormous hiss; she paused, listening to and watching the lonely street, but no one came to save her. When she got back to class, Brother Dobbs looked at her funny. She put her hand over her lower stomach, a gesture the old man could interpret in many ways, and took a new seat, closer to the refreshments.

. . .

"What did you learn tonight?" Jane asked in the car.

"Plenty," Theo said.

"Like what? Better yet, I want you to write me a paragraph about it when you get home. And I know that girl been calling my house and hanging up, bringing Satan all up in my home. You hear me?"

Most people didn't know that the spirit was housed between the skin and the muscle. An invisible razor was cutting Theo's loose. The feeling was excruciating but a blessing as well, because her skin had been so tight that it had been smothering her spirit. She dragged herself from the car. Inside, Roger popped out of the kitchen, wiping his hands on a dish towel.

"You feeling any better, girl?" he asked, as if she'd had the flu.

Theo was all set to walk back to her room like she hadn't heard him, but Jane stopped her.

"Don't you hear your daddy talking to you?"

It struck her then that Jane was absolutely Looney Tunes. Theo mumbled some answer to Roger, but he couldn't reply, given that Jane was kissing his jaw.

"Lord, I don't know what we gone do with that child," Jane said.

Later, Theo heard the pipes groaning as Jane ran her bath. She called Shirlee.

"Your mama tromped that ass, didn't she? You want to go to the mall tomorrow? I want some Sbarro's."

"No, Shirlee. I just . . . I just . . ."

Theo had known that the conversation would go this way. She didn't know why she'd even called.

"I'm 'bout to come over there."

"No!" Theo said. "Do. Not. Come. To. My. House."

"I don't know why I tried to hang with such a kid."

"I'm 'bout to go, Shirlee."

"What you call me for?"

"I don't even know, but I gotta go." But she didn't; she listened to their silence.

Shirlee's voice was a rush. "I miss you already. Please, friend. I'll come late."

"Real late," Theo said.

Long past midnight, there was a light tap on the window, and Theo jumped out of bed. She hadn't been asleep, but she hadn't been awake, either. She skipped shoes and slid out the back door. Shirlee was on the top step, lighting a cigarette. Theo had the urge to push her down the stairs.

"Step down with that smoking, girl."

"My bad. Scary ass." Shirlee laughed. "So we going to the mall tomorrow or what?"

She was puffing and walking around. Under that tree, they had lain in the dappled sunshine, their skin glued with sweat. That magic, Theo knew, was gone.

"Give me one of those," she said.

Shirlee swept a cigarette from somewhere and stuck it into Theo's mouth. She touched the place on Theo's cheek that had been bruised by the cord. It made Theo nervous and shameful and something else she couldn't identify.

"I-I-I can't hang with you no more," she said.

"You couldn't hang with me in the first place," Shirlee snapped.

Tears were in her eyes. Theo's heart quickened, but she didn't know the right words, so she didn't attempt any.

"So it's like that?" Shirlee said.

Theo shrugged, not wanting to cry herself.

"It's been real, girl." Shirlee nodded. "It's been really real."

And, like that, she was gone. No one would ever again cup Theo as tenderly as that girl had. The thought shook her from her daze, but when she jogged into the front yard Shirlee was already halfway up the street.

"Leelee," Theo called.

Shirlee started running. The T-shirt that had been knotted at her waist flapped loose behind her. Theo smoked the cigarette to the bitter end, flipped the butt into the grass, and brushed the ashes off the front of her nightshirt. She called her friend's name again but, this time, within her head.

Michael Deagler

The Pleasure of a Working Life

AT THE TIME of the adman's death, Gary Minihan had been with the Postal Service for thirty-five years. He spent the first thirty as a letter carrier in Abington, Pennsylvania, where his pragmatic father, who also carried mail, had persuaded him to take what was meant to be a temporary job at the age of twenty-two, after Gary had quit junior college for the second time. That was 1980. A first-class stamp cost fifteen cents. They gave him a walking route that included Paperbark Avenue, where he had lived as a teenager and where his parents still resided. He hoofed the blocks, kept the mail dry, and sweated in all weather—Gary had always been a large man. He did not like the work. He intended, always, to quit, at the end of this year or the next one. He imagined becoming a writer of some sort, of speeches or magazine articles. He brought his customers bills, catalogs, and greeting cards. At Christmas, they gave him Scotch and shortbread. He ate lunch at his parents' house and sometimes showered there when he got off work, even after he married and moved to Bucks County. As the years passed, the homes on his route were bought and sold, families moved in and out, children grew up and new children replaced them. The older people died, his parents included. In time he stopped thinking of the house on Paperbark as theirs, since the mail he dropped in the letter box no longer bore their names. He ate his lunch in his truck. By 2010, Gary was still a young man—too young, at least, to retire—but he was diabetic and his hips were shot. A friend with more political sense who had worked his way up at the Philadelphia district building found Gary a spot managing the small storefront post office in Kilntown, tucked away in a strip mall off Bethlehem Pike, between the Firstrust Bank and a hair salon. Such things were not usually done, Gary liked to point out. At the United States Postal Service, there were outdoor people and indoor people, and it was rare for an outdoor person to be invited inside.

Gary's new title was postmaster. Technically, he was the interim postmaster, which did not pay as well as a proper postmaster, but the job was his until he maxed out his pension. Kilntown did not offer mail delivery, only three hundred and ten PO boxes. These were rented primarily by small-business owners and a few wealthy people from Chestnut Hill who felt their post office was not well run. Gary had two clerks to assist him. Marla Towey was in her late thirties, with two children and an ex-husband who worked for SEPTA. She could not stay past two thirty in the afternoon because she needed to be home when her kids got off the school bus, and she lived all the way in Drexel Hill. Alondra Robles was ten years younger than Marla. She had three children, the smallest of whom was the daughter of a man she sometimes called her boyfriend but more often spoke of as though he were a chronic medical condition. Alondra also suffered from lupus. Marla had a herniated disc.

The PO boxes were in the outer lobby, which was accessible to the public twenty-four hours a day. Members of the local homeless population could sometimes be found sleeping there in cold weather. The business window was in the inner lobby, which was locked up every night, and behind it lay the work floor, where the employees spent their days. Things were busiest around eleven o'clock, when a line of ten or so customers would assemble before the window to buy stamps or mail packages. Monday was the most hectic, Tuesday the calmest. Often an hour would go by in which only one or two people came through the door. Gary manned the window on days when both Marla and Alondra were off or out sick. When one of them was in, he sat in the back, where, besides placing the presorted mail in the boxes after it was delivered in the morning and gathering it to be picked up in the evening, there was never very much to do.

The downtime proved an adjustment. All of Gary's working life, for ten hours a day, there had been something to march toward—this house and then that house, the next block and the one after. Now he spent most of the day sitting in the closet-size office at the back of the work floor, and hours passed in which he could not say that he accomplished anything at all.

"You're looking at this all wrong," said Chuck Feeney, his friend at the Philadelphia district building, when Gary called him at the end of his first week. "It's a low-traffic store. Basically runs itself."

"That's the thing," said Gary. "What do I do while it runs itself?"

"Got a library card?" asked Chuck. "Got a Kindle?"

The next day, Gary brought to work the first volume of Robert Caro's Lyndon Johnson biography, which he had bought not long after he was hired as a letter carrier but had never gotten around to reading. In his first attempt at junior college, Gary had been a political science major. In his second attempt, he had tried business administration, though it had never been a subject that excited him. His daughter, Caitlin, had graduated from Cabrini College with a degree in communications. Gary had always imagined she would go to a more prestigious school, but Cabrini had given her a field hockey scholarship, and he could not complain about that. He sat down to read the biography after loading the mailboxes and making sure Alondra was all right at the window. The volume was nine hundred and sixty pages long. Gary read four of them before he felt his attention waver.

He could hear Alondra at the window, agitated with someone. She hung up her phone as Gary stepped out of the office.

"How's Jeff?" he asked her. Jeff was Alondra's sometime boyfriend.

"Gary, you know I don't want to hear that name ever again." Alondra was on her feet, leaning forward against the counter. Her lupus caused her joints to cramp if she sat in a chair for too long. "That was my mother. Lucas is throwing up everywhere."

Gary couldn't remember if Lucas was the oldest child or the middle one. The youngest, he knew, was a girl named Jada. "Poor guy. Lucky he's got his grandma. I used to drop my kids off with my mom when they were sick. Grandmas make the best doctors."

"You know, Lucas is in first grade next year," said Alondra. "Am I gonna be able to leave at two thirty like Marla does?"

"I don't think we can have both clerks leave early every day," said Gary. "We need to keep the window open till four thirty."

"Why does Marla get to leave early?"

Gary did not have a satisfying answer. Marla's special dispensation was a holdover from the previous postmaster. Gary had not wanted to do anything to upset the order of things. Neither he nor his wife, Claire, who worked as a bookkeeper for a screw and bolt manufacturer, had ever been there when the children got home from school. Their kids had gone to a neighbor's house until they were old enough to watch themselves. But maybe Marla didn't have any neighbors who could watch her kids for two hours.

"Why don't you run home and check on him, if you're worried," suggested Gary. Alondra lived twenty minutes away, in Olney. "But you gotta come back after lunch if he's not too bad. All right?"

With Alondra gone, Gary took her place at the window, the Johnson biography spread open on the counter before him. Through the wide glass storefront, he had an unobstructed view of a construction crew digging up the thin strip of lawn next to the McDonald's across the parking lot. There must have been a pipe that needed fixing. The hole was deep enough that the man standing in it was visible only from the waist up. The other men lingered around the rim, paunchy in their sweat-stained T-shirts. For thirty years, people had said to Gary, "At least you're getting exercise," even as he stood before them in all his heaviness, growing wider by the season. It was a hot day for early May, with the sort of heat that a person walking in and out of buildings might mistake for beautiful weather. Anyone who had to dig a ditch would never mistake a hot day for anything other than what it was.

Alondra did not return that afternoon, nor did she call. Back when Gary told Claire he would have two clerks working under him, his wife laughed. "I'm sorry, Gar," she said, seeing the expression he must have made. "I just can't picture you managing people."

Gary had been at Kilntown for more than four years when the adman stopped in for the first time. He had read all four volumes of Caro's Johnson biography—he finished the final volume the same week it was released—as well as books about John Adams, Ulysses S. Grant, and Harry S. Truman. So far that summer, he had read about the Brooklyn Bridge, the Chicago World's Fair, and the Lewis and Clark expedition. He was halfway through a history of the Panama Canal when Marla told him there was a man at the window who wanted to buy ten thousand dollars' worth of stamps.

The Kilntown post office sold plenty of stamps, but most customers bought only a book or two at a time. A few local businesses purchased them by the roll. Sometimes the nuns from the Sisters of St. Joseph came to stock the mail room at the senior-living facility they operated on Wissahickon Avenue. It was always a pair of them, Sister Mary Elizabeth and Sister Agnes Marie, neither younger than eighty. They would arrive with a check for some arbitrary figure—ninety-six dollars and eleven cents, say—and the value of the stamps Gary sold them had to equal that amount, not one penny more or less. He would invite the nuns to sit with him at the table in his office as he counted out one- and two- and additional-ounce stamps, three- and five- and ten-cent stamps, fumbling with the math on an old RadioShack calculator. He felt like he was back in elementary school, with the nuns staring at him through the glare of their spectacles, embarrassed that he could not do the sums in his head, but he was responsible for every dollar exchanged in the building, and he did not trust himself to get the numbers right on his own.

"Now, this check isn't going to bounce, is it, ladies?" Gary would tease. "The Sisters of Mercy were in here the other week and warned me about you St. Joe's girls." Sister Mary Elizabeth would protest playfully whenever he said things like that, but Sister Agnes Marie never cracked a smile.

Gary stepped out of the office to see who it was who wanted ten thousand dollars' worth of stamps. A man stood across the counter from Marla in a loud blue suit with no tie. His face was flushed from the summer heat. It was July. The lobby was decked in patriotic bunting.

In the years since he had been at the Kilntown Post Office, Gary had come to think of himself as its proprietor, and he did what he could to make the store a more inviting space. He tried to keep the walls and counters neat, and he decorated for holidays, even the minor ones. All year long, he played music—Bill Evans, Stan Getz, things like that—using the iHome Caitlin had bought him several birthdays ago. Alondra said the jazz made her sleepy and asked if she could pick what was played on alternating days. Gary told her that, unfortunately, only the postmaster was authorized to select the music. The jazz made the post office feel like a café, he thought, even if no one hung out there except himself and the clerks. He had looked into putting a Keurig machine in the lobby, but he was told by his supervisor downtown that it was a potential safety hazard to have customers making coffee. Instead, he bought one for the employees to use in the back. He discovered after ordering it that Marla did not consume caffeine and Alondra drank only Diet Coke.

Gary invited the adman to sit in his office, at the table where he hosted the nuns. The office was not as orderly as the lobby—books and papers cluttered every surface—but Gary thought it was charming in its own way, like the study of a disorganized but respected professor. Only the table was kept clear, because it was needed to get the money together at the end of the day.

"I like that music you've got playing out there," said the man. He reminded Gary of someone, though Gary could not say who.

"I think that's McCoy Tyner," said Gary. The man asked what the song was called, but Gary didn't know. "I've just got them all on a playlist."

The adman's name was Jeremy Krukoski. He needed two hundred rolls of first-class stamps.

"We don't keep nearly that amount of stock in the store," explained Gary. "I can order it for you, but we don't keep that much lying around. That's a hell of a lot of stamps."

Jeremy worked in print advertising. He had business with Bausch + Lomb, the contact-lens people. Targeted mailings, postcards with discount deals, that sort of thing. Jeremy had asked an optometrist for his client list, only to learn that it was illegal for doctors to share such information. Patient confidentiality and what have you. Jeremy had the idea, then, of sending optometrists packs of the postcards pre-stamped, with the address line left blank. He took one out of his pocket and showed it to Gary. "The optometrist just has to fill them out with his patient's information and drop them in the mail. Bausch and Lomb makes money, the optometrist makes money, the customer gets cheaper lenses, and I look like I know what the hell I'm doing. Everybody gets theirs."

Gary inspected the card. Fifteen percent off a year's supply of contact lenses. Claire wore contact lenses, but Gary didn't need them. His eyes were about the only parts of him that worked as well as they ever had.

"Everybody gets theirs," Gary repeated. As he said, he could certainly order the stamps for Jeremy. The turnaround would be about a week.

"I knew you could help me. Soon as you came out there, I thought, Here's the guy I should be talking to." Jeremy took in the stacks of books around the office. "You writing a dissertation or something?"

"Just like to read," said Gary. "This place basically runs itself."

"Sounds like a dream. With me it's go, go, go, all the time. Nights, weekends. My doctor told me I should meditate. I said to him, 'Where the hell am I gonna meditate? On the Schuylkill Expressway?'"

"You're young," said Gary. "Things settle down. They did for me at least."

"Hell, they'd better," said Jeremy. "I got little kids, so that's part of it."

"That's part of it," agreed Gary. "It's a busy time of life. I have two, grown up now. It's like they were never in the house in the first place."

"That's what I'm waiting for," said Jeremy. "'A busy time of life.' I like that. I feel that, you know? So which of these should I read first, once my kids go off to college?"

Gary eased the Truman book out from under three others balanced on top of it. "Here's a regular guy who ended up becoming president. Sold men's clothing, originally."

"No shit?" Jeremy stared at the cover for a moment. It seemed as though he was going to ask a question about it, but instead he said, "We'll be doing a lot of business. It's Gary, right? Lot of business, Gary. You get a bonus for moving stamps?"

Gary did not.

"Well, you're gonna move a lot of stamps regardless. Enough that we should probably talk about discounts."

After the adman left, Gary sat thinking of his son, Colin. Colin worked in computers—medical software, something like that. He lived in Madison, Wisconsin, with a woman who did the same thing. Gary had asked him if he figured they would get married, but Colin said he didn't think so. Gary and Colin spoke every couple of weeks, whenever something needed to be said. Gary would usually tell him about the book he was reading, how Truman had done this or that. Colin listened, but Gary could tell he wasn't very interested. "You know, Truman was almost assassinated by Puerto Rican nationalists," Gary would say, and Colin would respond with, "That's great. Listen, Dad, I got this thing I gotta get to . . ."

When the window shuttered at four thirty, Marla sat in Gary's office as he closed out her drawer. Gary saw more of Marla in the summer, when her kids were out of school. That summer, her favorite conversation topic was her cousin, who flipped houses in the city. "You should see these places. Real shitholes. You would never think to live there. But he cleans them up and sells them for twice, three times what he paid."

Gary wished she would stop chatting as he added up the money. He counted it once, twice, three times and still came up short. "Marla, you're missing a hundred dollars," he said, doing his best not to sound accusatory.

Marla stared at him as though he hadn't said anything.

"You sold a hundred-dollar money order," he said, looking over the receipts. "Where's the hundred?"

"It's in there," said Marla. "It isn't in there?"

Gary counted a fourth time. He had never had a drawer short one hundred dollars before. The money went out with the mail on the evening truck. If it was short even one dollar, he would get a phone call in the morning. They looked for things like that, the people downtown.

"A hundred is a lot, Marla," said Gary. "That's a lot of money to lose."

"I didn't take it," said Marla.

"I didn't say you took it. Maybe go look around the counter and see if you misplaced it?"

Marla returned empty-handed, her face crumpled like she might start to cry. In his first few years with the post office, when Gary had made less money, he took a second job delivering pizzas at night. They had just bought the house in Bucks County and Claire was pregnant with Caitlin. A week into the pizza job, he misplaced a twenty—dropped it on the street, probably, trying to stuff it in his pocket—and the manager, a real bloodless son of a bitch five years his junior, deducted it from his pay. The guy acted as though Gary had taken it, as if he was not just a thief but a stupid one who hadn't realized it would be missed. Gary worked the rest of his shift and then made a big show of quitting. He told the manager he'd be waiting for him in the parking lot. He hadn't actually waited—he had just wanted to scare the kid. Gary had had more of a temper when he was a young man.

"It's all right," he told Marla. He went to the store's safe. Alondra often turned in her drawer with more money than it should have had. Four or five dollars over, never too much. Gary reminded her each time that she needed to be better about giving people the correct change, and then he placed the extra money in an envelope. On the night Marla's drawer was short, there were one hundred and eight dollars in the envelope. He counted out a hundred and slipped them into the bank wallet. "You gotta be more careful, Marla. Technically, they can dock your pay for the difference."

"I don't know what could have happened," said Marla. The threat of tears had passed. "I must have accidentally given it to somebody. Really what I'm most upset about is that somebody got an extra hundred bucks and didn't say anything about it. Just decided it was theirs to keep. You can't trust nobody these days, I swear to God."

"Yeah, you're welcome," said Alondra when Gary told her about it the next morning. "I'm the only one making this place any money."

. . .

Gary moved a lot of stamps.

Over the next five months, Kilntown became the third-most profitable store in the Philadelphia suburbs, behind only Chester and Lansdale—much larger operations—owing solely to Jeremy and his bulk stamp purchases. The higher-ups in the district building allowed Gary to keep three hundred thousand dollars' worth of stock on hand, a previously unfathomable volume for a tiny walk-in post office. It didn't mean any extra money for Gary, but even so.

"The district manager knows your name, Gary," said Chuck Feeney on the other end of the line.

"If we're so important, maybe they can get me one of those ergonomic saddle chairs so I don't have to deal with this broke-ass stool," said Alondra when Gary told her about it. He had tried not to sound too self-important as he did.

"We have a store budget," said Gary. "It has to be spent on improvements for the store."

"A new chair isn't an improvement for the store, but a coffee machine is? Nobody even uses that thing but you, Gary."

Jeremy used the coffee machine. He drank the breakfast blend with three packets of Splenda. He came in every Friday for his stamps, usually dropping thirty-five thousand dollars each time. Gary had been unable to secure him a discount—the Postal Service did not offer discounts on stamps—but the increased stock saved Jeremy from having to place an order and wait a week for it to come through. He acted as though Gary had pulled off a masterstroke of arbitration. "It pays to know a man on the inside," said Jeremy between sips from his paper cup. "My grandfather taught me that. Worked at traffic court. One of the greatest ticket fixers of the twentieth century."

On such days, Gary would sit nervously with Jeremy's check until he sent it off on the evening truck. He was plagued by an irrational anxiety, considering that it was simply a piece of paper, easily canceled and replaced if lost. Really, it was Jeremy who should have been nervous, driving off with thirty-five thousand dollars' worth of stamps in his car. But Jeremy never seemed nervous about anything.

On the evening of Marla's accident, Gary left work early for a wake. Mrs. Brown, who had lived on his route for a decade, had passed away from emphysema. She had always been kind to Gary, offering him a drink every time he stepped onto her porch. When he greeted her son at the funeral parlor, Gary told him, "I delivered your mother's mail for ten years." He had not expected much of a reaction to this statement, but the son seemed oddly moved by it. He ushered Gary around to his relatives, saying, with a gravity Gary found slightly embarrassing, "This is Gary Minihan. He delivered Ma's mail for ten years."

Gary was on his way home when he received a call—the first since he had left work—from a man who identified himself as Marla's ex-husband, Steve. "There's been an accident on the job site," he said.

Gary turned his Hyundai around and headed back to Kilntown. When he got there, a second sedan was idling next to Marla's in the rear parking lot. A man dressed like a train conductor leaned against the hood smoking a cigarette. Marla lay in the cabin, reclined on the passenger seat. She rolled the window down as Gary walked up to the car.

"You all right, Marla? What the hell happened?"

"I told you I need a key to the back door, Gary," she said without looking at him. Gary noticed that she was holding her neck rigid. "I've been saying it for years."

Marla had closed up the store, handing off the day's mail and earnings to the evening driver at five. She then locked the door between the inner and outer lobby, realizing a moment too late that she had left her car keys in Gary's office. "I must have set them down when I was getting the mail together for the driver. Like you *told* me to do, Gary." This shouldn't have been a problem—Marla merely needed to unlock the door she had just locked—but when she inserted her office key and gave it a twist, the blade snapped off. "It's in there now. Go on and look at it. The door's stuck in the locked position. So I was locked outside without my car keys. And I don't have a key for the back door, and I had to get home to my kids, and I didn't want to call you, Gary, because you told me you were going to a wake and I didn't want to be disrespectful." So Marla did the only reasonable thing, which was to climb through the package window that connected the outer lobby to the work floor.

"You went through the package window?" asked Gary. Not in a million years would it have occurred to him to try to crawl through the package window. Not that he could have fit, of course. It was a narrow aperture, about four feet off the ground, where people dropped off packages that already had postage. Just hoisting himself up to it would have been a challenge.

"It was the only way in, Gary!" cried Marla, her jaw jerking above her stiff neck. She had tumbled through the window head-first and landed upside down. Still she had not called Gary, out of respect for the dead. She called Steve. The smoking conductor confirmed the story with a nod.

"Jesus Christ," said Gary. "How did Steve get you out?"

"I had to crawl, Gary," said Marla. "I crawled all the way to the back door, like an invalid. I may be an invalid now."

"Well, go to the hospital," said Gary. "What are you doing in this car? Call an ambulance."

"We have a doctor we like," said Steve. He seemed unconcerned by the whole affair. "I'll take her in the morning."

"I won't be in tomorrow, Gary, if that isn't obvious," said Marla. "You need to call a damn locksmith."

"How's Marla gonna act so stupid when she's got a herniated disc?" wondered Alondra the next morning. "Even the homeless people who sleep in the lobby never try to crawl through the package window."

Gary paused as he was loading his coffee pod into the Keurig. The possibility had never occurred to him. If Marla could squeeze through the window, surely a homeless person could. People might be crawling in and out of the window every night, and he would never know. He should probably have a talk with Chuck Feeney. Maybe the union rep too. He didn't think he was liable for what happened to Marla, but who knew with things like that?

"The juiciest aspect of the whole thing is that she called Steve," continued Alondra. "I bet they're back at it hard. No way I would call Jeff in that situation. He'd just fuck it all up worse. Plus his license got suspended."

Around two o'clock, Jeremy appeared in the doorway of Gary's office, sweaty despite the December air. His suit was olive green. Gary was surprised to see him, as it was not a Friday. "We fucked up, Gary," he panted. "There's been a misprint emergency."

Gary set aside his John D. Rockefeller biography and gestured for Jeremy to sit.

"This guy," said the adman. "Dr. Vincent Wu—he's the biggest optometrist in Phoenix. He's got a fucking empire out there. I spent fifteen grand just on postcards for his clients."

"So?"

"So, I misspelled his name. I wrote Vincent *Woo,* with two *O*s. The cards are useless. I'm out fifteen grand on a fucking spelling mistake."

"We can figure something out," said Gary. "Some kind of buyback, maybe. These things must happen."

Jeremy's agitation seemed disproportionate to the severity of the loss. Sure, Gary would be in a panic over fifteen thousand dollars, but he would have guessed it was little more than a rounding error for Jeremy.

"Things have been tense at home," Jeremy admitted, rubbing his temples. "Between you and me, my marriage ain't in the best shape. Some other ventures haven't panned out like I thought they would." He picked up the Rockefeller book and flicked the cover open and shut. "You always keep a calm head, Gary. It makes me calm. You know, I'm thinking that after I get things straight I might expand a little. Maybe I'll put you on my war council. That'd be something, huh?"

Gary agreed that that would be something.

Gary had trouble returning to his book after Jeremy left. He kept thinking about the job offer—if that was what Jeremy had meant by war council—wondering whether it was serious. Gary had never intended to spend his entire career with the post office, confident that something else would come along. Most of the carriers he had known were not lifers. They had migrated from other occupations—construction, manufacturing, the army—or from jobs that didn't exist anymore. Telephone operators, electrotypers. A couple guys used to build ships at the shuttered navy yard. The post office was a decent place to land—job security, pension—but Gary had landed there so early. He remembered the day he realized that, since his raises were based on nothing but his length of service, he could calculate how much he would make every year for the rest of his life. It was a bit like learning the exact height of the sky.

Marla went on disability leave. The post office offered fifty-two weeks, and Gary was sure she would take all of them.

"So are we getting a new clerk?" asked Alondra. "Tell them to send someone who can count a drawer."

Gary cleared a buyback of Jeremy's misprinted stock for ninety cents on the dollar. It was standard practice, but Jeremy wanted to celebrate. He had Gary meet him for drinks at the pub just across Bethlehem Pike.

Jeremy looked sweatier than at their previous meeting. His tan suit appeared yellow in the dim light of the bar. He told Gary he was drinking Red Bull and vodka, but after the first round—a putrid combination that made his heart race—Gary switched to beer. Gary had never been a big drinker, and was even less of one since the diabetes. He had never been inside this pub, which was more upscale than he had imagined. Suit jackets and cocktails and huge potted ferns. He felt like he was at a wedding reception.

Jeremy had put back a few before Gary got there. "The wife's leaving," he said by way of explanation. "What can I say? I still like to party. But it's not a good time for a divorce, money-wise. Really fucking terrible time, right now specifically."

Jeremy ordered another round and sat staring at the sports highlights playing on the television suspended in the corner. "How is there enough time?" he asked. "I look at my kids and I barely recognize them. When I was a kid—well, my dad wasn't around, but my friends had dads. I saw those dads around. Dads used to be around more, didn't they? Where did they find the time?"

Gary didn't know. He thought there was a lot of time, almost too much of it. That was how he had read all those books in his office. But it hadn't always been like that, he supposed. He had lived most of his life in a different time, one that had ended only when he'd stopped carrying mail.

"You're easy to talk to, Gary, you know that?" Jeremy placed a wet palm on Gary's shoulder. "You remind me of a priest."

Gary chuckled. "A priest for the war council?"

"What's that?"

"The war council," repeated Gary. "Your next venture. You said you'd hire me for the war council."

"Oh, yeah. Yeah," said Jeremy. It was clear from his expression that he hadn't thought about it since he had said it. "If I could give you a job, Gary, I would. Maybe for the next thing. This Bausch and Lomb thing was a bust. Didn't go at all like I expected. But when I figure out the next thing, you'll be the first hire I make."

"To the next thing," said Gary, tipping his beer. He felt like a rube. What was he doing in that bar? he wondered. He needed to go home.

"Orthodontists, maybe," muttered Jeremy. "Invisalign."

. . .

Gary called Jeremy later in the week about returning the stamps. The misprinted postcards needed to be destroyed under postal supervision before a refund could be issued. The call went to voicemail, which was not unusual. Jeremy did not call back that day, which was.

He received a call three days later from a man who identified himself as Jeremy's brother-in-law. Jeremy had been found in the hotel where he was staying, dead of cardiac arrest. The man implied that drugs might have been involved.

"We heard your message about the refund." The man sounded irritated, as though this was not a job he thought should fall to him. "That's some good news, finally. Jeremy left a lot of debts outstanding. I can put you in touch with the lawyer who's straightening it all out. How anyone ever trusted that guy with money, I'll never understand."

Gary had planned to go to the wake. He brought a blazer to wear over his work clothes. It hung in the back of his car all day. But when the time came to turn west onto the turnpike, he found himself driving east toward home.

"What happened to the wake?" Claire asked when he walked into the house, his blazer undisturbed on its coat hanger. She was sitting on the couch watching something on her iPad. She wore one of those headsets with a microphone attached, like an air-traffic controller.

"I didn't feel like it," said Gary.

"I thought this was a friend of yours."

"Just a customer. Nobody there would even know who I was."

Claire frowned. "So?"

"So? What am I supposed to do, go up to his widow and say, 'Hi, I sold your husband stamps'?"

"I'm sure she'd appreciate the gesture."

"She was divorcing him. She could give a shit about who sold him stamps."

Claire turned back to her tablet. "Supposed to snow tonight," she said, after a moment.

There was a foot on the ground by 5 A.M., when Gary's supervisor called to say he needed to go in early and shovel the store's walkway. It fell to the postmaster to ensure that the building was accessible, a responsibility that seemed to Gary, on that particular morning, a profound injustice. Claire warned him not to have a heart attack and fell back asleep. Gary grumbled as he dressed, filled a thermos with coffee, and pulled away from his own unshoveled driveway to risk his life on the roads.

The rear lot was a sheet of white. He didn't bother to locate a space, stopping the Hyundai somewhere near the center and grabbing his shovel from the trunk. He trudged around to the entrance. A plow had cut a path through the main lot, kicking up an extra three-foot hump of snow in front of the post office that Gary would have to get through. The wind had blown a drift two feet up the glass door. Across the parking lot, barely visible in the predawn light, a teenager labored to clear the McDonald's sidewalk. With that sympathetic scrape echoing off the concrete, Gary lowered his shovel and went to work.

The snow was heavy, the six inches closest to the ground dense as wet sand. Once it was on his shovel, Gary had nowhere to put it. If he threw it to the left or the right, it would only become the problem of whoever showed up to dig out the bank or the hair salon. If he tossed it in the parking lot, it would impede traffic. The only spot available was the strip of lawn beside the McDonald's, where he had seen the men digging a trench that first week in Kilntown. He figured McDonald's wouldn't mind a bit of extra snow on their lawn. He would work it out with the teen if it came to that.

He went at it slowly, shuffling across the cleared lane and dropping snow on the McDonald's lawn one shovelful at a time. After the third trip, Gary was sweating beneath his coat. His hips were killing him; his arms and palms were immediately sore. He was too fat, too broken-down. He was fifty-six, but his body felt much older. Too old to be shoveling snow. He didn't even shovel snow at home—the Zieglers next door had a blower. There was no sound anywhere in the blind morning other than his scraping, the teen's, and his own gulping breath.

He had been a fool to think there would be an early departure, a special dispensation that would excuse him from his work, his real work, before they had gotten everything they needed from his body. He was only—had only ever been—a set of arms and feet, a back to lift and haul. A shoveler. A carrier like his father. A smarter man would have played his hand better. Cut corners, made a fuss, found a scam. He'd lacked the imagination for that.

As the sky lightened, the hump grew smaller. His shoulders burned, and the sidewalk gradually cleared. He turned finally to the entrance itself, just as the first SUV pulled up to the McDonald's drive-through. Gary felt his shovel scrape against the threshold. The drift that had formed against the glass crumbled into a pile of fluffy clods.

Then, like some religious visitation, the door opened from within. Gary stood there staring, his shovel laden with snow, as a figure sidled out of the lobby—his lobby, the lobby he had spent the past forty minutes making accessible. It was a woman swaddled in several old coats, her hair greasy beneath a stained knit hat, a hiking backpack slung over her shoulder. She shuffled past Gary without a look or a word, beelining for the road. His grip loosened and the shovel spun, spilling its contents back onto the pavement. Gary watched the woman float silently away down Bethlehem Pike and melt into the wintery day beyond.

After catching his breath, he scraped up the last of the snow and went inside to open the store.

In March, Gary learned that Marla had been fired.

"Faking it," said Chuck Feeney from the district building. "Faked the whole thing."

"The injury?" asked Gary. He sat in his office with the phone to his ear.

"The ex-husband, too, at SEPTA. Said he fell off a platform or something like that. He was out for a year, then applied for permanent disability. Social Security sent an agent to check him out, and not only is he full of shit, but Marla's full of shit, too. They're renovating a house together on Baltimore Avenue. The guy saw them hanging Sheetrock. Lifting, carrying, climbing, the whole thing."

"You know, I had my suspicions," said Gary. "Her story sounded off to me."

"Well Jesus, Gar, don't say that. There's gonna be eyes on your shop after this, especially with all that money you've been bringing in."

"That's all over now. The guy died. In fact, we still owe his widow a refund for some misprinted stock. It's getting shredded tomorrow."

"Probably for the best," said Chuck. "Too much excitement for a guy like you, Gary, just waiting out the clock. How much longer you got?"

"Five years," said Gary.

"I always knew she was a liar," said Alondra when she heard about Marla. "She'd lie about nothing. Miss 'I don't use caffeine,' then I come in after she's opened up and like two of my Diet Cokes are missing from the fridge. So, like, who took them, Gary? The Diet Coke fairy?"

The next day, Gary drove to the printer in Fort Washington to oversee the destruction of Jeremy's stamps. A rented shredding truck was set up at the far end of a small industrial park, the useless postcards stacked on a pallet. No snow covered the ground, but it was one of those wet, colorless days in March when it seemed as though the year had already exhausted itself. Two Postal Service representatives—Gary and a woman from the district building downtown—were required to witness the destruction and sign off on the refund.

"Who is Dr. Vincent Woo?" asked the woman, examining one of the postcards. She was younger than Gary and wore an expensive-looking scarf atop her suit. He would not have pegged her for a postal worker.

"Biggest optometrist in Phoenix," said Gary. "He oversees a vast empire."

The cheerful man who ran the shredder—he seemed, from the way he spoke and moved, to love his job—let them each throw a few handfuls into the maw of the truck. The cards vanished in a faint purr of dust.

"What's the strangest thing you've ever shredded?" Gary asked him.

"Five thousand origami cranes," said the cheerful man.

They left it to the man to carry on the destruction while they sat in folding chairs on the near side of the lot. It felt a bit like a tailgate. The woman, Gail, had brought coffee and breakfast sandwiches. They were there for most of the morning, chatting and comparing notes—Gail was a font of gossip about the district building, about Washington, about where things were headed. She took frequent smoke breaks down at the roadside, talking loudly to someone or various someones on her phone. Gary sat by himself and observed the pulverization, thinking, for some reason, of his father.

Years before, an elderly woman had come up to Gary at his father's wake with a letter folded neatly in her hand. She told Gary that, on the very last day that Francis Minihan ever carried mail, he had dropped a copy of the letter into each of the boxes on his route, and she had saved hers because it struck her as such a thoughtful and unexpected gesture. Gary stuck the letter in his suit jacket and read it in his kitchen late that night, thoroughly tired and slightly drunk. In the letter, his father reflected on how much he had enjoyed serving his customers and watching them grow over the years. How the job was hard, but how the people on his mail route were a source of fulfillment. How, when he had started with the post office, a first-class stamp cost only three cents. The last line above his signature read, "It was the pleasure of my working life to be among you." Francis had never been a talkative man, and Gary was astounded by how well he articulated his thoughts on the page. He was sure it was one of the best things he had ever read in his life. He decided then that when his own final day of carrying the mail arrived, he would do the same thing, for he felt, in that instant, those same things his father had. He would write his own letter and make a copy for every customer and set it in their mailboxes without a word, to let them know that he had been there among them and that it had meant something. Years later, when he was offered the job in Kilntown, the farewell letter was not on his mind. He only remembered it two weeks after he was situated as interim postmaster, and by then the moment had passed.

Lindsey Drager

Blackbirds

I

School, and she can't breathe, and she forgot her inhaler again. She keeps forgetting, can't keep things straight. Forgot her lunch last week, twice. The inhaler should stay with the nurse, but she needs it so often that she now keeps it in her desk, takes puffs once an hour or so between lessons. School, and she can't breathe, and all she does these days is fail to remember. The inhaler in her desk ran out yesterday, and this morning she left the new one on the kitchen counter. She is eight and wears her glasses on a braided rope around her neck so she won't lose them. She is in the bathroom trying to breathe, trying not to panic because she forgot her inhaler, and she gathers two paper towels and folds them, wets them with hot water, locks herself in a bathroom stall, and puts them to her face. She breathes through the paper towels. Breathes slowly, counts. It is worse when she gets herself worked up, she knows, because then the stress closes her throat. She has to relax. She has to breathe very slowly and count. She is eight and she is breathing in the bathroom stall, breathing through warm, wet paper towels. She imagines her mother at home, worries about the new baby. Her mother, the baby—she's worried, and this takes shape in the way that she breathes. Slower, more slowly, she tells herself. Count. Count numbers, make them go up. She sees someone has drawn a dinosaur bird—a pterodactyl—with a spike on its head on the bathroom stall door. It has been drawn with colored pens. There are these really delicate veins in the wings, and the ink is green and blue and pink, and she wonders for a moment whether the color is right. Because no human has ever seen a dinosaur, so how would we know? How would we know what the flesh of beasts looked like before our own species was born? The dinosaur is beautiful there on the wall of the door, but the counting isn't helping. She has to shift gears. The dinosaur's head looks like a hammer to her, and then she thinks, The alphabet. The alphabet, she thinks. She runs each letter through her mind, then winds back to the beginning. Her mother, the baby. Breathe. The wheezing stops then, her breath evens. The alphabet, she thinks, not numbers. Because she can see the end of the alphabet, like she can imagine the end of this asthma attack. That must be why numbers don't work: because they just keep going. But, she thinks, the alphabet—it ends. The dinosaur is beautiful, she thinks, breathing slowly now, steadier, and the alphabet ends.

II

Her mother said she was going down for a nap, but that was five hours ago. The baby is fine. She has been playing with him—first blocks and then an electronic book with the sounds of animals that the baby echoes in his baby voice. She pushes up her glasses with her finger, picks up her baby brother to go knock on her mother's door. She's got to try to wake her. The baby is nearly her size—the girl has slimmed down, has heard her grandparents ask her father on their rare visits, *Why do you think she's lost all that weight so quickly? Why?*—and she kind of shifts the baby to her hip and walks sideways to get her balance. He goes for her glasses, and she gives him a definitive *no* and offers him one of her braids, and he plays with it, and she lets him. She is walking to her mother's room, which is really her parents' room, but she doesn't think of it that way. The baby nuzzles his face into the side of her neck and then lays his head there, sighs loudly. She knocks on the door to the room, but there is no answer. She knocks harder, waits a beat, then yells, *Mom?* She says, *Are you awake? Mom?* But there is no answer. There was also no answer two hours ago, when she last attempted to rouse her mother. She tries the door handle again, but it is still locked. She weighs her options as she shifts the baby to the other side of her hip, looks at the digital clock in her bedroom. She has trouble telling time on the analog face of the clock, keeps failing her clock tests in school. The digital clock reads late, and she understands it is long past time for dinner, and she's worried if she doesn't wake her mother now, her mother will sleep until the morning. The baby yelps twice, and she says an empty, *Yep, that's right,* as she always does when he yelps, and— balancing the baby on her hip—she goes to her room and takes the paper clip she has stretched out into an uneven line from the secret drawer in her dresser. Also in the dresser: her collection of fossils; a card with an autograph from Annie Lennox, which she received in response to a letter she wrote her; and every pen her father ever got her from his business trips. When the baby starts to fuss—just the beginnings, just the very start of a fuss, a single unhappy grunt—she starts to bob him up and down on her hip. He is getting heavy, she thinks. She returns to the door and pokes the paper clip through the thin hole in the doorknob. There is a click, which is the lock releasing, and then she turns the knob.

Her mother is there, beneath a mound of blankets. She walks to the far side of the bed, her mother's side of the bed, and whispers her name. Her name, her name, the girl whispers, bobbing her baby brother on her hip. There is no movement, and for a moment she gets scared, a shiver of fear runs through her, and her throat tightens and she breathes deeply to ward off something more. Then she leans over with the baby and twists him a bit. She lets him sort of push on their mother, add pressure to her form.

Their mother stirs instantly, responds by jolting upright, snaps, *What?!*

Are you coming out? the girl says. She used to whisper this, but she doesn't anymore. She knows whispering when her mother is in this state gets her nowhere.

Please leave me alone, her mother says.

The girl rearranges the baby on her other hip now and leaves the room. She is halfway down the hall when her mother calls her back. *Close the door,* she says. *When the door is shut it's for a reason. Keep it closed,* her mother says, and so she does.

She puts the baby back in his bouncy chair, then wheels the chair to the kitchen so she can keep an eye on him as she's warming up a can of ravioli. She drags her step stool over to the oven, turns the electric stove on to medium heat. She's been in this pickle before, which is why she started asking for ravioli cans that have tabs like soda, because she can't use the can opener. Tried it once, cut herself. Never got that can open. Had to put waffles in the toaster that night.

The girl pops the tab of the can and curls back the metal lid, asks her brother in a singsong voice if he is hungry. He'll get Cheerios and a banana, cut up small. The ravioli is for her. She stirs the can's contents with a large plastic serving spoon, waiting for the food to heat up, and she peeks behind herself at her brother. He is smiling and bouncing up and down in his bouncing chair, his feet not long enough to stand, so they hang and jostle like he's on a ride at the fair.

The fair, she thinks. Her favorite is the Ferris wheel, because you can see so much all at once. She used to be scared of it, but not anymore. She stirs the ravioli and thinks about turning up the heat so it will cook faster, but she did this last time and she burned it. She keeps the heat on medium and keeps stirring. She is patient, she thinks to herself. She looks at her brother, his feet bobbing below him. Soon they won't, she knows—soon his feet will extend so that he will become mobile. He's already growing so quickly, she thinks. She's excited to help him learn to walk, but also nervous, because it means she'll have to keep a better eye on him.

She stirs the ravioli and starts to make the sound of animals from the digital book. She makes a single sound, and when she makes it her brother echoes her. She turns around and smiles at him. *Yep, that's right,* she says, and tries another. He echoes this one too. A cow, a cat, a duck, a dog. She pushes her glasses up her nose. The lenses grow foggy from the heat of the stovetop. *Yep, that's right,* she says.

The fair, she thinks, making more animal sounds. She does the math until next summer, which is eight months from now. She glances at the analog clock in the kitchen, tries to discern the time. The hour hand first, round down, then the minute hand—five ticks between the numbers, one minute for each tick. She thinks she's got the time, but when she looks at the stovetop's digital clock she's off by an hour and ten minutes.

She stirs the ravioli, makes the sound of a chicken. Her brother echoes her. She can't tell the time, she thinks. She just can't do it. The sound of the chicken again and again, and her brother echoes her, and she stirs the ravioli and tries to think about how she got it wrong, what the hour hand tells, where lie the minutes, until she is jolted back to what is before her, which is the smell of her dinner wafting up from the pan and her brother making the sound of a chicken, over and over again.

III

This morning her mother doesn't wake up. Or she wakes, but it's another bad day—two in a row. This is rare for her, but the girl is learning rare is something elastic, something that bends and stretches and folds so that what once felt like it seldom happened expands to become the new version of everyday. She can't get her mother to wake up, but she'll be roused enough to yell something at the girl, tell her to leave her alone.

The baby is still sleeping—thank goodness he is such a good sleeper, she thinks, which is a thought she's adopted from her grandparents. She didn't know other babies didn't sleep well until her grandparents mentioned that he did. Her mother isn't up, and she thinks about the baby. It's not a good day for her, but it is a Monday, and what is she going to do about school? There is something inside her that knows what she has to do is both wrong and right. It is both a lie and not a lie, what she's about to do. Or maybe that's the wrong way to see it. Maybe the question isn't about what's right. Maybe it's about what's necessary.

She pulls out the phone book and flips to the pages that share a first letter with the name of her school. She runs her finger down the long line of names on the left, then the long line on the right, and she sees that the sweat from her fingers has smeared the ink, so she presses more lightly. Now the ink stays put.

She flips the page once, then again—this is delicate work, the pages so thin, she has to be sure she doesn't tear them—and then she finds it toward the top on the left: the number for her school. She pulls one of the kitchen chairs from the table, drags it slowly, quietly, so as not to wake the baby, and puts it below the phone that hangs from the wall. Then she sings the numbers to herself in order to remember. Sings them again, then uses her finger to press the seven numbers in the order that she sings.

When the secretary gets on the phone, she fakes difficult breathing—she wheezes through her speech. *Another asthma attack?* the secretary asks. And then, *Why isn't your mother calling?*

She's loading my baby brother in the car, and we're headed to the doctor's, she wheezes.

Okay, well, we'll see you tomorrow, the secretary tells her, and the girl hangs up the phone.

She goes back to her bed then, crawls under her covers. She

has a quilt that is all dinosaur fossils, and on her ceiling live her collected images of the extinct beasts. She loves the dinosaurs with wings best, and she collects the images from books her grandparents give her from yard sales and book fairs, tears them out and pastes them to her ceiling. They are beasts from a time that is both imaginary and also real, a time before people. She won't be able to sleep, she thinks. She has lied, she thinks, but somehow it feels right. This dual sense of guilt and duty will be something she learns to navigate with great care in the months and years to come.

No, she won't be able to sleep, she thinks, but she can lie here and look up at the ceiling, at her dinosaurs and the proof of them all these millions of years later, their fossilized remains. She won't sleep, but she can look out her window at the sunshine and the way the breeze makes the tree limbs move. Later she can study the analog clock face, try harder this time. Try to do better. She won't sleep, but she can rest here, just until she hears the baby is awake.

IV

She is coming home from school and she spots in the gravel of the driveway a fossil. She picks it up and licks her thumb, smears it with her spit. There, pressed into the rock, are the delicate lines of some coral. It's a Petoskey stone, her state's rock. She had to memorize the state motto last week as part of social studies, and she says it to herself now. She lives in a place that was once a giant ocean, long before it was populated with people, and now the echo of coral lives all over the town she calls home. She pockets the rock and keeps walking, knows what she has found is dear because this particular stone is so hard to spot. It's hard to see the fossilization when it isn't wet, takes a real eye to find one. It's only after it's wet that the secret beneath is revealed—the tessellations of hexagons linked together, a network of ancient coral locked in rock that she can touch, that she can pick up and put in her secret drawer with all the others.

The state's motto, she thinks in her head as she's walking through her front door. She pushes up her glasses. She is walking through the door, preparing for whatever it is that will meet her on the other side. The motto, she says to herself, recites to herself, in her head, as she's calling her brother's name. The motto, she says over and over again, inside her mind: If you seek a pleasant peninsula, look about you.

V

It has been a good day, her mother up and around enough to order two pizzas and leave her a twenty and a ten-dollar bill to pay. Her mother is on the phone in the other room with the girl's aunt, her mother's sister. She is crying and saying something about wanting to go away, to leave, and what does that mean, and did her sister know the feeling after she had her second child, and nothing like this happened to her after the first, and what is she supposed to do, what will she do, what is she going to do, she's losing it, it's lost, she's got to get some kind of help. While it may have worried the girl the first time she overheard her mother have a conversation like this, that was months ago now. That was so long ago that the girl barely even remembers to whom she was talking. Instead, the girl is choosing to be excited because her mother let her try a new topping on her pizza. The topping is mushrooms. They are her father's favorite, and he says that they are a whole different taste, a taste that is fully its own. She knows the other tastes from class—sour, salty, bitter, sweet—but she has never tasted the taste of a mushroom. Her father says the taste is a word that sounds like *tsunami*, that scary water wall that was a problem for her father's friend from college in Hawai'i. But Hawai'i is another world away from where she is, and anything that threatens it doesn't threaten her, at least right now. Because she's in the middle of the country, far from any coast. Because you stay away from things that contain the propensity to hurt you. Because distance creates safety. This is something that she knows.

And she knows that she is trying mushrooms, trying something new. She cannot wait to taste this taste that she has never known.

Just then her mother raises her voice to the person on the phone. She must have hung up with the girl's aunt and dialed the girl's father, because this is a tone she only uses with him. The tone is a kind of moaning, a kind of groaning that reminds her of how she felt when she had the stomach flu and could only eat pieces of bread that were toasted but without any butter or jam. It's the sound of someone with the stomach flu, but she knows her mother doesn't have this ailment. Something is wrong, the girl knows, but it is a kind of subtle knowledge, a recognition of a pattern one notices in the world without the language to describe it. Like the way when she goes into different homes—her cousins', her grandparents', her dad's coworkers'—each house has its own smell. She suspects other people detect this too, but no one talks about it. Maybe it's because it's not considered polite. Something is wrong, she knows, but it lingers in the air undiscussed, the way the smell of someone else's house does. She's not sure if what is wrong is a sickness. She doesn't know enough about the body to know if it is, but she secretly hopes that it might be, because she is still young enough to believe all illnesses can be treated and—eventually—cured.

Then her mother screams into the phone, and the girl jumps from the suddenness of the sound, and her mother slams down the mouthpiece from her bedroom. The baby is in his Pack 'n Play in the living room, watching TV. Her grandparents say they shouldn't be allowed to watch so much television, but her grandparents are here so rarely. It's hard to abide by any kind of rules when no one is here to enforce them.

The pizza is coming—she is getting excited about the mushrooms. Will they taste bland or piercing? Like vegetables or meat? What is the taste that her father knows but she does not? What will she tell him when she tries it?

The phone rings then, but her mother doesn't get it, slams her door shut, and the girl can hear the sound of the lock. Her brother giggles at something on the TV and bangs two blocks together, yelps three times in a row. Then it sounds to her like he is talking to himself. Maybe, she thinks, he's making a decision. He must be old enough now.

The phone rings again, and she drags the chair under the phone where it hangs on the wall, reaches up, and answers. It is her father. He asks how it's going, and she has to do that thing again, has to negotiate the guilt with the duty. Because if she tells him the truth—if she tells him how it is really going—what will happen is that he will do a thing he threatened once last year, a thing that scared her so deeply, so fully, and so much that she spent nearly an entire night without sleep. She didn't sleep at all, sweating and breathing really hard as she kept thinking of the thing he threatened, and she watched on her digital clock as the hours moved through the night. What he had said was this: *If your mother can't take care of herself—which means she can't take care of you—then we'll need to put her in the hospital. And while she is getting better, you and your brother will need to stay with your grandparents.*

So she lies—it's deceit but it's in service of safety, the safety of their family, keeping them all under one roof. Because exchanging a situation that is really bad for a situation that is unimaginable is not an option for her just then. It's not an option yet. The problem with being eight is that the unimaginable is always scarier than what is right in front of you.

Everything is good, she tells her father. *Everything is fine.* She's okay, for now, she tells him, because she knows he won't believe her if she says she's great or well or better. She's okay, the girl tells her father in so many ways, spinning in circles, twirling the cord of the phone around her body even as she is on the chair. She turns the cord around her until it is tight and then untwirls it so that she is released. She leans toward the living room to peek in on her brother, who is raptly watching the television show, sitting inside his Pack 'n Play. It's been a good day for her mother. It was a good day today.

And then her father asks how *she* is doing—the girl—and

something inside her breaks open, blossoms and blooms. Because this is attention for her, not for her mother. This is her father asking about her and her alone—the girl—and no one else.

She tells him everything in a single sentence: about the bully at school who teases the kids who play four square; the response she got to her artwork from the teacher, who wants her to enroll in a special program next summer; her troubles with telling time on a clock face because she can't understand which arm is the hour arm and which is the minutes, and suddenly now the teacher has added a third arm, and she can't keep them straight, which is why she's had to retake the clock test twice; the state's motto; the new addition to her fossil collection; and the song she just learned in music that they sing in a round on the bus—she sings for him the chorus—and then she says, at the end, at the end of this monologue, as she is running out of breath, her breathing starting to get difficult, she says that she has ordered pizza and she got hers with mushrooms, just and exactly—precisely—just like him.

He is happy, and she can tell, and she is thrilled that she has pleased him.

When are you coming home? she asks him, and because even the topic, even acknowledging the topic of him being gone, creates in her a very instantaneous and visceral sorrow, she suddenly wants to cry. But she is fierce and she is fearless and she is resolute in her lying, and she knows if she breaks down he will know she's deceiving him. And if he knows she's deceiving him, her world order—her whole sense of the structure of her life—will unravel, fall apart. She holds the tears in by pressing the nails of her right hand into the very delicate flesh on the inside of her left wrist so that the sorrow is made minor by the pain. When the pain takes over, the sorrow is missing, and she can stop. This is how she does not cry.

The answer is next week. His return is next week, and man, does he miss her, he tells her, and she says she misses him too. *I got you a cool pen this time, a really stellar one,* he says, and she thinks of her pen collection in her room. She has never used any of them, not once, because that would break the spell of them. That would make the pens not gifts but tools, and that would change them from beautiful emblems full of meaning to practical instruments that are disposable.

Just then her father says he has to go and to kiss the baby, and she says okay and that she loves him, and he says he loves her too.

Oh, and, kiddo? her father says. *The third hand—on the clock. It's seconds. The short hand is the hour, the long one the minutes. The third hand is also long but skinny and counts the seconds as they pass.*

Oh, she says, sort of recalling the lesson but not really, because she then also recalls from that day, during that lesson in class, wondering why we would need to count the seconds. She would understand if life were some kind of race, but it's not, as far as she can tell. She wants to ask him why there's an arm for seconds, wants to ask him why we need the seconds, but he is telling her he has to go and he'll see her in a week.

And as soon as she hears the click of his phone, the line creates the sound of a kind of low, ongoing buzz. This is a sound she thinks should make her gloomy, but she loves it because it fills her with a sense of independence. For here she is, on the line alone. She is the only one on the call. She imagines a woman on the other end picking up then, a woman who is her in the future, and she would ask that woman, *What kind of person are you?* And maybe the woman would list all these qualities that are strange to the girl, but maybe the woman would just be a larger version of the person she is right now. Just a bigger, fuller iteration of the her she is today. She hangs up the phone then, and at the exact time that she hears the delicate sound of the mouthpiece fit into its cradle, the doorbell rings, and her brother yelps twice and claps and gurgle-laughs, and she is full of happiness for that fraction of a moment before she runs to the door. She is full of her father's voice and his promise to return—he will return, he will come back, this time with her mother isn't forever, isn't infinite—and her brother is healthy and happy and laughing, and her mushroom pizza—her first foray into choosing what she wants to taste—is on its way. She grabs the two bills she needs to hand off to the delivery person, and she knows to tell them to keep the change, and she runs to the door. And there is a lot of disorder, she thinks, a hugely massive degree of disorder in her life, but now, in this moment, everything feels like it is exactly as it should be. Everything feels just right.

VI

Home, and she can't breathe. It's another asthma attack, but this time in the middle of the night. She wakes up wheezing, and her pillow is soaked from sweat. She must have been struggling awhile, too sleepy to wake herself until just now. She is wheezing, but she knows she needs to be quieter or she'll wake the baby. She leaves her room and goes to her mother's, tries the door—it's locked. It's not worth spending time trying to wake her, the girl thinks. She walks to the other side of the house and pulls out her breathing machine. She flips open the box, plugs it into the wall. She uncoils the plastic tubing and presses one end into the machine, the other end into the cup part of the device. She screws the mouthpiece onto the lid of the cup, then pulls out a vial of her medication, twists the plastic to break the side of the vial, pours the liquid into the cup. She twists the bottom onto the top—she learned the hard way that you can't twist the top onto the bottom, because it's already attached to the tubing that latches to the machine—and as soon as the seal is tight, she flips the button, and the sound fills up the whole room. And then she puts the mouthpiece in her mouth and takes deep breaths.

She is facing the wide window, and the blinds are open—she forgot to close them last night. She keeps forgetting things. She needs to curb that. The blinds are open, and she can see the sun coming up, and then she inches closer to the window, looks outside. For there is something strange there, something otherworldly.

Her neighbor's roof is moving. It is shifting and moving and not staying still. And the neighbor's house next to that, and the one beside that too. At first she thinks the roofs have gone soft, melted. But then she realizes they are covered in birds. Blackbirds are all over the roofs of the homes in her neighborhood. Everything that has a surface outside that is high is blanketed by blackbirds. She cannot tell what is natural and what is artificial. It is all just a sea of blackbirds covering every roof, a canopy of blackbirds dwelling on top of every home. Every home, as far as she can see.

She breathes slowly and inhales the medication, and what she does then is this: she thinks about her own house—wonders if it, too, is covered in the birds. She wants to learn if her own house is also overwhelmed with this strange flock.

But how would she do that? She thinks. She is inside and at the back of the house and connected to the cord of her breathing machine. The sun is coming up, and she is breathing very slowly, sucking in the medication, letting it enter her chest. She looks at the birds covering every house on her street and gets a chill down her back, then another. She shivers and her skin tightens around her frame.

She wants to learn so badly if her house is also covered or if it has been spared.

But how would she know? Whether her house is the same as the other houses? If it's also encased by this phenomenon?

How would she know, unless she could somehow get outside, far enough away to turn around, see the house as a thing separate from her? Only then, with a great deal of distance, could she look back and bear witness to that which once hovered above her.

Clyde Edgerton
Hearing Aids

It occurred to Forrest that he needed to think about who he should leave his hearing aids to. His first thought was his brother, who had some cheap ones. But no, not him. He was thinking this while standing at the commode urinating. While his pee was hitting the water, making those sounds like a slow-running kitchen faucet into a pan of water, he sometimes liked to isolate one of the sounds and make a word out of it. Well, no. He didn't exactly *like* to do that. It was just something to do while standing there.

He listened . . . *prosecute*. Then . . . *scrambled*. He finished, flushed the commode.

He thought about Van, his neighbor. He could leave the hearing aids to Van. Last summer, out by the driveway, Van had said he couldn't hear shit. And then about two weeks ago, when they stood a short way down the road watching a bulldozer work, he said the same thing again.

If he left the hearing aids to one of his own children that wouldn't work because by the time they were needed they would be extinct, like a DVD player. He remembered the old man who used to sit in the lobby of the courthouse holding what looked like a hollow elk horn in his lap. He'd pull it up to his ear when somebody talked to him, and on more than one occasion Forrest's mother had said, "Go ahead over there, son, and say something to him. Say 'How are you today, Mr. Umstead?'" His mother had gotten him to step up to a lot of things that he was kind of undecided about. She'd pushed him into piano, and art lessons, and theater. None of it stuck. He'd joined the army, served thirty years, and then retired. His wives had encouraged him to get involved in several hobby-things that didn't quite work. All that—gone.

He thought now about how Mr. Umstead, the man with the ear horn, must have, as a boy, seen old men, maybe old women, sitting somewhere with an ear horn, and how then those people, as children, had seen old people with ear horns . . . and so on for no telling how many generations back—without change. Just plain and simple steady human stuff through time. He thought about his iPhone and the misery that had brought on, his hearing aids, his prostate, his dick, his elbow, his eyesight—about how his handwriting had started getting shaky, and then shakier, and how he'd clearly noticed the same thing when it happened with his mother, his father, and finally Frances. He wondered how many of those motherfuckers with ear horns in the last thousand years had been happier than he'd been. How many had died happy? Who died happy? Happy in general. How many had stayed happy all along? Had had somebody they were intimate with and laughed their asses off with right up to the end. If Frances were alive, he might mention that to her in front of the fireplace. If his army buddy, Talmadge Cochran, were alive, Forrest could call him and say, "Talmadge, you want my hearing aids?" They'd laugh about it.

By now he was in the backyard. He sat down in the outdoor lounge chair facing the morning sun, and he felt the warmth on his face and knees and chest. The morning was cool. An intense wave of sadness came upon him, then ached in his chest.

He couldn't get the hearing aids out of his mind. It occurred to him that there should be a long list of people to leave them to, but nobody much was coming to mind. And who would clean them and prepare them for the gift box? Maybe he should think of an organization, an organization that would give them away. He thought of Goodwill—some old lady shopping in there and looking into the glass case up front and saying, "Is that a pair of hearing aids?" And there they'd be, light gray, beside the necklaces and rings and earrings—there they'd be, all cleaned up, each with the little plastic string that you're not supposed to see, and the tiny speaker the size of a match head that goes into your ear canal. And the saleswoman says, "Oh, they're special. I think they retail for several thousand dollars and they are . . . what? Two hundred?" She and the old woman look into the case but the price tag has been turned over, so she pulls out her key ring and opens the glass case and turns over the price tag, and says, "Two hundred dollars. Yep, two hundred dollars."

Why isn't there a hearing aid bank? he thought. Think of how many perfectly usable hearing aids become available in funeral homes, for crying out loud. And think about what you go home to if you've got a job at Goodwill. Thank God he avoided that.

Forrest started to get up but sat back. He thought about how in the last year everything was going downhill. That song: "I'm on the Downside of the Downswing." He had noticed that even with the hearing aids in, he was hearing less and less well. But they were very fine ones, adjustable in sensible ways.

He heard the 11 A.M. train whistle. That was the slow train. The fast train was usually somewhere between two and two thirty. The slow-moving morning train would have all these clank and scrape sounds, and the fast train would have a kind of simple, very loud rumble-roar. It hauled ass. That's the one he liked to watch from up close. He wondered how those sounds compared with the ones from 1850 or whenever that final rail spike had been driven, in the middle of the country. And how many people on that very first cross-country passenger train ride had ear horns in their laps? He wondered if some people back then used ear horns that had been in their families for hundreds of years. Surely, they got passed down. Why didn't you see them in antique stores?

He thought about all those hearing aids that were the size of a pack of cigarettes and fit into a shirt pocket and had a wire running up to one ear. Back in the fifties. He didn't recall ever seeing a woman with one. They must have had them.

His helper, Sarah, would be by at noon, with his lunch and some paperwork to leave off. She was very faithful and a good worker. Finally . . . He had had to let three others go. He went back inside to wait for her.

He remembered that time he was getting an MRI for his prostate cancer—to see if, or how much, the cancer had advanced—and he thought of the sounds coming from the machine, a machine that had swallowed him. The sounds were unlike any other sounds. A high-pitched sound would be repeated for maybe fifteen seconds and then it would switch to a loud popping or some other sound, but the next sound might sound like two words: go man go man go man go man go man, over and over.

The doorbell rang. Forrest greeted Sarah. They walked into the kitchen and she set his lunch on the table and beside it placed the papers she had been working on. She asked him if he felt okay, and he said, "Fine."

Then he said, "Let me ask you an odd question, Sarah. Is there anybody in your family who is hard of hearing and might be interested in a pair of hearing aids?"

"Yes . . . Yes. My mother."

He got Sarah to write down her mother's name on his notepad and when Sarah left he wrote out a little codicil and paperclipped it onto his will—where there were several others clipped on. He'd told his children he'd be doing this from time to time. His lawyer had approved.

Suddenly he was very nervous and shaking some. He walked to the bathroom, took off his hearing aids, and placed them beside the sink. He looked at himself in the mirror. He saw and felt the great wide valley, the great wide, dark valley between him and Mr. Umstead, who was sitting way over there beyond the valley, on that hill. The valley had grown so deep and wide and was crammed so full of so many things, all those things that his mother saw for the first time, airplanes and automobiles, telephone wires, electricity, jets, wars, and wars, and his war, and marriages, and children. The valley had been expanding as if alive. If he could count on somebody to love him. If he gave a shit anymore for making love. If there were somebody to help him have experiences that he was kind of undecided about. If he could go back, or if he could only move forward a little bit.

Out back, he walked past the chair he'd been sitting in, and went to meet the train.

Dave Eggers
Sanrevelle

SANREVELLE SAID she would be at her boat, but she was not at her boat and the sky was darkening fast. The Procession of Illuminated Vessels had no set start time, so you had to be ready. Once the sky was black it began, and in December the dark could come at half past five.

Hop stood on the dock beside Sanrevelle's boat, a thirty-two-foot schooner called the *Cradle*, and saw no sign of her. There were no lights on in the cabin. He called her phone and got no answer. She'd said if she wasn't at the *Cradle* she'd be at the Waterfront Social Club, so he walked down her rickety dock, back to the rocky shore, past the ramshackle community garden and over to the Club. He had to think of a way to get past Walter, the bouncer, who'd done twenty-two years at Vacaville for armed robbery and checked Social Club membership cards at the door.

That the Waterfront Social Club had a bouncer at all was an act of great hubris, given that the Club was no more than a decommissioned barge sitting on the mud between the bay and the town. The interior of the barge looked like a seventies rec room. The floors were sticky; the beer, served in cloudy plastic cups, cost three dollars; and the food was warmed in a microwave by Walter's nineteen-year-old daughter. At high tide the barge briefly rose from the mud for an hour or two before settling again into the muck, which was gray and smelled strongly of fish, eelgrass, engine oil and gasoline.

When Hop reached the door, Walter was not perched on his stool as usual, so Hop quickly slipped into the Club unseen. He ducked past the big-screen television and around the lacquered tables, past the bookshelf filled with mid-century board games and 1870s sextants, and out to the back deck that faced the bay. A few dozen drinkers were gathered there, squinting into the night, waiting for the lighted boats to assemble and pass by like waterborne Christmas trees.

The parade had been going on since before electricity. Around 1880, a Norwegian seaman had decked his ketch out in candles and Chinese lanterns and had sailed around the town at night to celebrate the birth of Christ. His sail had caught fire and he'd almost died, but the tradition had carried on, and when not hampered by fog or war or local political rivalries, the parade produced otherworldly beauty for a few hundred shorebound spectators. Boaters decorated their sails, outlined their hulls in lights, bought inflatable snowmen and Santas; every year one tugboat carried fifty children, dressed as Mary and Joseph and sheep, all of them ghostly white against the dark, dark water.

Hop wove through the revelers in the Club, many of whom had brought their own beer to avoid the three-dollar charge. He didn't see Sanrevelle, didn't see any of her crowd. The parade watchers were a mix of aging hippies, salty and single, and the newer Club members, decades younger, with their very young children, who were crouching at the edge of the barge, using mussel meat tied to string to try to catch crabs amassed near the hull.

Then Hop saw Sanrevelle's skeptical friend Joy. She was drinking gin through a figure eight straw. Her eyes opened wide as she finished a long pull. "You just missed her," she said, and nodded toward the water. "Gwen came by on her skiff and Sanrevelle went with."

"Oh," Hop said, and looked out to the gathering of lighted boats in the distance, arranging themselves into linear form. From where he stood, the boats were like neon toys tossed into deepest space. He tried not to appear forlorn, but he was sure this was how he looked—like a desperate man of thirty-eight, arriving alone to a bar, looking for a woman out there, somewhere in the velvet black.

Hop worked as a paralegal for a personal injury law firm, and the firm was collapsing as its founder lost his mind. Hop walked in one day to find this sixty-four-year-old man, Sam Whistler, partner of Whistler and Wong, on Zoom, talking with a Turco-French psychic in Bordeaux. "That is exactly what happened," Whistler said to his psychic, voice awed. Hop had come to get clarity on an enigmatic invoice, but left his boss to his internet prophet. Later, Whistler came to Hop's desk. "That guy knew things about me that he simply could not know. When I'm done I want you to see him, too. He'll change your life."

Whistler began teleconferencing with the Bordeaux shaman daily. After a few weeks of readings, one morning he thrust a small toiletry bag into Hop's hand. "Take these away from me," Whistler said. Inside there was a business-style envelope full of psychedelic mushrooms. "That's about five thousand dollars there," he said. "I would have flushed them, but I thought you might want them, or know someone who would." He looked out the window, then down at the street far below. "And if my brother calls, tell him I'm out. He has cancer and I can't get involved."

The firm's offices were on the fortieth floor of the Millennium Tower, built on clay and sinking two or three inches every year. The engineers were baffled, the geologists amused, and the owners of the building were obliged to reduce the rent. Whistler had asked Hop to take over paying that and most other bills; he didn't trust Cecilia, his right hand, anymore. His medium in Bordeaux had a bad feeling about Cecilia, starting with her name—the letters, translated to numbers, added up to an unlucky sum.

The firm kept the lights on, but Whistler, far and away its most important earner, came and went at odd hours, and had stopped taking on new work. Soon the part-time help was laid off. Résumés were updated and attorneys fled. Whistler proposed dance parties and was visited by an eclectic parade of women of all ages with dangerously long fingernails. They arrived for lunch appointments in Whistler's office and he stumbled out afterward, struggling not to slur.

One day Whistler insisted that he and Hop become better friends. He'd read an article that said men needed friendships in middle age, so he brought Hop to a Giants game, and talked for three hours about his mother. He said he was working on himself. He said he was finding his own true north. He said he was microdosing and that most of the people in his life were toxic and manipulative. He asked not one question about Hop and stood up in the seventh inning, saying he needed to use the bathroom. He never returned.

"Hop, you're the glue that holds this place together," he confided a week later. The next day he said the same thing to his secretary, Janet, and then to Philip, the building's chief engineer, whose staff was unionizing. Soon they were on strike, and Philip had left for Cabo San Lucas. Only one of the eight elevators worked, and even then sporadically. The heat went off and on. There was no air-conditioning. The building was usually dark, half abandoned, and began to smell of hidden decay. The remaining staff of Whistler and Wong, most of them working from home, began to quit. Janet moved to British Columbia to become a wildlife photographer. No one saw the point in what they were doing in the Millennium, and Whistler didn't seem to, either.

But someone had to stand guard over the remnants of the firm. "Will you live here?" Whistler asked Hop. "There are no guards in the lobby and the electronic locks don't work. I have to leave the doors open or else I'll never get back in. Can you move in? I'll get you a bed. Sublet your place. Make a profit."

Hop moved into the tower but kept his apartment. He thought it would be a week, maybe two. But after six months Whistler had become even more elusive and vague, and Hop left his apartment and its $3,400 monthly rent. He lived for free on the Millennium's fortieth floor and had most of it to himself, his bed in a former conference room, a vast kitchen, long carpeted hallways he traversed on Whistler's pristine mountain bike; Hop had been given this, too. When the phone rang, usually Hop let it ring, but occasionally, for a lark, he picked up.

"Does anyone work there anymore?" the caller invariably asked.

"No," Hop would say cryptically. "I am alone in the tower."

During the day he pressed his forehead to the floor-to-ceiling glass and looked out at the vast blue bay, wanting to be there, on some boat, and not here, in a sinking building whose windows didn't open. He would spot some tiny sailboat, just a bright white shard against the sea of hammered blue, and would picture himself on it, sea spray in his face, roaring through whitecaps, yelling greetings and admonitions to fellow sailors, heading through the Golden Gate and into the madness of the Pacific.

One Sunday he found himself in a ramshackle marina in a brightly colored little town, waiting in his car for a sailing instructor. He'd been told to arrive at 9 A.M. but at 9 A.M. he saw only a raggedy-haired woman wearing mismatched layers, wools and plaids, struggling with a locked gate. He thought she might be trying to break into the place.

Finally she looked up and at him. Her face opened into a wide smile and she crossed the parking lot in a few long strides and was suddenly at his window.

"Hop? Are you Hop?"

He rolled down his window.

"I'm Sanrevelle," she said. "You ready? You're still in your car."

He'd expected an older, sunburned country-club gentleman, but Sanrevelle was frizzy, sturdily built, a few years older than him. Her skin was olive colored and taut and her hair was a swirling black mass. He half expected her to pull things from the thicket—pencils or maps or food.

"I'm thinking we just go out and learn as we go," she said, and led him around the gate she'd been trying to open, down a battered gray dock, and to a catamaran, its flat surface no bigger than a child's trampoline. She fitted him for a life preserver. There were no safety talks, no questions, no instructions.

"Sit there," she said, and he scooted from the dock and onto the catamaran. She stepped onto the other side, sat down and took the line of the sail—he didn't know the right term and she didn't tell him—and they were off. In seconds they sped a hundred yards into the bay. "Can you swim?" she asked. They were pointed toward Alcatraz. He said he could, and he squinted into the sunlight on the water, the way it moved like a flashlight zigzagging in the dark. He was momentarily hypnotized, taken out of time. He lived in that golden flickering for a while, and found himself closing his eyes, feeling the shimmer on his face, his eyelids. They'd been sailing for ten minutes and he was already changed by these colors, this abandon. There were no lanes on the bay, nowhere to be or not to be. They were shooting diagonally into a manic light.

"Hold on," Sanrevelle said, and tacked to get out of the way of a thunderous yellow-and-black ferry loaded with tourists, and when it had passed and they crossed its wake, Hop got soaked, the water icy and seizing every part of him—hands, feet, bones.

"Gusts over there," she said. She spoke this way, in fragments, leaving out words. "Porpoises," she said a few minutes later, and Hop saw two of them, their curved dorsal fins riding a swift current west. When he turned back to Sanrevelle, she was looking at his footwear.

For the lesson, Hop had bought, online, a kind of sneaker that had separate homes for each toe. He thought they might help him avoid falling off wet and slippery boat decks.

"I've seen pictures of those, but never in person," Sanrevelle said. "Are they comfortable?" Her tone was half amused, half aghast.

"They feel very strange," he admitted. "Almost lewd."

She laughed. "You don't need gear to sail."

"Okay," he said.

"Like you don't need tight shorts to ride a bike."

"I know."

"Take them off then," she said, and removed her own shoes. She tied her sneakers, canvas and torn, together and to the mast. Hop took off his shoes, too, and tied them to the mast, too, making an awkward mound of footwear around the clean aluminum pole. The trampoline surface of the catamaran felt good under his bare feet, like the skin of a snake.

"Indoor feet," she said about Hop's. Hers were calloused and blistered, and she was missing two toenails.

"I take it you work in the city?" she asked.

He pointed to the Millennium Tower and explained that he worked there and lived there, too.

"The one that's sinking?" she asked. "You have an escape plan?"

Hop told her about Whistler, how he'd lost his mind, and how the building staff had quit, and how Hop dreamt most nights that the tower was collapsing. In this dream, his face was pressed to the glass as the building fell toward Market Street. He could only watch as the pavement swung up to smash him.

"And then you wake up," she said.

"And then I wake up," he said.

"You could move," Sanrevelle said, and a gurgling sound caught her attention. "Look," she said, and nodded to a polished black orb that had just emerged from the bay. "That's probably Sarah." Sarah was a seal and the orb was her head. She followed them for a few hundred yards before disappearing into the reflection of the sun. They tacked awhile near Alcatraz, the waves rolling under them with growing power and menace.

"So is Hop short for something?" Sanrevelle asked.

"Family last name. Hopland. I think it means that somewhere, at some point, we grew hops."

Sanrevelle has lost interest in the history of his name. "Check it out," she said, and nodded toward a dark blur coming from the southern sky. "Supposed to rain. We'll head in." She turned the catamaran around and they skipped along the surface like a water bug. They got to the dock just as the rain began to come down, a silvery torrent that drenched them as they tied up the boat. He paid her in cash, $120 for two hours, and he asked when they could go again.

"Like a weekend or a weekday?" she asked.

Hop wondered to himself whether Whistler would care if he skipped a day or a month. No, he thought, he probably wouldn't notice. "Any day, anytime," Hop said. "No one cares anymore."

Even after the first lesson, he knew that Sanrevelle was the last capable and sane person in his life. Everyone else was lost, medicated, overwhelmed, drawn endlessly to their past, searching fruitlessly for clues as to why they were who they were and not someone else. Whistler hadn't been seen at the office in six weeks. The staff was down to seven, all but Hop working from home. There was one practicing attorney, Gilbert Escovedo, who was looking for a new firm and one day brought movers to the building and took away much of the furniture. Hop didn't know if Whistler had approved this or not, and he didn't have the standing to challenge it.

The last time he'd seen Whistler, he was deep in a new therapy, unlicensed and run by a group calling itself the Urgers, that sought to redirect adult lives by finding "microfaults" in the patient's parents. Whistler had prepared a list, four pages long and growing, of the mistakes his parents, dead before the turn of this century, had apparently made; he asked Hop to make three copies. Hop had glanced at the top of the page, where Whistler had written "Not enough botany." His parents had encouraged him to go to law school, and this, Whistler now surmised, was an act of great evil. Turns out he should have been a sculptor; the internet psychic had uncovered this. Had it not been for his parents, he was certain, he would have been Rodin. Whistler was sixty-four years old and had become a grievance-based adolescent, casting about for complaints against the defenseless dead.

But Sanrevelle was not confused about herself or her place in the world, and was not at war with her long-gone progenitors. Every day she sailed passengers into the bay, sometimes under the Golden Gate Bridge, then sailed back. She was paid to show people the sea, and every morning she had a plan, to sail and show and keep her passengers from harm. She waved to the Coast Guard. She checked life preservers. She trimmed sails and filled her tank with gas. She battened hatches.

And she wanted to sail to the Sea of Cortez. She hadn't done it yet, but would do it—probably in the new year, maybe even January. She'd been planning it, and needed a crew of two plus herself. She told Hop this on their second lesson, when they shot across the bay to the point of Tiburon and for a while, when the wind died, they just sat, bobbing on the water's silky surface.

"If I knew you better, I'd take you," she said. "You're easy to be around." This was the first time she'd made any assessment of him; it seemed to be the first time she'd noticed him as anything more than a client, a passenger with bad shoes.

"I'd go with you," Hop said, trying to sound casual. "I haven't sailed to the Sea of Cortez, either. I can cook. You need a cook?"

She took off her sunglasses and assessed him. Her eyes were green, bright, hiding under squinty folds. "Maybe," she said finally.

And Hop knew that that's what he needed to live for—to be chosen by Sanrevelle, to sail to the Sea of Cortez as her mate. He knew little about sailing, and nothing about sailing to the Sea of Cortez. Was it dangerous? He pictured hundred-foot waves and orcas, maybe sea dragons. Did people really sail in little boats all the way to the Sea of Cortez? It seemed unnecessary, and long, and likely tedious, all those weeks without land. But he would follow her anywhere.

On their third lesson she took him out on the *Cradle*, and they sailed around Angel Island. The wind was light and westerly, so when they sailed to the eastern side of the island, they were protected and the temperature seemed to double; she dropped anchor. They took her tiny dinghy to the beach and sat together on that empty shore, facing Berkeley and El Cerrito, and she drew up her bare feet, sole to sole, and told him about growing up in Lisbon, at least till she was ten, then finding her way to Maine, then Indiana, then Coral Gables, then finally to California. She'd been married once, to a man who worked in marine construction and lived in Alameda. Hop sat and listened and tried to seem professionally aloof, but he was very much in love already, and then she took off her hoodie.

She wore hoodies always, usually navy blue and bearing her company logo, a signal flag and the words SAIL WITH ME! But that day on the beach was warm, and the wind suddenly died, and then she was taking the sweatshirt off, and while her face was hidden in the cottony folds, he glanced her way and saw her shape, her full breasts and lean muscles and soft belly and a ragged purple scar running from her left elbow to her palm. He looked quickly away, but thought then, and for weeks after, of the fool he'd been as a young man, assuming that anyone in their thirties or forties was wrinkled and saggy, when the miracle of it was that he was thirty-eight and hadn't changed much at all, and Sanrevelle's own shape was surely more interesting now than it had ever been—bursting with contradictions, soft and hard and fleshy and full of intrigue and power.

"Should we swim or would that be crazy?" she asked. It was the first time she'd expressed any doubt about anything.

They waded into the cold, cold bay, and dove and stayed in the shallows, swimming and diving. Her nest of black hair was briefly wet, shrinking like wool, but seemed to dry in seconds. Her T-shirt clung to her, a dark-colored bra beneath. She pulled at her shirt to separate it from her soaked skin, and then excused herself to walk up to where the beach met the trees. "Gonna wring this out," she said, and he stared at the water, and glanced at the Bay Bridge, where cars, just glistening dots, moved sluggishly into the city. When he looked back, she'd put her hoodie back on and was dragging the dinghy back to the water.

"Yeah, I could never date a middle-aged thumbsucker," she said. She seemed to be concluding a conversation she'd been having with herself. She dropped the bow of the dinghy in the water and covered her eyes with a stiff hand to look at him. "You're not a middle-aged thumbsucker, are you?"

"No, I'm not a middle-aged thumbsucker," he said.

"You're not working out mommy issues in your forties?"

"I'm not," he said.

"Get in," she said, and with one long sandy stride from Sanrevelle they were afloat. Did this mean she saw him as a romantic prospect? By nature, he was dense about such things. And she was the captain, the teacher. Maybe she was just thinking aloud—something she often did.

"Jump out first," she said.

They'd reached the *Cradle* and soon she was onto other things—the bad weather coming in from the west and the location, somewhere under the sea near Angel Island, of a safe containing $1 million in gold bullion, lost in a shipwreck from 1913. "How hard could it be to find it?" she asked. "The bay is big, but not that big."

Then she was onto the topic of tabernacle masts. She planned to replace one of the *Cradle*'s with a tabernacle mast, she said, once she got to Mexico.

"Cheaper down there," she said, and she could sleep on the beach while the shipwrights worked. The wind picked up just then, and her black hair spread like ink all over the sky. "Let's head back in," she said.

After each lesson he would return to the city, exhausted, sun-soaked, his shoes wet, his skin dry, his hair full of salt, and he would feel braided into the earth and sea. He would feel that this was the only way, so obviously the right way, to live—to spend the days out on the water with Sanrevelle, every spray of the ocean like a baptism. And then he would park on Market Street and walk into the Millennium Tower, would be seized by its sour suffocated smell, its wretched stained carpet, the elevator like a coffin rising to his floor, where he would rush back to the wall of windows and look back to the sea below, wanting to be out there in the fight and flow.

Joy knew his intentions. He was sure of it. She lived on a different boat, a converted pontoon cruiser a few docks away, laden with potted plants, and she called Sanrevelle "Revvy." She saw through Hop, seemed to have gleaned the exact moment when Hop knew he was in love. Hop had been following Sanrevelle down the dock after a lesson, carrying his life vest and backpack, and he must have been staring at Sanrevelle's shape, her sprightly, purposeful walk, her jogging shorts and tanned legs.

"Hi, Hop!" Joy had said. She'd come out of nowhere and was quickly between Hop and Sanrevelle, looking at him like she'd caught him at something. "Good lesson, Hop? Enjoying your lessons with Revvy, Hop?" Joy was far younger, maybe just thirty, and looked upon Hop as a sad sack, a city guy hopelessly out of place.

But now, this night of the Procession of Illuminated Vessels, as Hop was staring out at the distant neon lights, thinking he had no way to get to them, Joy said, "You know . . ." Then she sipped from her figure eight straw and closed one eye, as if looking at him through an invisible telescope. "You could go find her. Borrow something. That canoe will get you there."

She pointed to the Waterfront Social Club's lower deck, where a dozen kayaks and canoes and paddleboards were stacked without care. Members of the Club were allowed to keep them there, provided that they be available for other members to borrow freely. It was a hippie system that worked for everyone but resulted in profound wear and tear to the vessels involved.

"She's probably not far," Joy added, and took another long pull on her straw. "Take the canoe."

Hop walked down the ramp and turned the canoe over. A small creature, a chipmunk or crab, scurried away. Hop dragged the canoe loudly across the deck and into the water, looking for signs of Walter.

"Just take it?" Hop asked.

"Jesus, Hop, yes," Joy said.

Hop set the aluminum canoe into the black water. It bounced like a baby on a bed. He looked for a paddle and found a heavy wooden one, old and splintered, in a nearby rowboat. He crawled into the canoe, wanting to do as Joy had said, to seem confident, and so pushed off with the end of the paddle, realizing too late that he wasn't dressed for the bay in December—he was wearing jeans and sneakers and a canvas jacket—and he hadn't brought a life vest. It was too late to go back, he decided. And yet the canoe was no more than a concavity, a half tube of metal, a noncommittal promise of protection. In it he was dry and safe, but all around was icy water; he'd be hypothermic in minutes.

He left the lights of the Club, the shrieking laughter and muffled sound system growing fainter as he paddled into the dark. He looked toward the scrum of bright lights in the distance, and paddled—two strokes on the left, two on the right. The water was calm, the wind light, but the air couldn't have been more than fifty degrees, and felt colder with each lunge deeper into the bay. The whinny of a small motorboat startled him, and he watched as a single man in a tiny skiff crossed his path, a dog sitting upright on the bow. The boat's wake gave a shimmy to the canoe, and Hop set the paddle across it, steadying himself.

Passing a long dock running parallel to the shore, Hop saw a series of beach chairs occupied by dolls.

"Where are you going?" a boy's voice asked. They were children, not dolls. They appeared to be about six or seven. He couldn't see the boy's face, only his silhouette. There were no parents in sight.

"This way," Hop said, and pointed with his paddle.

"Are you cold?" the other child, a girl, asked.

"Not yet," Hop said.

"You don't have any lights on your canoe," the girl said. "You're supposed to have lights."

"That's where I'm going, actually," Hop lied. "To get some lights at the light store." He pointed into the bay. "Where are your parents?" he asked.

"There's no light store out there!" the boy said, but Hop had already paddled away. He was headed toward a big red tugboat called the *Excelsior*. Its owner was a friend of Sanrevelle's, and Hop thought there was an outside chance she'd be on board. Though it was moored to a long dock, and not decorated for the parade, there were figures in the bright windows and he heard voices coming from the deck.

Hop was halfway to the tug when a herd of watery ravers came his way. They were paddleboarders festooned with glowing necklaces and bracelets and hats, their boards outlined in pink and purple LEDs.

"There's a guy in a canoe," a voice said from the dark, and they paddled past him in silence, seeming wary. They were heading south, to the central parade-viewing area in town, and when they were gone, Hop was alone, and he looked into the sky to see a one-quarter moon set within a gauzy ring, a promise of rain tomorrow.

The rumble of a small motor brought his attention to the piers behind him.

"Who's that?" a man asked. The man's voice was parched, reed thin.

"Just me," Hop said, though he realized that his answer would not clarify much.

"Me who?" the man asked, and now Hop could see a hunched figure at the back of an aluminum boat, its outboard no bigger than a vacuum cleaner.

"I don't think you know me," Hop said. "I'm just here for the parade."

"No, no. Your voice sounds familiar," the man said. "What's your name?"

"Peter," Hop lied.

"Peter Pumpkin, or Peter Pan?" the man asked, his voice taking a hard turn.

"Just Peter," Hop said, and paddled in the direction of the tug. "Have a good night."

"Peter Pumpkin or Peter Pan?" the man yelled to Hop's back.

Hop paddled hard for the tug, which seemed to rise higher as he got closer. A gust of wind came down from the headlands and someone from the tug yelled, "Put a weight around it!" Hop looked up to the deck to find two people wrestling with a six-foot penguin, a lawn decoration, lit from within. The two people were attempting to fasten it to the stern of the tugboat. But then the wind gusted again and lifted the penguin into the air and—"No! No!" a woman screamed—it arced downward, slowly and almost gracefully, onto the surface of the bay, where it quickly deflated, went dark, and began to sink.

The two figures leaned over the edge of the tug, laughing hysterically, slashing a beam from their flashlight into the obsidian water. And then they saw Hop.

"You! Save our penguin!"

"Yes, can you?"

They thought this was beyond funny, that the penguin might be rescued by a guy in a canoe. Hop paddled to the plastic mess, and found it stiff and heavier than expected, but easy enough to save, and when he had the penguin safely inside his concavity, the light within it went bright again, as if resurrected.

"He got it! He got it!" the revelers roared from above. "It's a Christmas miracle!" they yelled, and then laughed till they were breathless. By now, there were a half dozen people on the deck of the tug, wanting to witness the rescue. Hop paddled closer to the *Excelsior* and a rope was lowered. He tied it around the waist of the deflated penguin and it was lifted, still lit from within, up to the tug, and once it was aboard, a roar of applause burst out.

"Thank you, Paddle-to-the-Sea," he heard a woman's voice say. "Can you come aboard? Just tie up at the pier and use the gangplank."

Now Hop could see faces, beautiful faces, above, and in the portholes at eye level, everyone fascinated by the man in the canoe who had saved the illuminated bird. Hop wanted to paddle off, like a cowboy would, but then remembered why he'd approached the tug.

"Is Captain Sanrevelle aboard?" he asked.

"Is Captain Sanrevelle aboard?" the woman repeated to the people assembled on the deck. She seemed to know Sanrevelle, and her tone implied there was a real possibility she was there on the tug. For a moment Hop felt sure that Sanrevelle would be there—the tug was owned by her friend, and it was a logical place from which to watch the parade. The penguin salvation, too, now seemed inevitable—a logical step to him finding her, proving himself while she was close.

The woman returned. "Nope," she said. "Paulie saw her on the shark-yacht, though. You know that one?" She pointed out into the bay, to the tangle of bright vessels struggling to get themselves into parade order. "Come aboard anyway," the woman said. "We have glögg here, and . . ." She retreated again and emerged holding a bottle of gin. "Locally made!" she said. "You know Scott?"

Hop did not know Scott, but thanked her and said he was moving on.

"Wait!" the woman said, and shone a flashlight on herself. "We're sending you off with a gift." She wrapped a bottle in a beach towel and tied a line around it. She lowered the bundle to him, and because it was too complicated to refuse it, he thanked her, sent the line back to them, and turned the canoe around and pointed himself into the bay, where the procession of lighted boats was newly in a semblance of a line.

"Goodbye, penguin savior!" a man said, and Hop looked back to see that they'd arranged the penguin upright again, and someone was making the bird wave down to him. Hop raised his paddle to the penguin and the *Excelsior,* and then startled when a loudspeaker burst to life with a deafening scratch.

Hop turned to find an enormous white yacht approaching, bright with a thousand tiny white and pink lights. It looked like a casino unmoored, and the speakers sent a mid-century holiday song into the air. It was Dean Martin's "Let It Snow!"—brassy and even a bit lewd, a distinctly adult, nightclub version of the song, though none of the words had changed.

Hop had to paddle backward quickly to stay out of the yacht's path. The passengers couldn't see him, would have no chance of seeing him so far below, given he was so small, without lights, and drifting in the shifting shadows. As the boat passed, he saw fifty or so people aboard, wearing antlers and necklaces of alternating lights. The mass of guests on the main deck yelled "Woo!" to no one in particular, while a small group sat still on the bow, all clad in white gowns—ghostly costumes of sleep or the afterlife. Hop assumed they had something planned for the judging stand a half mile south, though for the moment they looked dour and cold. The yacht passed, and its wake tipped Hop's canoe left and right, left and right, and the bottle of gin rocked on the floor, tempting him.

Hop picked it up and took a sip. It was bitter but sugary, too—dangerously easy going down. He took another sip and recapped the bottle.

"Heads up, bro," a man's voice said, just behind Hop. He turned to find an inscrutable pattern of lights approaching. There were two horizontal blue stripes near the water, and above them, a zigzag of fast-moving yellow lights. It was a small craft, just big enough for the one man.

"You know how much farther to the reviewing stand?" the man asked, panting hard. By now Hop saw that he was wearing a wetsuit festooned with LEDs, and was pedaling a bicycle mounted on pontoons, each of them strung with lights, too. The contraption was wildly inefficient, a desperate sort of locomotion.

"You're almost there," Hop said, while knowing that at the man's plodding pace it would take him another hour.

"Thanks bro," the man said. "You good?"

"I'm good," Hop said.

"You don't have any lights," the man said. "Scary for you."

"Just looking for a friend on the shark-boat," Hop said.

"What friend? Clara?"

Feeling he had nothing to lose, and because this man seemed anxious for conversation, Hop said he was looking for Sanrevelle.

"Captain Sanrevelle?" the man asked. "I just saw her twenty minutes ago. She was on Maya's boat. See?"

Hop sensed that the man was pointing, but because his arms weren't lighted, he couldn't know for sure.

"Over there. Little dinghy with the light rings. Near the Christmas trees."

"Was she with Gwen?" Hop asked, and immediately realized that this did not matter.

"I don't think I know Gwen," the man said. By now his continued pedaling and conversation had exhausted all his breath. He was hoarse and heaving.

"Thanks," Hop said, and let him pass.

Beyond the pontoon man, on a promontory jutting into the bay, there was a small operation selling Christmas trees. From the water it looked like a tiny forest, the tree line orderly and lit from above by garlands of white lights. Against their glow, a small boat with two figures aboard was moving out from the rocky beach. Even from a hundred yards away Hop could tell these figures were women, and of course one was Sanrevelle. The pontoon man had just seen her.

With a new sense of mission, Hop paddled quickly toward the skiff, and as he got closer, there was something in the posture of the rear figure that reminded him of Sanrevelle, something eager and muscular. He could see the shape of a hoodie, too, so he stroked hard, his paddle clunking against the hollow aluminum, announcing his arrival. Now he was sure that it was Sanrevelle; he could almost see her smile, and as he drifted closer, only ten yards away, he saw what appeared to be a mound of neon treasure in their boat—rubies and emeralds and amethysts emitting a powerful glow.

"You want one?" a woman's voice asked. The voice came from the bow and was not Sanrevelle's.

Hop was now close enough to leap from his canoe to their skiff, but he couldn't make out their faces. The woman in the bow held out a piece of plastic jewelry, an oversize diamond ring lit from within. As he took it, the tip of his canoe touched the rim of their boat in a baritone clunk and the woman's face was briefly illuminated in gold. Hop saw that it was neither Sanrevelle nor Gwen.

"Thanks," Hop said, and put the ring on his fourth finger.

"Not a problem," she said, "but don't think this means we're married." Meanwhile, the figure steering the outboard made no sound, her silhouette still opaque to Hop. "Sanrevelle?" he asked.

This rear woman said nothing, but the woman in front shook her head. "No Sanrevelle here," the first woman said. "Sanrevelle? Is that a name?" She didn't wait for an answer. "You stay safe out here, you hear? Keep that ring-light where people can see it."

And they puttered away, heading toward the assembly of glittering boats. By now the parade was a straight line, extending half a mile into the distance. Six boats away he could see a yacht with lights arranged in the shape of a jagged mouth. The penguin people had said Sanrevelle was there. The parade would pass right by him. All he had to do was wait.

"We can't wait!" Whistler had said the last time he'd seen him. Whistler was trying to get him to come to Florida with him, to a compound—at first Hop had heard commune—where they could do ayahuasca guided by experts in Further Father.

"Further father?" Hop had asked, and wondered if that was capitalized. Whistler had been discovering new terms, new theories, weekly, and this was another. Whistler's father had been dead for decades. Did this mean the founder of the fourth-largest personal injury law firm on the West Coast missed his daddy? Could this happen to Hop, too? Would he turn fifty or sixty and suddenly need to be coddled, to make lists of childhood grievances, to be dazzled by theories because they almost rhymed?

On the other hand, there was this. There was water and light, there were oceans and holidays and sharks, there were people communing, there were boats and seals, there was Dean Martin, there was Jesus, there was now. Hop reached down and felt the cold water, brought some to his face, and felt newly awake. A sailboat was approaching, its sails outlined in purple lights, its mast entwined in white. On the bow, a teenage ballerina was holding a swanlike pose, her hands using the halyards for balance. The next boat was a three-story pleasure cruiser, lights like icicles hanging from every level, and a solitary couple, an older man and woman, dressed as Santa and Mrs. Claus, sat high in the cockpit.

The shark-yacht was now approaching and a dread came over Hop. Did she want him to find her? After all, she'd told him she'd be at her boat and she had not been at her boat. She'd said that as a last resort she'd be at the Waterfront Social Club, and she hadn't been there, either. And she hadn't answered her phone. So the cues were clear. She was not looking to spend time with Hop this night or any night.

A foghorn sounded nearby, as if to punctuate this revelation. Hop stopped paddling and coasted for a moment, the heavy oily sea beneath him like the scaly back of a vast sleeping monster. He turned toward the shore, knowing he should go home. Read the signals, he told himself.

But he had a tendency to invent reasons to go forward, to

ignore obvious discouragements and press on. When he was thirteen, old enough to know better, he'd decided he would be a hurdler. He'd seen Edwin Moses run, Edwin Moses with his receding hairline and goggle-glasses, looking so professorial and utterly out of place, and Hop had decided then that he would be a hurdler, too. He signed up for an open track meet at his school, pestered his mother to buy him spiked shoes, and at the day and time, Hop lined up with every other runner, mimicking their stretchings and other preparations. When the gun went off, he was fine, he pumped his legs and arms in a convincing way, until the first hurdle, which collapsed upon him like a bear trap. When he got up, he was bleeding from the nose and knees, but still he got up and attacked the second hurdle with fervor. This second hurdle caught his instep and threw him to the red clay, clavicle first, forehead second, and that was the end of his hurdling dream. No one clapped, no one told him "Nice try." He simply made his way back to his duffel bag, stuffed his shoes inside, and walked home barefoot.

This quest in the black water was no different. He would arrive at the shark-yacht, and Sanrevelle, if she was there at all, would be shocked, mortified, and would, at best, wave to him and tell him she'd see him another time, at their next lesson—some way of redrawing their boundaries. Nothing would be lost.

But then again, hadn't she given him occasional encouragement? During their last lesson, in the first week in December, it had hailed as they were coming in, but she still let him steer as she reefed the sails, let him steer the *Cradle* all the way into the marina. And afterward she'd invited him down below, to wait out the storm in her musty cabin, and they'd had tea, and she'd offered him a blanket, and she'd served him zucchini fritters. Surely she didn't do this for just any student.

"I'm actually going to the Sea of Cortez," she said. "Soon. January. So . . ." And then she'd looked at him for just a beat longer than she ever had before. Then she lowered her eyes, back to her tea. "It's open-ended. I might stay down there awhile. Just in case that matters."

In the moment, Hop hadn't read much into it—he'd assumed she was talking about a long pause in their lessons. But his Edwin Moses mind emerged in the days afterward, until finally he was convinced that she wanted him to come with her to the Sea of Cortez. And that she was leaving soon, and she might not be back anytime soon, so if he wanted to come, he'd damned well better make his intentions clear.

And what if she did take him? The thought of waking up on her boat, crawling up to the deck, seeing her at the helm, sailing into the sun—my god, he thought, could the world ever be that good?

A splash behind him turned his head. He assumed it was a seal, but he found a man in a small aluminum boat. Hop hadn't heard him approach.

"Peter Pumpkin!" the man said. "What are you doing now, Peter Pumpkin?" The man was close now, so close Hop could smell the medicinal stench of fermenting booze. He wasn't just passing by. He'd come to investigate. "Peter Pumpkin, you're not the one who's been poking around the *Sequoia,* are you? You can't go creeping around people's private boats, private homes, Peter Pumpkin. You know that, don't you? Are you smart enough to know that?"

"I'm not whoever you're looking for," Hop said. "I don't even know what the *Sequoia* is."

"We've seen a canoe like yours a couple times, and then afterward we keep finding certain things missing. You know anything about that, Peter Pumpkin?"

"I just borrowed this canoe tonight, from the Club."

"Okay, and maybe you borrowed it another time, too."

"No," Hop said. "You're wrong and I'm—"

"Shut it!" the man snapped. He took a few long breaths. "Okay, Peter Pumpkin. But I'm not the only one watching what you're doing. And I'm not the only one willing to protect the *Sequoia* you say you don't know anything about. Just know that it'll be dangerous for whoever comes close again. Have a nice procession, Peter."

"Shut the fuck up," Hop said.

"What?" the man said.

Hop had no idea where his own words were coming from. "I said shut the fuck up or I'll drown you." The threat came from some volcanic place within him, and the man went still, his mouth open. Any menace he had presented to Hop was gone, but his skiff was still between Hop and the parade.

"I'm looking for Captain Sanrevelle," Hop said, "and I need you to get the fuck out of my way before I put this paddle through you."

Without a word, the man put his motor in reverse and his boat gurgled backward. "Jesus, man. Don't get so harsh." He seemed near tears. "She's my friend, too." A long silence stretched between them, and the man's face slowly grew bright under the lights of an approaching yacht. "I'm Tyler," he said. "I've known her twenty years."

"Hi, Tyler," Hop said. "Sorry for what I said."

"She's right there, anyway," Tyler said, and pointed to the enormous boat passing before them. It wasn't the shark-boat. This one was far brighter than any before it, ten thousand bulbs in red and white and green, and soon it was above him, and there was no boundary between sky and water, day and night. All was kaleidoscopic color, and laughter and music echoed across the bay and against the far hills. And then he saw Sanrevelle. She was among a dozen people inside, everyone in gold and white, and was she wearing antlers? She was.

"See?" Tyler said.

Hop began to paddle, but the yacht she was on was moving briskly. In seconds it had passed them and was speeding away. Somehow Hop hadn't thought of this—the fact that the parade was moving too fast, that its boats had engines, that he couldn't possibly keep up.

"Fuck, whatever, I'll pull you," Tyler said. He was quickly in front of Hop's canoe, and threw him a line from the stern. Hop grabbed it and the man gunned his little outboard. They followed the vast casino-ship, its lights shimmering wildly in its frothing wake.

"You didn't have to get so harsh," Tyler said again as they gained on the yacht. Hop apologized once more, and as they approached the yacht's stern, Hop had to think of exactly what he'd do when they got close. Jump from the canoe?

"What're you gonna do when I get you close?" Tyler asked. His face was bathed in the yacht's white light now; he looked like a neon Jesus, so gaunt and exhausted, and yet willing to make one more attempt at majesty.

He was pulling Hop's canoe, and the canoe was bouncing madly in the bright wake, and Hop thought he would have to somehow crawl forward in his canoe, and then jump to the man's boat, and then make his way from stern to bow there, and finally, if they could get close enough, he'd jump from the skiff to the yacht . . . Good Christ.

But he could do it. He was still young enough to do it, and he felt a strange calm about doing it. The skiff in front of him was weaving in the wake, and his canoe was shuddering and swerving, but Hop felt a serenity in knowing without doubt that he would make it across, dry and unharmed. He was about to explain the plan to the man but then Sanrevelle appeared. She was standing at the back of the yacht, on a low platform, bathed in red light.

"Ty? What're you doing? You okay?" Now she was kneeling, ready to grab a line offered by Tyler.

"I'm fine," Tyler yelled. "It's this guy who needs you." And he threw a thumb over his shoulder toward Hop, bouncing in the wake.

"Is that Hop?" she said, squinting, and her mouth broke open into a wide, crookedly confused grin. "What is happening back there?"

And then he knew she would come with him.

And then she did. After some pleasantries with Tyler, and after she bade goodbye to her hosts and retrieved her backpack, she climbed down onto Tyler's skiff and crawled from bow to stern, and then crawled into Hop's canoe, and they cut free of Tyler—at some point she lost her antlers—and Hop paddled backward, and the canoe drifted from the wake of the bright boat with its thousands of lights, and they floated quietly out of the channel. Soon the water was calm and the parade moved almost silently in the distance, a gorgeous pageant of irrational color in the darkest night.

"Show me that you're not wearing those weird shoes," she said.

He showed her.

"Good. How'd you know I was out here?" she asked. "You're not wearing a life jacket."

"I asked around," Hop said. "And you're not either."

"So weird," she said. "I had a dream you'd find me out here."

It was so quiet and so black. Her face was purple in the light of the ringed moon. She was grinning impishly, looking so young, so happy, so tired.

"I know a place we should go," she said. "You have another paddle?"

"I don't," he said.

"Well, you can take me this time," she said, and she arranged herself on the floor of the canoe, facing forward, and slowly, blessedly, she lowered her wild mane of hair into his lap. "I'll tell you where we're going, and when we get there I'll kiss you, okay?"

And so he let her guide him.

Madeline ffitch
Stump of the World

AT THE STOP SIGN before the library, Emma saw Gallo painting his yellow line as he had painted it for thirty years. The line highlighted a ten-foot-long crack in the road, a rogue speed bump that, unpainted, might do some damage to your car or your neck or your teeth or your coffee. The crack had been there as long as Emma could remember. Gallo had too. Emma had watched Gallo from a young man to an old man painting his yellow line. She had watched him reletter his sign when it became tattered: DONATE TO UPKEEP THIS OUR ROAD. Gallo had a son Emma's age, and Emma had watched Gallo teach him to paint the yellow line, to fly the sign, to approach each car's window with his cashbox. But Gallo's son was grown and gone. Emma hadn't seen him since her own sons were small. Now only Teddy, her youngest, still lived at home. Emma drove him to the library Saturday afternoons because he had been caught skipping high school and shoplifting again. At the library, Teddy helped unwilling children learn to read. If he helped enough of them, he might still be allowed to graduate.

Emma rolled down her window and handed Gallo her ones. Gallo had a boyish face gone liver spotted. A banana is too green to eat, until one day it's overripe. Traditionally, Emma and Gallo exchanged grave nods as neighbors watching each other age but this time she said, "Where's your son these days?"

Gallo opened the cashbox and slipped Emma's bills inside. He locked the box with his tiny brass key. He leaned against the car window. "My son," Gallo said, shaking his head. "Where is anyone's son? Where is your son?"

"Here," she said. "Right here. This is Teddy." Gallo shaded his eyes. Teddy was slumped in the back seat.

"Hello, Teddy," Gallo said.

"Teddy," Emma said. "Say hello." Teddy mumbled something and didn't sit up.

"Teenagers," Emma said. Gallo waved and Emma pulled the car forward.

"Pathetic," Teddy said, a word he used for everything lately, especially himself. "If he actually wanted to fix the crack in the road, he would do it."

"He's not trying to fix the crack in the road," Emma said. "He's trying to warn people about the crack in the road."

"Then why doesn't he use better paint, and only paint it once? Or once every few years?" Teddy didn't ask why Gallo didn't call the city. There was no city.

"That's not his goal," Emma said. "His goal is to make a living."

"So it's a scam," Teddy said.

"Have you ever considered how you might make a living?" Emma said.

"No one makes a living," Teddy said. "Uber, envelope stuffing, pyramid scheme."

"No one makes a living?" Emma said. "What about me and Grandma?"

"Grandma can't even afford to live in her own house," Teddy said. "That's why she lives with us." He pressed his inflamed cheek against the lock button to make it click back and forth. Teddy had the unreasonable teenage belief that he should not be interpellated, which Emma had to google to learn that he felt he should not be collected into a humanlike image by the rods and cones of others.

Emma worked in produce, always had. Teddy's skin was like the skin of an avocado or a Seville orange.

Emma's mother worked part-time at the library. When they arrived, she was distributing reluctant kindergartners to delinquent teens. Candace (fistfights), Bryson (selling cigarettes to middle schoolers), DeAndre (running a plagiarism business in the locker room). Emma watched Teddy turn on his music so he wouldn't have to talk to anyone. "Teddy. Headphones. Now," his grandma said. He took them off. There was no city, but there was just enough of it left to punish people. "Reading is not punishment," Teddy's grandma said. The kindergartners and the teens let her say it.

While she waited, Emma helped her mother clear the overfull bulletin board. Only one flyer had nothing to sell:

> Wanted: Grandparents. I am a woman in my midthirties. I am estranged from my parents and have no close family. I am seeking a man or a woman (couple is fine too) to *adopt* me as their grandchild. This would include giving me advice, celebrating *some* holidays, passing down traditional family recipes, possible movie watching, slow walks, etc. Call Jessica.

Jessica's phone number fringed the bottom. Emma's mother reached past Emma and tore one off.

"You already live with one of your grandchildren," Emma said. "And you barely spend time with him."

"To be honest," her mother said, "he's annoying. Just a little bit."

"Teddy's not annoying," Emma said. "He's sullen. He's disengaged."

"That annoys me," her mother said.

"That's not what *annoying* means."

"I don't like to think of Jessica out there, grandparent-less."

They tore down flyers whose dates had passed. A pricey parenting workshop offered by the worst parents in town. A restorative yoga class, twenty-five dollars a session. The teacher liked to relax on cushions. So did everyone. White ancestral healing with Lindsay, sliding scale. Pathetic, Teddy would say. White nonsense. Emma thought they weren't allowed to teach kids things like that in school anymore. Things about race. But Teddy skipped school.

Skipping school was new, but shoplifting was not. At age six, Teddy had stolen a long green ribbon from Joann, then a hanger from Marshalls, and later a tape dispenser from Staples. He liked collecting stray objects, exfoliated from the world. Emma had, too. For her, it had been a package of paper clips, red as forbidden berries, toppled off the drugstore shelf. Her mother had dragged her back and watched, arms folded, as Emma returned them and stammered her mortified apology. Emma had intended to pass this shame on to Teddy, but when it came time for her to explain why he shouldn't steal, Emma figured she could do it later. Now it was later, and Teddy was an unhappy seventeen-year-old with no driver's license and severe cystic acne, addicted to stealing sheet masks from Rite Aid. Teddy said the masks made him feel better, his face but also behind his face, his brain. When he was done with one, he hung it someplace he shouldn't. You'd open the refrigerator or the mailbox to stare into an eyeless white visage, gelatinous and nutrient-dense as kelp.

Emma's mother rode home with them. The kind of rain previously called a downpour now lingered for days or a whole week. Teddy filled the car with the smell of his wet socks. Gallo was still on his corner, where the stop sign stood before a shaggy apartment complex, protected from the road by a fence of spindly pines. The crack crawled from the curb into the road, away from Gallo, who had opened an umbrella and donned a voluminous black poncho. He was staring at the ground.

"Is Gallo's yellow line longer than it was this morning?" Emma asked.

"So he can scam more money," Teddy said, but he craned out of the window, letting the rain in. "You're right," he said. "The crack's growing. It's wider and longer."

"That crack has been the same my whole life," Emma said. "It's been there even longer than those hideous apartments. Those pines were bottlebrush."

"Everything changes," Teddy said. "Blah blah it's the one constant."

"Not everything," Emma said. "Not the crack in the road. Not Gallo's yellow line."

"DeAndre has better headphones than me," Teddy said.

"So get a job and save up," Emma's mother said.

"There are no jobs," Teddy said.

"Have you looked at the bulletin board?" she said. "If you're willing to be creative, there are all kinds of ways to earn money."

"The bulletin board is pathetic," Teddy said. "No one signs up for those workshops. Their market is each other. It's a big stupid circle."

"Everything's a big stupid circle," his grandma said. "Rain, the earth, life, death."

Emma watched in her rearview mirror as Gallo walked to where his yellow line ended and the blank crack began. He wielded his paintbrush. He dripped yellow beneath the dripping sky. You can't paint in the rain, but Gallo was going to try. Emma adjusted her mirror so she could see Teddy, the way his chin, cupped like a plum, deepened its crease when he refused to cry.

Jessica was the name of someone who'd had a side ponytail and a sweatsuit with a top and bottom that matched, pink piping up the side. Jessica had a My Little Pony birthday party. Jessica's scrunchies were real velvet. Jessica had a hat like Blossom's hat. Jessica was the name that Emma had decided to go by for three weeks when she was nine. Emma was not enamored with the trendy multiverse the way Teddy was, so she couldn't know that she'd created Jessica, like Athena from the head of Zeus. Emma's mother invited Jessica over for tea.

Emma helped her mother clear the house of used sheet masks: watermelon, cucumber, pumpkin, Mickey's Smooth Strollin' squalane and tea tree, Cryo Rubber with firming collagen, Hello Kitty Ready Set Glow, Unicorn Glow Hologram, activated charcoal, retinol, acne repair. Emma and her mother unstuck them from the walls, unhitched them from the lampshade, peeled them off the coffee table.

"This is annoying," her mother said. "Teddy should be doing this."

But they hadn't seen Teddy in two days. The high school had sent a letter. The state test is imminent, the letter said. It's unlikely your child will graduate.

Emma had called Martin, Teddy's older brother, who drove for Uber far away.

"Teddy's on drugs," Emma said. "Or, I don't know, sex? What if he's being used by someone older?"

"Possibly," Martin said. "Does he have any friends?"

"Yes," Emma lied. "DeAndre, Candace, and Bryson."

"I'll talk to him," Martin said. But Emma knew what that meant. Would you rather piss shit or shit piss, would you rather be a ball of snot or a storm drain, would you rather live inside an owl pellet or a placenta, would you rather be a human beehive or a termite mound with legs? The likelihood of Martin having a forthright and sensitive talk with his younger brother was roughly the same as the likelihood of Martin moving back to the city, and there was no city.

The doorbell rang. The kettle boiled. "That's Jessica," Emma's mother yelled from the kitchen.

"She's your guest, not mine," Emma called back. She sent herself to her room and made herself small again. Then she sneaked halfway down the stairs and peeked through the railing. Her mother ushered Jessica into the living room and Emma was relieved to see that Jessica was a dingy adult like Emma, a dish-soapy little bottle of a woman, a wrung-out rag, all pulled-down edges.

"I've been doing a lot of personal work," she heard Jessica say.

"Paid?" Emma's mother asked. She poured tea. She served jam cookies.

"Thank you," Jessica said. "But I don't eat jam."

Emma stifled a mean-spirited laugh.

"What was that?" Jessica asked. "Is there someone else here?"

"It's no one," Emma's mother said.

After Jessica left, Emma's mother cleared the teacups while Emma bit her nails on the bottom step. "How do you think Teddy's going to feel about Jessica?" Emma asked.

"There's no need to be jealous," her mother said, eating a jam cookie. Jealous of dishrag Jessica? If anyone was pathetic, it was Emma. The door opened and Teddy came in. "Mom," he said. "Why are you crying?"

"Teddy," Emma said. "Where have you been?"

"Everything's all right, Mom," Teddy said. "Don't worry." He knelt on the bottom step and took her into his arms. Teddy held Emma and patted her back like she was his baby and not the other way around. Sheet masks slipped out of his back pocket and shushed across the floor.

Driving to work, Emma saw that Gallo had sunk a tree branch down into the crack in the road. He had strung Christmas lights along its skeleton scarecrow arms. The yellow line now extended bravely across both lanes of traffic. The crack opened up into a monster mouth. Gallo sat in a lawn chair next to his sign, hands clasped placidly across his cashbox. Emma waved and Gallo waved back, bowing his head.

In produce, Emma sorted bad apples so they wouldn't spoil the whole bunch. Jazz went mealy faster than Cosmic Crisp. WildTwist stayed crisp longer than its child, Cripps Pink. Envy apples were fragile, the sweetest of all. Emma loved her aisle. Privately, she spelled it *isle*. On the other isles, food was static, part of no circle. Emma's isle was a special archipelago along with Ericka's and Dave's (dairy, meats), the people whose food rotted. Voyagers to Emma's isle expected a mushroom textured like a pink eraser, cilantro not accidentally filed as flat-leaf parsley, flavorful blueberries out of season. No one wanted to notice a road, a potato, a banana, a mother. If they didn't notice it, it meant it was working. Teddy had been gone almost four days this time.

Emma's phone vibrated in her apron pocket. It was the manager of Epic Adventure, the sporting goods store at the mall.

"I had no idea you were still open," Emma said. "Are people still buying sporting goods?"

"Your son isn't. He tried to steal an inflatable raft," the manager said.

"Are you sure? He usually doesn't."

"Next time, I'm calling the cops."

"I'm sorry. He's in a program. At the library."

When Emma arrived at the mall, which was abandoned except for Epic Adventure, Teddy was sitting on the curb with his chin on his chest. Emma hugged him in full view of the manager.

"I thought your thing was sheet masks," she said, once they were in the car.

"People change, Mom," Teddy said.

"Why do you always get caught?"

"It's a numbers game," he said. "And I'm bad at math. Are you taking me back to school?"

"Well," she said. "I could use some ice cream. How about you?"

"Ice cream's not good for my skin," Teddy said. Emma handed him a bad Envy, nearly alcoholic.

"If you got a job, like Grandma said, you could save up for

that raft," Emma said. "Though where you would float it, I don't know."

"They weren't even using it," Teddy said. "It was just sitting there."

"Teddy, I'm here to help," Emma said. "I'm your mother."

"Why do you always say that?" he said.

"Say what?"

"'I'm your mother,'" he said. "When you say it so often, it sounds like it's not true. It sounds like something a robot would say."

"I'm not a robot," she said.

"A robot would say that," Teddy said. Emma was pretty sure he was joking. She was pretty sure he wasn't going to become a mass shooter, because she was pretty sure he was gay and she was pretty sure gay teens didn't kill other people, they just killed themselves, and then she had to pull over and put her head on the steering wheel. She looked up and there was Gallo. He waved. Since the morning, he had changed his sign. Now it read GUESS THE DEPTH OF THE SINKHOLE AND YOUR MONEY BACK. Emma lowered the window.

"Hazard a guess?" Gallo asked, leaning in.

"Not today, Gallo," she said. He saw her red-rimmed eyes, and Teddy beside her, gnawing on the apple core.

"Being a parent is the price you pay so that one day you can be a grandparent," Gallo said. "The joy without the trouble."

"Do you have grandchildren?" Emma asked.

"Sadly, no," Gallo said. "My son was unable to . . . before he . . ." Emma handed him a five-dollar bill.

She pulled back onto the road, following the yellow line safely around the sinkhole. Teddy twisted around to watch it go by. "I'm surprised Gallo doesn't advertise on the bulletin board," he said. But Gallo had been painting his yellow line long before the informal economy had come to the underqualified yoga teacher, the bad parent, the wounded white descendant. Gallo's vocation grew in proportion to the sinkhole, more vital each day.

. . .

Jessica this, Jessica that. Jessica recommends sleeping with your mouth taped shut so that you are forced to take deep cleansing breaths through your nose. Jessica says it takes a lot to be vulnerable. Jessica thinks that if libraries were invented today they'd be jailed for treason. Jessica was probably right. Emma's mother and Jessica spent more and more time together. They needed their intergenerational fix, they said. Tonight, Jessica was coming to dinner and Emma's mother was inventing a traditional family recipe. Three cans converged in a pot. Tomato paste. Chili powder. "Ethnic stew, your grandmother called it," Emma's mother told Emma. "I'm pretty sure." She ripped open a bag of shredded yellow cheese. "Jessica says I should run for city council," she said, stirring the stew as if there was a city.

Emma rinsed sandy spinach, sliced hairy carrots. The definition of being annoying was sharing too many opinions or asking too many questions or speaking too loudly or too softly or too close to someone or too far away from them or finishing someone's sentences or being surprised about unsurprising things or watching a movie and saying oh yeah like that would ever happen during every scene. Teddy walked into the kitchen and slouched into his seat at the dining table. Teddy was a malcontent. Teddy was a pirate. Teddy was a walking statistic. Teddy was a teen with a gold sparkly face. Teddy was not annoying.

"Jessica's annoying," Emma said.

"You're too hard on Jessica," Teddy said. "She's not that bad."

His grandma looked at him. "You'll take that mask off before she arrives, won't you?" she asked. Teddy peeled. His acne glowed.

Jessica brought them special salt, salt with deeper meaning. Emma doled out raw vegetables. Emma's mother ladled ethnic stew. Jessica said grace.

"Grandmother tells me you have a test coming up," Jessica said, once the candles were lit.

"What," Teddy said.

"Every kid in the state," his grandma said. There was no state, but it seemed rude to say that.

"We can help you study for it," Jessica said. "I was an honors student. Right, Grandmother? It's what families do."

"Here's a test," Teddy said. "Name the signs of a sinkhole."

"Cracks," Jessica said.

"That's good, Jessica," Teddy said. "Cracks in foundations, cracks in interiors. Anyone else?" Teddy ticked on his fingers. "Doors or windows that become hard to open or close," he said. "Trees or posts that tilt. Rapid appearance of a hole in the ground."

"Rapid appearance of a hole in the ground?" Emma laid down her fork. "That's like saying that a sinkhole is the sign of a sinkhole." The edge in her voice was as sharp as the carrots should have been but were not.

"It's from the U.S. Geological Survey website," Teddy said.

"So the USGS is paying someone to publish circular definitions," Emma said. "Just like everyone else, monetizing something they're shitty at. Might as well put it on the bulletin board."

"Mom," Teddy said. "Everyone has to get by."

"You've changed," Emma said. She brandished the salad bowl over Jessica's plate. "Gallo told me he wants a grandchild. His son never had any children."

"Being a grandchild is a lot," Jessica said. "I don't think I have the capacity to do it for more than one person."

"Most people are more than one person's grandchild," Emma said. "Many people have up to four grandparents."

"Emma, did you hear her?" Emma's mom said, reaching for Jessica's hand across the table. "She said she doesn't have the capacity."

"My mother already has grandchildren," Emma said. "Gallo has none." She tipped the salad bowl. Spinach curled onto the tablecloth. Bits of bitter cucumber bounced into Jessica's lap.

"Mom," Teddy said. "Stop." But Emma didn't want to stop. Teddy was still the child and Emma was still the mother. He was still the grandchild and she was still the daughter.

"Gallo is lonely," Emma said, setting the bowl down. "And it's so sad, what happened to his son."

"What happened to his son?" asked her mother.

"Death," Emma said. "Maybe. Or prison. Gallo couldn't even talk about it."

"Death?" Emma's mother said. "Prison? Gallo's son went to school for IT and moved to Springfield. He's fine. Tomas. You were in the third grade together."

"I don't remember that," Emma said. "I still think it's not a fair distribution. Of grandchildren."

"Why is it always about fairness with you?" her mother said. "Relationships aren't like oranges, interchangeable."

"Oranges aren't interchangeable," Emma said. She stabbed a carrot. She checked Teddy's chin, a cupped plum. She noticed Jessica's chin, similarly cupped, similarly plumlike. Trembling. So what? Was she meant to fall into sympathy? You might have a sinkhole if you sense an earthy switch to the scent of rain. If your yard begins to smell like a garden. Jessica ate the cucumber from her lap. They finished their salty meal.

Teddy hadn't been home in two weeks. Emma called the high school. He'd been ejected from the library program. He'd missed the state test. He wouldn't graduate. Emma called Martin. Martin had talked to his younger brother the Friday before last. "He told me he'd rather not choose between arsenic on the back of a postage stamp or cyanide on the tag of a teabag," Martin said. "He said he'd rather find a third option, one he actually liked. Which is not in the spirit of the game." There was no one else to call unless Emma wanted Teddy to be punished.

Jessica now came to dinner each night. "I'll put this in terms you can understand," she told Emma gently. "When it comes to your family of origin, sometimes the flesh is too easily bruised. Grandmother needs my support." She stayed late and snuggled on the sofa beneath an afghan, watching true-crime shows.

Emma called in sick. Ericka and Dave dropped off a box of lumpy dairy, iffy meat, but Emma wasn't hungry. At a library computer, she made a poster with Teddy's face on it. Teddy would no longer consent to have his picture taken, so the photo was from early sophomore year, the year Martin left home, the year her mother moved in, the year Teddy's face began to sputter and grumble. Emma's phone buzzed, but it was just the supermarket reminding her she was running out of PTO. How did the world continue without her knowing where Teddy was?

"On the other hand, you'll spend your life not knowing where your child is," her mother said, punching her employee code into the library Xerox machine. "You'll have to get used to it."

"Did you get used to it?" Emma asked.

"Why do you think I decided to live with you?"

"Because the library cut your hours back and you couldn't make rent," Emma said.

"Jessica has invited me to move in," Emma's mother said. "I've been waiting for the right time to bring it up with you."

"And leave me alone?" Emma said.

"I'm not rushing into anything," her mother said. "She needs to know by next week."

Emma tacked a poster to the bulletin board. Teddy's face was surrounded by opportunities for people to pay to churn butter or buy old textbooks or go on a long walk through the natural world. Emma had sold her first vegetables at fourteen, tomatoes she'd grown herself, an heirloom variety called Stump of the World. She'd set up a folding table in the front yard, Magic Markered a cardboard sign. Now she built beefsteak tomato pyramids and could almost forget they were for sale. DeAndre paused on his way to his miserable six-year-old. He took off his shiny headphones.

"Really," he said.

"What?" she said.

"That poster makes it seem like Teddy was kidnapped by a cave troll or something. He's not a baby. He's not going to accidentally drown in the bathtub. Teddy doesn't want to be found."

"DeAndre," Emma said. "Do you know where Teddy is?"

"Do I look like a snitch?" he said.

"DeAndre."

"But I don't, anyway," he said. "And that photo. Looks like you paid for airbrushing."

"If you hear anything," Emma said. She pressed a poster into his hands.

Emma drove the streets of the noncity. The stop sign was tilted. The ground beneath it ebbed. Gallo's yellow line had become a yellow amoeba, expanding. Gallo waved traffic around orange cones. He had added taller branches, longer strings of Christmas lights, caution tape, a new sign: BEAUTIFY THE SINKHOLE YOUR DONATION APPRECIATED. The branches were hung with wind chimes and mittens, prayer flags and pinwheels, a boot and a baseball glove, a single striped sock. Beside Emma, on the passenger seat, Teddy's face repeated and repeated. Emma was not a robot. She was thousands of roaring fans in an enormous arena and Teddy was the only one on the field.

Emma parked her car in the lot of the apartment complex and walked through the pines. At the edge of the sinkhole, she offered Gallo a ten-dollar bill. She showed him the poster. "Please," she said. "Could I hang this from the Christmas lights?"

"That is not what Teddy looks like," Gallo said.

"It's the most recent picture I have," Emma said. He wouldn't take the bill but then he took it.

Dangling from one of the skeleton branches, a golden mask whirled against the wind. Emma's heart turned to the kind of grapefruit they call Ruby Red. When Teddy climbed out of the sinkhole, a headlamp elasticked around his greasy teen hair, Cotton Candy grapes rolled through her. Teddy didn't see her and while she watched, he handed Gallo a small rock caked in mud. Gallo polished it on his shirt. Gallo and Teddy gave each other the secret side-hug handshake of men. Only then did Gallo nod in Emma's direction, so that Teddy looked her way. The opposite of a sinkhole is a volcano. It was not a fact you could put on any kind of test, but Emma felt it to be true. She was as angry as she had ever been.

"How long has my son been here?" She turned on Gallo. "Why didn't you tell me?"

"I got a job," Teddy said. "Like you and Grandma wanted. Gallo's going to teach me everything he knows."

"Didn't anyone ever teach you right from wrong, you little shit," Emma said. "Do you think you're the only person who actually exists? Do you even notice me?"

"Mom, you should see what we're finding down there. So many crystals it's almost boring," Teddy said.

Emma was so angry, but Teddy wouldn't stop talking. "I'm learning so much, Mom," he said. "I never knew where the term *grassroots* came from. I thought it was just a term people put on the bulletin board. But it actually means the roots of grass. And I've been beneath them." He switched his headlamp on. "Let me show you." Teddy sat on the concrete and swung his legs over the edge of the sinkhole.

"Get back here," Emma yelled at him. "Not one more step." There was no way she was letting that little bastard out of her sight again.

"We're going to install ladders," Teddy said. "Maybe even stairs." He grinned. "But for now it's the old-fashioned way." Teddy pushed himself forward. Concrete crumbled into the depths. Teddy slid into the hole. Emma teetered at the edge.

"It's hard to get your children to do what you want them to do," Gallo said. "Especially at this age. It was the same with Tomas." Gallo handed Emma her own headlamp. He turned back toward the traffic. He guided the public around the sinkhole as if he believed he could stop it from swallowing them.

Crumbs of soil and concrete eroded under Emma's feet. Teddy

had left a narrow trail. The sinkhole was funnel shaped, wide and shaggy at the top, smoothing as it sloped. The surface was crunchy. The inside was creamy. A tunnel, a cave, a tunnel again. Emma climbed furiously but Teddy kept ahead. Emma reached out for roots. She put her feet where Teddy's feet had been. She passed loose change, soda-can tabs, worms, a mole, some kind of den. Was she beneath the apartments? "Teddy, you listen to me when I'm talking to you," she screamed. But Teddy talked fossils, limestone, salt beds, carbonate, shit left over from the Ice Age. "We're going to charge for tours," he said. The water had polished the soil away and now it was all rock. It was porous and breathy, cool to the touch.

"Goddammit, Teddy, I'm warning you," Emma roared, but Teddy would not be interrupted. Emma followed Teddy down. They descended lower. Lower still. What the hell was he thinking? He was in so much fucking trouble.

At the bottom of the sinkhole was a young forest. Moss of iridescent green condensed on wispy saplings. They twisted toward a hazy light that filtered in through the cavern's ceiling. The floor was wet. Emma had heard about gases in caves, but the green made it so she could breathe.

"This grove has been here all along," Teddy said, not stopping. "Growing in the dark. That light comes from the opening on the other side of the apartments by the drainage ditch. Talk about a microclimate!" When Teddy was four and sleeping in his own bed for the first time, Emma had stood at the door of his and Martin's room. Martin had the top bunk, and Teddy slept on the bottom, beneath his moon-and-stars quilt. Emma had waited for the moon and stars to move. She needed to watch Teddy breathe. She needed to make sure he was working.

Emma chased Teddy through the trees, desperate to catch up. She followed his narrow, breathing body to where the lake began. Steam lifted, a miasma. The lake smelled like the runoff from the road, like the drainage ditch. It smelled like yellow paint. Emma wasn't supposed to like the odor but she liked it. She was going to punish Teddy when she caught him. She was going to punish him so bad. The inflatable raft waited on the shore, price tag still attached. Teddy climbed aboard. He'd be sorry when she finally got her hands on him. Teddy turned to his mother and held out his hand. Emma followed her son to the center of the earth.

Indya Finch
Shotgun Calypso

We were on our way from Huntsville to Houston to pick up Lonnie because it was Saturday, and it seemed like every Saturday we were dragging our asses to River Oaks, wearing shoes without holes like we were going to church. Sometimes, if Mrs. Vanessa was out of town for work, we'd stay the night with him and build a blanket fort in the unaired guest room with the plain white crib in the corner. Today he wanted to come over to barbecue. As if someone had asked him to do that, as if we wanted to pretend we liked his tasteless meat.

I rode shotgun whenever Lonnie wasn't around. When it was just us, Ma let me put my feet on the dash if they didn't leave any marks on the windshield. She didn't want to clean them off, and despite my own insistence on being uncivilized, the least I could do was pretend like I wasn't so people wouldn't call her an unfit mother. I don't think of myself as wild—wearing shoes just isn't my thing.

I was trying to enjoy the last moments of the front seat and outstretched legs before Lonnie blocked my view and leaned his seat back against my knees. Clio was laid out on the stained back seat, etching cuss words into the fabric before dragging her hand across to erase them. Ma was singing along to "End of the Road," by Boyz II Men, which meant she was about to start babbling about the time she got invited to their after-party in '94. Michael, the bass, could've been my father, and she almost named me Michelle instead of Calypso. There were other options. Daddy liked Diana, but Ma spared me a lifetime of being called Dirty Diana, and she told him Billie Jean and Annie were out of the question too. In the one college class she ever took, they read the *Odyssey* and she decided right then that's who I was. Why wouldn't she want a goddess that men feared for a daughter? My birthright was women who trapped love and took it by force even when men cried—even when they couldn't afford to stay one more minute, they stayed eight more years. She'd told me these stories a million times, but I didn't ever stop laughing or gasping when the moment was right. I didn't know what else to do.

On another day the music would've been cut lower, and the three of us would've been talking about the new man we saw coming out of Ms. Winnie's apartment and our pride at her still pulling men at the age of seventy, but that day Clio and Ma were still mad at each other. For the billionth time Clio had complained that I always got to ride up front, and for the billionth time I said she could sit in the front when her birthday came before mine. Instead of accepting as she had done so many times before that her lot in life as my younger sister is to take the things I don't want, she got mad. She reached her hands around the seat and gripped both of my cheeks and dug her nails in. Clio always went for my face, always scratching me as hard as she could. When we were younger and would fight, Ma would make us both put on one of Daddy's oversized shirts he left behind and hug underneath it. Clio would grab the skin at my sides and pinch and scratch me until I bled, and I hugged her like I was supposed to. I wanted to cry, but I never did because if Ma saw tears she made us stay in the shirt longer.

Ma didn't pull over, but she did slam on the brakes, and the tires screamed like she'd peeled off their skin. Ma pulled her arm back and hit Clio in the mouth so hard her bottom lip burst open and bled. She didn't even whimper. Her face scrunched up into a Raisinet of squinty almond eyes and purple lips, and she smacked them even though she knew Ma hated that, and Ma popped the other side. She didn't mean anything by it, and neither did Clio. It was just their way. They're so much like each other. Clio's lip healed. She has a crescent-moon-shaped scar there now, but she doesn't remember from what. The car was mostly quiet as we drove up I-45.

Ma never hit us in front of Lonnie. He didn't agree that children needed to feel pain to learn how to behave. If Ma wanted to hurt him she would ask him where he got off giving advice when he didn't have any children he could point to. But she didn't want to hurt him often. Even though Ma said he was a trick, like all the men she courted, she used some restraint.

That didn't mean she wouldn't give us a look that said she'd cataloged our poor behavior and we weren't getting off scot-free. Once on a school night we made a trip to Lonnie's. It got late as we waited for him and Ma to come out from his room, and by the sound of things we knew they were almost done. We passed the time by carving butterflies into the legs of his table. It had been Clio's idea. Later we learned it was a table his grandfather brought back from the war. Lonnie never said which war, but from what Ma says, some brown family generations later were still eating on the floor. Even though Clio was mostly responsible, we got whooped together. Ma says all the time that it hurts her more than us, but I think that's bullshit. We're the ones with welts trying to hold back tears so she doesn't give us something to cry about.

Lonnie wasn't forever. We all knew that. But I think she loved him. In the way you can love a rich married man who pays your rent when you're short. Which is why we hated to have to spend so much time with him: Ma didn't need our help convincing Lonnie to stick around. If we could've stayed home with our neighbor

Ms. Denise, we would have. She made butter beans to die for, we rode bikes and raced through the neighborhood with her son Cameron, trying our hardest to keep the fastest-on-the-block title. She would watch us from the stoop of her apartment, drooling, and leaning on the rail for support.

But Ma had a fear of the three of us dying separately, so we went where she went. Sleeping on the floor of the carpeted conference room or late at night helping her sweep the busted tile of the gas station and filling the beer coolers with ice so we could get home quicker.

I always wanted him to at least offer to sit in the back when he rode with us. He was the grown-up, so I know Ma never would've let him, but I hated how he could just change everything without even knowing that when we were alone, the three of us, we had different rules, different traditions. He never thought he was disrupting, and I wished he knew he was. We'd squish ourselves into the back seat, whispering to each other even though we saw Ma cast her suspicion through the rearview mirror. Every time Lonnie fell down into the passenger seat, we watched him while he checked his teeth in the passenger mirror, ran a hand through his hair, and put his seat back so far he could look out our windows. I think it's because he thought it'd make him look slimmer, and his belly wouldn't protrude so much from between the straps of his seatbelt. Or maybe he just didn't want to be seen leaving his place in a car with chipped paint that always took a few tries of starting before the engine turned over, with a nappy-headed woman and her nappy-headed kids. I hate the way people stare, as if it isn't embarrassing enough we can't afford to fix everything wrong with our Chevy at once to make it run like it's supposed to, but they gotta let us know they see how poor we are.

He made sure to humiliate us in public too. If we were at the grocery store, he cracked stupid jokes the cashier didn't laugh at, he blew his nose into a handkerchief he stuffed right back into his pocket, and he wore white socks that went halfway up his calf. And whenever he got in the car with us, he smelled like cigars and cinnamon. Me and Clio couldn't stand it. We'd all but cover our noses with our T-shirts because Ma didn't like to roll the windows down when Lonnie rode with us. She said it'd be a waste of her perfume, the one she got at the dollar store. And even though that sugary cotton-candy scent clawed at her throat, made her sneeze three times when she sprayed it, she wasn't in the habit of spending dollars recklessly, she was gonna make sure he noticed she put it on.

I never looked forward to that change. When Ma stopped being my ma and became someone's lady.

I looked over at her and saw the sun shining on her face, her red lipstick, her left leg kicked up onto the seat, and the sparkle of the small diamond necklace he got her for her birthday. A big semitruck rambled up beside us. Ma tried to slow down to get out of his way, but the red-faced man in the car behind us started honking as soon as he saw brake lights. So we kept driving next to it while she mumbled a curse on his family pets. She wanted them to contract worms and shit all over his house.

"I hope he has a white carpet."

I looked at Clio through the side-view mirror and tried to get her to laugh at Ma's fantasy of a shit-covered home, but she didn't. She just stared at me and didn't let me in her head.

The truck driver was hunched with one arm slung over the steering wheel.

"Oh, Ma! Can I do the thing?" I tapped her arm, and she shrugged it off.

"What if you would've made me swerve into traffic and kill us all? And you know I don't like to be touched."

I looked at her.

"I don't care, Calypso. Do it."

Clio sat up and moved over to the passenger-side window and we gestured frantically, pulling on imaginary horns until he noticed. He brought his V-shaped fingers up to his mouth and wiggled his tongue up and down.

Ma saw and honked her horn. He snapped back to the road with a little less boredom in his posture.

"What's that mean?" Clio asked.

"It's disgusting is what it is. Men are disgusting, don't ever forget that," Ma said.

"What about Mr. Lonnie?" I asked.

"He's a man, ain't he? Roll your window down."

I complied, and she handed me her lukewarm coffee.

"Throw it."

We hit a pothole and the coffee jumped ship. It ran down my hands and onto my ironed pants that smelled like I had left the heat on them too long.

"Throw it," she said again. I peeled the lid off and tossed it at the semi. It splashed all over the shiny red coat of the truck. Ma sped up to pull into another lane as he rolled his window down to shout.

"That's not fair, I wanna throw something!" Clio shouted.

"Hurry up and do it!"

Clio settled on her half-eaten sandwich that we packed from home. The soggy wheat bread slapped against the windshield. He turned the wipers on, melted cheese and bologna grease smeared across the glass. He probably could barely see. I didn't know if mustard could stain glass like it could clothes, but I still hoped it washed off soon after. Car washes are bad places. We found a body in one once, and the woman from 911 said Ma should do mouth-to-mouth, but Ma said no because the woman was already blue and stiff. I doubted the truck could even fit in one of the brick stalls. He'd have to climb up and scrape the congealed cheese with his hands and get it under his fingernails, and he'd remember us and feel hate, especially if he found a body too.

We turned into Lonnie's bougie neighborhood, the kind the Obamas could live in and the rest of the neighbors, Lonnie included, would love and adore them, but they would whisper about the maintenance of the lawn and complain about how many strange cars were parked around whenever the Obamas threw a party. River Oaks was full of cookie-cutter houses that all looked the exact same, with identical neighborhood watch and homeowners' association posts stuck into the ground. Ma wants a house someday. Our landlord stands outside the kitchen window sometimes, and we have to act like he's not there. She's tired of renting. I hope she never gets a house like these. I like columns. If we ever have money someday, I want her to buy one with columns, and I want it to be different from everyone else's on the block.

Clio sat up and pressed her nose against the window, her breath frosting in pointed arrows on the glass.

"Pirates, ye be warned," Clio said.

"The fuck did you just say?" Ma asked.

"Nothing."

"Don't get smart."

Clio rolled her eyes.

"Do it again," Ma said.

Me and Clio looked at each other.

"Why she always tripping?"

"I don't think she knows she ain't always got to be crazy," Clio thought.

Ma smacked my leg. "You know I can't stand when you do that." She looked at Clio in the rearview mirror.

"Do what?" I asked.

"You know what. Y'all get on my last nerves talking above my head," she said. She hit the brakes a little too hard at the stop sign and stuck her arm out to catch me, but the seat belt was faster and snapped me back when my body lurched forward. Someone had tagged the sign with *Get Fucked*. I had never thought about getting fucked before. Seemed like from what Ma said, it was never something you got, more that you gave, and always felt like taking back as soon as you handed it over. 'Cause these boys out *here*, she would say, wouldn't ever really know what they were doing. So why bother with it, Caly? Just be a lesbo, at least then your pussy will get ate, and that's half the battle won.

The paint was still fresh, beads of it still dripping doing their best to dry. I always thought graffiti was cool. Conceptually, I mean. When I look at it too long, especially if it's chaotic and too many words, my brain starts to hurt a little. But I thought the boys, probably boys, who did it were brave in a way. Except of course that they were in the suburbs and probably put their half-used paint cans back in the garage when they were done. We took a left onto Panther Paw, the houses like perfect rows of multicolored teeth. Ma slid a glance at the white people sitting outside on their porch swing. They swirled the little umbrellas in their tea glasses by touching them every couple of seconds to make them rotate in the other direction, faces puckered at the smoke billowing from our tailpipe. Ma won't admit this, but white people make her nervous. She almost can't control herself when she's around them because she's too busy thinking about what they're thinking. Ma didn't like white men normally. She said Black men were the only real type of men she had any eye for, but Lonnie was built sturdy and had a charming smile. And what wouldn't you do for a good smile?

One of Lonnie's neighbors knelt in his yard, measuring the height of the grass with a ruler, while a young man covered in sweat waited to hear what the owner thought of his mowing skills. We stopped at Lonnie's door. I unbuckled my seat belt and clambered into the back seat; Ma slapped my backside the whole time.

"I told you to stop climbing over like that!"

I fell onto Clio, and we stifled our giggles and struggled to sit upright. Ma honked the horn, and out sauntered Lonnie. He had just gotten off work; he was still in his blue button-down shirt, black slacks, and brown loafers. Me and Clio didn't know much about Lonnie, or Mrs. Vanessa for that matter, but we knew they must not have loved each other for a long time, that their marriage had been over well before Ma, even if neither one of them wanted to do anything about that fact. And we knew he must not have had a mother, or sisters, or really any other kind of family. If anybody cared about him, they would've taught him not to wear brown shoes with black pants.

He held a cold Pretty Lady in his left hand. He leaned into the passenger-side window, and Ma tried to give him a kiss.

"You're a little early," he said as he bopped her nose instead. "Vanessa's still here. She should be finished packing in about fifteen more minutes. Circle the neighborhood a few times. I'll call when you can come inside."

"We're not coming inside. Just tell her your friend is here and you're going to go. I don't wanna drive around till she's gone," Ma said.

In the back seat the two of us sat boring holes in his cheeks. He winked.

"Hey, girls."

We mumbled a greeting, and Ma cut us with a sharp eyebrow raised halfway up her forehead.

"Try again," Ma thought.

"Hey, Mr. Lonnie. How are you?" I asked.

"Can't complain, sweetheart. I missed y'all."

He stuck his arm through the window and pinched my cheek. His fingers were damp and sticky with some of the Pretty Lady he must've spilled on his hand from the walk across the lawn. He left it there, and I wanted to wipe my face but I knew how it'd look if I did. I also knew I'd have a pimple in a few days. My skin was too sensitive for his bullshit. No one ever tells you how bad puberty is. Ma told me I was becoming a woman, but if all it took to be a woman was oily skin I should've been worth about three or four then.

"I want you to come inside," he said.

"For what?" Ma asked.

"I've got something for you," Lonnie said.

"Oh yeah?" Ma asked.

"Yeah, and the girls too."

"For us?" Clio asked. She sounded skeptical, but I knew she was intrigued. Clio was a hard person: she didn't like most people, sometimes I wasn't even sure if she liked me. She was mostly mean and sometimes funny. She got that from Ma. But if she didn't fuck with you, she didn't fuck with you. The only way to change that was to give her money or a gift. She got that from Ma too.

We did three circles around the neighborhood, and after Ma saw that Mrs. Vanessa's car was still parked in the driveway she drove us to the nearby playground. She didn't let us get out because she didn't want to have to wrangle us up again and couldn't we just be patient for once.

Ma leaned against the hood of the car while she chain-smoked. She wasn't gonna be able to sneak any more until we got home and Lonnie was watching TV with us. So she crammed one in for now, the car ride home, and before they started drinking for the night.

I missed her old guy Charlie. He was fun. And he didn't have all the rules that Lonnie came with. We couldn't spend the night unless Vanessa was out of town, he couldn't spend more than $500 from their joint account on us at once, none of us were allowed to go into their room or touch her things, holidays were a hard no. Vanessa didn't ever want to be put into a situation where she had to look at us, but if they ever crossed paths he couldn't touch Ma in front of her. Lonnie had to vacuum after we'd been there so that she wouldn't find our hair everywhere. Charlie could be with us whenever he wanted to; he took us to amusement parks, he used to tell knock-knock jokes, and I'd tell him some too. He used to laugh really hard. Ma said that he was faking. I didn't think so, though. I think he thought they were funny, even though most of them I got from Laffy Taffy wrappers and Popsicle sticks. Some of them I made up. Those were the ones he liked the most.

Knock knock.

Who's there?

Calypso.

Calypso who?

How many Calypsos do you know?

Lonnie never felt like the kind of guy I could tell jokes to.

There were a million reasons to dislike Lonnie and his house, but the doorbell was high on the list. When you rang it, it played a song we always heard in church.

"For still our ancient foe," Clio sang.

"Doth seek to work us woe," I finished.

Lonnie opened the door and kissed my mother full on her lips. Ma nudged our heads past the two of them and pushed us into the foyer. He had taste. I couldn't explain in those artsy terms what style anything in his house was, but he had a foyer. When he and Ma would fuck, me and Clio'd warble at the high ceilings and it would catch our voices and they were beautiful.

Clio blew past me, clutching her purse strap between her fingers as she made a beeline for the bathroom. I skipped behind her. Ma and Lonnie were giggling like the cool kids did in the parking lot at school.

I shut and locked the bathroom door behind me. Clio was already on her knees, digging in the cabinet underneath the sink. She pulled out six rolls of toilet paper, and this was not just any toilet paper. This was the fifteen-dollar, multiple-ply, lavender-scented toilet paper. The good stuff.

I opened the floor vent and waited for her to finish sliding the cardboard out from inside the rolls before she tossed them to me. I ripped the cardboard into small pieces and stuffed them inside the vent. I fiddled with the fan switch and made sure no pieces flew past the open slats. We were always careful to cover our tracks. We couldn't use the trash can—too obvious—and we could have held on to them but we needed every inch of space we could get.

Clio set the rolls neatly in her purse with space in between each one. I opened the medicine cabinet while Clio opened Daddy's old Crown Royal drawstring pouch. We grabbed different bottles of pills and dropped a few of each into it. We squished the pouch inside a roll of toilet paper. After enough visits out here, we'd figured out how to minimize the rattling of stolen goods. Inside toilet paper was soundproof.

Clio popped open an empty travel-size mouthwash, poured some of their tall bottle of Listerine into it, and spilled some on the counter. I wiped it with one of their decorative hand towels, and we refilled the bottle back up with water, the concoction a little less blue than before.

"That it?" Clio asked.

"I think Ma said to grab her some tampons."

We opened drawers and grabbed little extras. Tiny bottles of lotions and a bar or two of soap. The tampons were in the bottom drawer; we took half the box and left some loose ones rolling around on the inside.

"You think she wants any of this?" Clio pawed through a drawer full of mascaras, eyeliners, lipsticks, and eye shadow palettes.

"Does Ma wear makeup?"

I picked a tube of lipstick labeled British Red. "You think this would look good on me?"

"Lipstick can't fix all that," she said while drawing big circles around my moon face with her hands.

"Fuck you."

"I'm telling!" Clio tried to run out, but I grabbed her by her wrist and we tumbled to the hardwood floor. Shock ran up my elbow to my shoulder.

"I take it back!" I squealed, but that was not enough of a surrender for her. She jammed her fingers in my nose, her sharp little shovels scratching the inside.

"Say uncle!" she demanded.

I would've died instead. Though Clio was younger by a year, I never felt like the older sister, especially in moments like these. I slipped the cap off the lipstick and painted broad strokes of red on her face. She screeched as if it had been a sword. She crawled backward, sputtering and spitting the whole way.

"Why would you put this on me? They make these out of aborted babies!"

"Who told you that?" I asked.

"Minnie."

"Minnie Fischer? Minnie Fischer wasn't even allowed to watch *The Little Mermaid* with us 'cause her folks said it was unholy. She don't know nothing. And she always smells like cat pee."

Clio calmed down. "Most Baptists do," she said. I grabbed a wipe and approached slowly. Clio looked at me like a wounded deer, ready to flee if need be.

"Lemme fix it." I wiped away the streaks gently, and she hated me less. "You should put some on for real though."

"Ma will be mad," she said.

"Nah, she won't be," I said.

"I don't know how."

"Me neither," I said.

She sat mostly still while I applied it. Her top lip British Red and the bottom Nude. Clio gave me Divine Wine. We pursed our lips in the mirror and posed, over and over again, each one more dramatic than the last. We thought we looked like Naomi Campbell, when she was twelve and eleven at least. We pressed our fingers into Mrs. Vanessa's eye shadows and left fingerprints in the mauve and matte blues. We poked each other in the eye more than we actually applied anything, but our eyelids were peacocks. We revealed our flashy colors to each other. We covered ourselves in glitter body spray and couldn't stop smelling the parts on our wrists where the perfume clung the most.

We returned the bathroom to its former virgin state. The drawers and medicine cabinet closed, leaving no trace of the deflowering we'd done. Ma and Lonnie were still pairs of legs on the couch, Ma's painted toes caressing his hairy hobbit ones.

Lonnie and Mrs. Vanessa's bed was always made just right. I thought they must have never slept in it. Some of Vanessa's dresses, still on their hangers, were laid out on the bed. They must have been the ones she chose not to take. Lonnie was probably supposed to hang them back up, but he hadn't. We hoped for his sake that when she came back on Tuesday, he would have. We crinkled the blanket and creased her clothes with our bodies, rolling around on top of them.

The dresses slipped on easily over our heads, though they hung too long and too loose. So suddenly, we were women. Clio's dress had silver buttons all the way down the front. She shoved her hands into the two front pockets and admired herself from every angle in the floor-length mirror. Mine was yellow, with a hole in the back where my birthmark was visible. I remembered how Ma said that God made yellow just for Black girls. We couldn't walk in Vanessa's shoes, they were too high, but we could stand for a few seconds before our ankles wobbled enough that we fell back against the bed, laughing.

"What's going on in here?" Lonnie asked.

We froze, sure there was only trouble to come and thinking of the best way to get out of it. Clio, certain that as long as Ma didn't see, there was no evidence, began undoing the buttons.

"No, no, no. Don't worry," Lonnie said. He helped her button them back up. Her hands hung in the air, the barely visible hairs standing straight up. His knees popped as he leaned down, his face a few inches from mine. Some of my curly baby hairs about to brush against the coarse unshaved shadow of a beard, the Pretty Lady tickling my cheeks when he spoke.

"You little ladies having fun?" he asked.

"We'll take it off," Clio said.

He brought his thumb up to his mouth and sucked on it for a moment. He slowly swiped the curve of my bottom lip with his wet finger.

"This stuff's tricky. You'll get the hang of it. You want me to teach you a trick? Gimme your hand."

My limbs stayed stuck to my sides, tingling to the edge of pain, going numb until I couldn't remember whether it was a symptom of a heart attack or a stroke. Ma had tried to make us memorize what signals our bodies would send under life-threatening causes so that we could save each other, but right then, when it mattered, I couldn't tell you what was wrong.

"No?" he asked.

Lonnie gently pressed his finger against my lips, probing for resistance. "Just open."

I don't know what magic prompted my mouth to pop open. He put his thumb in my mouth, and my lips closed around it. Ma says the best way to get a man's attention is to put something in your mouth. She and my aunt Tonya had been walking back home after the concert; they were young, sixteen or seventeen. A limo pulled up, the window rolled down, and a Black hand with a Rolex around the wrist beckoned them both closer.

Ma leaned into the car, breasts first. They were still perky then, not yet ravaged by Clio and me. Michael, the bass, was her favorite. She was glad he was the one doing the talking. His voice slid over her like silk pajamas and soft red-carpet gowns. He promised champagne and a late night, but all my mother heard was a baby if she played her cards right. No more sockets that spit fire when you tried to plug something in, no more falling onto the floor while the men outside shot the building full of holes, no more hoping that the old woman next door wasn't the one to catch a bullet in the neck, no more splitting a one-bedroom apartment with four sisters and two cousins.

Once, she had sent us to bed while Aunt Tonya was over and they laughed about how stupid they were then. Me and Clio lay on the floor, heads rubbing together while we peeked through the slip of light at the bottom of the door. They were dancing, with hips a little wider and less flexible than they used to be, but me and Clio could imagine them then, curly hair in nineties asymmetrical cuts, small dresses, borrowed shoes, and Bath and Body Works Japanese Cherry Blossom perfume. Tonya said they should've done it all differently. She would've never met LeRoy and wouldn't work at the chicken factory now if she had just let one of them take her. Ma said she would take her life as it is because sleeping in that other room would probably be a Michelle and a Holly. And who the fuck would they be? Not those girls. Those weird, smart, fucked-up girls. I had never known that Ma liked us. Loved us, of course, but not liked.

"Besides," Ma laughed, "who's to say even if we did, they wouldn't have just dropped us off at the nearest Scrape 'N' Save and kept on moving?"

They both knew she was right, but a ho life past is still a life mourned.

"Purse your lips," Lonnie said.

"What?" My voice was muffled.

"Purse your lips."

I couldn't. So he used his other hand to squish my face, and he pulled out his finger with a definitive pop. A ring of purple around his thumb.

"This way it stays off your teeth," he said.

I nodded.

"Valentina's in the backyard. She's got your present back there."

It was a trampoline. Ma was smiling in the backyard with a beer in her hand while she clapped her hands and said things like "This is so nice of him!" and "Tell him thank you. He didn't have to do this." When we didn't fall all over ourselves in thanking him, Ma looked at the two of us hard.

"The least you can do is act grateful," Ma thought.

So we were grateful. For hours we were grateful. Clio pushed through the mesh net and pulled me through. I crawled my way across the smooth landscape until Clio jumped and I fell face down. The canvas was hot and burned my face.

I saw Ma sitting on Lonnie's lap; they leaned back in a lounge chair as she kissed his neck. His eyes were on us. We bounced together and didn't stop when they laughed, or kissed, or when they disappeared inside, and we bounced to feel like we weren't alone. The blinds were partly open, so we bounced to feel like they were closed, and we bounced to feel like we couldn't see inside. We bounced as the sun went down, and we bounced when they asked if we wanted to order pizza. We bounced until the food came, we took our portions and lay on our backs, breathing heavy from our tiredness. We bounced and promised each other when the rapture happened the last thing we put our eyes on would be each other. We bounced until the neighborhood went quiet, and the moon hung, we bounced while we held hands, we bounced while Clio wiped a stray tear from my cheek, we bounced and watched the whole families in their own private spaces, we bounced while I asked Clio if she thought our father ever really loved us, we bounced until Ma told us it was time to go home.

I let Clio ride shotgun. The stop sign that said *Get Fucked* was gone. A new one was already in place. I remember rolling the back seat window down and wondering if I was gonna forget someday, about him, lipstick, trampolines. I did. For a while. And then, it came back. Three days ago, on my fifteenth birthday, I kissed a boy, Cameron. When his tongue slipped past my lips, I found it there behind my teeth. I was surprised he didn't pull away, that he couldn't feel it.

Alice Hoffman
City Girl

New York City, 1987

My father told me never to cross Tenth Avenue, but I didn't listen to him. I loved and honored him, but he didn't know me the way he thought he did. I had studied ballet from the time I was ten, and we told my mother that was why we had to live in the city instead of moving to Connecticut or Long Island or New Jersey, but that wasn't the truth. That was a lie my father and I shared. We loved the city, even though it was dangerous. In the year I turned sixteen the population decreased by a million people and the homicide rate skyrocketed. No one with any sense walked in Central Park after dark. I snuck into the downtown clubs, Limelight and the Roxy, Tramps and Palladium. I was a dancer, so they let me in. I only felt alive when I was dancing, and so of course, my mother thought she should put an end to it. She said it was unhealthy for me, and that I had become too thin and too bruised, but my father always defended me.

My parents had two other children after their marriage, and I was not my father's blood relation, but I knew he loved me best, even though I would break his heart. I was that sort of girl, the kind who refused to listen to anyone. My father likely saw me out on the streets with my wild friends, not wearing coats in the winter, smoking cigarettes. I ditched the ballerinas and my private school classmates and hung out with kids in our neighborhood at the Hudson Guild. I liked to watch the boys play basketball. I wore mascara and eyeliner that made me look like a cat, and huge gold hoop earrings. In time my mother got her way. We moved to a house in Greenwich and my little brothers went to school there, but I commuted with my father into the city every day, for school and dance lessons. Sometimes I'd call his office and say I was staying over with my friend Daisy and wouldn't be driving back to Connecticut with him, but that wasn't the whole truth. I was on the street or at the clubs, and if I bothered to sleep, it was on friends' couches in their families' apartments in the projects down on Ninth Avenue. Mostly I stayed with my friend Daisy, who I knew from dance class. Then she told me she'd give anything to live in Connecticut and I stayed with her less often after that. I realized we didn't understand each other at all.

Across the street the Maritime Union building had been sold to Covenant House, and I watched the drug addicts milling around outside. I saw a young man with a shaved head depart from there one day when I was leaving Daisy's apartment to go uptown to school. I walked beside him, silent, until he realized I was there. He was about twenty and had blue eyes that were cold and flat and beautiful.

"Did they shave your head in there?" I asked.

"Go away," he said. He turned into a bodega and got in line for coffee. I did the same. My heart was pounding. I felt as if I had entered into a bubble. I ordered a sweet coffee with cream, but he got his black coffee and took off, so I did too, with the counterman yelling at me in Spanish when I slipped out without paying.

"You should go home," the young man said when I caught up to him. But of course, back then, I never did as I was told. It was freezing and he was wearing a T-shirt and jeans. I had an extra sweater in my backpack, which I took out and gave him. He looked at me, then accepted the sweater and pulled it on. I thought he was the most beautiful person I had ever seen. People often fell in love with me, men in the clubs, boys at school, but I ignored them all. I don't know what I was looking for, but I had suddenly found him there on Ninth Avenue. We went to a coffee shop and I bought us breakfast. He told me he was an actor, and his setback was temporary. He had nowhere to live, and before I could think straight I took him up to the penthouse where we used to live before my mother forced us to go to Connecticut. My father kept it for weekends and when he had to stay in the city, and it had a deserted feel.

"Wow," Cooper said. That was his name. Cooper Dunn. He'd changed it for professional purposes. We sat on the couch, close together. I knew I wasn't going to school. I was going to have sex with him, there in our living room, with all the lights turned off and rain hitting against the windows, while my father was working downstairs in the office. Cooper pulled off my clothes and fucked me; he did it as if he was drowning and it scared me and tied me to him and made me cry. It was my first time and there was blood on the couch, which I cleaned off as best I could while he took a shower. I turned the pillow over. I looked at myself in the mirror and saw a sixteen-year-old girl with long dark hair and all at once I knew I had done this because I could never be a dancer. I wasn't good enough, I was too awkward and too tall, nearly six feet. My stepfather came from a line of giant men, he was six seven, and even without any DNA in common I seemed to have inherited that trait.

I washed my face and braided my hair. I found Cooper in the kitchen, drinking scotch and eating a peanut butter sandwich. He left the bread out on the counter, so I wrapped it up and put it away. My father always kept food there for me in case I got hungry after school and wanted to stop in for a snack.

"They're going to kill me when I go back," Cooper said of the drug rehab house.

"No," I said.

"Oh, yeah. They'll tie me up and dunk me underwater until I can't breathe. Maybe they'll let me live. Maybe not. If I do I'll have to wear a sign around my neck. *Coward, thief, motherfucking liar.*"

He had a soft voice and his eyes pierced right through me. My natural father had been an actor in England who had brought us to California and dumped us there. Sometimes I saw him in a movie, and every time I did I thought he was too handsome to be real.

I stayed the night with Cooper in my parents' bed. I told my parents I had night classes and was staying with Daisy, and I guess they believed me. I knew how bad I was. In the middle of the night Cooper fucked me without asking, and he wasn't very nice about it, and afterward I went outside on the terrace where my father had said he'd often stood in the snow with his grandfather who had owned the building and passed it down to him. It was snowing that night. We had a tall fence made of barbed wire between our patio and the one on the penthouse next door so no one could get out or in. Two people had recently been murdered in the neighborhood, men who had brought people back with them from the clubs and been killed in their own beds. I took a shower and got dressed. Cooper was sitting in the living room waiting for me. He had taken some tinfoil and made a pipe and he was smoking something that smelled harsh and bitter.

"Get over here, girlfriend," he said. I did so because I wanted to, not because he told me to. That was so unusual for me. "You're going to love this," he said. "You're going to fall so hard and so fast you won't know what happened to you."

I saw the little white rocks and I knew it was crack. I'd seen it in the clubs.

"I've got to go to school," I said.

"Miss schoolgirl," he said. He pulled me toward him and had his hand in my pants before I could stop him.

"Really," I said.

"Really, truly," he said.

I did it when I knew I shouldn't. I did it knowing I had done a terrible thing. I leaned back into the couch and I could see birds outside and the Hudson River in the distance and I didn't care about them or anything else. We were there for four days, smoking, and when we had no more left, Cooper took a silver vase that had belonged to my father's grandfather and traded it for more so we could smoke again. The world was a snow globe; it was so far away I didn't care if I couldn't be a dancer. The telephone rang but I didn't answer. I fucked Cooper when he wanted it, but I couldn't even see his eyes anymore. He wasn't the handsomest man I had ever seen, I'd seen better, but who cared about such things anyway.

I forgot everything but the here-and-now, and then the door was thrown open and I knew who it was before I saw him. My father, the giant. Cooper looked up and panicked when he saw him. He ran out to the terrace as if he might jump, but my father caught him and hit him and threw him in the coat closet, which he tied closed with an electrical cord.

I was naked and cold. I grabbed a coat from the coatrack and banged on the elevator and got in just before my father could get to me. I was thinking that I would disappear onto Eleventh Avenue where the hookers stood waiting for someone to want them. How could I think I would be a dancer, that I was somebody special? My own real father hadn't wanted me; my mother loved her baby boys. I ran down the street barefoot. People shouted at me but I didn't care. There was neon everywhere, in every drop of snow. I ducked into the door to the building with the pool, running past the doorman. It was the best pool in New York City. It was steamy and hot in there and I could feel myself melting. I thought I saw a little girl who turned and stepped into the deep water. That was when I jumped in.

There were bubbles and then a whoosh. My father had leapt in, still wearing his coat and his shoes. He lifted me up and deposited me on the edge of the pool, where I lay on my back trying to get my breath. He got out and sat beside me, dripping water.

I wanted to tell him how sorry I was. How I'd ruined my life and I was only sixteen and I was most sorry that he wasn't my real father because he looked at me as if I were. The police took Cooper away. I was in the shower when it happened. Years later, my father told me he'd told the officers he'd found Coop robbing the apartment. He didn't mention me, and if the officers heard the shower running they didn't ask who else was there.

We drove to Connecticut through a snowstorm. My father had a Mercedes station wagon that could get through bad roads. It was dark and difficult to see. All of us kids called my father Gig, so I said, "Gig, where are we going?"

I thought he might be getting rid of me. I was craving what I had been smoking, and I was shivering and sweating and I felt like I could possibly hit him and steal the car and go find what I wanted. But we pulled into a long driveway. It was a hospital.

"Don't tell your mother," Gig said. "We'll say you went on a trip with the dance class. To California."

"All right," I said.

I had to stay there for two weeks. It was expensive, and I would have my own room and a therapist every day, and they would help me get over being sick.

"That guy was a bum," Gig said. "You know that, right?"

I shook my head. I didn't know what I knew.

"My grandfather told me the most important quality in the person you wind up with is a kind heart."

"You didn't listen. You married my mother." My mother wasn't very nice to him; even I could see that.

"Because she had a little girl with a kind heart."

I started crying. I tried to hide it by looking out the window at the hospital. I wished so much that Gig was really my father instead of that actor who'd never even called me on the phone.

I stayed at the hospital for two weeks, and when Gig picked me up spring was starting. There were some ferns growing in the hollows. I had decided that I liked Connecticut. I liked walking along the muddy paths. Some daffodils had already opened, and I thought about the little girl I had seen at the pool. My doctor said it was me, me before Gig, when my mother would leave me alone when she went to work and I sat in one place, terrified, until she came home. And then one day I walked out the door, tired of being terrified. I decided I wouldn't be a child anymore, I would do as I pleased. I would step out of the world and make my own way. I didn't have to ruin myself to do it, that's what my doctor had told me, and maybe someday I'd believe it.

I said goodbye to the staff and my doctor and met Gig in the hall.

"Ready?" he said.

He looked solemn. I felt that if I said the wrong thing I might just destroy him.

"I am," I told him. "I'm different," I said.

"Not too different, I hope." He smiled and we walked out to the car. I dodged puddles. I loved the way the air smelled and I thought maybe I could do it, be the girl I could have been if I hadn't been so terrified back then when it was just my mother and me. We got into the car and that's when I saw the crate in the back seat. Something was snuffling around. I climbed over into the back and saw a little white rabbit.

"What?" I laughed and took it out to hold. I could feel its heart beating in my hands.

My father had decided I would go to school in Connecticut. For now. I would have to give up New York. But he didn't want me to feel alone, so he had gotten the rabbit. I remember that when he had first met my mother he said he'd come out to California to find himself. My mother had fallen in love with him because he was tall and strong and willing to take care of her. But I loved him because he had an old rabbit he kept out in his yard, beneath a eucalyptus tree. He fed him water with an eyedropper as only the most kindhearted person would ever do. Because my rabbit was an orphan and I sat up nights feeding it, it followed me wherever I went, and even when we were outside in the woods of Connecticut it never ran away. Maybe I had told my father the truth. I suppose I had changed, because I never went too fast when I went into the woods with the rabbit, and I always looked behind me on the path, to make certain it hadn't strayed.

Jane Kalu

Sickled

THE FIRST TIME I ever saw an owl was in the backyard of our childhood home in Enugu. That afternoon, my sister, Ije, stood by the guava tree feeding corn seeds to the stray pigeons at her feet while I leaned on the back door so that I could watch our dinner cook and keep an eye on her. The theme music of *The New Masquerade* reached us from the living room, where my mother watched TV with nothing but a wrapper tied around her. Soon our father would come home and complain about her indecency while he sat at the dining table in his boxer shorts.

The heat and humidity were excessive that year. It rained weekly, yet nothing but hot air rose from the ground. Children littered our street, shirtless. Grandparents and babies were brought out to the porch for their naps. Even as I stood there, the late afternoon's gentle breeze sweeping over my face, I could feel sweat pooling under my arms. I knew it was useless, but I called to Ije, "Isn't it time to come in?"

She rolled her eyes and murmured, "Tufia. Ima enye nsogbu."

This was the way of our relationship. I fussed. She cussed. She was born with sickle cell disease, and, at sixteen, only a year older, I was used to caring for her. I came to know the disease better than she did. Better than our parents. And this is what I learned: Ije had crescent-shaped red blood cells. Without their roundness, the cells lose their wholesomeness and ability to maneuver, triggering pain as they travel through the veins. Sickled blood cells break down and die early, resulting in anemia and a weakened immune system. And when she got sick, Ije ran a fever, triggering the death of more blood cells. When she overexerted herself, it increased blood flow, risking a blockage called a crisis—which can be deadly.

Everything could lead to death, was how I came to think of it. And maybe it was this knowledge that placed the burden of her sickness on me. So that I was the one who listened when the doctor said, give her paracetamol when the fever starts, and put a cold cloth on her head, and if she's too hot, make her bathe, and mind you, she must drink lots of water, and if it persists for more than six hours, take her to the emergency room, okay? During those hospital visits, my father was often preoccupied with praying the crisis away, and my mother, well, she followed his lead.

Ije went on cooing at the pigeons.

"You're so stubborn," I mumbled.

"Did I beg you to follow me around like a fly?" She threw more seeds in the air.

A white bird with wings much bigger than the flycatchers that populated our guava tree swooped down, picked up a seed with its beak, and flew up to a tree branch. The sun shone orange behind it, and it looked like the apparition of an angel.

Ije whispered, "Do you see that, too?"

I nodded, though both our eyes were fixed on the bird. Ije stepped forward, her gaze never leaving it.

"It's an owl," she whispered, and waved at it. She touched the tree trunk gently, but the owl flapped its wings and flew into the pink sky. "How spectacular!" Ije sighed.

The bird really was beautiful. It flew with grace—its wide and arched wings not flapping, just soaring.

When it was finally out of sight I said, "You know that owls spell bad omen, abi?"

Ije ignored me. She continued to search the sky and scattered more seeds until her bowl was empty.

I went in to check on the yam boiling on the stove and turned off the flame. As the bubbles slowed, a sobbing sound echoed from somewhere in the house. I was certain it wasn't the TV, where Zebrudaya and Ovularia bickered as always. I tiptoed down the dim hallway and ducked my head into the dark living room. Against the light of the screen, I could make out my mother's silhouette shaking. I was taken aback. I had known she was sad, but there was something about her crying alone in the dark that caused my eyes to water.

She had lost her job at the electoral office six months earlier. It was right after General Abacha took over the presidency and scrubbed the country clean of all democratic commissions. She went from running out the door every morning in wonky-heeled shoes that koin-koined on the gravel in the yard to dragging her feet up and down our hallway with a pained face. Our father, instead of getting a job, took on more duties in church, insisting that we needed God's intervention. He remained adamantly unemployed, despite my mother's failed attempts at finding work, a failure fueled by her not having a college degree.

There was a sense that year that we were headed toward an event, the climax of something. But the dread I felt wasn't just about our dwindling finances. There was something else—a spirit that hovered over us. Sometimes I felt it in the hallway on my way to the bathroom at night. Sometimes, I imagined hands reaching out of the framed Bible quotes my father hung on our walls. It didn't help that my mother began to keep the curtains drawn. Migraines, she complained. Or the birds were too loud, she would say. She would have asked my father to cut down the guava tree out back had Ije not loved it so much. "Oh, leave her alone," she said once when I complained that Ije spent too much time out there in the sun.

I could see how our mother thought it was good for her. Ije had suddenly grown from a child who was constantly in pain to one who stared at the sky and admired its blueness. She pointed out wild mushrooms and beautiful moss I had never noticed in our backyard. She fed birds food we didn't have and talked to lizards as they scurried about. I wish I could have told my mother that it was a boy who made Ije happy, and not the tree she kept alive.

My mother's sobbing grew deeper, as if she were trying to reach the pain inside and get it out. I wanted to hold her hand and tell her not to cry, but she would have been embarrassed, annoyed even, if she'd known I had seen her. Not that she hadn't cried in front of us before, but it was often at Ije's bedside while Ije lay writhing in pain. Only Ije moved her. And I would not understand until much later that her sadness through those months was not about her losing her job at all. I stood there and waited until she finally stopped. Even though she had not known it, I felt I had shared the moment with her and consoled her by being in the room. I watched as she raised the edge of her wrapper to wipe her face. Then she flipped the channel to ETV, where General Abacha sat at the head of a table lined with other military men in uniforms. "Ekwensu," my mother hissed, and changed the channel back to NTA. Even she must have confused the weight of her hatred for Abacha with the weight of her guilt.

That night, as we lay in the darkness, Ije would not stop talking about the owl. I pushed her voice far away and instead recalled the image of my mother sobbing. My parents slept on the other side of the wall, but when I put my ear to it and listened, I did not hear my mother weeping quietly into her pillow as I imagined. I could make out only my father's soft snores.

"There is nothing else that looks like an owl, isn't that fascinating?" Ije said, refusing to accept my silence as a reluctance to participate in a conversation. "Absolutely nothing looks like an owl."

Her spring bed whined as she turned to face mine. "Do you think it was trying to tell us something?" she asked.

I raised my eyebrows at the excitement I heard in her voice. I believed that God spoke to us in different ways, but I knew deep down that he would not speak to us through a strange bird. Anything the owl had to say came from the devil. That I was sure of, which was why I didn't mention it to our parents.

The door opened. It was our mother. Though I did not turn toward her, her smell—sweat mixed with the Morning Glory talcum she poured all over her body to soak up the wetness—filled our room.

"Are you girls still talking? Go to sleep," she said in a low voice.

"Good night, Mommy," I said.

Ije remained silent, and our mother hesitated, then I thought I heard her inhale sharply before she gently shut the door.

My mother and Ije had had a quarrel a couple of months earlier—a quarrel that I didn't think at the time bore much weight with our mother. It happened just a month after our mother lost her job, toward the end of the school year. That day, Ije had stormed out of her biology class and came racing into my math class, crying. The teacher had excused me without hesitation. Everyone in our school knew about her illness, and whenever she as much as coughed, they'd say at me, "Is she having a crisis?"

And no, she was not having a crisis that day. At least not a medical one. She'd just learned that sickle cell disease was genetically transferred. Her eyes were red when she said to me, "Did you know it's Mommy and Daddy's fault I am this way?"

"What are you talking about?" I said, buying time to think of a response. She asked if I knew that the best way to avoid having a child with sickle cell disease was to select a spouse who, when their genotype crossed with yours, wouldn't produce a sick child.

"My teacher said that some churches even make you find out your genotype before they agree to wed you. Is that why Mommy and Daddy ran away?"

She studied my face. "They knew?" she snapped as if I were somehow implicated in our parents' decision.

I was surprised Ije hadn't pieced it together sooner. Our mother often told the story of how her parents cut her off. She and our father were supposed to be married in her parents' church, but the priest had decided, just weeks before the wedding, that he would no longer conduct the ceremony. So, instead of breaking up like her parents and the church urged, they eloped and got married in my father's church. My mother never told us why the leaders in her parents' church had changed their minds, implying it was because of my father's poor background. But I filled in the gaps in the story after I heard nurses whisper behind their clipboards about how irresponsible our parents were. It was through them that I learned some churches didn't like to be culpable.

After school, we came home to our mother in the living room watching *Willie Willie*. The TV framed the ghost in a white flowing gown and ridiculously large wig, and the piercing sound of piano keys, designed to instill dread, became an ironic backdrop to the horror that unfolded with Ije's accusations.

"How could you marry a man with an AS genotype when you knew you also had an AS genotype?" she asked.

My mother looked at me in surprise, but I shook my head, refusing any responsibility. Instead, I tried to take Ije's hand, but she stared at me with murderous eyes and jabbed a finger toward me. "If you dare touch me again!" she warned.

I backed away.

My mother took a deep breath. "Ijemma, don't let the devil use you."

"Don't let the devil use me?" Her eyes stayed half shut, the veins on her temples pulsing. "You mean the way he used you?"

My mother sighed. "There's a reason for everything."

"Don't start that nonsense Bible thing with me!" Ije yelled. "What you and your husband did was wicked. Wicked!" And then she marched out of the room.

"Bia . . . ," our mother called after her, her voice shaky.

"I hate you!" Ije screamed, and the slam of our bedroom door reverberated through the house.

My mother took a deep breath. "Make sure your father doesn't hear about this, okay?"

I nodded, as if my father and I had conversations in which I brought up how horrible he was for marrying my mother.

Ije did not speak of it again, but hatred grew inside her and festered into rebellion. I, on the other hand, did not disagree with our mother. I believed that there was a reason God allowed her illness. That Ije might have lost control had she not had the disease to hold her back. There was, already, all that frivolity in her eyes. What might it have grown into?

The owl didn't return despite Ije's scattering all the corn seeds she could find in the yard, and it was not until she gave up the idea of ever seeing it again that it came back with a screech.

My mother and I were in the kitchen the evening it showed up. She stood by the sink, lost, looking out at the weeds. There was a pot of jollof rice on the stove filled with whatnots we could find: half a small tin of tomato, a shriveled onion bulb, palm oil scraped from a discarded bottle, and a dash of crayfish. The smell of frying tomato filled the air as on the morning of a traditional wedding, only there was no party. We worked in silence as we often did until we heard the screeching and my mother awakened, her body moving faster than it had in months. She placed the bowl she held in the sink, rushed to the back door, and locked it.

With the light that came through the door gone, the room dimmed and the smell of soot from the kerosene stove intensified. I took my mother's place by the open window and found the eyes of the owl on the back fence where it perched. I could make out the pattern of its feathers more clearly than the day Ije and I first saw it. It was white mostly, but there were light brown specks here and there. Its face scared me, so I didn't dwell on it, but I had noticed its pointed beak before I averted my eyes to the clawed talons. My mother reached over my shoulder and closed the opaque louvers. Then she declared that we must all stay inside the house and wait for my father to come home.

She abandoned the simmering rice on the stove and went into her bedroom. I was surprised that she did not ask us to pray right away. But there were many firsts with her in those days. For instance, she stopped washing our father's laundry but asked me to do it with the wave of a hand. Showed no concern that I didn't weed the yard weekly. No longer took care to dress up when we went to church but kept her hair tied in a loose knot. No braids, no twists. These things I had considered inconsequential.

I looked for Ije to tell her that the bird was back and found her curled up in bed, running a fever and shivering. It felt pretty low, still, so I fed her paracetamol, then touched her arm gently and said, "Tell me right away if it starts to hurt," which was unnecessary because the aches could be so severe she'd roll on the floor and scream when they hit her. The screaming only stopped when the oxycodone, or, sometimes, morphine, kicked in, or in the worst cases, when she passed out from the pain.

"Leave me alone!" she mumbled, and shook my hand loose. "Don't you have anything else to do?"

Ije liked to accuse me of suffering from her sickness more than she did. And maybe she was right. Maybe I should have gone out to the street and said to the first person I saw, does that shape in the sky look like a man or a fish to you? Maybe I should have climbed trees when I was younger or kicked a spoiled orange with other children until my toes bled. Maybe I should have been born into a family who sat about doing nothing but laughing and holding hands. But it's not like anybody gave me a choice, did they? So I leaned forward and said, "I'll leave you alone when you learn to take care of yourself."

"So, this is my fault?" she said tearfully.

I wanted to tell her that it was. That if only she followed the rules, that could keep her from having a crisis. If only she did not push her thin, frail body beyond its limits. It made me so mad when she forgot to drink water or take her folic acid or nap in the afternoons. I wanted to grab her hand and yank until she got it. I wanted to say how stupid she was to believe that a successful life did not acknowledge pain. She was ready to die whenever, wherever, she claimed. I wished I could tell her to go ahead and die. It would make our lives better, wouldn't it? But I simply touched her warm forehead and said, "Of course not. I didn't mean it that way."

I didn't want Ije to die. I was just annoyed at her for thriving when I didn't. Couldn't. That year she turned fifteen, she morphed into a young woman in a way that I hadn't yet. Where I walked by simply throwing my legs carelessly out in front of me, Ije's gait emphasized how her waist moved and the bouncing of her small breasts. She began to tilt her head this way and that when she talked. When she listened, she hung her hand, limp and suspended in the air, a smile lingering at the corner of her lips in a way that suggested the possible release of something concealed.

It began with books, this metamorphosis. First, there were the romance novels with covers that displayed bare-chested men clutching blond or red-haired white women. Those novels drove down the neckline of Ije's blouses, and her skirts lost a few inches. She suddenly wanted pantyhose, holes in her earlobes, extensions in her hair, makeup, nail polish. She coveted hair straighteners and relaxers. She wanted to ride on the back of a motorcycle with wind blowing through her hair. All the things our parents said were worldly. She secretly altered her school uniforms, shortening the skirts and making the shirts tighter. I caught her many times staring at a boy, her eyes darkening, her nipples under the school shirt pointing forward, inviting his gaze. I watched, not sure when to tell her to stop being an akwuna. When she began to linger in the bathroom mirror, staring at her breasts? When she stuffed tissue in her bra? Moaned in her sleep?

"'Eat, drink, and be merry, for tomorrow we may die,'" she quoted to me one evening, a book on Epicurus lying on her chest. It was a few months before the owl. The year was still young. We had just declared our new year's resolutions. Hers was to do whatever she wanted, sickness or not; mine was to bring her closer to God. I believed in the undefeatable power of God. I believed in miracles. I believed that God could heal her if only she believed. I knew that if she were healed everything would be better for all of us.

"You should be reading the Bible," I said, exercising my resolution.

"Do you think God is deaf?" she asked.

"'Pray without ceasing,'" I said.

"'Rejoice always, pray without ceasing, give thanks in all circumstances; for this is the will of God in Christ Jesus for you.' Why do we ignore the other parts of that verse?"

Defeated, I snickered.

Ije was brilliant. She was going to study to be a doctor. But when I closed my eyes, I could never see her in a doctor's coat. I could never see her older than our present day at whatever age we were. Sometimes I wondered if she understood how close she came to dying during each crisis. If she knew there was a high chance she wouldn't live past her forties no matter how many gallons of water she drank a day or how conscientious she was with her folic acid. We argued about her coughs, her running a fever or waking up breathless, but we never talked about her emotions. Sometimes, I wanted to look into her eyes and ask how she really felt about being the one to get those genes. If she knew that I sometimes wished I'd gotten it and not her.

"We have to keep praying," I replied. "What else can we do?"

"I can kiss boys," she whispered, and laughed. "Like Bube."

I eyed her. Bube was the boy who often visited his grandmother next door. His parents lived in America, and he oscillated between his grandmother's home and his uncle's in Lagos. At first, we didn't really know him, just as we didn't know any of our neighbors. We knew who lived in which house, who moved out or moved in. But we didn't know them the way you would walk up to a neighbor's door and ask if they could spare you a cube of Maggi. When we drove past them, we didn't wave. We were the family on the street that wouldn't be unequally yoked with unbelievers. Our parents made sure we avoided sharing spaces with *sinners,* which was how they referred to anybody that wasn't a member of our church. You never caught us at neighborhood meetings or saw us lingering on the sidewalk talking to someone across the street.

But Bube I got to know, and I got to know him first, albeit from a distance. I knew he woke up around seven every morning. That his bedroom window faced our yard, and that once he was up in the morning, he would pull his curtains open, yawn, and stretch his shirtless body, pushing his chest forward. I knew he was tall and thin, and I imagined wrapping my arms around him and placing my face where his heart beat. I knew that he sometimes swept his grandmother's yard, and that if he caught me staring, he would smile and wave and I would stand there, mute. After he was gone, I'd swear that I would talk to him the next time, and then the next time and the next time, until one day, he was standing there smiling at Ije, and she was smiling back shyly.

He looked at Ije in a way that suggested he knew something she didn't. He told her that death was not the main event, living was. If you live your life constantly afraid of dying, you have allowed death to win twice, he told her. She fell in love. I imagined he didn't. That she was just a project.

"Now you're fantasizing about kissing Bube," I said to her that day in our bedroom, trying to keep a cool voice. "Do I need to tell you that Daddy will kill you?"

"Oh please, I already kissed him," she said.

"You what?" I clasped my hands to keep them from shaking.

She laughed even harder, amused by what she thought was my concern for her soul. She didn't worry about our parents' finding out because she knew I would never tell. That I would hold her secrets because if they came spilling out, I would be blamed. It had to be me. Our parents could never bring themselves to flog her with a cane or ask her to spend the week digging out the weeds around our compound in punishment.

When my father came home that evening, my mother told him about the owl, though the hooting had stopped. He marched straight to the back door, but his hand lingered on the handle and what might have been fear flashed across his face. He took a deep breath and composed himself, then went to the window and looked out. The crickets and frogs hidden in the onugbo shrubs serenaded him. My mother stood tentatively by the kitchen door, and I was behind her, watching him from under her arm.

My father, doubtful, turned around with a frown, but the owl screeched and he jumped, knocking down the plastic bowl my mother had forgotten by the sink.

"We need to go to prayers immediately," he said, and marched into the living room.

My mother and I followed.

"The devil wants to attack this family. He plans death for us!" He freed himself of his yellow-and-brown tie. "We all know what that evil bird represents."

"That's what I thought," my mother said.

"So why didn't you pray?" my father retorted.

This was my father's tactic. He liked to throw accusations our way, as if his closeness to God, as a pastor, gave him insight into how we spent our day without him. My mother lowered her eyes, and my father looked at me, standing there in the doorway.

"Ije is not feeling too well," I blurted out in a bid to shift the conversation.

"My God!" my father cried. "It's already happening."

"Why didn't you tell me?" my mother snapped, possibly to prove to my father that she would have prayed had she known all the facts. My father hurried to Ije, his bottle of anointed olive oil and large Bible tucked under his arm. Ije was asleep and stirred when my father waved the Bible over her.

"Out!" my father spat, speaking to the demon or spirit or curse.

Ije opened her eyes and glared at my father, then at my mother and me. She tried to move away from the Bible, but my father held it in place and poured the oil into her hair, drenching the pillowcase with it. I sat on the bed and took Ije's hand. She tried to pull her hand away, but I squeezed hard, and she winced.

My mother thought it was the beginning of vaso-occlusive pains and began to sob. "Stop it!" my father snapped at her. "You better not bring fear into this atmosphere for we do not operate in fear but faith."

My father prayed through the night. I woke up around 2 A.M. to check if Ije's chest was rising and falling, and he was still muttering in the living room. This was not unusual. Staying awake and praying was the mark of a true believer, he often said to us. My father was wrinkled and bony at forty-three. I know now his body must have been worn down by all that prancing and jiggling he did while praying, not to mention the constant fasting. I don't remember my father eating at all.

"It's so funny how he prays so hard for the impractical solution when he can just simply get a job himself," Ije said once.

Since my mother lost her job, our father prayed many hours at a time, not pausing even to eat. Over and over, he prayed for General Abacha to die. Die, die, die, he would cry until I became cursed with an earworm. I wondered how he could go on for so long without his tongue drying out. I agreed with Ije that he probably needed a job, but some things were not meant to be said out loud.

Ije muttered in her sleep now, and she kicked about restlessly. Though her body had cooled, I put a wet cloth on her head, in case the fever returned, and sat by her bed. I must have dozed off because when Bube called her name from outside our window, I jumped, startled. The night was calm. Even the frogs and crickets had gone to sleep.

"Ijemma," Bube said again, this time a little louder.

Angry, I threw open the French wooden windows.

"Are you mad?" I whispered. "What are you doing here?"

In the darkness, the fair skin of his bare chest glistened. He must have just showered. Who did he think he was, showing up at somebody's house shirtless?

"She didn't meet up with me yesterday evening and I've been so worried," he said. "She's having a crisis, isn't she?" He didn't wait for an answer but climbed through the window, forcing me to step back. His arm brushed against mine, and I placed my hands on the wall to hold steady.

"What are you doing?" I whispered, turning my head toward my father's voice.

"I'll be quick," he said, and then he looked me over. I tried to stick out my chest, braless under my nightgown, the way Ije often did it, but he went and knelt by her bedside. I wrapped my arms around myself, ashamed.

I watched Bube as his features contorted at the sight of Ije's swollen face and labored breathing. He brought her hand gently to his lips. He had never seen her having a crisis. For a second, I felt sorry for him. I knew how difficult it was to see Ije weak and defeated, completely devoid of her liveliness.

"Hey, beautiful," he whispered, and Ije batted her eyes open.

It wasn't until Bube came into our lives that I saw how beautiful Ije was. We were both dark like our mother and had her oval face and full lips and round, bright eyes. But even though I was the curvy one, and Ije had thin long legs and a slightly protruding belly, I was too shabby to be noticed. I was not yet aware of my body, at least not in the way Ije was of hers. I wore our mother's old clothes and kept my hair wrapped in a scarf most of the time. Ije, on the other hand, insisted on getting new clothes every Christmas. She was feisty and loud and funny. She wore hairstyles with colorful beads at the tips.

She was not surprised to see Bube. She sat up and touched his cheek. "You came," she said in a tired voice.

"Shush," he said gently. "Remember, it's all here." He tapped his head.

Bube's parents were philosophy scholars. They sent him long letters instilling in him their Epicurean beliefs. When he wrote back that he missed them, they taught him about finding pleasure in little things in order to live a life without bodily pain. Ije told me all this about him. He taught her the same things, and she believed them. Yet, I understand now that to Ije, it wasn't simply about overcoming the disease. She was also just a girl who had a boyfriend she hadn't thought she could ever have, and now she believed that anything was possible.

During that period, with my mother lying around half asleep and half awake, Ije went out whenever she wanted. I imagined Bube sneaking her past his grandma, dozing in the living room, and into his bedroom. I imagined Ije lying on his bed with sheets that reeked of him. Before she left, she'd probably walk around his bedroom, touching his things to establish a co-ownership. When she snuck back home, she sang about his love for her. She told me he would marry her and that they would have children running around their white-and-blue bungalow. I wondered how Ije managed to live outside of her illness completely. As I sat and listened, the only thing I could think about was her condition and how Bube would eventually recoil from its reality. One day he would see her lying in bed, her face ashen and twisted in agony, and the image would become forever embedded in his memories, remaining there no matter how much she smiled after the pain was gone.

"Think about the birds," he said to her now. "Go to a pleasurable place. I know of one you could think of."

"Oh, Bu," Ije said softly. Even in sickness, she flipped her braids to one side and narrowed her eyes. They shared a giggle. A secret I was not a part of.

"Time to go," I hissed, and as if on cue, our parents' bedroom door opened. My mother's feet shuffled down the hallway and into the bathroom. I tugged at Bube.

He leaned in and kissed Ije on the lips. I yanked at his arm. "Go! Now!" I whispered.

After he left, I quickly closed the window and checked the hallway to make sure neither of our parents lurked there.

"Relax, you look like you might have a convulsion," Ije said, amused.

"This thing with Bube ga alaputa gi," I snapped. "It's gone too far!"

"Maybe." There was a twinkle in her eyes, and before she said it, I knew. "We had sex," she said.

I collapsed on my bed, and she burst into giggles, pleased by my shock.

"Why do you refuse to be helped?" I asked, taken aback by my teary and weak voice.

"It's not a bad thing, Ada, haba." She shook her head at me. "Is pleasure not better than pain?"

The owl resumed its cries in the morning, and my father invited the church prayer group to our house. He asked my mother to set out refreshment: Fanta and cabin biscuits or bread. Maybe malt drinks, he said.

My mother eyed him. "Where will I get it?"

He shrugged and quickly hurried into the bathroom. We arranged the dining chairs in between the settees and carried out the small center table to make space for my father or whoever led the prayers to pace while they spoke. I could not imagine how hot it would become with twenty people fitted into that tiny living room. We left the two windows open, and with just my mother and me in the room, I could already feel the heat sticking to my back. "We have biscuits left from the last meeting, should I bring them out?" I asked my mother, fanning myself with my hand.

"Adamma," she replied. "Do we have any food for breakfast tomorrow?"

I shook my head no. "I'll save the biscuits then."

"Good. You're going to run your home one day. You have to learn now how to manage your kitchen."

"Yes, Mommy," I said.

She sighed. "Your father has to ask the church for support. I don't know what we will do next week."

I knew she wasn't expecting me to respond. She was only thinking aloud. Still, I nodded.

As soon as the prayer team arrived, one of them, a woman, declared my father had done the right thing. Not just because it made logical sense to bring in reinforcements, but she had had a dream. A revelation. Our house had been on fire and vultures, many vultures, hovered in the sky. Vultures were evil birds, a striking similarity to owls that we shouldn't ignore. In this dream, someone inside our house had set the fire, though she couldn't tell who it was.

My father tightened his bony, already sweaty face into a frown and glared at me. He asked what sin I had committed that let the devil in. Tongue-tied, I could only shake my head at him. He turned to my mother, and she raised her eyebrows in warning.

"Your prayer life has been waning, Gladys. You must have let the hedge down and now the enemy is here," my father spat. "Don't you understand that you have to be an example to our daughters?"

My mother's mouth dropped open slightly.

"Both of you better stay and pray with us." He clapped rapidly and began pacing, signaling the exercise was about to commence.

My mother snuck away and sat with Ije, who was asleep. After running a fever, Ije was often very tired and would sleep for days until her cells regenerated and she regained her strength. I stood by the door and watched my mother's small hands caress Ije's forehead. I wondered if she was ashamed or even annoyed at my father. How could she let him humiliate her? I don't know what I expected her to do. I had never seen her question him. It would have shocked me if she had confronted him, and yet I stood there hoping she would do something. Hoping she would be somebody else for once.

My mother took her hand from Ije's face and beckoned to me. I went to her, and she reached for me, but I stepped back in surprise. Only Ije she touched that way. I don't remember her hugging my father or ever holding his hand. I thought her to be a melancholic woman, but I see now how she came to be without happiness. How she became incapable of loving my father and me. There must have been space only for Ije.

"I know you're worried about your sister," she said in her calm voice. "Sit down. Stay here with us. You don't have to pray with them."

I nodded and sat on my bed.

This was her way of rebelling against my father. It made sense that her revolt would not be frantic. She was a quiet and slow woman. I had never seen her hurry even when we were running late to church. It was as though she lacked the ability to do anything at a quick pace. She was not a big woman, so it was not her physical features that held her back. She was petite with short thin legs that one would at first expect to move swiftly. I admire that slowness now. How she remained unfazed by my father's complaints of her sluggishness. She would ignore his bickering and carry on with whatever she was doing until she was ready. It was the only confrontation she had in her.

Ije opened her eyes, and when she saw my mother holding her arm, she shrugged her off. My mother reached for her again.

"Leave me alone!" Ije snapped.

My mother's lips quivered, and she stood. "Sit with her," she said, and hurried out.

I waited until my mother slammed the bedroom door shut and I said to Ije, "Why are you mean to her, Ijemma? It's not fair."

"Well, they were mean to me first," she said in a dry croaky voice.

I gave her some water to sip.

The prayer went on all afternoon and with it the crying of the owl. Ije was sleeping again. She thrashed her legs and punched the air.

"Ije," I called. "How are you feeling?"

She stretched out her hand to me with her eyes half open. I put my face inches from hers, and her breath was warm against it. She tried again to open her eyes, but her stare was unfocused. She grabbed my hand and squeezed. My heart plunged into my belly.

"Ije!" I shook her. "Ije!" I didn't understand my own panic. She was moving. Was not screaming in pain. Was not having a fever. And yet, "Ijemma," I called again.

Finally, she looked at me, but without the amusement with which she usually observed everything. This was not the worst of her crises. I had seen her on the floor and screaming from pain. I had seen her eyes red, swollen shut. I had seen her face nearly drained of life. But when she looked at me this time, something in her expression, something from the inside, maybe the bond we inherently shared as sisters, called to me for help.

I ran into the living room and told my father we had to take Ije to the hospital immediately. Somebody in the prayer team waved me off and said we needed prayers, not a doctor.

"She told me herself that we have to go to the hospital," I lied. "I think it's serious."

"Don't bring your lack of faith in here," my father bit at me.

My mother ran out of the bedroom in a wrapper that hung

loosely above her breasts. Some members of the prayer team averted their eyes.

"If Ije wants to go to the hospital, then we are going," she said.

At the hospital, as we helped Ije out of the car, my father's hands trembled from what I thought to be anger, but it must have been from fear. It must have all been from fear. The desperate need to exert his power over the disease, his insistence on keeping himself detached from our world in order to remain resident in one that relieved him of the consequences of his actions. It was all fear. All of it.

As we wobbled into the building with Ije leaning on us, it occurred to me that these few minutes when we carried her into the hospital together were often the most affectionate I ever spent with my father.

"No, go this way."

"Be careful, Adamma."

"Ije ya? Good."

All mere instructions he gave me as we walked, but ones I cherished. In the hospital room, he stood in the corner clutching his Bible in one hand and the anointed olive oil bottle in the other, his lips moving silently. He must have loved Ije as much as my mother did.

Ije lay on the table while the doctor examined her. The portrait of Abacha in his military uniform adorned with stars hung above Ije's bed, his lost, watery eyes staring down at us. I caught my mother looking at him a few times before quickly averting her gaze. If we stayed longer than one night, as we often did, she would take down the portrait and stick it in a drawer.

"How much will all this cost?" my mother asked the doctor a few more times than she probably realized.

The doctor ignored her as she listened to Ije's chest and belly. An ultrasound machine came barging into the room and along with it a nurse in a white dress, a small white cap perched atop her head and kept in place with a cluster of hairpins.

"It appears there's a heartbeat in your daughter's uterus," the doctor announced after rolling the probe around Ije's belly.

Everyone looked from the doctor to Ije and back.

"She's pregnant," the doctor finally elaborated. "About eight weeks."

My parents' eyes immediately flew to Ije's belly, which always protruded anyway because of her enlarged spleen, one of the symptoms of her disease. I reached for the door frame to hold steady. My mother left Ije's side and sobbed into a wall. Ije's eyes met mine and for the first time there was fear in them.

"Who did this to you?" my father asked.

Ije did not break eye contact with me as she replied, "Please. Stop."

Our mother turned to me. "Do you know this person?"

Ije shook her head at me.

"No," I replied, and looked down at my shaking hands, ashamed that my lie was to protect not Ije but Bube.

The doctor sighed again. "We would have to take out the baby. At her age, with SCD, it could kill her."

"I'm not going to approve murder," my father said, shaking his head. "God will take care of this."

"But I don't believe in your God," Ije blurted out, and even the air in the room froze.

I clenched my fists and felt my heart thumping in my chest. I waited for my parents to turn to me, to ask me what I had done to my sister, but my father stormed out of the room and my mother followed.

I may have seemed like the sane one, because the doctor came closer and spoke in a low tone. "We really need to move fast. She's already severely anemic. You see how yellow her eyes are."

I ignored her, too angry to speak, and she left.

"Well, they took that well," Ije said.

"Did you really have to say that?"

"Why do you always side with them?" she asked.

"Why do you like to hurt them? You think you're smart because you read a few books. You're just an idiot."

She snickered. "You just think they'll like you if you do everything they say."

"That's a lie," I whispered. I felt tears roll down my cheeks.

"Whatever." She shrugged nonchalantly, but there were tears in her eyes too.

"You're so ungrateful. They give you everything." I was angry now. "They love you—"

"And yet they're willing to let me die." Her voice broke. "You heard your father."

"You should have thought of that before you opened your legs to the first boy that talked to you."

"So you want me to die too?" Ije snapped.

I ran out of the hospital room and went to the bathroom down the hall, where I heaved but nothing came out. In the whole frenzy of the day, I had not eaten, and my tummy growled. My father would be pleased I had fasted with him. The Lord will heal her through our starvation and suffering, he would say. I splashed water on my face and took a deep breath, avoiding my eyes in the mirror. When I pushed the door open, I came face-to-face with Bube and jumped.

"Jesus Christ!" I cried.

"Sorry, I saw you run in and—"

"Why won't you leave her alone?" I said, and started to walk away, but he took my hand and stopped me.

"How is she?" he asked. "Do you think I could see her?"

His hands felt warm in mine, and I began to sob again. I grabbed him and hugged him and put my face in his sweaty neck.

"What is it? Is she okay?" he asked.

I shoved him away.

He raised his eyebrows, and I took his hand again, craving his soft skin against mine.

"Ada, what's going on?"

"She's pregnant with your baby, and she needs surgery to take it out."

He let go of my hand and it dropped to my side with a weight that surprised me. I stretched it toward him and hoped he would take it one more time, but he wasn't looking at me. He stared down the hallway and then toward the door, frantic.

"She's pregnant?" he said.

I sighed and let my hand return to my side. "Yes."

He grabbed his head, and I thought he might cry.

I looked away, embarrassed. When I turned back around, he was hurrying down the hallway toward the exit. It was the last time I would ever see him. Later, when I told Ije that he came to the hospital but ran off when he learned she was pregnant, it was with relish. Of course, she would not believe it.

Back in Ije's room, everyone had reconvened. My father kept his head bowed. My mother was crying. The doctor kept her eyes on the clipboard.

"What is it?" I asked.

"The placenta has ruptured. I may die whatever they do." Even weak and breathless, Ije's voice held a hint of sarcasm.

"Is it true?" I asked the doctor.

"Please just let them do the surgery," my mother begged my father.

"It really doesn't matter," Ije said. "Death is better than this anyway."

"What has come over you? Don't say that!" my mother cried, and reached out to touch Ije, but she slapped her hand away.

"What's going on? Somebody talk to me!" I barked.

"Your sister is bleeding, and we—"

As she spoke, Ije's eyes rolled to the back, and she lost consciousness.

My mother screamed and told the doctor to do everything to help her, but my father stood between the doctor and the bed.

"Daddy?" I yelled, and pushed at his arm. "You can't do that. She's going to die."

He began to speak in tongues and my mother grabbed his shirt. "Shut up! Just shut up! No more prayers!"

My father stepped away from the bed, shocked.

"I'll sign the paperwork. I'm her mother," my mother said to the doctor, giving my father one last glare. "Please help her," she said to the doctor again.

This was not the year that Ije died. She only lost the baby. For the three weeks that she stayed in the hospital after the surgery, everything returned to normal at home. Normal being that the hospital incident never happened, and Ije was never pregnant. Crisis, we told everyone. We couldn't even look in each other's eyes as we passed in the hallway, let alone talk about the truth.

But Ije's pregnancy is not the main reason I tell this story. Something more important happened the morning she returned. Our father was in church for a prayer meeting, and our mother decided to stay home and cook something hot for Ije. It was left to me to get her from the hospital.

When we got out of the taxi, Ije had insisted I first take her to Bube's house, where his grandmother told us through her parted orange drapes that Bube had left. Her grandson was visiting his uncle, she said, and would be leaving for America from there. She hissed the words out, her eyes moving from Ije to me, perhaps trying to work out who the wayward one was. She peered at us as we walked toward home, and not once did she call us back to ask why we both had tears in our eyes.

Ije asked that I take her to our backyard, where she sat and sobbed into her palms, her body shaking so much I wondered if the stitch in her belly would tear. But I felt sorrier for myself than I did for her. I'd had no hopes that, after Ije, Bube and I would be together, but I'd taken consolation in the glimpses of him I caught from across the fence and was mourning my own loss.

When we finally went into our house, we met a quiet kitchen. There was no yam pepper soup sizzling on the stove. There was no water boiling in the kettle for Ije's bath. Ije looked at me, but I turned away, allowing my eyes to travel down the hallway toward our parents' bedroom door. We could have touched the fear we shared if we'd stretched out our hands in front of us. We walked down the hallway, me first, and Ije behind. I knocked, and when nobody answered I pushed the door open. Our mother was lying in bed peacefully, Ije's oxycodone pill bag empty on her chest.

I don't remember what happened after we found her. I don't remember what was true and what I fabricated. Whether it was me or Ije who grabbed the pill bag before we called on the neighbors. Whether it was me or Ije who found the note scribbled on the torn page of her Bible. Whether I ran all the way to the church on bare feet to get my father or if a neighbor took a car to ferry him home to his dead wife. Whether it was my father who declared that Abacha had killed her or a member of the prayer team. I don't remember what we ate. If we ate. How we slept. If we slept. I don't remember who cared for Ije in the days that followed. I don't remember who stayed with us, if we were left alone with our father. I don't remember her body being moved. How many people it took. If they stuck her in the back of a neighbor's car or if an ambulance came.

But I remember standing over her body and wondering when she had done it. Her hand in mine was still warm. Perhaps she was still breathing when we got out of the taxi. Perhaps she only died a few seconds after we walked into the house. I would spend every day wondering what might have happened if she had lingered. Waited for us to find a pulse.

But these are things I try not to think about so that I can make space for the one image that kept me from wrapping my hands around Ije's thin body and squeezing until there was no breath left in her. A memory from before we entered the house. Before we discovered our mother's lifeless body. Before we found the note in our mother's handwriting that said, *I am very sorry, Ijemma.*

I was about to push the back door open when Ije asked me to wait. She quickly wiped her tears with the edge of her T-shirt and smiled a smile that didn't reach her eyes, practice for when she greeted our mother. She took a deep breath and had just reached for the door handle when the owl cried behind us.

Ije spun around. "It's still here? After three weeks?"

I nodded.

"I want to see it," she said.

We approached the guava tree where the owl sat in a nest on a low branch. It stopped crying and watched us cautiously, its eyes shining from within the leaves. We crept closer and closer until we could see that there were two eggs peeking out from beneath it.

My hands flew to my mouth, and I said, "Poor Daddy!" and Ije burst into hysterical laughter. This is the memory I play and replay: Ije laughing and laughing. Her thin, frail body bent forward and jerking uncontrollably. Her hollow eyes filled with happy tears, and her arm stretched out, reaching for me. I had taken her hand and laced my fingers between hers and for a fleeting moment—one that I would try to replicate many times for the remaining years that Ije lived—I loved her and could have forgiven her anything.

Thomas Korsgaard
Translated from the Danish by Martin Aitken

The Spit of Him

KEVIN DIDN'T HAVE a rain jacket and for that reason he wasn't wearing one. A pair of *Bananas in Pyjamas* pajama bottoms bunched over the shafts of his rain boots. From his left shoulder, a flat laptop bag dangled. It had been consigned to his school's lost-property box and had remained there more than four months before he'd claimed it for himself. Now it flapped rhythmically against his hip. It contained next to nothing, but he felt that it lent him a professional air.

It was a Tuesday, early evening, and Kevin was the only person out. Darkness had descended upon him since he'd left home. Drizzle beaded his face.

He'd told his father that he was going out to get some fresh air. He wasn't actually sure that his father had even heard him. His father never heard anything when he was gathering his deposit bottles.

Anyway, there Kevin was, walking along the side of the road. Occasionally, he looked up to see if there were any cars coming. Only a single truck had gone past in the half hour that he'd been walking.

He was approaching the neighboring village. He'd never been

this far. It was actually quite near his own village, but his father never took him there.

"What would we want to go there for?" his father had said when Kevin pointed at a signpost over by the church one day and asked if they could drive in that direction for a change. "It's a piddling little place with bugger all to see. All it's good for is driving through."

It couldn't be that little, Kevin thought now, as he passed a sign with the village's name. There were lampposts, too, with soft pools of light. White lines ran down the middle of the road. And soon there were houses, set rather far apart at first, then closer together.

Lettering was peeling off from the front of one. COFFEE. TOBACCO. BETTING. There were some lights on inside. He went up to a window where a small sheet of paper with some handwriting on it had been affixed. The letters got smaller and smaller as they neared the edge of the paper.

Open by appointment.

But there was no telephone number to ring. Kevin stood on his tiptoes and leaned forward. There was a slight bump as his forehead touched the pane. The shop window was crammed with china dolls wearing crocheted bonnets. Shoulder to shoulder they sat, staring out empty-eyed at the road. Two Madam Blå colanders, also, and a pair of hospital crutches. Farther inside, an old-fashioned spinning wheel and a desktop computer with its keyboard. There were price stickers on everything.

Someone sneezed. Then sneezed again. It sounded like a *no*. Kevin dropped onto his heels and went round the side of the house. Some tall steps led to a door. He went up them and considered for a moment a teddy bear crafted from moss that sat at the top. He raised his hand and gripped the knocker. It was made of brass and looked like a boot. But before he could bang it against the door the lights went out inside, one after another.

There were so many people you would never meet. Most, in fact. He returned the brass boot to its resting position and went back to the road.

In front of the next house stood a figure of a stork, with a pink ribbon around its neck. There were no lights on. Nonetheless, he went up to the door and knocked a couple of times. He stepped back and was trying to remember what he'd decided to say when a voice behind him said, "What can I help you with?"

Kevin spun around to see a square-shouldered man with a crew cut standing before him.

"It's because I'm out selling stickers . . ."

The man bent forward, his eyes seeming to fix on Kevin's wet hair. He looked Kevin up and down, then zipped his coat. It was the local sports club's coat. Various sponsor logos were emblazoned on the front. Kevin recognized some of them.

"And what would your name be?" the man asked.

"Kevin."

"Kevin what?"

"Jørgensen."

"You've got some guts," the man said, and folded his arms.

Kevin looked him in the eye. He'd heard that eye contact was important, but then the man's eyes moved.

"You can wipe that grin off your face, too, if you know what's good for you."

A baby started crying inside, and a woman's voice called out. The man went in and quietly shut the door behind him. A little click of the lock, and then the light came on in the hall. Kevin went down the drive until he reached the road again. The rain was heavier now. His boots chafed at his ankles. He paused to empty out some grit.

· · ·

Kevin walked on through the village and, after a while, came to some houses that were being built. Cable drums occupied the pavement, which appeared to be new. Some of the paving stones wobbled under his feet. One house looked to be finished. It had big picture windows. There were stickers on several panes, featuring the name of a security firm and warnings about CCTV and Neighborhood Watch. The hedge had only just been planted. In the garden, perennials poked out of various sacks, waiting to be planted. Flagstones on a pallet, and a soil compactor. It was a two-story house. A few lights were on, and a flame flickered in a pumpkin lantern on the doorstep. Its lid was rotten and sinking. Three printed lines on the letter box:

Candle Showroom
&
The Rønbjerg Madsen Family

Kevin knew that their first names were Birgitte and Henrik. Every year, they donated some boxes of Advent-calendar candles to his school, Christmas gifts from their factory.

He stepped up to the door and wiped the rain from his face. Readied his teeth and pressed the bell. An intricate melody played, but no one answered.

He pressed again, leaving his finger on the bell this time. The music started from the beginning, but there was still no answer.

After a while, he stepped back, and he was about to walk away when a light came on behind the frosted glass.

A tingling sensation spread across Kevin's cheeks as a shadow loomed. And then a woman wearing an apron was standing in front of him.

"Yes?" she said.

"Yes" was all Kevin could say.

"Adverts, is it?"

"Adverts?" he said.

"Just drop them in the letter box over there," she said. "We haven't got a slot."

She gestured to show him where and turned to go back in.

"Actually, it's not adverts."

A pleasant smell came from inside. He tried to sniff it in without making a sound. Cinnamon and something else. He could see behind her and into a mudroom with shiny tiles, and a long staircase going up.

"What do you want, then?"

Birgitte pushed a strand of hair behind her ear.

"Well, you see, it's . . . just a second," Kevin said. His hand found his laptop bag. The Velcro from the flap made a rasping sound as he reached inside to produce a smooth plastic sleeve.

"There," he said. "They're a bit hard to separate in this cold weather."

"You should be wearing something warmer."

"No, I'm fine," Kevin said, in an older-sounding voice. "But I'm out selling something, you see."

"And what might that be?"

"These stickers here."

"Stickers?"

"Yes."

"What for?"

For every sheet you sold, you could keep five kroner. The rest went to a good cause. He'd been given two thick folders full, but not that many people lived around here.

"You can put them on your Christmas cards," he said.

"Christmas cards?"

"For example, yes."

He handed her a sheet. She looked at it, then handed it back.

"Christmas is a long way off," she said.

"Forty-eight days."

"As many as that."

"You can put them on ordinary letters, too."

"Oh, yes?"

"Oh, yes," Kevin said. "It's completely up to you."

And, because he stayed put, she eventually turned her head and shouted into the house.

"Henrik," she shouted.

For a second, neither of them spoke. Music was coming from upstairs. A man's voice was singing along.

"Henrik," she shouted again. "Henrik, turn that down. Have we got any change for some stamps or something for our Christmas cards? Turn it down so you can hear me, or else come downstairs. I'm asking if we've got any money for a sheet of stamps. There's a boy here."

"It's only twenty kroner a sheet," Kevin said. "And it's for a good cause."

"It's twenty kroner a sheet, Henrik."

"Yes, all right," a voice shouted back, and the music stopped. There was a thudding of feet on the stairs and a long sigh as someone came down. A man in a checked shirt appeared in the hall. He looked inquiringly at Kevin and then at his wife.

"Have we got twenty kroner?" she asked.

"What for?"

"The boy's making an effort to earn some pocket money."

Henrik extended a hand into the rain.

"What terrible weather," the man said. "A good thing we took the washing in."

"We?" Birgitte said.

"Summer's long gone," Kevin said. He felt a drip run down his neck.

"Birgitte," Henrik said. "Why don't you fetch those cookies?"

"They're supposed to be for later."

"Fetch them, go on."

She stepped past him and disappeared from view.

"The proceeds go to—" Kevin began, only to be cut off. It was Birgitte, back already. Her hands held out a baking tray. She gave it a little shake and the cookies loosened from the greaseproof paper.

"Take one," she said, looking at Kevin and then at her husband.

"Just the one, mind," Henrik said.

Kevin's fingers hovered over the cookies before selecting a medium-sized one.

"Thank you," he said, and popped it into his mouth.

He shuffled forward, slightly out of the rain. Under-floor heating streamed from the house and warmed his face.

"I know who you are," Henrik said.

Birgitte looked at her husband in surprise.

Kevin was going to say he knew who they were, too, only his cookie was in the way.

"There's no mistaking it," Henrik said, his eyes finding Birgitte as if he wanted her to say something, too. "Can't you see?"

She scrutinized Kevin.

"It's Åge Jørgensen's lad," he said.

A little gasp escaped her. A snap of breath.

"It is, isn't it?" Henrik said, and then seemed to examine Kevin's clothing. A moment passed in which Kevin munched and pointed at his mouth, munched and pointed.

Kevin swallowed at last and smiled with pride.

"Yes," he said. "I am."

"I hadn't realized," Birgitte said. She kept looking first at Kevin, then at her husband.

"Do you know my dad?" Kevin said.

"Oh, we don't *know* him," Henrik said, his expression changing. "But we know who he is."

Kevin gave a puzzled look.

"From when he used to live here," Henrik explained.

"Here?" Kevin said.

"That's right," Henrik said.

"But he's never lived here."

They all went quiet.

"You'll be Jan," Henrik said after a second.

"Not Jan, Jon," Kevin said.

"Jon," Henrik said.

"Jon, yes," Kevin said. "He's my younger brother."

"Yes, you would have a younger brother," Henrik said, glancing again at Birgitte.

"Two, in a way, if my dad's new girlfriend's boy counts. But they live in Pattaya," Kevin said. "It's in Thailand."

"You don't say," Henrik said, and laughed as if what Kevin had said was funny.

"Have you been there?" Kevin asked. He smoothed the front of his top.

"No," Henrik said, rather quickly. "We certainly have not."

"Me neither," Kevin said. He could hear his father's voice in his head: Someday we'll go there together. Only it's a bit expensive if we're all going to go.

One of the candles on the chest of drawers in the hall went out. Birgitte opened a drawer, took out a long-necked lighter, and lit the candle again.

"They're very nice candles," Kevin said.

"We produce them ourselves," Henrik said.

"I know."

"It keeps half the village in work," Henrik said. "But what's your name, if it isn't Jon?"

"Kevin Jørgensen."

"Kevin," Henrik said.

"Yes."

"Birgitte," Henrik said, placing a hand on her shoulder. "Offer Kevin another cookie, would you?"

Birgitte held out the baking tray. He chose another one and put it in his pocket.

"Thank you very much," he said.

"Take a couple."

Kevin studied the cookies again.

"In fact, you can take as many as you like," Henrik said, and so Kevin took one, two, three more cookies and put them in his pocket.

"Are you sure that's all? Go on, have some more," Henrik said.

"I don't mind if I do," Kevin said.

"I thought so," Henrik said.

Kevin didn't know what else to say. Fortunately, Henrik did.

"You're the absolute spit of him," he said.

"The spit?"

"That's right. You look just like him. Your dad, that is," Henrik said. "It's amazing, when you think about it, that a person can look so much like somebody else."

Kevin's father was tall and hairy. His forehead was creased, and the creases never went away, not even when he relaxed. His father had five DVDs of porn hidden under the mattress and a bat next to his bed. His father walked with a slight limp and coughed up mucus into the bathroom sink every night without washing it away. His father hated the government, which made people work for their disability benefits. His father was a Libra. His father had green eyes.

"I've got my mum's eyes," Kevin said, widening them so that both Henrik and Birgitte could see.

"It's your honker that gives you away," Henrik said, tapping the side of his own nose with a forefinger. "What's he doing with himself, anyway?"

"Now, you mean?"

"Yes, now."

"I can phone him, if you like. But I don't think he'd answer."

"I'm sure," Henrik said.

"It's because we've only got one charger at the moment."

"Ah."

"Our dog keeps chewing them up."

"I see. That's not very good."

"No, he chews everything up."

"Dogs need to be trained, or else—"

"Or else what?" Birgitte said.

"Well, or else you shouldn't have one."

"He just needs to learn, that's all," Kevin said. "He's only a puppy."

Birgitte was about to say something, but then her husband did.

"I saw that advert your dad put in the local paper. What was the slogan, now? It's slipped my mind."

"'Cow-hoof trimmer? Åge's no beginner!'" Kevin said.

"That was it," Henrik replied with a smile. "Priceless."

Kevin smiled back.

"It's just something he does on the side," he explained. "To earn a bit of extra money. He's been looking for something more permanent, only jobs are hard to come by if you can't work full time."

"Are they really?"

"Yes, and employers can't even be bothered to take five minutes to reply to an application."

"Can't they?"

"No, they're too stuck-up."

"Plenty of work to be had for those who want it," Henrik said.

Kevin pictured his father making candles for Henrik and Birgitte, twenty hours a week in a factory hall with tall chimneys. He imagined him having his lunch in a cafeteria and then coming home and talking about how his day had gone. Getting paid once a month and taking Kevin to the cinema.

"That'll be why he's driving again, I suppose," Henrik said. "I hear he drives a brown Lada now, with commercial plates. With loud music coming out of it. Is that right?"

"Yes, it's got a really good stereo," Kevin said.

"There you are, then," Henrik said. "Spotted on the main road a couple of weeks back."

"Says who?" Birgitte said.

"Says Svenne, the carpenter."

"Well, do you know what I think?" she said, folding her arms across her chest. "I think Svenne should get a life. And I think you should lay off the lad. It's hardly his fault."

Henrik scrutinized her for a moment.

"He's not responsible for his dad," she said.

"I could come back another time, if you like," Kevin said. "Nothing we can do today that can't be put off until tomorrow."

"How old are you, anyway?" Henrik said.

"Ten," Kevin said.

"Ten," Henrik said, in a strange voice, as if he could tell by looking at Kevin that this wasn't entirely true.

"Or nearly ten," Kevin said. "Nine and three-quarters, actually. But I'll be ten next year. The eighth of February."

"You'll be having a party, then?"

"Yes," Kevin said. He could feel his cheeks growing warm. Under his bed, he kept a birthday box. In it were some drinking straws with little umbrellas attached, leftovers from last New Year's Eve. There were fifteen in all. He dealt them out in his head. Dad and Jon and himself. Granddad in Thisted, if he could get someone to drive him. Mum, if she and Dad were getting along. Henrik and Birgitte. Kevin smiled at them, and Birgitte smiled back.

"It won't be a big party," he said.

"Won't it?" Henrik said.

"Not this time. It's the half-term holiday, you see. People will be away. Besides, it's too much fuss for my dad. I'm sure it'll be a nice day, though."

"Too much fuss? His son's birthday?"

"It's not because he doesn't want to," Kevin said, shaking his foot inside his rain boot. It had gone to sleep from standing still so long.

"Have you ever heard the like?" Henrik said, looking now at Birgitte. "His own lad's birthday."

"He's got an old concussion," Kevin said.

"I'll bet."

"That'll do," Birgitte said.

"And dodgy knees," Kevin said. "It's not easy for him."

The wind gusted in the dark. Farther away, something made a commotion. It was the sound of an object dislodging, a roofing tile or a satellite dish, perhaps, falling to the concrete and breaking into bits. The lawn was saturated. There were big muddy pools in the grass. The rain sheeted down.

"Come out of that weather," Birgitte said. "You'll be drenched." She took Kevin's arm and drew him a step closer. "Now, about those stamps you were selling."

"They're not stamps exactly. They're—"

"To think," Henrik said, as if to himself. "More than ten years ago now."

"Henrik," Birgitte said. "I think you should go inside." She made as if to bundle him away from the door, but Henrik stayed put.

"Philip," he said calmly, pensively, and shook his head.

"Henrik," Birgitte said. "Inside."

"Philip?" Kevin said.

"Yes, Philip," Henrik snapped back, like the name belonged only to him.

"It's a nice name," Kevin said, sensing that he ought to say something but unsure what it should be.

"He was only on his way home from handball practice," Henrik said. "It wouldn't have taken five minutes on an ordinary night like this, especially when the weather wasn't as bad."

Kevin could hear himself breathe.

"It was an accident," Birgitte said.

Kevin dipped a hand into his pocket and was about to produce a cookie but thought better of it.

"An accident?" Henrik said. "Is that what you call it?"

"Yes," she said. It sounded almost as if she were crying. "A terrible accident that we needn't talk about now, Henrik."

"Getting behind the wheel of a car when you're pissed out of your mind?"

"Henrik," Birgitte said again. She took his hand and gave it a squeeze. "The boy obviously knows nothing about it."

"About what?" Kevin said.

"Let me see those stickers you've got," Birgitte said, smiling at him now. He'd nearly forgotten about them.

"It wasn't what *I* would call an accident," Henrik said.

Then Kevin said what his father usually said whenever there was a program about such things on the television: "How terrible."

"You think so, do you?" Henrik said. Birgitte put the flat of her hand against his chest to shove him inside.

"I'm talking to the boy. I'm allowed to, you know," Henrik said.

"Not about this, you're not."

"Like I said," Kevin said, and gave his laptop bag a pat. "I'm out for a good cause."

Henrik was breathing heavily.

Then gradually everything went quiet.

"All right," Henrik said at last. "What sort of good cause?"

"I can't quite remember," Kevin said.

"You can't remember?"

"It was something to do with children . . ."

"Save the Children?" Birgitte said.

"That's it," Kevin said.

He wasn't sure what more to say. Henrik looked out at the garden.

"These are the stickers, if you'd like to see them first," Kevin said, and handed Henrik a plastic sleeve.

Henrik looked through them.

"Actually," he said, "I'm not sure we're interested."

He handed them back to Kevin, though without returning the sheets to their sleeve. Rain washed over them. Colors started to run. Angels dissolved into clouds, chimney sweeps became black blotches that seeped into toothy mice, then trailed over stars and Christmas hearts and trees.

Henrik went inside for a moment and then came back.

"You're in luck," he said. In his hand was a small cylinder wrapped in brown paper.

He squeezed the cylinder between his fingers and out popped first one, then two, three, sixteen coins in all into Kevin's outstretched hand.

"We'll take the lot," he said.

Shiny and new, the coins lay in Kevin's palm, the queen's head on top.

"All of them?" Kevin said.

"That's right," Henrik said. "All of them."

Kevin handed him the soggy sheets of paper.

"Thank you very much," he said, and dropped the coins into a pocket in his bag.

"On one condition," Henrik said. "You do me a little favor in return."

"Of course," Kevin said.

"Say hello to your dad from Henrik Rønbjerg Madsen."

"There's no need for that," Birgitte said.

"You stay out of it," her husband replied.

Birgitte huffed and went inside, her feet thumping heavily.

"Henrik Rønbjerg Madsen." Henrik pronounced the name slowly and deliberately, almost sounding it out. "Have you got that, do you think?"

"Yes," Kevin said. "Henrik Rønbjerg Madsen."

"Right," Henrik said. "It's a deal."

"Right," Kevin said. "I'll tell him. Have a nice evening, and thank you for your business."

"My pleasure," Henrik said.

. . .

For a moment, Kevin remained standing at the door that had now closed on him, as if he were waiting for something more to happen. As he went down the drive, he turned and looked back, and in an upstairs window he saw Henrik flop down into an armchair. Seconds later, the music started again, the volume turned up a notch. Kevin arranged the strap of his laptop bag more comfortably on his shoulder, then carried on along the road.

Slowly, slowly, he walked.

He counted his steps to put his mind on something else.

One, two, three.

He passed the first of the houses he had seen when entering the village and was soon well on his way. A wind whipped at everything that was not rooted or lashed to the ground, rivulets of rain ran toward him on the road, and his pajama bottoms felt sodden and heavy. He sat down on a bench inside a podlike bus shelter. At his feet was an empty tobacco tin. He kicked it away. An out-of-date timetable was fixed to the inside of the shelter. Beside it, some words were scratched into the fiberglass:

S+T
torkild lund is a joke
BIG BASTARD GOT HIS HEAD KICKED IN
HERE 13.8.2007 WELL DESERVED
Thanks for info
BEST FUCK RING 97528252
Fake
Not fake
Number not working
Not working
Number doesn't work :-(

His fingers were numb. He wondered how much rain it took to make a flood. The dike could burst. The roads could turn into rivers. The bus shelter could be swept away with him in it. The rain drummed against the roof.

Apart from that, there were no other sounds. He craned his head to look at the sky. His father had once told him about the moon in Pattaya. It was big there, and as orange as an orange. Here, it was small and pale.

Ling Ma
Winner

I HADN'T RETURNED the keys because the landlord hadn't returned my security deposit. That's how I remember it, though it'd been a long time since I'd moved out. I came across the keys again when I was rifling through a desk drawer one day, looking for something, batteries maybe. There were three in the set—one for the building entrance, another for the mailbox, and the last for the apartment unit itself.

I would not have recognized the keys if not for the daisy key chain. I closed the drawer again, not wanting to touch them. The deposit didn't matter by this point.

A week passed, then another, before I thought to return them. It was the most karmically clean solution. But maybe I just wanted to go back.

Where I live and where I used to live aren't that far apart. The distance is less than a subway stop—if you took the train, you'd overshoot it. I don't remember the last time I was there. "There is no time like the present" is something my therapist tells me, although I guess that's a common adage. It was midday on a Friday. I put on my shoes and took a walk.

My old neighborhood has become gentrified like anywhere else. The assisted living facilities and retirement homes, outdated even when I lived there, have been converted into luxury condos and rentals. The laundromat has been replaced by an eco-friendly dry cleaner. I missed the Indian takeout place that sold, next to the front register, these big samosas under a heat lamp. In the winters, getting off the train from work, I would buy two for $5, before hitting up the liquor store at the corner for a beer on the way home.

The liquor store was still in business, repainted with a selfie-bait mural of animals punching each other in a rainbow boxing ring. Inside, the inventory had been completely revised. There were shelves of celebrity tequilas, and in the fridge section, wellness drinks replaced the old Mistic juices and Coke varieties, those thick Goya nectars. I took a bottle of mushroom-infused water that was inexplicably $7.99, and when I went to check out, I saw that they still had not taken the banner down. There was a photo of me on it, shaking hands with the owner, as we both looked at the camera. My old bangs, my greasy skin.

WINNING LOTTERY TICKET SOLD HERE!!! $$60 MILLION!!

Sixty million is Britney Spears's estimated net worth, I read somewhere, maybe in an article about myself winning the Powerball. The amount was inconceivable to me, but for Britney Spears, it somehow didn't seem enough. I hoped she would never have to work again if she didn't want to. I myself have not worked in years.

"There's a surcharge of three percent," the cashier said. "Our policy for credit card purchases under ten bucks. Is that okay?"

"Sure, that's fine." I needed to make a habit of carrying cash. "Can't get out of surcharges," I added.

"What's that?" He looked at me.

"Nothing." I looked away. It was unlikely he would recognize me from the banner. The girl in the picture had ascended into lottery-winner heaven. She was ziplining through a Colombian jungle, or Birkin shopping in Paris. Or she had joined the fate of most lottery winners and fallen into destitution. When you are struck by the lightning of extreme fortune, there is no middle path forward, only the paths of extremes.

"There's an ATM in here if you want to do cash," the clerk said, then remembered something. "But there'd still be a withdrawal fee."

"It's fine. Thanks." Suddenly I wanted to get out of there. There's a feeling I have sometimes that, having narrowly escaped my life, I am about to be found out. I brace for a blow that never comes. I don't know why. Being lucky isn't a crime.

He rang up the water. "You want a bag for this?" He gestured toward a stack of black plastic bags, with a wry smile. "It's seven cents, but I won't charge you."

"No thanks." I took my water and backed away.

I half expected the old apartment building to be razed and replaced with new construction. But like the liquor store, it was still there, different and only slightly recognizable. Walking down the block, I almost passed its new brick façade. The building had been repainted a neutral Dilbert gray that covered up its confusing fleshy yellow shade. Someone had planted hedges along the front; only up close could you tell that they were plastic.

I couldn't find the rental office, where the landlord used to sit at his desk, watching baseball on a small, goofy TV, discarded fast-food wrappers everywhere. When you went in to ask about repairs, he would only half listen, his eyes darting between you and the game. We called him Mr. B. We didn't know his surname, but it was just as well. He had inherited his family property and had mismanaged it into shambles.

A management firm had mounted a sign with its contact details near the entryway. Mr. B had finally sold the building, I assumed, and the new owner had contracted the firm to maintain it. When

I lived here, we heard rumors that Mr. B was going to sell it to a developer and retire—a matter of when rather than if. I thought to call the listed firm to return the keys, but the idea of leaving them with an anonymous company based out in the suburbs held no meaning. It was unlikely that the missing keys had been registered in the sale and transfer of the property.

I stood on the sidewalk, gathering neck sweat. It had gotten hot. I had come out all this way, and I had no one to be accountable to.

At the building entrance, I tried the keys. The door opened easily. I stepped inside. The musty smell of that foyer, the mailroom, the hallways, was so familiar—marine air freshener and faint secondhand smoke. Technically I was trespassing, but it didn't feel like a crime. You can't trespass into what's familiar.

I walked up the stairs to the second floor. It was a small studio at the end of the hallway, next to the janitor's closet. From inside, I always seemed to hear the elevator chiming in the night and early morning. I lived in that place through most of my twenties, working at an insurance brokerage firm the entire time. My supervisor was what we would call "abusive" and "toxic" now. When I wasn't at the office working, I was at home, blanked out, sleeping or watching TV. Those were the only two modes.

The door had been repainted gray, a lighter shade than the building's exterior. All the doors had been. I recognized the dent along the bottom of my old door, from having kicked it in anger one night. The unit, spelled out on the door, was 205—loser numbers that I'd incorporated into my Powerball entry as a joke.

When I tried the key, the door opened just as easily as the one downstairs. Someone lived there, it looked like, but no one was home.

That night, lying in bed beside my husband, I couldn't quite slip into sleep. One trick to relaxing, my therapist advised, is envisioning a familiar space. You imagine yourself walking around, taking inventory of every detail. As my husband's breathing deepened into little snores, I thought back to my old studio that, hours earlier, I had broken into.

The unit had seen some updates and renovations, a development probably effected by the management firm, not Mr. B. Aside from the new paint job, it had updated light fixtures, a new fridge. Something else, too. The grime, the general mustiness, had been dispelled. The place was tidy and pleasant, if a bit impersonal with its soft, muted tones—ocher curtains, heather sheets. The framed photos of natural wonders—a cactus palm, a seaside cliff—could have been stock images.

The occupant had organized the space more effectively than I had. I respected that they had opted for a twin-sized bed, which allowed for a desk and sofa within the three-hundred-square-foot space. The American choice would have been to sink a space like this with an extravagantly large mattress, so that all other functions—eating, watching TV, surfing online—would have to be conducted from where one slept. It is not choosing the "big" things that is fundamentally American but the blind insistence on grandiosity despite the reality of circumstances. It's not living beyond your means, it's the unceasing, headless insistence on "the best," whatever that is.

The biggest compliment my supervisor used to give me was "You're no American." It meant that I had a work ethic adapted to what is necessary, that I was not blind to circumstances. My supervisor often told me this in the evenings, when I was staying late at the office at her encouragement, or rather at her demand. It was typical for me to stay two or even three hours after everyone else left, before returning to the studio to collapse into my small, hard bed.

My supervisor was born and raised in the country of my parents. I wondered if that was why she had hired me. At times, I conflated her approval with that of my parents. That may be the reason I stayed at that job for as long as I did, the only full-time job I have ever held in my life. I thought her toughness, her demanding nature, would improve me. The chosen metaphor was of a blade forged by fire, a necessary tempering, when the more fitting one was that of a tree slowly burning to death. Not being American, according to her, was also being able to take suffering.

In our bed, my husband stirred. "Go to sleep," he murmured groggily. His voice sounded distant, blurred out by the sound of the AC.

It literally took winning the lottery to quit that job. And even then, I stayed another month to ensure a smooth transition. "You'll never make it," my supervisor said to me routinely, casually, at unexpected moments. Only toward the end did I question what "it" was. I didn't have ambitions to climb to the top of the company, and I wasn't committed to the field of insurance brokerage, which was ugly and corrupt, like all things healthcare-related in the United States. What did "it" mean?

When I told my supervisor I had won the lottery, she was confused at first. We were in her office. She wanted me to explain how the Powerball system worked, something I didn't totally understand myself. So we looked it up on her desktop. We googled it. We read guidelines for lottery winners ("Avoid sudden lifestyle changes," "Diversify your investments"). We pored through the articles for some time. She was both solemn and overzealously congratulatory. But I was tasked with working through her confusion with her. Her continual, now incessant, questioning began to feel exaggerated, pointed: any good fortune could not have occurred unless she had personally verified it. I began to feel trapped. I had planned to give notice, but it would have to wait until another time. When she asked, "Why you?" I said, "I don't know."

The next day was Saturday. Montessori was closed. We did family time—some configuration of stroller walk, coffee shop, farmer's market, and playground. Maybe a brunch restaurant. A nice, middle-class family doing nice, middle-class activities. Then we returned home, where my son took his nap while I played video games, shooting out tanks and personnel carriers in a DMZ-like setting. My husband read the news in the other room. It began to rain.

In the afternoon, we took our son to the library. In the children's area, I read him a picture book about a zoo filled with sad animals, which turned out to be about climate change. We were interrupted by an eerie, synchronized beep—a flash flood warning on everyone's phones. When we prepared to leave, our kid protested with whimpers, then screams; we had to drag him out. He darted into the parking lot, splashing into a puddle before my husband grabbed him, wet and wailing.

On the drive back, my husband fumed. "We're doing it wrong," he said, echoing his mother's stance, which is that it is unnatural for our lives to revolve around entertaining a two-year-old.

"Whatever," I said. "Drive to the toy store."

Our son had been placed in the NICU after his birth, and for a while it was very touch-and-go. His thighs, the only puffins of fat left, were punctured with needles and IVs. I kept a notebook, a narrative of his condition, because I did not believe that the system, a scattering of nurses and doctors tending to multiple patients, would be able to keep it straight. I stood next to him, reciting the narrative, making sure they didn't miss any details. At one point, the doctor said they had done all they could. "It's up to him now." Only at this crucial moment did they recognize his agency.

It was winter. I looked around, trying to find something that would tip the scales in favor of living. The paper cups of coffee, the linoleum-tile flooring, the bouquet of spray carnations that had come, questionably, with a white CONDOLENCES balloon. My husband had taken the balloon out of the room and was looking for somewhere to throw it away. He had been gone for twenty minutes. Outside the window, the hospital parking lot was covered in a porridge of gray snow and slush. A cluster of coats waited at the bus station across the street. There was nothing I could convincingly point to.

But I spoke to my son through the plastic. I said that from his vantage point, the world might not seem like an inviting place. But if he was willing to wait, strange, spectacular things happened every day. Like his birth, for one, and everything leading up to it. I said that the chances of winning the lottery were extremely slim, but it had happened, and the money was what had made his conception possible, the fertility treatments and so on. If anything, the extremely narrow odds leading to his existence meant that he was supposed to be here, that he deserved to be here. So I hoped that he would stay.

I was surprised by this line of reasoning as I spoke. But his little face, closed up like an old fist, seemed to relax at the sound of my voice.

Finally, I said that if he could keep going so we could leave this hospital, I would use the lottery winnings to make his life great.

The toy store was closing early when we got there, due to the extreme weather. But the clerk opened it and I managed to grab a Duplo set, along with a mock smartphone that played musical notes and something called a Pop-a-Balls Push & Pop Bulldozer, at the clerk's recommendation. Rushing out into the rain, I put the shopping bag into the back seat instead of the trunk, which was a mistake.

"Wait to open the boxes when we get home," my husband instructed our son.

"Don't make a mess!" I chimed in, getting into the passenger seat. "You can hold the toys, but don't open them yet."

In the rearview mirror, we watched helplessly as he tore into the boxes. He was surprisingly strong, with fast-growing nails I could barely keep up with trimming. "Yeahhhhhh!" he yelled, waving the toy over his head, like an eighties wrestler. "Yeahhhhh!"

We drove home slowly as our toddler rampaged in the back

seat. The streets were eerily empty, and though the rain was heavy, the gutters weren't overflowing. I didn't think the conditions warranted this kind of response, but we were all primed for catastrophe now.

"We're doing it wrong," my husband repeated, looking straight ahead at the road.

"There is no right way."

"I might not know what the right way is, but I definitely know we're doing it wrong."

"Yeah, you keep saying that." Outside the window, even the parking lots of box chain stores were deserted.

"Look, if a kid is screaming and being disrespectful, he shouldn't get rewarded. It's as simple as that." He gestured to the back seat. "If he's throwing a tantrum at the library, we don't need to take him to the toy store right after. It just encourages bad behavior."

I glanced in the rearview mirror. "Maybe those are two separate things. We went to the library, and we went to the toy store. Not everything is cause and effect."

"That's not how it comes off to him." My husband turned into our driveway. "He needs to learn about consequences. We need to instill some kind of moral code." He paused to locate the clicker for the garage door. "We need to teach him that, you know, you don't just get rewarded for nothing. That's chaos."

"Okay," I said, as we pulled into the garage of our house, a three-story refurbished single-family home with a rooftop deck, dual-zone heating and cooling system, and landscaped bamboo courtyard. "I hear what you're saying."

On Monday, I received an email from my former supervisor. It read, *How are you?*

Occasionally, I still get emails from her. They come unpredictably, every few months maybe. They are not sent from her work address, which I blocked long ago, but from one of multiple personal addresses. It is always a brief message, often a question or a leading statement. Sometimes it is an inside joke we once shared. A few times, it was a news link asking my thoughts about something related to insurance.

In all cases, I delete the message. The thought crosses my mind that I should keep them as evidence, but evidence for what? I have to get rid of it, or I'll keep thinking about it.

How are you?

I deleted this. Then I emptied the trash folder. I did this from the comfort of my old studio, which I had snuck into again.

The space was just as clean and tidy as it had been last week. There were no dishes in the sink, no dirty cereal bowls or coffee mugs abandoned before they rushed out the door to catch the train. The white countertops looked smooth and spotless. The bed was made. Who did that? Who kept their apartment that clean on a Monday morning? This time I felt like an intruder. But I didn't leave.

This time, I had brought an iced coffee and my laptop, which I set up at the desk. I planned to apply to jobs that morning, something I had been procrastinating on for weeks. There was just no urgency when I worked from home.

In my old apartment, I updated my résumé. Mostly, I just refreshed the design; I didn't have much to add. I constructed a template cover letter, describing my work gap as a decision to spend time at home as a new mother, without any mention of the lottery. If an employer googled me and figured out who I was, then fine. I looked up various postings and bookmarked a few positions I might have a chance at interviewing for. Most of these were entry-level communications-type jobs. None were in insurance brokerage. I created a LinkedIn page, as advised by job-hunting articles, and sent former coworkers, but not my former supervisor, requests to connect. This was the most productive I had been in months. The longer I stayed, the less I felt like I was intruding. And when I was done, I cleaned up after myself, making sure not to leave anything behind, including trash. As I exited the building, a neighbor coming in smiled at me. I almost froze, but I smiled back. "Have a nice day," I said.

The next few days passed in much the same way. After I dropped off my son at Montessori, I would come to the apartment and work on job applications. On one of those days, I even did my virtual therapy appointment from the studio.

"I'm cat-sitting at a friend's place," I explained to my therapist.

"That's very nice of you," she said. "But is this something you wanted to do? Walk me through how this request played out." The previous week, my therapist had given me a chart on the four communication styles. We both agreed that I resorted to my default "passive" style too often and needed to practice "assertive" style.

"My friend asked me a while back and I agreed. They live near me, so it's not a big chore." I was unprepared to make up more lies on the spot, but I tried to convey that I had not been finagled into this by my passivity. "I just feed the cat and spend time with her. She's sweet."

"I thought you were allergic to cats."

"Not, like, super allergic. I can be around them for a couple of hours." Then, switching gears, I added, "I've been using the time here to start applying to jobs."

She nodded in approval. Finally, some progress. We had recently come to the conclusion that I should seek out gainful employment again. It was a grounding measure, a way of ordering my days, which had become increasingly slippery and meaningless. "How is that going?"

"I've sent out a handful of applications so far." I chuckled uneasily. "It's been so long since I worked. I don't know if blind applications are the way to do it anymore."

"Well, regardless. This is a great first step. I'm proud of you."

"I'm a little worried because I don't have a lot of references. And I don't want to put my former boss's name down."

"What do you think would happen if you asked her to be a reference?"

"I don't know. She might feel that I owed her. I'm afraid that . . ." I trailed off. It sounded ridiculous to say that I was afraid she might come back.

"Are we dealing in fears or plausibilities?"

"I'd rather not even open that door," I said. "It's why I have been applying to entry-level jobs. I'd rather just start over."

"What would happen if you were to approach her?"

"I don't know." I didn't want to engage in more thought exercises. "I think she's still angry at me."

"Why does she still feel angry toward you?"

"Because . . ." I struggled to find the words. "Because I escaped, and by escaping, I upended the order of things. She wielded her power over everyone. Especially me. But suddenly I had an escape hatch out of that whole system."

"Lots of people quit their jobs."

"But it was almost as if, by quitting, I was saying that the system, the one in which she reigned, was stupid. That anyone would leave if given the chance."

My therapist paused. "How do you know she feels this way?"

"I just know . . . From working with her for all those years. I know how she thinks."

"You've given a lot of thought as to how she might feel toward you. Tell me how you feel toward her."

"She was a mean-spirited person who made my life hell in subtle ways at first and, as time accrued, more obvious and egregious ways. But by that point I was used to it, and so I just took it."

"So you feel angry."

"I feel angry," I said, then added, "But I've been very lucky."

"You're minimizing yourself." She jotted something down. "You don't have to minimize your anger. The more space you allow yourself to take up, the more this world will accommodate you." She paused. "And the less angry you will feel."

I sighed. "That line of thinking seems so American, though. If everyone gets to take up space, it would be . . ." I searched for the word.

She laughed, a little bit. "Yeah, tell me. What do you think would happen?"

"It would be . . . annoying." I wanted to say *disgusting*.

"News flash," my therapist said. "You're an American."

Leaving the studio that day, I saw that the door to the janitor's closet was open. It emitted a dim, orange light, incongruous with the cool, white lumination of the hallway. Peeping inside, I saw a single bulb dangling low on a string. It was jiggling, as if someone had just turned it on. But there was no one around.

Even when I lived here, I had never seen inside the closet, which was the size of a homey walk-in. There were a few shelves of cleaning sprays and bottles, some brooms and vacuum cleaners, and a floor sink where the mops were washed out. Nestled amongst these was a little cot with a wrinkled floral sheet spread over it, lilacs against a white backdrop. A McDonald's burger, unwrapped from its wax paper, had been left on the cot, alongside some fries.

When the elevator pinged, I moved toward the stairway.

The next week, I was in the studio, in the middle of writing an email to follow up on an application, when the door opened. I turned around, bracing myself.

The person at the door was an older man. There was a pause. "Well, you're not supposed to be in here," he said, only mildly surprised. It was Mr. B. Which was also surprising. I'd assumed he'd retired.

"Oh, hi, Mr. B," I said, for lack of anything else to say. He looked smaller. He still wore the same thing—white T-shirts, yellowing around the pits, tucked into belted chinos. I'd forgotten about the white tube socks and black Reebok sneakers.

"You're not supposed to be in here," he repeated. "There are showings here tonight."

"Oh, okay." I tried to recover from how startled I felt. "Are you trying to find a new tenant for this place?"

"No, the showings are not for this unit, they're in this unit," he said, impatient. "This one is not for sale. This is the sales model."

"Oh, really?" I reassessed the studio again. It made too much sense—the sterile tidiness, the framed stock photography, the impersonal décor. I could have figured it out.

"You're lucky no one lives here." He chuckled. I did not seem to be in any trouble. "This studio is too small to rent out. Hasn't been lived in for a couple of years. So they spruced it up as a sample."

"But I used to live here." I wondered why they would use the smallest unit as a sales model.

He looked at me, incurious. "Okay, well. That was probably a mistake."

I didn't know how to respond to that. "I used to live here," I repeated. "Like, for six years. Back when it was your building."

"Ah, the good old days." He squinted as if trying to place me, but I don't think he remembered. "Why are you here now?"

"I was going to return the keys." It wasn't exactly an answer, but I fumbled through my bag. "Here," I said, holding them out to him. As if I had been waiting to do this all along. "I held on to the keys because I never got the deposit back."

He did not move to take them. "Did you come back for the deposit, then?" he asked, and I knew that I had remembered correctly, that he had never returned it.

"Don't worry about it." I still held out the keys.

"Because if you're asking for your deposit," he continued, as if not having heard me, "first of all, there might be a statute on that.

I don't know, I can't say one way or the other. But you're going to have to go through management, not me. They own this place now."

"Do you work for management?"

"I don't work for anyone," he said, bristling, before launching into a long-winded explanation. He had an arrangement with the property firm to help maintain the building. It sounded like light janitorial tasks. He swept the front entrance, he made sure no packages were left outside, he tidied up the sales model, et cetera.

"Do you still live in the building?"

"I live in the Fairview. Do you know where that is?"

"Yeah, that's not far from here."

"It's just down the block." Mr. B was uncommonly proud. "Never thought I'd end up there."

"I heard it's really nice." Fairview was an expensive senior living facility, one of the last in the neighborhood that advertised hotel-quality amenities. There was a well-pruned courtyard and a restaurant on the first floor. Walking on a winter night, I once spotted, through gauze curtains, white-gloved waiters moving from table to table, ladling soup from a cart.

"Well, I sold this building for . . . a tidy sum, you might say." Propriety prevented him from disclosing the exact amount.

"I thought you'd be fully retired by now."

"And what would I do all day?" he said, suddenly indignant. "Watch TV?"

I bit my tongue. That was literally all he did when he was the landlord: watch baseball in his office.

He continued, "This building has been in my family for generations. I know it like the back of my hand, and you can't buy that kind of knowledge. They know that. They're the ones who keep asking me back!" Sharpened by his irritation, he zoomed in on me. "And now I'm going to have to ask you to leave, please."

"I'm going, Mr. B." I had been holding the keys the entire time, keys he hadn't accepted, and I put them in my bag. "It was nice to see you again."

He grunted in return, neither confirming nor denying.

In the hallway, the janitor's closet was open again. I didn't peep inside this time.

I went down the steps to the foyer, then through the front doors and down the streets of my old neighborhood. I went past the station where I used to catch the train to go to work and the new bus stop that accommodated an express line going directly downtown. I hadn't even clocked the new shoe store or the fine jewelry shop. When you come into a big windfall, the impulse is to convert the money into material things. But I think the real trick is to convert money into time.

I walked until I arrived back at my house, new construction that, according to our agent, accrues at a higher rate than most properties in the city. I punched in the security code, and when I opened the front door, the blast of air-conditioning felt bracingly, refreshingly minty. In the foyer and living room, I negotiated the labyrinth of paintings and sculptures, silently accruing value day by day, hour by hour. Also accruing along the hallways were rare first editions entombed inside closed bookcases, titles I have never touched, let alone read.

I climbed the staircase to the master suite, where I found my king-sized bed dressed with sheets the color of pistachio ice cream. Even if I don't know what to do with time anymore, I still want it. It is mine to waste. I smoothed out the pillowcase. I got underneath the covers. I closed my eyes and went to sleep.

Anthony Marra
Countdown

THEIR UK VISAS were all of five hours old when Sonya's husband, Alexei, looked up from the computer and announced they would never escape Russia.

"Come on," she said. "Ticket prices can't be that bad."

By now, Sonya was inured to Alexei's bouts of melodrama and declarations of doom. He was the sort of easily persuaded catastrophist who sourced his medical advice and political opinions from Reddit.

Sonya set her passport on the kitchen table. She'd been smelling the visa itself, which had the fresh, fibrous scent of a newly minted banknote. According to the lady at the British embassy, the paper was fitted with microchips for enhanced security. Paper that was part computer: what better gestured to the brave new world awaiting them in England?

"We're not going to England," Alexei repeated. "There are no fucking flights."

"Language," Sonya said, nodding to their six-year-old daughter, Masha.

"Since when has she ever listened to me?"

"Fucking, fucking fuck," Masha said.

"See?" Sonya said. "She's a sponge, Alexei. Yesterday in the car, she was giving other drivers the middle finger."

Alexei refreshed the page again. "There are no flights."

Sonya leaned over his shoulder, assuming, not without reason, that he had no idea what he was doing. The perpetually astonishing fact that her husband, a philology PhD who kept his log-ins and passwords taped to his computer monitor, had found work as a cybersecurity consultant spoke both to his natural charisma and to the wishful thinking of his superiors. Befuddled by entertainment systems with multiple remotes, powerless to disable Siri after weeks of effort, he had—while in the throes of postdoctoral desperation—applied for a job in IT at the headquarters of a grocery chain a few hours east of Moscow. "An arrest for buying cocaine on the dark web doesn't qualify as IT expertise," Sonya had told him. But she'd underestimated his talent for bullshit. Of course she had. She'd married him. No one at his office knew enough to know that Alexei knew nothing.

"Refresh it again," Sonya said. Alexei did, but the website still showed no available departures. "Even flights to Pyongyang are fully booked. What the fuck?"

"Language," Alexei said. "Maybe someone broke the internet."

"You can't break the internet. That's a meme. It's not something that happens."

"Who's the IT professional, me or you? In my professional opinion, someone broke the internet."

"The internet's not broken," Sonya repeated, though her husband wasn't as idiotic as he sounded. Since the first days of the war, everything reliant on Western technology had begun breaking down. The shift was neither immediate nor dramatic, a gradual regression rather than a total collapse, as if Putin were less the president of a nation than the conductor of a time machine reversing into the past. Two years earlier, they could have relied on airfare aggregators to filter and sort flights based on departure and arrival times, layover durations, baggage allowances, legroom.

Now that sanctions had severed the Russian banking system from the international economy, the only options were easily hacked .ru e-tailers that catapulted pop-up ads across your screen and planted malware in your hard drive.

"This is the best one I could find," Alexei said, highlighting an itinerary that swelled to sixteen days, thirteen connections, and sixty-three thousand euros. "We should have left months ago."

"We had to wait for our visas."

"We could have waited for them in Georgia or Kazakhstan. Somewhere with airplanes."

Sonya glanced to the kitchen table, where Masha was watching TV: the misadventures of a dim-witted cartoon bear and his gaggle of woodland pals.

"We agreed that we didn't want to disrupt her schedule," Sonya said.

"Masha is about to become a six-year-old exile, and you're worried about disrupting her schedule?"

"It's harder for some of us to simply pack up and leave," Sonya said. She was referring, of course, to her mother, who'd been diagnosed with dementia the prior spring and wouldn't understand—or if she did understand, wouldn't remember—why her daughter, son-in-law, and granddaughter had to emigrate. She would assume they'd forgotten her, at least until she forgot them.

"I'm sorry," Alexei said. "Let's not fight. This whole year. Jesus."

Sonya touched his arm, felt him recoil and then relax under the heat of her hand. "I know it's a lot to ask, but do you think Galina could help us again?"

Alexei had said he would reach out to Galina a few months earlier, after the Kremlin had begun insisting it had no intention of ordering a general mobilization. Sonya thought he was joking because, come on, who was Alexei Kalugin—with his air of cheerful failure and his unaddressed eczema—to slide into Galina

Ivanova's DMs? Like most of their generation, Sonya could still quote lines from *Deceit Web,* a movie of unremitting stupidity and irresistible nostalgia. Following its release, Galina had enjoyed a couple years of cultural ubiquity before marrying an oligarch and fading from public view.

"I knew her in Kirovsk," Alexei had explained.

"Bullshit."

"It's true. She dated Kolya in high school."

Alexei rarely spoke of his older brother, who'd returned from the First Chechen War transformed. When the Russian army reinvaded in 1999, Alexei was eighteen years old, a chronic underachiever with no prospects, and no capacity to survive Putin's murderous imperial project. That he evaded conscription was due entirely to Kolya, who reenlisted as a contract soldier and leveraged the hefty signing bonus to buy Alexei's way into university, a guarantee of military deferment. All this history complicated Alexei's natural inclination to avoid compulsory service in Ukraine, a war he found as politically senseless and morally repugnant as the one that claimed his brother's life, deep in the Chechen highlands, on a summer day in 2000.

Sonya recalled Alexei taking a few belts of vodka after DMing Galina. An unpracticed drinker, he misjudged the effects of mixing alcohol with the prescription sleeping aid on which he depended for his eight hours, growing increasingly loopy and confessional.

"Who are you most afraid of turning into?" he asked.

"I don't know. My mother?"

"Your mother's sweet."

"Only because of the dementia. She's forgotten that she's actually a monster."

He rattled the pill bottle. "Why'd the doctor say not to take these with booze? It's great. Hey, would you brush my teeth for me?"

"I'm changing my answer. The person I'm most afraid of turning into is you."

"Come on. The bathroom's so far."

"Didn't you accuse me of infantilizing you the other day?"

"Doesn't sound like me."

Sonya rested her head on his shoulder. "Oh no. That doesn't sound like you at all. You know your six-year-old daughter can brush her own teeth?"

"She has to keep that filthy mouth of hers clean."

"You're the one teaching her curse words."

"Not me. She's self-taught. Like Van Gogh."

"Our daughter, the Van Gogh of vulgarity. Terrific." Sonya sighed. "What about you Who are you afraid of turning into?"

"My brother."

Sonya didn't respond, turning her eyes to watch him.

"He was a murderer. He murdered people."

"He was a soldier."

"Semantics."

"You're a lot of things, Alexei, but you're not a murderer."

"Yeah? How do you know?"

"You're a vegetarian."

"So was Hitler."

"But Hitler had ambition."

"Kolya did, too. He had hopes—for after."

"You know what else Kolya had?" she said, taking the pill bottle from his hand. "A good heart. And you have a good heart. At least you did, before you started playing pharmacist."

To Sonya's surprise, Galina not only responded to Alexei's message the next morning, she offered to help. While her popular profile had evaporated in the two decades since her name last topped the marquee, her actual stature had materialized. She'd relocated to London with her husband, and their sixteen-room Knightsbridge residence had become an informal seat of Russian influence in the UK. Sponsoring visas for an old acquaintance and his family was so easy Galina didn't even consider it a favor.

. . .

Alexei stood from the computer, opened his Instagram account—@AphorismsByAlexei—and tapped out a message to Galina. He was dressed in a rumpled linen shirt and faded jeans, his hairline receding, his temples graying, the fifteen kilos he'd vowed to shed for the duration of their marriage still anchored to his waistline. Prescription lenses magnified his eyes, emphasizing his expression of genial naïvety.

Five days before, Sonya had returned home from dropping Masha at school when her phone dinged with the news of Putin's partial mobilization order, mustering young men and ex-cons. Alexei was still asleep, his glasses on the nightstand. She didn't wake him, as if she could stay the next chapter.

"Is Galina online?" she asked.

"I don't know. She's not responding." Alexei grabbed his jacket. "How much cash do you have on you?"

"Check my purse. There should be a few thousand rubles. Why?"

"Maybe I'll have better luck at the airport ticket counter."

"Alexei. Don't be an idiot."

"I'm losing my mind here. I can't just sit around refreshing Instagram all night."

"What if the police pull you out of line? I read Moscow has stationed recruitment officers in the metro."

"There won't be police at the airport."

"It's an international fucking airport—"

"Language," Masha chimed in.

"—of course there are police. I'll go, okay? I'll go."

Alexei stuffed the cash from Sonya's purse into his pocket. "What about Masha's homework?" he said as he walked out the door. "We don't want to disrupt her schedule."

"Asshole."

It felt wrong to think in such terms, but the war had likely saved their marriage. Or postponed its dissolution, at least. Masha's birth had clarified certain matters for Sonya: namely, that she had two children, which wouldn't have been an issue if she weren't married to one of them. In the course of dead-end arguments, Alexei accused her of changing—*I don't even recognize you, you've changed, Sonya*—as if maturation were a character flaw. Yes, in a normal world, she would have left him. Yet in this grotesque and precarious one, she was leaving Russia with him.

"Okay," Sonya told Masha. "That's enough TV for today. Let's do your homework."

"It's boring."

"I know it is."

"Then why do I have to do it?"

"Because enduring boredom with good cheer will serve you well for the rest of your life."

And for the next twenty minutes, Masha plodded through a passage glorifying the genocidal exploits of Peter the Great. She'd always struggled with reading comprehension, even in her native language; God knew how she'd fare in British schools. Sonya was trying to coax an answer from her daughter about the vanquishing of the evil Swedes when she heard footsteps in the hallway. They stopped at the door. The intensity of her relief startled Sonya: Alexei had come home. She listened for the jangling of his keys. Instead, a knock.

Sonya crossed soundlessly to the door and peered through the peephole. If not for their uniforms, she would have assumed the two military recruitment officers were food deliverymen: one officer straining under the weight of four bags bulging with groceries, the other flipping through a folio stuffed with what she first took for receipts, until recognizing them for draft notices. The latter brought his fist to the door and pounded so forcefully the peephole's metal collar bruised her eye socket. She stepped back and bumped the coatrack.

The pounding stopped.

"You can open the door, or we can break it down," said the blue-eyed officer brandishing the draft notices. "Please choose how we come in."

So chivalry isn't dead, Sonya ghoulishly thought, as she opened the door. "I'm sorry. I didn't hear you."

"She didn't hear us, Boris," the officer with the grocery bags deadpanned. "That's the fourth flat in a row. Do you suppose this is a home for the hard of hearing?"

"There's a plague of deafness going around, Sasha," said the officer with the draft notices. "It's a miracle we can still hear ourselves think. We're here to serve . . . Alexei Kalugin. He about?"

Sonya shook her head.

"Imagine that," said the officer with the grocery bags. "C'mon, Boris."

The two men pushed past Sonya, trailing cigarette smoke, waffling the floorboards with grimy boot prints. Masha slipped behind her mother.

"Good evening, little person," said the officer with the grocery bags. "Is your father home?"

Masha shook her head.

"Imagine that," said the officer with the draft notices. "Like mother, like daughter."

"We should check the kitchen, Boris. Just to be thorough."

"Right you are, Sasha. It's the burden of perfectionism."

Sonya watched the two officers commit a home invasion of her refrigerator. While one rooted around the crisper drawer, the other enumerated the provisions pilfered from her neighbors.

"Lettuce, tomato, onions, mushrooms, hard-boiled eggs, black bread, smoked trout, ham, chicken breast, mayonnaise, mustard, butter, caviar—perhaps enough for a sandwich."

"Nonsense. We haven't any cheese."

"There's a jar of pickles in back. Pass it here."

Mashing the fifth spear into his mouth, the officer called Sasha noticed a photograph stuck to the fridge door: Alexei on his thirty-eighth birthday. "Look here. I found him."

"Poor fellow," said the other, as he added a bottle of horseradish and a jar of chutney to their haul. "Don't suppose he'll live to see his next one, do you, Sasha?"

"Not in front of the missus, Boris. It's unprofessional."

"But she's deaf, Sasha—remember? She can't hear us at all."

"Is that orange juice fortified with extra vitamin C?"

"You tell me—you're the health nut."

The officer called Sasha tipped the carton to his mouth, and Sonya watched the juice spill over his cheeks, staining his uniform and splashing across the floor.

"You know, Sasha, I've always had a kind of affection for Ukraine."

"You have relatives there?"

"My father. He's buried in Odesa. Killed himself on a family vacation."

"How awful."

"Oh, it was. His wife found him hanging in the closet of their hotel, then found out about my mother at the funeral. I'm not sure which upset her more."

"At least he killed himself with his other family, Boris. At least you have that."

"It is a consolation, though hardly the sort of thing printed on a sympathy card."

"Perhaps there's a market. These days, the most calamitous stories are often the most common."

"Hard man, my father. Survived three years in Afghanistan and eight years in a Siberian prison, but no more than a few days on the Black Sea with his other family before deciding to end it all. And if that's what Ukraine did to him, just imagine what it'll do to a fat, middle-aged IT worker with ten days' training."

"So why the affection for such a place?"

"Because my father was a motherfucking prick."

"Language, Boris. The young are so impressionable."

"Okay, Sasha, okay. Let's see if"—the officer flipped through the draft notices—"Dmitry Morozov next door has any brie."

. . .

"Why did they come here?" Masha asked once the recruitment officers had gone.

"They were hungry," Sonya said.

"But why did they want Dad?"

"Your father makes the best sandwiches. Isn't that what you're always telling me?"

Masha nodded.

How much did she understand? Sonya and Alexei had tried to shelter their daughter from the turmoil. The move to England wasn't a harrowing escape, but rather a thrilling vacation. Masha was too young, and Sonya wouldn't burden her with the truth of a world she would learn about soon enough. And yet protecting Masha meant replicating the Kremlin's distortions, denials, and silences within their home. Lying to her became inseparable from loving her: how else could they keep her safe?

"Shall we call your father and see where he is?" Sonya suggested.

Alexei's line went directly to voicemail.

"Where is he?" Masha asked.

"On his way home." Sonya tried to smile. "C'mon. Let's read a book while we wait."

"Okay. *Curious George*."

Alexei had purchased *Curious George* as part of a campaign to improve Masha's English, and for the prior few weeks, Masha had asked Sonya to read it to her every night. There were only so many times Sonya could recite the misadventures of an inquisitive primate before hoping the poachers would show up. But now, as Masha curled beside her, she wondered if her daughter wished to return to this story precisely because she already knew it by heart. In a reality where recruitment officers could barge into your flat, demand your father, and steal your pickles, what was better than a fantasy swept clean of uncertainty or suspense?

Footsteps boomed down the hallway.

Masha's grip tightened on Sonya's wrist. How many fathers had been marched out into the dull daylight by uniformed men? How many mothers had sat in darkness in this very flat, silently praying the footsteps wouldn't stop at their door?

The footsteps stopped at her door.

Then, thank God, the jangle of keys, the lock snapping open, and as Alexei appeared, bearing more disappointment—sanctions prevented Galina from wiring money into Russia, and every international flight was sold out anyway—Sonya and Masha embraced him as if he'd delivered the best possible news.

It was two in the morning when they finally finished packing the car with one suitcase, four cardboard boxes, and eight trash bags. Their most valuable possessions—the family photos—lived on their phones and in the cloud. Alexei hauled the television down the apartment stairs, only to find a dozen of Masha's stuffed animals occupying the last of the back-seat real estate.

"Are you really sure you need to bring all of them?" he asked.

"I'm really sure," Masha said.

"It's just that this is beginning to look like Noah's Lada."

"We can't leave anyone behind."

"What the hell," he said, setting the television on the sidewalk. "We watch too much TV anyway."

He wrapped an arm around Sonya's shoulder, and when she didn't shrug it off, Alexei chose to interpret this as the most positive omen. Perhaps a new age of peace and harmony was dawning. A new city, a new country, a new life.

They climbed into the car, Masha in back with her menagerie, Sonya riding shotgun, trash bags of clothes obscuring the rear window. It was a twenty-seven-hour drive to the Georgian border, and Alexei couldn't remember when he'd last changed the Lada's oil. Crossing into the Baltic States or Finland would save hours, but on Telegram, Alexei had found conflicting reports on European port-of-entry closures. Were he an actual cybersecurity expert, he might have known if any were from credible sources.

"You ready?"

"No," Sonya said. "Not remotely."

"Me neither."

He put the car into gear.

They stopped for gasoline in Tula, bathrooms in Voronezh. Everywhere, Alexei saw men in need of a shave, a shower, a nap. Men much like himself, driving to the border, alone or with their families, their earthly goods jammed in the trunk, tied to the roof, left by the side of the road. Swiping at their phones at the gas pumps, spreading news of traffic, apprehensions, closed crossings, each one bleary-eyed, exhausted, kept alert by cigarettes and energy drinks and adrenalized panic. The simplest questions of basic time and space—*where will I be tomorrow?*—became existential mysteries. The known world receded, and no matter what Yandex Maps suggested to the contrary, it was all uncharted wilderness.

Sonya yawned and rubbed her eyes. "How long was I out?"

"A couple hours."

"You want me to take over?"

"I've got it," Alexei said. And he did. The difficult conversations he and Sonya would have down the line, none of that mattered. What mattered was shrinking the distance to their deliverance.

"How long has the motor been making that noise?"

He'd hoped she wouldn't notice the clang coming from the . . . well, whatever those parts were called.

"A couple hundred kilometers."

"When'd you last have it serviced?"

"I've never had it serviced."

"Alexei."

"If I'd thought we'd be driving this shit-box across half of Eurasia, I'd have brought it in for a tune-up first."

"Those gun-nut survivalists in America convinced the world is about to end—what do they call them?"

"Republicans," Alexei said.

"No, the ones who can build an internal combustion engine out of the odds and ends they hoard in their bunkers."

"Oh, preppers."

"That's right—preppers. I used to think they were crazy," she said. "Maybe they're just early."

"They're definitely crazy."

"Perhaps, but while we still have a signal, I might search the internet for one of their diatribes on fashioning a fan belt from a pair of stockings."

"You know what the real culprit is?" Alexei said. "DIY. You start baking your own bread, and you end up living in a basement with a few thousand rounds of ammunition and a filtration system for drinking your own urine."

"Is this how you justify abstaining from your share of the cooking?"

"All I'm saying is that I've never seen a person who makes their own clothes and thought, *Now, here's someone in full control of their faculties*."

"What are we even talking about?"

"The end of the world," Alexei said, as rain detonated against the windshield. Several silent kilometers passed before he spoke again. "My brother and I used to pretend that the world was ending. We were preppers before the internet made it fashionable."

"What, you collected canned food?"

"We built a spaceship."

"Excuse me?" Sonya stared at him with genuine curiosity, trying to recall the last time he'd surprised her in a good way. "How have you never told me this?"

"It was just a bunch of junk we cobbled together and wrapped in tinfoil."

"A DIY spaceship. And here you are sneering at people who make their own clothes."

"We'd pretend that the Americans had launched a nuclear attack, and we had to blast off before the bombs landed."

"The two of you floating around in space, huh?"

"No, just one of us. There was only one seat in the capsule. So one of us would escape, and the other, well, you know. I remember the countdown. Those last moments together."

"You never talk about your brother."

"What's there to say? I hate him for what he did because he loved me."

"Look," Sonya said, nodding to the rearview mirror. "She's finally asleep."

Alexei listened to their daughter snore in the back seat while the wipers sloshed rain across the windshield, and hoped the clanging engine wouldn't wake her.

"We're here," Alexei said.

Sonya stirred and looked at her phone. "The map says we're still thirty kilometers from the border. There must be an accident."

Alexei opened the door and peered ahead. The highway was bricked over in taillights to the horizon. "I don't think there's an accident. I think this is the line to leave."

Hours passed. Alexei measured distance not in kilometers but in car lengths. Sonya asked again if she might take over.

"I'm good," he said.

"You haven't slept in two nights."

"I'll rest once we get through," he said. He unzipped his cassette case, popped a mixtape into the tape player, tapped his thumb on the steering wheel to the beat.

Finally, the border came into view: a line of security fencing, sheet metal, stripped paint. Signage with clear instructions belied the general disorder. He counted the cars ahead: twenty-eight, then twenty-seven, then twenty-six.

"We're nearly there," he said.

"Who are they?" Sonya asked.

A half dozen uniformed officers had pulled the driver, a young man, from the next car in line. After glancing at his passport, they hauled him to a bus idling on the other side of the road. A bus with bars over shatterproof windows, pointing opposite the fleeing traffic.

"Turn around," Sonya said.

"We're so close." Twenty cars. Nineteen. Eighteen.

"Turn around, Alexei. We'll find a different way. We'll cross into Kazakhstan."

"Not in this car. It's got nothing left."

"Then we'll go back home. Masha's only missed two days of school. We'll go back to the way we were. Just turn around."

The alarm in her eyes made him feel bewilderingly, unjustifiably loved.

"You have Galina's address," he said. "She'll ensure you have everything you need in London."

"Turn back, Alexei. Please."

Seventeen. Sixteen. Fifteen.

An officer tapped on Alexei's window.

"You're right, Sonya. You should take over driving for a while."

Make something of yourself. These were the last words his brother had spoken to him, at a bus depot in Kirovsk, before beginning the journey that would end ten months later in a mined pasture south of the Terek River. And they were the words by which Alexei had—in the twenty-four years since—measured his failures.

Now, as the officers wrenched him from the driver's seat, he gazed back at the distraught family he'd delivered to the border—a thirty-three-hour slog without pause except for gas and bathroom breaks, and he'd driven every kilometer. That was something, surely, but was it enough?

The wind was kicking Sonya's hair all over as she stood in the road, her fists balled, her eyes radiating desperation. *Don't turn back,* he thought. *Please.*

The driver behind the Lada laid on his horn, and Alexei watched, heartbroken, as his wife froze, flustered and uncertain, with this asshole's impatient clamor blaring in her ears.

Then the Lada's back door flung open, and Masha stepped out, flipping off the driver and uncorking a torrent of the most magnificent profanities. *Oh, my little vulgarian, you make your father so proud.*

By the time Sonya managed to corral her, there were only four cars ahead.

Alexei stared through the window of the army bus.

Three cars.

I love you.

Two.

Just go.

One.

Lori Ostlund

Just Another Family

MY FATHER SPENT the last year of his life discontinent. He'd always had trouble with prefixes. The day after he died, I entered my parents' house—the house I grew up in—to the smell of piss, the humid night air thick with it. "It's the mattress," my mother explained, and I said, well, then the mattress had to go.

I tried to haul it out right then, just dropped my bag and went down the hallway to their bedroom. I started with the soda bottles. There were five of them, scattered beneath their bed, three with urine still sloshing around inside from when my father had relieved himself during the night. I used a broom to maneuver them out while my mother watched, lying on the floor on the far side of the bed, peering at me across its underbelly and demanding that I call them pop bottles. She was sure that I was saying *soda* to bother her because she said there was no way a person could grow up saying *pop* and then find herself one day just thinking *soda*.

As I knelt beside their bed, I felt something hard beneath my right knee. "Why are there cough drops all over the carpet?" I asked, using the plural, for I could see then that the floor was dotted with them, half-sucked and smooth like sea glass washed up in the dingy blue shag of my parents' bedroom.

"Your father coughs a lot at night. He sucks on them until he's just about to doze off, and then he'd spit them on the floor," my mother explained, her sentence beginning in the present tense but ending in the past, because that's the way death worked, the fact of it lost for whole seconds, whole sentences. "I used to pick them up in the morning, but he'd get after me for wasting perfectly good cough drops."

"Bettina's not here yet?" I asked. My sister lived just an hour away, so I was annoyed that she had not arrived, but I was also admitting defeat: the mattress was too much for me to handle alone.

"You know she has a family," my mother said, by way of excusing her absence.

Rachel and I had been together eight years. We had a house, jobs, two cats, and a dog, so I thought of myself as having a family, also.

"You know what I mean, Sybil," my mother replied. I did know. She meant that I didn't have children, but mainly she meant that two women together was not a family.

"Well, if she's not here in the morning, I'll call a neighbor to help," I said, but my mother did not like this plan. She felt a mattress soaked with urine was a family affair.

My father was dead, I said, so what did it matter, and she said, "Why can't you say 'passed away' like everyone else?" This was a good question.

From where she lay on the floor on the far side of the bed, she announced that she was putting me in my old bedroom. "So you'll be comfortable," she added, and I did not say that I had never been comfortable in this room and could not imagine I'd start being comfortable in this room now, nor did I remind her that Rachel would be arriving the next day, which meant that I would not really be in my old room long enough to get comfortable because Rachel and I always slept in the basement, in the rec room that my father had built years ago with teenagers in mind. My parents did not approve of us sharing a bed, and the rec room was a compromise: it allowed us to sleep together, a technical win for us, but together on separate sofas, unlike my sister and her husband, Carl, who slept upstairs in her old room, in a double bed that my parents had purchased for this very purpose.

"Why are you lying on the floor?" I asked, bending low to peer beneath the bed at her.

"You're getting rid of my bed," she said, and then she pulled herself slowly up, using the mattress as support, and I picked up my bag from where I'd dropped it and went down the hallway to the room my mother somehow imagined I would be comfortable in, this room that I had spent my childhood in: with walls that my father had painted pink as a surprise, the orange shag carpet, the framed print of a child kneeling to pray.

Years ago, soon after I brought Rachel here to my parents' house for the first time, I'd returned for a solo visit having to do with one of many health scares related to my father. Though my parents had just met Rachel, they did not engage in even the basic courtesy of inquiring how she was. Then, on my second night here, my mother came into my room, *this* room, to announce that she—and not just she but everyone she knew—was ashamed of it. She was carrying Bibles, a stack of three, as though they did not all say the same thing.

"It?" I said. "What, exactly, is *it*?"

"You know what *it* is." This was what an education had done to me, she said. I couldn't just talk about stuff like normal people.

"Well, then I guess I'm not normal," I said, "because I want you to say what this *it* is that you and every single person you know is so ashamed of." I was speaking to her from the bed I had occupied as a child, before I went away and became the kind of person who thought of her life as something more than *it*.

"If you can't say what you mean," I said, "then we're not going to talk about it."

My mother had left, but not before turning to set the Bibles, stacked atop one another, on my dresser, where they have remained these seven years; on the nightstand, a fourth had been added—just in case.

Now, beneath the praying child, there was something new, pointing upward: a row of hunting rifles, six in total, butts nestled in the orange shag rug.

I went into the kitchen, where my mother was doing something with cottage cheese.

"Why are Dad's guns in my room?" I asked.

"They were in the entryway, but you know how your sister gets about the kids."

"You mean how she gets about not wanting them to blow their heads off?" I said.

Earlier that evening, after a day spent flying backward from Albuquerque to Los Angeles in order to get a flight to Minnesota, I had stopped to pick up my rental car at the airport, and the young man at the counter asked whether I was here on vacation. He was making small talk, but also, he didn't think I was from here, for reasons having to do with the way that I speak, the Minnesota accent that I no longer have. I had not made a point to lose it, not that I could recall, though Rachel says that by the time we met, it was already gone. Sometimes, my mother says she can't understand me anymore. "It's your brogue," she says, as if I have suddenly become Scottish.

"Actually, my father just died," I told the young man, which surely struck him as further proof that I was not from here, because if you were from here, you knew not to say such things to strangers. Quickly, he handed me the keys, and I got into the rental car and drove two hours up the interstate, exiting onto the highway that led through my hometown. All around me was darkness, but I knew what was out there: lakes and fields, cows and barns and silos, the occasional house. Three miles out of town, I turned onto a gravel road and then, half a mile later, into the driveway, at the top of which I shut off the engine and rested my head on the steering wheel, the way one does at the end of a long trip, especially when there's more to come.

I lifted my head, and there was my mother, staring in at me like all the gas station attendants of my youth. I rolled down the window. "Fill 'er up," I said, but she didn't get the joke, or maybe she did get it but didn't get why I was making a joke at a time like this, with my father so recently dead.

Passed away.

"Oh, you're awake," she said. "I thought you were planning to sleep out here."

My mother often said things like this, things along the lines of suggesting that I might be planning to sleep in a rental car in the driveway. My father and I had been alike in the way that such things irritated us. "Why would I sleep in the car?"

"I thought you might be tired from the drive," she said.

"I am tired," I said, and then I tried to play the game where I kept my mouth shut, just once—the game I always lost. "But why would I sleep in the car?"

"Shirley's been at it again," my mother said.

Shirley Koerber lived on the lot behind my parents, her sole companions a band of dogs at which she yelled for various infractions. She was a stout woman with legs that bowed severely, as though she were straddling an invisible barrel as she walked, and she possessed a deep hatred of small animals—squirrels, chipmunks, birds—all of which the dogs chased with limited success and at which she shot with far greater. As a child, I'd awakened often to the sound of her gun, rising to watch from my window as the dogs circled the felled animal, howling, while Shirley rode her imaginary barrel toward them. Once when I was hanging laundry on the backyard line, a bullet whizzed past my head and I ran inside, leaving the basket of wet clothes behind. When my mother came home and asked about the abandoned clothes, I explained that Shirley had been shooting again, and my mother nodded as if I'd said it had started to rain, my options akin to opening an umbrella or going inside, for there was no option that involved making the rain stop.

"This is crazy," Rachel said the first time she visited my parents' house, a visit that I kicked off with a tour of the bullet holes speckling the back wall. "Why didn't your parents do something?"

Rachel grew up in the suburbs of New York, in an intellectual Jewish family with parents who were refugees from war and violence. Until she met me, Rachel had not known people who discussed guns in a personal way, as objects they owned and fired.

"What could they have done?" I asked, trying to see the bullet holes through her eyes. Until I met Rachel, I had not known people who had never held a gun.

"What could they have done?" Rachel repeated, sounding incredulous. "They could have called the police."

"And what could the police have done?" I said, equally incredulous. "Take the gun?"

"Yes," Rachel said. "They could have taken the gun."

I made a list once—pre-Rachel—a list of the things that I considered nonnegotiable in a partner. It was a short list, reasonable in its expectations. I met Rachel just two months later, at a lesbian potluck of all things. Not long after we moved in together, I read an article in *The New York Times*—back when we used to have it delivered instead of reading it on the computer—about professional matchmakers, all of whom said that the key to successful matchmaking was to pair up people with the same pasts, people who recognized themselves in their potential mate's childhood and family and beliefs: Italian Catholic from Long Island with Italian Catholic from Long Island. People want familiarity in a mate, want to recognize themselves, their youth, in the other person. That's what all the matchmakers said. It's not that I didn't believe this. I did—maybe especially of the sorts who would consult a matchmaker—but I also believed that matching a person with someone who resembled a cousin more than a lover suggested a lack of imagination. Until then, I'd assumed, naïvely I suppose, that most couples were like us, drawn to each other precisely because we were so unfamiliar.

At night, when we lay in bed, Rachel told me stories about her family's arrival in this country, and I listened. Her father and grandparents had fled Russia because they were Mensheviks, one of her stories began; she dropped in *Menshevik* as though the word were common knowledge. This was right after we had sex the first time, so I did not say, "What is a Menshevik?" though later I realized that nobody knew what Mensheviks were, that Mensheviks were not common knowledge, except in the very specific world of Russian Jews in exile.

Her grandparents had first gone to France, where they continued to be Mensheviks, and then came to this country, where they kept on gathering with other Mensheviks. Even after her grandparents were dead and her father had his own family—Rachel, her mother, and her sister—the tradition continued. One of the other Menshevik offspring had a house on the Hudson River where all of them would meet on weekends in the summer to eat and drink vodka and discuss Russia, its past, its future. Once, Stalin's daughter was there, Rachel told me. This was after a different night of sex. She wasn't Jewish, of course, Stalin's daughter, but she was Russian and in exile. Imagine growing up with parents who knew Stalin's daughter. I couldn't imagine it, not at first, but I wanted to, just as she could not imagine parents who rose at dawn, who did not smoke or drink, who did not speak of ideas or question God, his existence or his decisions.

My great-great-grandparents left Sweden in 1867 after the crops had failed yet again, failed because so much rain fell that year that the potatoes rotted in the ground. They left with eight children and arrived in Minnesota a year and half later with five, two of whom eventually continued on to Washington, where they became fishermen, while the other three settled in Minnesota and resumed farming, the two factions forming—or so I like to imagine—a poetic yin-yang of land and sea. According to my father, the Minnesota side never forgave the Washington brothers for choosing water, not after all the misery that water had brought to their family: first, the absence of it, droughts that stole the crops year after year, and then the abundance of it taking their crops yet again, and finally the water that surrounded them during those agonizing weeks at sea as they crouched, vomiting, between decks, and watched three children die.

By the time that I was born in this same small town in Minnesota, my father had long ago given up farming to run a hardware store that he purchased in the late forties, soon after he came home from the war. He had enlisted right out of high school, but when the war ended, he had gone no farther away than Florida, where he was being trained as an airplane mechanic. Something about the experience unsettled him greatly, put him off the world. He came home to this town and never left again. He spoke of this as the best decision he ever made. I suppose that there is a sanity in this, in claiming to want what one has, and yet, perhaps because my father and I were alike in all of the most problematic ways—stubborn yet shy, prone to solitude, sarcastic at moments when it did not behoove us to be so, overly fond of the subterfuge of words—I thought that I understood things about him that others might not: that is, I believed that he was not beyond regret, regret for a life that he—to be fair—never alluded to but that I sometimes imagined for him, college in place of family, in place of us.

For starters, he took no pleasure in family time. Every evening of my childhood, he went back to his hardware store, where he watched television and tended to the books, and though I was relieved at his chronic disinterest in us—for the house took on a different shape when he and his anger were part of it—I wondered at his decision to become a father in the first place, especially as he had waited forty years to begin. Occasionally, well-intentioned people—people who are parents—ask why I do not have children, referring to the fact that I am "good" with children, that I like them. "No," I tell these people. "I like some children." You see, I am selfish, but just unselfish enough to accept that I would not be a good parent. I never wanted to be a parent. In this way, I suspect, my father and I were also alike.

Thus, when he ridiculed me for going far away from this town and the world of hardware and childbearing, I could not help but see his ridicule as an expression of his own remorse. I imagined that my father would someday speak to me with an openness that belied the daily narrative of this place. He never did, so what remains is the narrative, a fairly standard one for those who grew up how and where I did, about hard work and toeing the line. Still, I do not think it possible to tell the story of my father's death without first telling the story of how we came to be in this country, this place, the place my father ran back to, the place I ran away from.

Early in our relationship, Rachel and I decided that the best way to keep our relationship sound was to live a plane flight away from our families. This, we believed, would save us from middle-of-the night phone calls from a parent who needed help relighting the heater or procuring medicine that had "suddenly" run out. Of course, this was a plan built on logic, and middle-of-the-night calls—middle-of-the-night anythings—are not. They are built on the fears that daytime holds at bay, fears that do not keep company with reason. I say this not in a critical way, for I am not impervious to the terror of deepest night, but perhaps I am just hopeful enough, still, to know that morning will come.

The night that my father died, Rachel and I had returned from New Jersey, where we had been visiting her mother, and when we got home, the pet-sitter had refused to leave. She just sat there, telling story after story of all the adorable things our pets had done in our absence, and when she was finally gone, Bettina called, but, by then, we had vowed not to answer the phone for the rest of the evening. I did not even listen to my sister's message, but Rachel said that there was something odd about her tone and that I needed to call her back at once.

Bettina answered in her usual way, a hello and then right down to business. "So, I just talked to Mom, and she said that Dad might be dead."

"Might?" I said, seizing on this as the starting point.

She explained that my mother had called her a few minutes earlier, and when my sister asked, "What's up?"—brusquely because she'd been trying to get my mother to stop calling at the kids' bedtime—my mother had said, "Oh, not much," and then, "Dad's not doing so good." My sister thought this meant that my father's cough had worsened or that he was just being his usual cranky self. "What's wrong with him?" she'd said.

"Well," my mother had said, "he's on the floor, and the paramedics are working on him, but it's been an hour, so I think they think he's dead."

My sister and I were both laughing. Rachel was not.

"Let me know when they're sure," I said.

An hour later, my sister called again. My father was definitely dead.

I would like to say that I did not sleep well that first night back in my old room, but I did. The night before, by way of letting Rachel know that I had arrived, I texted her a photo of the guns lined up beside my bed with the caption "Fresh sheets." I awakened in the morning to a text from her letting me know that she had finally managed to locate a house-sitter—she had given in and called the same loquacious woman we had been unable to get rid of two days earlier—and was on her way to the airport at last. Of the photo and its caption, she said nothing.

Then, I called the neighbor, and he said that he would come

right over to help me with the mattress, but by noon the neighbor had still not arrived. My mother set the table with food that people had dropped off: hotdishes and Jello salads made with walnuts and sour cream and shredded carrots, the kind of food that I had grown up on, that we ate in the basements of churches and brought to others. Protestant food, I described it to Rachel.

The night before, I'd found a pair of suede mittens in a drawer, and I had them on now, despite the heat. I could not eat with them on, but I liked the way they felt.

"What was his last meal?" I asked.

"He had a frozen pizza around five," my mother said. "Then a couple of potpies at six. There was a TV dinner in the oven when he had the heart attack. One of the paramedics smelled it, or it might have burned down the house."

When I was two months old, my father came home from ice fishing one Sunday to find me in the oven. "She wouldn't stop crying," my mother had explained as my father lifted me—like a Thanksgiving turkey!—from the bottom rack.

That was the way my father told the story, making my presence in the oven sound festive. My mother never told the story.

"Did he always eat four dinners?" I asked.

"He didn't actually eat the TV dinner," she said. "Why are you wearing mittens?"

The neighbor arrived then, bringing a jar of sauerkraut made by his wife. He and I turned the mattress on its side and carried it through the house while my mother stood in the entryway holding the door for us. As we passed through, I saw that she was crying, but I said nothing because what came to mind to say was "It's just a mattress soaked in piss." That is the person I am here. When I'm not here, I tell myself that the person I am here is not who I really am. Rachel is the only person who knows both, and that is no small thing.

"Your father was really proud of you girls," the neighbor said.

"I don't think he was *that* proud," I said. My mother cried harder.

The neighbor was Bettina's age—not some old man is my point—and I wanted to say something about his use of "girls," but he'd come in the middle of a busy workday, so I didn't. This, I thought fleetingly, was how injustice grew.

On three, we heaved the mattress into the bed of my father's truck.

"You're pretty strong," said the neighbor. He meant for a girl. "So, did you ever end up getting married?"

"End up?" I said. I understood the way his mind worked.

"You know what I mean," he said.

"Not really," I said. "Anyway, I'm a lesbian, so I can't get married. It's against the law." I knew that he knew I was a lesbian. Everyone in town knew, despite my parents' best efforts.

"Tell Bettina I said hello," he said.

I had forgotten until then that he and my sister had once dated. Not exactly dated—they snuck out at night sometimes and met in the woods between our houses, his the house he still lived in these twenty-five years later. They met in a fort that we had all built together, and when I asked Bettina what she and the neighbor boy did in that fort on the nights they met, she said that they played house, which I had taken to mean that they sat around eating the cans of baked beans that we stole from our parents' cupboard and stocked the fort with so that it would feel real, like a place we could live if we needed to, if the rapture happened or we ran away from home.

I slammed the tailgate of the truck. "Thank you for your help, and thank your wife for the sauerkraut. I'd forgotten how neighborly everyone is."

The neighbor looked at me uncertainly, as if he thought I maybe meant something more by this. "I'm sorry about your father," he said at last.

I'd last seen my sister six months earlier, a visit that ended abruptly because of what happened on Christmas Eve. The evening had unfolded as usual—supper, church, the midnight opening-of-gifts, a progression of events throughout which we acted like just another family together for the holidays, ignoring slights and feigning enthusiasm for our gifts, most of them chosen with little regard for the recipient's taste or needs. Only Rachel was safe from having to pretend, for she never received gifts from anyone in my family.

When I'd pointed this out once, early on, my mother said, "But isn't she Jewish?"

Rachel was Jewish. This did not stop us from spending every other Christmas with her mother in New Jersey, alternating under the pretense of fairness, though I suspected that it was Rachel's way of minimizing the time spent with my family, not because she disliked my family but because she disliked who I was when I was with my family. I felt similarly, so I should have been better disposed toward her position, but mainly I brimmed with unjust thoughts: that if Rachel really loved me, she would love me *most* when I was around my family, saying and doing awful things.

On the night that would turn out to be our father's last Christmas Eve, he sat in his recliner opening gifts: a shirt, gloves, another shirt. He studied each, demanded loudly but of no one in particular, "What do I need this for?" and then, with a solid drop kick, sent it ricocheting off the ceiling and tree while we, his family, continued to unwrap our own disappointing gifts.

For several years, our father had been relearning Swedish, which he had spoken as a child, so in the weeks prior to Christmas, I'd gone to every used bookstore in Albuquerque, searching for something, anything, in Swedish. I'd finally found Zola in hardcover for ten dollars, which seemed like both nothing and a lot, nothing when considered against the fact that it was the seventh bookstore I'd tried, a lot when I stopped to think about how few people in Albuquerque would be interested in Zola to begin with, in Swedish to top it off.

My father tore the wrapping from the book with his usual angry haste, and I braced for the sound of his shoe on hardcover. For several long minutes, he stared at the cover, taking in the words in Swedish, and then he began to read. Eventually, he rose from his recliner and went, with Zola, to his room. He had had enough of Christmas, enough of us.

As my mother scurried around retrieving his gifts and sobbing while the rest of us sat watching her, Bettina turned to me from where she sat on the sofa. "The Swedish book was my idea," she said. "I was the one who said the only thing he cares about anymore is Swedish."

This was true. She had said it during a telephone conversation that summer, not as a gift idea, but as a complaint. She had taken the kids to visit my parents, and our father had barely spoken to any of them. He just lay on his bed listening to Swedish on tape, hitting pause to yell for my nephew and niece when he needed something, another cup of coffee or a jar of herring.

"The important thing," I said, looking up at her from where I sat on the floor, "is that he actually got one gift he didn't kick. What does it matter whose idea it was?"

And just like that, she was on me.

To be clear, I don't condone fighting, but neither do I think it's worse for two women to go at it than two men, even if those two women are "sisters who should love each other," as Rachel kept saying afterward, after she and Carl had pulled us apart and the two of us had gone down to our rec room quarters. When we undressed for bed, she pointed at my arm, at the scratches from the tree that Bettina and I had rolled against, nearly toppling it as we each struggled to get on top.

The next morning when I awoke, Rachel's sofa was empty. I went upstairs, and there they were, the two spouses huddled together at the table, between them the leftover potato sausage from supper, which they began—only then—to eat. When I sat down at the table, they pretended that they had not been talking about what happened the night before. Carl took out a shell casing and showed it to Rachel, who touched it the way one would a talisman, as though it contained power that should not be doubted or taken for granted. Did Rachel even understand what a shell casing was, I wondered, that it was what remained behind, empty, after a gun had been fired?

My brother-in-law was once a large man. He woke up on his twenty-fifth birthday and decided that he did not want to be large any longer, so he picked up the first object he laid eyes on—a shell casing from the top of his dresser—and put it in his pocket. Whenever he felt like eating, he had once told me, he reached into his pocket and the casing acted like an electric shock, the memory of his life as a fat teenager and then a fat man jolting his resolve.

My sister had not known her husband then, and when he told us—my mother, my sister, and me—the story of his weight loss, the way that half his body just melted away, he explained it like this: "When I was twenty-five, I lost my twin brother."

We were driving in his van at the time, and my mother, who was in the passenger seat, turned and stared at him with a stricken look. "Carl," she said, "I didn't know you had a twin."

We all laughed, except my mother, who liked things to mean what they meant.

I knew that clarity often arrived unexpectedly, a moment in which one saw one's life plainly—that it was not working, what needed to be done to fix it—but these moments were fleeting. This was what I admired about my brother-in-law, that he could hold on to his moment of clarity all these years, was still holding on to it.

I sat at the kitchen table with him and Rachel in silence, watching them pretend to enjoy the potato sausage, until Bettina appeared. She went directly to the toaster, inserted a slice of bread, then stood awaiting its transformation.

"Remember when you tried to smother me?" I said.

She laughed. "Of course."

I laughed also.

The first year of my life, Bettina and I had shared a room, the room that now houses my father's guns, the room that Rachel and I are forbidden to sleep in together. This—the story of what happened in that room, which is the story of why Bettina was moved to her own room, the room with the double bed purchased for her and Carl by my parents—was one of the stories that Rachel did know about my childhood, but Rachel did not think the story was funny.

What happened was this: Our mother found Bettina inside my crib one morning, holding a pillow over my face. "I want to smother the baby," she'd explained. She was not yet three, but she knew not only the word *smother* but apparently how smothering worked, for she'd brought a pillow with her when she crawled up and over the railing and into my crib.

"Maybe she meant *mother*," my grandmother said when the adults whispered about it in the years to come. "She heard all this talk of mothering and got the word wrong." Nobody stated the obvious: that *mother* was not a verb, not where we came from.

"She had a pillow over her face," my mother had asserted once. Just once.

As we retold the story that morning, Bettina and I continued to laugh. Our spouses continued not to laugh. They did not approve of the way that our family settled problems: the way that we downplayed one egregious event by invoking a time when our behavior had been even worse. Had the outcome been different, our response might have been different, but you didn't respond to the thing that hadn't happened. You responded to what had, and what had happened was nothing. We were just another family whose members had not killed one another.

We'd never liked each other, my sister and I—who knows why, animosity is nearly always harder to explain than love—and Christmas, with its expectations of good cheer, seemed only to intensify our hostility. Indeed, I could not recall a Christmas when this tradition of ill will had not made itself known. The year that I was ten, Bettina twelve, we were ordered to help with the erecting and trimming of the tree, a task that began with the two of us standing behind our crouching mother, each plotting how to make the endeavor unpleasant for the other, while our mother hacked away at the trunk with a flimsy saw, paring it down to fit into the stand, a tripod with three large screws. Our mother had a vision, I think, of the three of us tightening the screws just so to achieve a perfectly erect tree, of us working together.

As she sawed, I selected a small glass ornament from one of the boxes and put it in my mouth, then smiled at Bettina, my lips pulled back to reveal the smooth green glass.

"Mom, Sybil put a bulb in her mouth," Bettina reported, as I knew she would.

"Sybil, spit out the bulb," our mother said, her weary voice muffled by the tree, and Bettina smiled at me smugly.

I chomped down hard. I had a plan—fuzzy at best—to assert that my sister had smacked the top of my head, causing the bulb to shatter.

My mother stood up. "Spit it out," she said again, cupping her hand beneath my mouth. She did not yet know what I had done.

I opened my mouth wide. I could see the fear in my mother's eyes, feel it in the way that she gripped my head in the vise-like bend of her elbow and worked like a dentist on my mouth, all the while pleading in a loud, panicky voice for me not to swallow.

Just over my mother's shoulder, Bettina peered down at me, smiling.

This was not our first glass scare of the year. The first, just months earlier, was on a Sunday, steak day at our house. After church, Bettina and I set the table, which we managed to do quietly—in deference to our father—though we circled each other warily, using our hips and elbows to force each other aside. Bettina, because she was older, carried the steak knives, marching toward me with the blades pointed out in a game of cutlery chicken. Meanwhile, our mother stood before the oven, its door cracked open as the steaks crackled and smoked beneath the broiler. It was then, as she bent to peer inside, that we heard it: a small pop, our mother's "oh no." The bulb in the oven had exploded.

"A little glass isn't going to kill anyone," said our father when he saw the glittering steaks. "We're not wasting perfectly good meat."

Our mother did not argue. She went into the front yard, held the steaks up beneath the brilliant sun, and—in a dress rehearsal for what she would do with my open mouth just months later—extracted shards. Then she came back inside and set the platter of lukewarm meat on the table, crying just a little. We ate tentatively, except for my father, who acted as though there was nothing he welcomed more than the opportunity to eat glass.

I had not told Rachel either story. I knew what she would say. "How is it possible for a family to have two stories about eating glass?"

Six weeks after the ornament incident, on a morning during which we had been tasked with removing the remaining Christmas decorations, Bettina and I took our Christmas gifts—tennis rackets that we had begged for, separately, after watching Wimbledon on television—and practiced our swings against the tree that our mother had tried, without success, to teach us to erect together. In a rare display of teamwork, we backhanded and lobbed and forehanded until entire boughs of the desiccated tree were bare, their needles embedded so deeply into the shag carpet that the vacuum, which my mother drove frantically around the room, proved useless. Bettina and I spent the afternoon on our knees, extracting needles by hand and dropping them into the large bowl generally reserved for popcorn, but when we went to report that we were finished—arguing about who had done more—we could not find our mother anywhere.

"She's gone," one of us said, and seeing nothing more in our mother's disappearance than possibility, we went into our parents' bedroom to snoop. We tried first to shake quarters out of the large plastic piggy bank in the corner and, after failing, spent several minutes jumping on the bed. Bored, we began opening dresser drawers, looking for something that would shock or appall us, though we did not know what.

"What's that?" Bettina said. We'd both heard it, a sound that seemed to come from beneath the bed.

"Maybe we broke it when we were jumping," I said.

We lay on the mattress and hung our heads over the side. There was our mother, lying perfectly still beneath the bed. She did not turn to look at us, did not acknowledge our presence, and finally Bettina asked, "Are you dead?"

I laughed, not at the thought that she might be dead but at the silliness of the question.

"Go away," said our mother, still not looking at us. "I'm sick of you both."

She began to cry then, and we did not know what to do, so I said to Bettina, "It's your fault," and she replied that it was mine, and we went back and forth like this for several minutes so that we would not have to think about the fact that our mother was lying beneath the bed.

Three hours later, our father's headlights came up the driveway. We always dreaded his arrival because whatever we were doing—watching television, playing games, reading—made him angry. That evening, we were sitting at the table, waiting.

"Just sitting there doing nothing?" he yelled from the entryway as he took off his coat and boots.

We told him that our mother was under the bed.

"Under the bed?" he said, sounding more confused than angry.

"She's hiding," Bettina explained.

"From us," I clarified. "She's tired of us."

"Who isn't?" said our father.

Our father was afraid of nothing. When a noise awakened us in the middle of the night, he got out of bed and went directly toward the source, catching over the years bats and squirrels, even a skunk that had worked its way into the dryer, but that night he stood staring down the hallway toward the room in which our mother, his wife, lay under the bed whose urine-soaked mattress I would find myself removing nearly three decades later. Finally, he turned and went into the living room, where he sat in his recliner, the needleless tree nearby, and read the paper. After a while, our mother came out from under the bed and went into the kitchen, and when supper was ready, we all sat down at the table and ate the meal that she had crawled out to prepare, and we asked nothing about why she had been under the bed to begin with.

It was past two when Rachel pulled up in the driveway. She got out of her rental car, and my mother came out of the house, and they stood ten feet apart, greeting each other like two people on opposite banks of a fast-flowing river. Rachel extended a card, which my mother reached toward her to receive, still holding the door ajar behind her; then, without inviting my partner of eight years to follow, my mother turned and went back inside, where she would add the card to the stack that I had pulled out of the mailbox that morning. I rolled my eyes at Rachel, and she did not roll hers back at me.

Inside, my mother stood beside the pile of cards, and when Rachel asked what she could do to help, my mother told her to open each of them and log the donation amount, and Rachel set down her bag and began—using a steak knife supplied by my mother—to do just that. I sat with her, not asking about her flight or making any of the small talk that people make. I did not want my mother to think we had a relationship that in any way resembled what my mother believed of relationships.

Most of the cards contained two one-dollar bills, but when Rachel opened her own card, I saw that inside was a receipt for a $100 donation to Amnesty International in memory of

Harold Berglund. I did not know which seemed more absurd—the amount or the organization, which my father would have suspected, as he did most charities, of being communist. She looked at me, then slipped the receipt into her pocket, replacing it with two bills. On the log that she was keeping for my mother, she wrote: "Rachel $2."

She made a point to read each of the cards, and I made a point not to. I could not help but feel that the task felt to her anthropological, a study of this place that she often described to others, our friends, with succinctness: "It's the most foreign place I've ever been that does not require a passport."

"What do you think this means?" she asked, and she read from a card that said, "Once we visited your family and Harold told us about the Amish."

"How would I know?" I said, meaning that I did not want to be made the expert.

When we finished, my sister was still not there, so Rachel and I got into my father's truck and drove to the town dump, where we paid a small fee to discard my father's urine-soaked mattress amid appliances and furniture and bags of clothing, the detritus of his neighbors' lives.

"I can't believe this place," Rachel said. "It's so strange to think this is where you're from."

"I'm not actually from the dump," I joked. I tended to fill silences with unfunny comments when things between us were tense, which seemed the case now, even if Rachel had reached over and twirled my hair while I drove. "I did learn to shoot here, though."

This was true. When I was twelve, my father had enrolled me in a gun safety course and we'd practiced here, in this place where we could do little harm because everything around us was beyond fixing.

"Have you talked to Bettina?" Rachel asked.

"Why?" I said.

Rachel sighed. "She's your sister, your only sibling, and you just lost your father."

We climbed out of the truck's cab and into the bed, where we strained to expel the mattress.

"I talked to Carl," she said. "On the phone last night."

"Carl?" I said. "Since when do you and Carl talk on the phone?"

"We're worried," she said.

I wanted to ask which of them had placed the call because that would indicate which of them was more worried, but I knew she would say that it didn't matter who had called. It mattered that they were worried.

"Carl told me about your mother," she said quietly. Quiet definitely meant angry.

"What about my mother?" I said, but I knew what Carl had told her. "The oven wasn't even on," I added, though I imagined she knew this was untrue. I laughed suggestively, but she looked at me as if I were the crazy one.

"It's not funny," she said, and then, "Are you worried?" She meant worried about my mother, now that my father was dead.

"It was a long time ago," I said. "Anyway, that story is none of Carl's business."

"What do you mean?" she said. "He's part of this family."

I thought about the way she said "this family," including herself even though I had done everything I could to make her feel outside my family because I could not imagine her wanting to be inside. I reached into the cab of the truck, behind the seat, where my father kept a rifle and a box of ammunition. "Do you want to try?" I asked, holding out the gun.

Rachel stared—at me, at the gun.

"There's no one around," I said. I pointed at the mattress, which lay where it had landed, propped against a doorless refrigerator. "It's your chance to finally shoot a gun."

I said this as though shooting a gun were something she had

aspired to, a bucket list item that I was giving her the chance to tick off.

Rachel looked around the dump rather than at me, this woman with whom she lived who was now offering her a gun, this woman whose mother had tried to bake her. "How is it that we've been together eight years yet you've never told me that story?" she asked softly.

I walked out into the distance with my father's rifle—away from the mattress, away from Rachel—and knelt behind an abandoned bathtub, loaded the gun, and pressed the butt to my shoulder.

"What are you doing?" Rachel yelled, and I pulled the trigger. Even from a distance, I could see the hole that it tore in the stained yellow mattress.

Each year on my mother's birthday, my father and mother would go into the aisles of the hardware store devoted to household goods, and my father would instruct my mother to pick a gift out for herself. One year, she chose a vacuum cleaner, another year a coffeemaker. "This doesn't seem like a birthday present," I said the year of the Crock-Pot. "It's really a present for the whole house. I mean, we all eat. Plus, it comes from our store, so she already owns it."

I would like to revise history, to claim this comment as a reflection of my nascent feminism, but I know better. I was simply stating the obvious, for I was that sort of child, one who embraced logic (though if I were going to belabor the point, I would note that feminism is simply that: a stating of the obvious). I was ten at the time, still of an age when presents meant something. An appliance was not a gift. I suppose all children feel this way about adults. They watch them stare at the news or listen to them speak of what milk costs today and what it cost a year ago, and feel nothing but amazed horror, and soon enough they stop listening because they understand that from adults nothing interesting can be expected.

After just a few meals, my father had unplugged the Crock-Pot from the wall. "Nothing tastes right," he announced. To be clear, the Crock-Pot had produced meals far better than those on which we usually dined, and I could not imagine that my father did not agree. What I have come to suspect is that he took offense at the very thing that attracted my mother to the Crock-Pot in the first place: it made her life easier.

The next morning, he took the stew-encrusted Crock-Pot with him when he left for work, placing it on the seat of the truck that, all these years later, Rachel and I used to drive his mattress to the dump. This is what it means to have a vertical history: your family arrives in a place and stays, and everything gets built on top of itself so that the dump where you take the mattress might also be the dump where your father took the Crock-Pot all those years earlier, which might also be the dump where your partner, watching you with a rifle pressed to your shoulder, thinks that she has had enough.

She did not actually say that she had had enough. What she said was "I don't understand you people." What she meant was that I was one of *them*.

When we got back to the house, Bettina, Carl, and the kids were there, and Bettina greeted us by saying something about how we should not have run off and left my mother all alone, and I said something about how she should not have taken her own sweet time getting there. Then, we sat down to eat dinner, in silence, but after several minutes Petra, my niece, set down her fork and asked, "Were Sybil and Rachel born together in a big bubble?"

She was seven, trying to make sense of our relationship, of the way that we disappeared into the basement while the rest of the family stayed aboveground. I thought of my mother saying, "Everyone's ashamed of it."

"Yes," I told my niece while the others looked down at their plates. "Rachel and I were born in a bubble, and every day we wait for it to burst."

. . .

The next morning, my mother came into the dining room, where we all sat eating various versions of breakfast, and stood before us holding one of the Bibles from my childhood room, the room she now occupied because I had taken her mattress to the dump and shot it like an old horse being put out of its misery. I preferred to think of my actions that way, as vaguely beneficent. Of course, Rachel was the only person who knew that I'd shot the mattress, and we had not talked about it since. We had not really talked at all. She was waiting for me to explain not just about the mattress but about the fact that, years earlier, my mother had put me in the oven and turned it on, granted with the door ajar, my father arriving and plucking me out before it had time to get hot. Really, though, she was waiting for me to explain why I had not told her any of this.

My mother did not greet us or ask how everyone slept. She simply cleared her throat and began reading to us from the Bible. We all stared at her, not listening exactly, except when she paused to tell us that at night when she and my father lay in bed together, this is what they did. They read scripture. Once, years earlier, when my sister and Carl were first dating, my mother gathered the two of us—her daughters—and explained that sex was only for after marriage, but also that it was very important to marry someone with whom you were sexually compatible. When I pointed out the contradiction her advice involved—for how were you to know that you were marrying a sexually compatible partner if you did not have sex with that person, pre-marriage, to determine it?—my mother became indignant and said that this was why she did not talk to us about such things. We always thought we knew better. Then, with a note of finality, she said, "Your father and I have always been compatible in bed."

All these years later, I no more wanted to know that they read Bible verses in bed than that they had sex. I did not want to hear about the intimacies of their relationship. That is what it came down to.

Rachel is a nurse, which means that she knows how to take charge and provide comfort, so as our mother stood in the middle of the dining room, reading from the Bible and sobbing, and Bettina and I looked away in Protestant embarrassment, Rachel said, "That's lovely. I think it would be nice for the service."

We were leaving soon to meet with the minister, who was not the minister of my youth, that benign figure who had overseen my baptism and confirmation, the singular most interesting thing about him being that he wore platform shoes because there was some notion that he would be better served by height, that parishioners did not want to look down on their pastor. This new minister, my mother had told me repeatedly, led letter-writing campaigns to stop other Lutherans from embracing homosexuality. Who were these Lutherans that they were writing to, I had wondered. Was there a mailing list of homosexuality-embracing Lutherans?

"What is the purpose of this meeting with the pastor?" I asked warily.

My mother stopped sobbing but continued to stand before us in her frayed robe, the Bible aloft in her hands. *Apostolic* was the word that came to mind, though I knew that this was anachronistic thinking. The Apostles had not had Bibles because the Apostles wrote the Bible.

"We have to talk about our ideas for the service," my mother replied. "You know, your father's favorite hymns and verses. Maybe you girls have some anecdotes for the eulogy."

"What does *eulogy* mean?" my nephew asked. Lars was nine, the sort of child who liked words purely for the pleasure of knowing them—not as weapons, that is. The adults looked at him the way that adults often look at children who ask perfectly good questions.

I said, "In Greek, *eu* means 'good' or 'true' and *logos* means 'word,' so 'good word.'"

You see, I did regard words as weapons; early on, when I was first figuring out who I was in the world, I decided to make myself unassailable—unassailable in my new life, that is, the world of books and words and people for whom education was generational, a given—and so I became a student of grammar and etymology, both of which had contributed to my "brogue" and my very specific and unlucrative skill set.

My nephew appreciated my response, as I knew he would. Children like to be taken seriously. "Does that mean that they can't lie about grandpa?" he asked, and I said that, on the contrary, lying was generally required in eulogies, that it is nearly impossible to speak words that are at once good and true about any of us.

Needless to say, I was not keen to meet the new minister. Bettina said that he was fine, but Bettina had a tendency to set the bar low and also to enjoy the low-hanging fruit of normalcy that heterosexuality conferred upon her. The spouses remained behind with strict orders to keep the children out of my room, which was now my mother's room and—more to the point—the room that housed my father's hunting rifles, so it was just the three of us knocking at the pastor's office door. He immediately called out for us to enter, not pausing the way that people usually do as they shift from their private to their public selves.

As we pushed open the door, an overwhelming stench greeted us, leapt at us like a badly trained dog meeting guests. Perhaps the minister had been snacking on cheese, I thought, the stinky kind, but the minister explained, without being asked and with disturbing unselfconsciousness, that it was his feet we smelled. My mother responded to this news as though it were not news at all—as though her pastor's foot odor was common knowledge. She shook her head sympathetically and told him that the whole prayer chain had been working on it.

"You've been praying about his feet?" I said.

When I was young, the phone rang frequently with such requests, mainly involving illnesses and accidents. Even then, I was an inveterate eavesdropper, so I knew the drill. Before sitting down to pray, my mother dialed the next three members of the chain and described the nature of the request—a church member with a weak heart or Delphin Bergstrom's brother, who had run over his bare foot with the lawn mower. Regarding the chain, two things struck me: that a prayer chain seemed nothing more than God-sanctioned gossip, and that the most interesting subjects of it lived elsewhere—a nephew in Fargo who had begun tattooing his body with strange symbols; a brother-in-law who had been arrested in a park in St. Paul. I had tried to imagine what could be done in a park that required the police or prayer or the hushed tones with which my mother spoke of it to others, but I could not, nor could I ask my mother, who had already explained that some requests were almost beyond prayer. Once, my mother caught me listening and suggested that I join in. "The more prayers the better," she said. I asked whether God had a number in mind, but she said that praying did not work that way—did not require a consensus of opinion—which I imagined was part of its attraction.

"It means a lot to me that your mother and the other ladies pray for my feet like this," the pastor said solely to me, and then he turned to my mother. "The doctor says it's probably some sort of fungus, and the hot weather's sure not helping."

The three of us were still standing, but instead of inviting us to sit down, the pastor rose and came out from behind his desk. He was barefoot.

"Maybe we can get down to business," I said, because I feared where this was headed: the four of us, heads bowed, hands joined as we prayed together for what? Less humidity?

"Business?" said the pastor.

"I mean my father's funeral."

"Oh, yes. There's plenty of time for that," he said, "but I hope you won't mind if I offer my condolences first?" He opened his arms wide and asked whether he might hug me specifically, as though I were the only one with someone dead.

Mine was not a world of huggers but of people who greeted

one another from a duelers' distance, twenty paces, so I suspected that his plan was to draw me in and hoodwink me into letting down my guard, at which point he would turn the conversation to that whole trite dichotomy of sin versus sinners—of hating one and loving the other—which would end with me saying that, first of all, sin was a construct, and that moreover the two were inextricable: how could a sin even exist if there was not a body to accommodate it? It was like the fungus on his feet, in need of a host.

This was a conversation that would not end well. I knew that. So as he lunged confidently forward, I stepped swiftly aside, directly onto his foot, his funky, fungus-ridden foot. He yelped, and Bettina laughed, and my mother looked at once horrified and ashamed, as though she could not believe the hand God had dealt her—burdened with a clumsy, solicitude-adverse lesbian of a daughter.

"My mother has ideas for Bible verses," I offered instructively, and the pastor limped back behind his desk. The three of us, taking this as a cue to be seated finally, settled on the folding chairs arranged before it. "And I've got an anecdote," I added, looking at neither my mother nor my sister before I plunged ahead:

"We used to have steak every Sunday after church, and one Sunday the bulb in the oven blew. The steak was covered with glass, but my father made us eat it anyway. He said he wasn't going to sit by and watch us waste good food."

The pastor studied me for a very long time. It was a sympathetic look—I could see that, could see that my anecdote or possibly the fact that I felt driven to offer it stirred in him feelings of pity, but just as I understood the absurdity in speaking of sin as separate from sinner, it struck me as impossible to accept this sympathy as sincere, proffered as it was by someone whose life's work was to make my life more difficult.

"Can I pray for you?" he said.

"I'd prefer that you didn't," I said.

"I will anyway," he said.

. . .

Rachel and Carl were at the dining room table with the kids, all four of them drawing. I sat down and took a sip from Rachel's coffee, and Petra said, "Look, Aunt Sybil. I drew you and Rachel in the bubble." She held up a piece of cardboard on which she had sketched two stick figures with breasts holding hands inside a clumsily drawn circle.

"I love it," I said. I did love it.

"Rachel said she's going to frame it and hang it in your bedroom so it's the first thing you guys see every morning when you wake up."

"Well, if Rachel said it, then it must be true. Rachel does not lie."

Rachel gave me a sharp look, as though she thought I meant something more by this, but I didn't. Rachel does not lie.

"Care to descend with me into the Infernal Region?" I said to Rachel, which was how we referred to the basement—hell, Hades, the Infernal Region—and she rose from the table, promised Petra that she would be back up to claim her drawing, and together we descended.

"How were things while we were gone?" I asked. Really I wanted her to ask me how things had gone with the pastor, but Rachel instead chose to answer my question.

"Carl is a mensch," she said.

"A mensch?" I said.

She started to explain what a mensch was, and I said that I knew what a mensch was, that my consternation had to do with the fact that I had never once in all of the years we were together heard her use *mensch,* or really anything Yiddish for that matter.

"I use *schlepp* all the time," she said.

"You do," I agreed, "and your response has confirmed my point."

"How does proving to you that you have heard me use Yiddish somehow prove that you have not?" she asked.

"Because you know I'm right, so you reverted to the exception."

"Okay," she said. "I get it. You're mad that Carl and I are friends."

"I'm not mad," I said. "I'm not."

"Okay."

"Anyway, you're not friends. You're in-laws."

"The two outsiders, you mean. Is that your point?"

"I don't really have a point," I said. As far as I knew, I didn't.

"You don't have a point, and yet here we are, talking about why I don't have the right to call Carl a mensch or a friend."

"I'd hardly call that a point," I said.

"I give up," she said. "I hate coming here. It's like you disappear right in front of me."

"You mean that I become one of 'you people'?" The sentence was a syntactical mess. I knew that.

"So that's what you're mad about? That I said I don't understand *you people*?"

I had hoped that she would not understand my reference, which would mean that her comment at the dump the day before was nothing more than a fleeting moment of frustration, but she did remember, and this gave it import. "I told you I'm not mad," I said again.

"That doesn't mean you aren't. It means you don't want to accept that you're mad. What I don't understand, I guess, is who you're mad at. Me or them?"

"The meeting was all a setup," I said, and when she looked confused, I clarified, "Just now. With the pastor."

"What do you mean a setup?" she asked.

"To get me in the anti-homosexual letter-writing pastor's office so that he could exorcize my Sapphic demons."

Rachel laughed, and though I had meant for her to laugh, her laughter galled me.

"It's not funny," I said.

"So what are you saying? That your father's death was purely strategic, a tactical move designed to get you back here and into that man's office?" Her tone was at once incredulous and amused.

"It's possible," I said.

"Yes," she said, "I guess anything is possible."

I hated when she said stuff like this, placating clichés that meant I was being ridiculous, and hated it even more when I knew I was being ridiculous.

"Do you remember the shell casing that Carl showed you?" I said.

"What are you talking about?"

"The shell casing that your mensch friend Carl showed you at Christmas? Remember when I came upstairs and the two of you were talking about how crazy your spouses were, and then he showed you the shell casing that he carries to remind him not to give in to temptation?"

"The talisman?" she said.

"Yes, the talisman. It's from a gun, you know."

I could see from her face that she did not know.

"How would I know that?" she said. "I know nothing about guns. You know that."

"So Carl didn't tell you where that shell casing came from?" And then I proceeded to tell her the story of Carl's uncle, how Carl had gotten off the school bus one afternoon and come home to find his mother and sister in the kitchen drinking coffee. "You'll need to clean up the mess," his mother had said, nodding toward the living room. The mess was his uncle. While Carl was at school that day, his uncle had shot himself in the head.

I looked over at Rachel, who was lying on her sofa, perfectly still, breathing in and out, in and out.

"So, you see, Carl is just as crazy as the rest of us. He's one of us."

"Okay," she said.

I looked away. "Okay," I replied.

. . .

Fathers die first. Rachel and I both knew this to be true. Her father had died four years earlier, after several months of rapid decline. Just before he died, he announced that he and Rachel's mother would be moving out of the family home, the house in which Rachel and her sister had grown up, and into one of those upscale retirement residences in a neighboring suburb. We could not imagine him in such a place, so we knew what this meant: that he was ready to die and that even now, at the end of his life, he was doing what he had done throughout it, taking care of Rachel's mother, who lacked skills of the sort that would have allowed her to continue on in that house alone. She did not drive, never had, mainly because she lacked any spatial sense whatsoever, including the ability to find her way home amid the familiar topography of a place where she had spent most of her adult life, nor did she know how to shop for groceries or how to combine the discrete elements of the refrigerator and cupboard into the simplest of meals. Within weeks of completing the move, Rachel's father got pneumonia and rode it down.

Now, when we visited Rachel's mother, we stayed in one of the guest suites at the retirement residence, a place that was like a cruise ship—people eating and playing bridge, socializing and hooking up on the sly—except on this cruise ship everyone was old and Jewish, and they never set sail. Rachel, her mother, and I ate breakfast each morning with her mother's three usual breakfast companions, all six of us wedged in around a table meant for four, while her mother's friends tried to remember whether Rachel was Rachel or her sister.

"And who are you?" they asked me each time.

"Rachel's friend," her mother replied each time, in a way that made clear that she had not told them about Rachel.

Once, I suggested to Rachel, unhelpfully perhaps, that maybe this wasn't proof of her mother's disapproval so much as her mother's general lack of interest in her life. "They probably don't know you're a nurse either," I'd added.

On our last visit, the one we returned from the day that my

father died, one of the servers came over and scolded us for having too many people at our table. Even one extra chair at the table was not safe, she said, and we had two. I stood up to move, but one of the women ordered me to sit down. She said this loudly. These women said everything loudly. Just a few minutes earlier, they had pointed to a woman at the table next to ours who was missing an arm. "Look," they screamed. "She's missing an arm but you'd never know it, the way she eats." Everyone turned to look at the amazing one-armed woman who was eating her eggs like someone with two arms.

One of the breakfast companions, Helga, was reading a book as thick as an encyclopedia, which turned out to be one of those large-print tomes. In addition to her eyesight, Helga's memory was going, just the short-term, which meant that she could talk as though it had happened yesterday about walking, orphaned, back to Berlin after the camps were liberated; about arriving in England and going to live with a family that refused to let her speak, ever, of her life before she came to them. She did not hold it against them, she said, because that was the way people thought then, that life was best treated as a series of doors slamming shut behind you. She could remember that her sons were both dead and that she had wanted girls, that her husband, who was also dead, once baked a birthday cake for her out of potatoes.

A man pulled up a chair—a seventh chair!—and sat down. "You've been reading that book forever," he said to Helga. Rachel's mother had told us about this man. His name was Saul, and he was courting someone at the table, though they did not know which of them it was.

"Yes," Helga said. "That's the good thing about not being able to remember what I read yesterday. I just start over on page one every morning, and it feels like a new book." We all laughed, and Helga looked pleased. I thought about this, about how her brain did not forget that she was funny, did not forget the subtleties of delivery or perspective that contributed to humor.

Saul read the title of Helga's book aloud. "*The Good German?*

Does such a thing exist?" he asked, and the women laughed. I laughed.

Rachel gave me a look. "What?" I said. "I'm not German."

"I'll have orange juice," Helga told the server who had scolded us, and Rachel's mother reminded her that she had given up orange juice because it was hard on her stomach.

"Is that right?" she said thoughtfully, as though being introduced to some delightful fact about someone who was not her. "Grapefruit juice?" she said then, uncertainly, and Rachel's mother gave a small shake of her head.

"You hate grapefruit," she said. "You better stick with the cranberry."

Helga turned to the server and said brightly, "I will stick with the cranberry."

How did it feel, I had wondered, to exist, increasingly, from outside oneself, to rely on others to tell you who you were, to lose the secrets that you had told no one, the secrets that defined who you were, for better or worse, because they belonged only to you.

The morning of my father's funeral, I woke up on my sofa and turned to Rachel on hers. "Did you bring the purse?" I asked.

Normally, we had pockets, which was another lesbian thing about us, not that straight women don't have pockets, but lesbians seem more likely to prioritize practicality over fashion. Every once in a while, though, we went somewhere in clothes without pockets—the opera, for example—and for those occasions, we had the purse. We called it "the purse" because it did not belong to either of us, which meant that often we would arrive back at our car and realize that everything we needed, beginning with our car keys, was in the purse and the purse was somewhere else, usually under the seats that we had just occupied. We would argue about whose fault it was, but it was both of our faults and neither. That is the reassuring part of having a collective purse, a collective anything, I suppose.

Rachel sat up on her sofa and said that she had not brought the purse. What she actually said was "You didn't tell me to bring the purse." She still felt some sort of way about the events of the last few days.

It was true that I had not asked her to bring the purse. I had not thought about the purse until that very moment, when I woke up the day of my father's funeral and saw dangling haphazardly from an unused nail the skirt that I had emergency-purchased the evening before. It was long and drab and pocketless, and I had already determined that I had no need of it in my regular life. I would leave it here, hanging in the closet of my childhood room for when I needed it the next time: when I returned to bury my mother.

Already, the day was humid, and what came to mind was the pastor's feet. I did not want to be thinking about his feet, certainly not now, hours before my father's funeral, but once I started, I could not stop. Everything reminded me of them—the constant patter and thump of my family above us, the rancid moisturizer that Rachel found in the bathroom, shoes, oatmeal, the buttermilky tang of the kitchen sponge.

Around ten, we loaded everyone into Bettina and Carl's van and Rachel's rental car, because they were parked last in the driveway, and we drove the three miles into town. My mother insisted on riding in the van, and I did not argue with her, even though I knew it was because she did not want to arrive at the church in a car driven by lesbians. The businesses in town—there were only six or seven of them—were all closed for two hours to give the 418 people enumerated on the population sign the opportunity to attend my father's funeral; my parents had owned their store for fifty-five years, so they were known.

My parents' store—Berglund Hardware—was permanently closed. The sign on the door read CLOSED UNTIL FURTHER NOTICE, but everyone knew what that meant. My father had planned to keep it going until he died, but a few years earlier, he had begun sleeping much of the day, not out of laziness but because his body's needs had shifted—he was like a cat, napping for hours and then awakening to a terrible desire for protein. The preceding winter, just two days before we wrestled beneath the Christmas tree, Bettina and I had staged an intervention. We told our father that our mother was too old to keep the store going, biting our tongues to keep from adding "by herself," though that was what it had come down to. Our father was not ready to let go of it, for reasons that were probably symbolic but felt to us like hubris. He accused us of meddling in their marriage. While we pleaded with him to consider the burden that it placed on our mother, she sat in the other room. She knew what we were up to, but she did not know how to say these things herself. "Lunchtime," she called out instead, working against herself. Bettina and I had given up, accepted failure, gone into the kitchen to eat. We did not speak of it again. Then, months later, it became clear to us that the store was closed. There had been no formal announcement by either of them, just the use of past tense instead of present when they referred to it.

Halfway through the service, I feared that I had not silenced my ringer. I took out my phone, the eyes of the congregation on me. I believed that they thought of me—on the rare occasion that they did think of me—as someone who had left a place she considered herself too good for, which is to say that that morning they looked at me, phone in hand, and surely saw a woman bored by her own father's funeral.

I began to laugh. Beside me, Rachel turned, which only made me laugh harder.

The minister, busy eulogizing, announced that he had a story about my father, a memory that the deceased's younger daughter had shared with him the day before, a memory that said a lot about who Harold Berglund was. I stopped laughing.

"Every Sunday after church, the Berglunds had steak." From his pulpit, the minister looked around the church. "Every Sunday," he repeated. He nodded deeply, at once sanctioning the story and letting us know that it was over.

I began to laugh again, and soon my sister joined in. Rachel once more turned to regard me, to regard us both.

Those were the good words about my father. And why not? Every Sunday we had eaten steak. Only once had there been glass.

When Rachel told me that I needed to talk to my sister, truly talk to her, I was not troubled. That is, I did not read into her suggestion anything that seemed to imperil the agreement to keep our families at bay that we had made all those years earlier. It was the day after my father's funeral, and we were standing out in the driveway, wedged between her rental car and my father's truck. She was going home to our dog and cats, leaving me behind with my mother who did not think that I had a family to go home to. Bettina, Carl, and the kids were leaving also, and when I pointed out to Rachel the unfairness of this, that my sister had come late and was leaving early, Rachel said that I needed to consider that children, even those as delightful as my niece and nephew, were not always what one—by which she meant my mother—wanted to deal with in the midst of grief.

"I mean it," she said. "Talk to Bettina. Soon it will be just the two of you."

I was staying, simply put, because my mother did not seem capable of being alone. I watched her banging through her new life, lost amid the detritus of the past; it was a lostness that I at least recognized, an unmoored look in her eyes that she used to get on the rare occasion that my father had to be away. My parents did not take vacations, but each fall my father drove off with a group of other men from town to hunt. They would be gone for two or three nights, and each time my grandfather came to stay. Later, I would realize that my grandfather came because it was understood—by everyone but Bettina and me—that my mother could not be left alone with us, could not be left alone with herself.

But Bettina and I did not sit down and talk, at least not then, because even as Rachel and I were saying goodbye, Bettina and Carl and the kids came out and said that they were also hitting the road. The kids laughed because they thought that "hitting the road" was funny, and then they both flopped down on the driveway and proceeded to pummel it with their fists and scream, "I'm hitting the road. Look! I'm hitting the road!"

Rachel glanced over at me as if to say, *You see?*

I had been waiting to see how Rachel would say goodbye, whether she would tell me she loved me or skip that part, and whether I would believe it to still be true either way, but then the kids got up from the driveway—well, were yanked up—and before I knew it, everyone was driving away except me.

That night we sat alone together—my mother and I—she at the table eating microwave popcorn and reading her Bible. One of her Bibles.

"I'm going to call Rachel," I announced, and stood up, and she looked at me as though she had no idea what I was talking about. "Rachel," I said again. "My partner. The woman I have been with for eight years." I huffed off, down to the basement.

I did not call, of course, even though I wanted to know that she had arrived home safely, wanted to know how Gertrude and Alice and Frederick the dog were doing, whether they missed me. But I was waiting for *her* to call, and I fell asleep waiting—fell asleep on Rachel's sofa, which was where I had decided to sleep because the basement frightened me in ways that it did not when Rachel was there with me.

Deep in the night, my cell phone rang and I sat up, thinking it was her, but it was my mother's voice whispering into my ear: "Someone's here. There's a car in the driveway. I'm scared, and your father's gone."

It was not clear which meaning of *gone* she had in mind—whether she thought that my father was off hunting or whether she knew that he was dead.

"I need you to come home," she said. "Right now."

I started to say, "I am home," but caught myself. "I am here," I said instead, worrying about semantics even as my mother was going crazy above me.

"I've got the gun," she said.

"Which gun?" I asked softly.

"The pistol," she said, referring to the gun that my father had always kept, loaded, above the stove, believing that his children would never be stupid enough to touch it. It turned out I was stupid enough. The Sunday we ate glass, after our parents disappeared into the bedroom to rest, I climbed up on the stove and stood with my feet on the burners that were still warm from string beans and potatoes and took down the loaded pistol, two stupidities rolled into one. I pointed this gun at any number of things—the toaster, the relentlessly dripping faucet, a loaf of whole wheat bread—and when my sister came in from outside and saw me there, standing atop the stove with the gun that we were forbidden to touch, she said, "I'm telling," and I turned the pistol on her.

"That gun is loaded," I said, speaking loudly this time, fearfully.

"They're in the basement!" my mother cried out, both into my ear and through the floorboards. "I hear them talking."

"There is no one down there," I said, whispering again.

And she said, "I'm going down."

"Do not go down there," I said. "Do not."

We were both silent for a moment. Above me, she paced.

"I'll call the police," I told her at last, and hung up, and then I called Rachel, who answered on the fifth ring, sounding not at all groggy, though it was after midnight back home. I described the situation—that my mother had become confused and mistaken my rental car for the car of a stranger, an intruder whom she believed to be in her house at this very moment.

"She's got the pistol," I said, but the pistol was one more story I had not told Rachel, one more story at which she would not have laughed. I wanted her to laugh, even though I could see what laughing meant, how it allowed us to live with everything that was wrong. I backtracked to explain only that such a pistol existed, that my mother was holding that pistol now.

"Do not go up there," Rachel said. "Whatever you do, do not go up there." On the other end of the line, in our home miles and miles away, Rachel began to cry.

"I won't go up there," I said, but she did not stop crying. "Hey, I'm sleeping on your sofa," I said.

"Are you all crazy?" she said. She wanted an answer.

"Yes," I said. "We are all crazy." But she only cried harder.

We will steal the gun together, Bettina and I. That is what we decide when I call her at dawn after a sleepless night spent listening to my mother above me. My task will be to get the gun, to physically remove it from my mother's room, my old room, and then baton it off to my sister, who will take it away with her, though not home to the house where she lives with children whose heads none of us want blown off. My sister says she cannot be the one to take the gun for reasons having to do with the Ten Commandments—the one about stealing, I wonder, or about obeying your mother and father?—and I cannot be the one to dispose of it, for reasons having to do with the fact that neither I nor anyone I know possesses knowledge of this sort. And so, my sister and I will work together.

My mother does not seem surprised to see me when I come up for breakfast, nor does she mention her middle-of-the-night call. She is in her robe, the one that had seemed apostolic just days earlier, but now seems simply ratty. She is not carrying the pistol. I do not mention that Bettina is coming, but when she pulls into the driveway at lunchtime, my mother says, "You see? Your sister is here." Perhaps she has been expecting her all along. Perhaps in some tucked-away corner of her brain, you called one daughter and both appeared.

Then, while Bettina distracts our mother, I go into her bedroom, my old bedroom, and rummage around. The six rifles still stand at attention; the kneeling child still prays over them. If my mother discovers me, my plan is to pick up one of the Bibles and pretend to be reading it. She will believe it because she will want to believe it. But my mother does not come in and I do not find the gun. When I'm about to give up, I kneel beside the bed, like the girl in the picture, like the girl I used to be. In this way, my trip has symmetry: it begins and ends with me kneeling.

I lean sideways. Beneath the bed are old newspapers and shoes, broken toasters and irons, boxes of ammunition, presumably for the six guns leaning against the wall, but it's hard to know whether the ammunition was placed there with proximity in mind, or simply abandoned there years ago for no other reason than that there was space.

What there is not is the pistol.

As I rise, my arm rests briefly atop the bed, atop something hard. I pull back the blanket: nestled like a kitten or a hot water bottle is the loaded gun.

"Have you heard of the Mandela effect?" I ask Bettina.

Four hours have passed since she arrived, four hours during which we ate lunch and stole a gun, and now Bettina and I are standing in the driveway, pretending to say goodbye but really trying to hand off the pistol. If there is anything that should make my mother suspicious, it is this, her two daughters making a point to bid each other farewell.

As I waited for my sister to arrive this morning, I graded papers, for though a substitute was covering my four freshman composition classes, the grading was all mine. The assignment was to write about something they knew nothing about, something they had never even heard of before, an assignment that angered them greatly, for how—they had wondered aloud at the beginning and middle and end of each class for two solid weeks—were they supposed to arrive at a topic they did not even know existed. In response, I said all of the annoying things that they expected me to say: that instead of asking this same question over and over, they should simply get started, that this was meant to be an exercise in exploration or learning or curiosity, that they had come into this world knowing nothing and look at them now. Of the one hundred and three papers submitted, only one introduced me to something new: the Mandela effect.

Bettina says that she has not heard of it, glancing past my shoulder at the doorway, and I say, "It's when a whole group of people remembers something that never actually happened, a collective false memory, like Mandela dying in prison."

"He did die in prison," my sister says.

"No, he didn't," I say. "That's the point. He got out and became the president of South Africa."

She is quiet for a moment, not thinking about Mandela specifically, I suspect, because my sister is not the sort to know much about Mandela, but wondering why I have brought this up now, as we stand here attempting to pass off my mother's loaded gun. My sister likes to figure out what people are thinking and why, without having to ask, though eventually she will ask.

"Why are you telling me about this right now?" she says.

"I don't know." This is true. Partly true. "I guess I'm just trying to imagine what it's like to have a memory that you're so sure of, and that all these other people have also, but the memory's wrong. I mean, how is it possible that all over the world people share the memory of Mandela dying in prison?"

"And?" she says.

"Sometimes, I think we're like that."

"We?" she says. She knows that I am referring to our family, though not whether I mean all four of us, or just me and her. "What memories do we have that aren't true?"

She is right. We are the opposite: a family with memories so true, so vivid, we rarely dare to recall them.

I say, "Remember when Mom put me in the oven, and Dad came home and took me out?"

"Like a Thanksgiving turkey," Bettina says.

Rachel believes that I did not tell her this story because of her, but the truth, I realize only now, is this: the child's mind cannot live in a constant state of contradiction. I could not sit down at the table each day of my childhood to eat the food that had come from that oven—food that had been prepared and placed inside it by my mother—unless I chose not to think about the fact that, once, my mother had placed me in that same oven and turned it on. In this way, perhaps childhood always involves a degree of Stockholm syndrome.

"I like Rachel," Bettina says then, as if she is reading my mind.

"I like Carl," I reply, even though I know that compliments given in response to compliments always sound insincere. But it's true. I do like Carl. Carl is a mensch. He grew up with his own crazy family, but he is still willing to deal with ours. This is probably how it will always be with my sister: we will always like each other's spouses better than we like each other. We will always exist at this one degree of separation.

I look back over my shoulder at the house to make sure that my mother is not watching, and then I slip the gun out of my hoodie pocket and hold it out to my sister, and we stand like that for a moment—me holding the gun, her on the other end of it—and I know that we are reliving the same moment.

Then, she takes the gun, opens the large tote bag that she brought with her for this very purpose, drops the gun inside, and extracts a cardboard tube, which she holds out to me.

"I promised Petra that I wouldn't forget, and then I nearly did," she says. "Petra was very upset that she forgot to give this to Rachel."

Later, I will take the drawing out of the tube and unfurl it, and I will see that Petra has made some changes. Rachel and I are still there, of course, two stick figures with breasts, but Petra has added two cats and a dog, and has fortified the circle around us with a series of thick crayon lines. Across the top she has written *The Bubble Family*. This is how Petra sees us, I think. We are just another family.

I take the tube with my niece's drawing from my sister. "Well," I say. "A gun for a drawing."

Bettina laughs, and I laugh. It's a good trade.

Tomorrow, I will leave behind my mother and her failing mind and go home to the bubble that has still not burst and tell the woman I love the story of this place, which is the story of who I am:

The father who plucked me from the oven fed us steak peppered with glass, and the mother who placed me in that oven removed that glass, shard by shard, in the bright light of a Sunday afternoon.

Above that oven was a loaded gun, and it was meant to keep us safe.

Once, I pointed that gun at my sister, but did not pull the trigger.

Once, my sister tried to smother me.

Once, together, my sister and I stole a gun. We left six more behind.

Ehsaneh Sadr

Mornings at the Ministry

It was the memory of Ms. Musavi's arrogant eyebrows, rising up toward her chador like two sideways parentheses, that made Amir lift a hand to strike his twelve-year-old daughter for the first time.

Amir and his wife, Seema, had never hit their children, not even a light slap of the hand when chubby fingers reached for something dangerous. Amir himself had grown up with plenty of well-deserved smacks, a few twisted ears, and even a hard kick to the rear once when his father was trying to break up a sibling tussle. So he'd been surprised to discover, when he became a parent, that he simply couldn't bring himself to inflict physical pain on the small beings in his care. And he was grateful that his wife felt the same, in part because the children were Seyed-e Tabatabaee, descendants of the Prophet through both parents. To hit them would be wrong, she said. It would be like injuring the Prophet himself—peace and blessings be upon him and his family.

Besides, Amir and Seema had been lucky to have good kids, who were quite responsive to gentler forms of discipline. Even the two boys, more rambunctious than Fatimeh by far, were easily extricated from inevitable conflicts without any need for violence.

If they fought over a toy, it was simply taken away. If they hit each other, they were separated until they cried to play together again.

When the boys were ten and eleven, Mohammad came home one day with a swollen cheek from a classmate who'd heard the boys had never been beaten by their father. Over dinner, Mohammad described how the boy had said that they needed to know what a good licking felt like. Morteza, younger than Mohammad by only fourteen months, leaned his head onto Amir's shoulder and said, "I'm glad we don't have hitting at our house," while dear little Fatimeh—then a precocious five-year-old—stood on her chair, chanting "No hitting! No hitting!" and waving her hands like an orchestra conductor until everyone sang along.

And yet, hitting his beloved only daughter was exactly what Amir now found himself compelled to do. Fatimeh would one day be a Ms. Musavi, in name as well as prospects, and Amir was determined to save her from the other Ms. Musavi's fate.

Ms. Musavi and Amir shared the same last name, although they weren't related. They'd met when they overlapped at the University of Melbourne during Amir's last year. At the time, Amir and Seema had been so overwhelmed with school and their baby boys that they hadn't been as welcoming as they'd have liked to the new Iranian student whose headscarf indicated that she shared their loyalty to religion and culture, even outside the country. They'd never even gotten around to having her over for a meal before they returned to Tehran, earlier than planned, so Seema could have the help and support of her family as Amir finished his dissertation from afar.

Five years later, Amir had been surprised to see Ms. Musavi introduced at the weekly staff meeting of the Ministry of Reconstruction Jihad's Rural Research Center. The surprise wasn't just at the unexpected—but welcome—crossing of paths with an old acquaintance; no one had bothered to tell him that his division would be expanding. It was great news, but he'd have appreciated a heads-up to prepare the team, particularly as Khanoom Doktor Azadeh Musavi was joining as a research specialist, level III. New PhDs usually started no higher than a level II. When Amir himself had joined the RRC, it had only been as a research specialist, level I. He'd worked hard to prove himself before moving up the two additional levels and becoming the division lead for the level IIIs.

Of course, unlike Ms. Musavi, Amir hadn't come on board as a full PhD. When he and Seema had returned to Tehran, he'd thought it would take six months, at most, to finish his dissertation. But his professor had ambushed him with additional research demands after Amir had submitted what he thought was the final draft. Between work and family, it took another two years to finally become a *doktor*.

Amir went out of his way to help Ms. Musavi settle in. He introduced her to her new colleagues, he showed her around the library, and he made sure she got one of the new roller chairs with levers to adjust seat height, armrests, and even the tilt of the cushions. Amir had suffered for years in a Soviet-style steel chair with the stuffing leaking out of its mustard-colored nylon backing before the new ones were made available to those with the most seniority. But Ms. Musavi, as the only woman in their division, deserved some additional comforts.

"I don't know how she does it," Seema said when Amir told her about Ms. Musavi that night, as they were getting into bed. "Wearing a heavy chador all day long around those men! If I was going to work outside the house, I'd get a job at a women's spa or girls' school, where I could be comfortable."

Amir yawned as he leaned against his pillows. "A women's spa probably doesn't need a specialist in rural economics."

"Is it confusing having two Dr. Musavis at the office?" Seema asked, brushing her long hair out as she always did before bed.

Amir chuckled. "Not really. I'm Dr. Musavi and she's Khanoom Doktor Musavi."

"That makes it sound like she's your wife," Seema sniffed, setting the hairbrush down on the vanity table.

Seema was right. *Khanoom doktor* could mean "wife of the doctor," and Seema herself was often called Khanoom Doktor Musavi. But it could also mean "lady doctor," signifying a woman who had attained the rank of a doctor. In the context of the ministry, it was a useful way of differentiating between Amir and his new colleague.

"And how did she end up a level III, anyway?" Seema asked as she took off her house robe and clambered into bed beside Amir. "Does she know someone?"

"See, now you're just being sexist, assuming a woman can't get ahead on her own," Amir chided as he pulled his wife near, enjoying the feel of her silky nightgown over her swelling belly and wondering if baby number three would be the girl they were hoping for, the girl they would name Fatimeh after the beloved Prophet's daughter. "Maybe she's just exceptionally smart and talented."

"Oooh, you seem to admire Ms. Musavi a great deal," Seema said, beating on his chest lightly with one fist.

"Not nearly as much as I admire you," Amir growled as he nuzzled his wife's soft neck. The truth was that he did admire Ms. Musavi, though not in the way his wife suggested.

During Amir's years abroad, a few of his Western colleagues had been bold enough to ask pointed questions about Seema's hijab, implying that veiling diminished women and cemented a second-class status. Amir and Seema would disagree, vigorously, but Amir wasn't sure they were ever able to convince Westerners that the chador actually elevated and empowered women by protecting their delicate and yielding parts behind an impenetrable, iron curtain.

On an intelligent woman, like Ms. Musavi, a chador made her even more intimidating and powerful as she interacted with the unveiled and vulnerable men that were her colleagues. It also—contrary to his wife's teasing—made it impossible for Amir to have any sort of sexual feeling toward her. It was exactly as God intended when he made veiling compulsory as a gift, not a burden, to women.

No, Amir's admiration for the young woman was entirely professional. Five years was a blistering pace for her to have completed her PhD, even if her adviser had a reputation for leniency. And the hours the woman worked were impressive. Amir had always been the first one in the office, so he could leave early every day to get home to Seema and the kids. But Ms. Musavi arrived as early or earlier than him and still, Amir heard from the janitor, didn't leave until the building was locked up for the night.

In meetings, Ms. Musavi was concise and to the point. She never added unnecessary chatter like some of their colleagues did when, say, chiming in with unoriginal arguments in favor of a village electrification project that nobody opposed. When Ms. Musavi spoke, it was because she had some fresh insight or information to offer that might move the group in an entirely different direction, such as asking whether the villagers themselves ranked electricity among their top needs or if they understood how the introduction of television and other electronics might impact their children and families. When Ms. Musavi spoke, everyone listened. And while some of that might have been due to the natural respect accorded the sole female in the room, the bulk of it was because of an impressive combination of charisma and intelligence that Amir, as his wife noted, greatly admired.

When Charles Roberts, a British field researcher who had popularized the concept of participatory rural appraisal, traveled to Iran to conduct a workshop on his techniques, Amir appointed Ms. Musavi to serve as the visitor's guide and primary counterpart. He knew Ms. Musavi would challenge Dr. Roberts's assumptions and stereotypes about Iranian women and what they could achieve. Plus, Ms. Musavi's English was impeccable. She'd somehow conquered the weirdly soft Western *R*s, with their flat edges, and even managed to keep her pronouns straight—a task that was especially challenging for Iranians, whose language had only one pronoun for all genders. Ms. Musavi impressed and charmed the foreigner so much that he offered the team a scholarship for three ministry colleagues to travel to his institute in Lexington for a workshop on PRA's application in semi-rural settings.

Her only misstep, Amir thought, was an inability or unwillingness to make friends at the ministry. Of course, as a woman, she did have some additional challenges. She wasn't able, for example, to join the men in certain spaces, like the lunchroom where Amir and the other level IIIs and IIs came together every day over herbed rices and stews to talk through work challenges or simply relax. But even in their shared office space, where conversation and banter would be allowed—expected, even—she was all business, all the time. She never asked anyone about their children or holidays. She never joined in when everyone else pushed their chair away from their desk to take a break over tea and swap stories about experiences out in the field. If she passed a colleague in the hallway, she might nod or say hello but would never smile. A few of Amir's colleagues started to call her the Robot behind her back.

On an early morning in September, just a few months after Ms. Musavi had started at the ministry, Amir decided to say something—in the spirit of an older brother or mentor guiding a younger colleague.

"Khanoom Doktor," he called to her, and she swiveled in her chair immediately. She looked at him with intense focus, as if certain he must have something important to say, something worthy of interrupting the precious morning hours in which the absence of their colleagues' chatter and clatter gave them quiet time to concentrate. Amir momentarily lost his nerve.

"Ahem," he cleared his throat as he chose his words. "If I can be so bold, I wanted to offer a small word of advice to you, my dear sister. You might try getting to know your colleagues better and becoming—you know—friends with everyone."

"Friends?" Ms. Musavi repeated, her lips curling. "You think I should become friends with all the men in this office?"

Amir felt the blood rush to his face. Why did the idea suddenly sound so dumb? "Not friends, exactly," Amir backpedaled. "Just have friendly relationships. So that—you know—when the inevitable work conflicts arise and people disagree—well, that way people won't take things personally, you see?"

As Ms. Musavi looked at him steadily, Amir noticed the perfect shape of her eyebrows and how symmetrically they spread right and left, almost like the wings of a bird without a body. His wife was vigilant about keeping her own eyebrows in a similar shape, wielding her tweezers and razor against errant hairs as they appeared. Did Ms. Musavi do the same? Amir dropped his gaze and looked at the woman's feet.

"What do you think would be said about me if I tried to be friendly with all you men?" Ms. Musavi asked. She made it sound as if Amir was encouraging her to flirt with or even, *astaghfirullah*, God forbid, sleep with her colleagues. Amir's scalp burned.

"That's not what I meant," Amir sputtered. "It's just, well, people will be more receptive to your ideas if you . . . Look at Ms. Khoini in the library. She always has a kind word and a smile for everyone. And in return, no one takes offense if she tells us that we can't take items out of the library or that our research plan doesn't make sense. We would do anything she asked. She's like our . . ."

Amir stopped and looked at Ms. Musavi. She raised an eyebrow at him. It was as if the bird across her brow was dipping one wing, circling for an attack.

He'd been about to say that Ms. Khoini, who could always be relied upon to help researchers dig out village maps or lists of grain disbursements or other necessary items from library archives, was like their mother. But therein, perhaps, lay the reason for her ability to be so comfortable and, yes, friendly. She was older than most of the researchers by at least a decade, maybe two. And she was married. Ms. Musavi was neither.

"You do whatever you want," Amir said, shrugging as if he couldn't care less. "I was just trying to—"

"Dr. Musavi?" Amir was cut off by the mail boy, who stuck his head in their room.

"Which one?" Ms. Musavi asked. The boy squinted at the white envelope. "Dr. Amir Musavi," he read, and Amir reached forward to take the letter. It was from Bangladesh, perhaps an answer to his application to travel to the Grameen Bank for a training on microcredit.

"Anyway," Amir said to continue the conversation. But as he turned toward her, he saw that Ms. Musavi had already swiveled away from him, her head bent over her unadorned table.

It was simply unnecessary, Amir thought in the days that followed, for Ms. Musavi to be so hostile, so critical, when he was only trying to help. Yes, perhaps he didn't quite understand her situation, and he could see that it might have been presumptuous of him to think he had any worthwhile advice to offer a young woman trying to make her way in a male-dominated field. But his intentions were good. Didn't that count for something? And by being so dismissive, so scornful, Ms. Musavi was simply alienating someone who was on her side.

In the months that followed, Amir was less inclined to choose a charitable interpretation for behaviors he'd previously noticed and forgiven. Like the way she charged through doorways as if she were the queen, never pausing to offer those she walked with the opportunity to go first. Of course, her male colleagues would have uniformly insisted she precede them, so Amir had initially appreciated her inclination to avoid wasting time on the Iranian custom. But really, oughtn't she at least pause a bit or nod to acknowledge the fact that she was given the honor of going first? And for colleagues that were more than twice her age, shouldn't she at least make a pretense of insisting that they go ahead?

And then there was the matter of how she treated students. PhD candidates from the University of Tehran often worked as research assistants, some of them even recruiting ministry employees to their dissertation committees. Most of Amir's colleagues went out of their way to be encouraging and kind to these young people who brought fresh eyes and opinions to their work for little compensation. But not Ms. Musavi. She worked every one of her students up to the maximum limit of twenty hours a week. There were even rumors, which Amir had initially been inclined to dismiss, that some of them ran personal errands for her, like shopping for food items or picking up dry cleaning in between pulling articles and drafting arguments.

Ironically, Ms. Musavi seemed to be hardest on her female students. One day, Amir overheard her berating a young woman in the library. "Are you even trying?" Ms. Musavi spat, her voice so loud that everyone turned to stare. "Do you think the *Journal of Applied Economics* will accept something that sounds like a high schooler wrote it?" Then Ms. Musavi threw the manuscript to the ground and stalked out of the library, leaving the humiliated young woman to pick her papers off the ground as she wept into her chador.

But the thing that bothered Amir the most—as he observed Ms. Musavi closely in the weeks and months following their awkward, early morning conversation—was the obsequiousness with which she interacted with senior leaders in the ministry. Ms. Musavi, who was known to eviscerate colleagues and pick apart arguments with a flick of her chador, suddenly became all smiles and big eyes whenever the vice minister or assistant vice minister stopped by. The most pedestrian, and even incorrect, points these men would make were met with words of praise one never otherwise heard from the woman. "Wow, you're absolutely right," Ms. Musavi would gush. "How did you come up with that idea?"

It was sickening. Worse, it was entirely unethical. Research specialists were hired for their brains, and their responsibility was to share an honest assessment, politely, of the ideas presented before them. To do otherwise for the purpose of currying favor was to sacrifice the common good for personal advancement.

So it wasn't just jealousy that made him do what he did on

that terrible Saturday morning. Amir had already decided that he disliked Ms. Musavi for her pride, her selfishness, her boundless ambition, long before she was promoted over him to deputy division manager.

But the jealousy wasn't irrelevant. When Ms. Musavi's new role was announced at their weekly staff meeting, envy crashed down on Amir with a force as immobilizing as the powerful ocean waves that hit him the first time his friends had taken him surfing in a small town outside of Melbourne. Both experiences were all the more overwhelming for being entirely unfamiliar.

Amir had never been a jealous person. Life had come easily, and he'd had so much to be grateful for. He'd been at the top of his class in every grade, winning an all-expenses-paid slot at the University of Tehran and then a scholarship to fund his studies abroad. Given his academic success, he'd been in school all throughout the war and, therefore, was never in danger of being conscripted or expected to join the war effort. He'd married a distant cousin, whom he'd admired from afar, and they'd turned out to be incredibly compatible in a joyful marriage. And he had three children—the boys plus their long-desired little sister—whom he adored. What was there to be jealous of?

Amir hardly recognized himself in the months following Ms. Musavi's promotion. It was the injustice of it all that inspired a barely suppressed rage and an obsession with plotting a million small and large ways in which he would get revenge. The fact was that he was the better person for the job. His colleagues knew and liked him, and he already inspired their trust in his leadership, even without the additional title. He was the one who was able to bring the team to consensus on things like which villages would get their roads repaved in the spring. He listened, asked questions, helped opponents find the overlaps in their positions where they could agree, and then nudged the group to a final decision, which, if not unanimous, was at least understood by all who participated and made them feel included in the process. Skills like these were decidedly not in Ms. Musavi's repertoire.

It was true that Ms. Musavi had an impressive number of publications in prestigious international journals—including the most recent one she'd worked on with the female student she'd berated in the library. But this was only because, as a young, unmarried woman, living with her parents, Ms. Musavi had so few real responsibilities. Once she married and had children, she'd slow down like the rest of them, probably even more so given the additional burdens of childcare for women.

What Amir suspected, and what made him so angry, was that her false praise for the senior leaders at the ministry had worked. Her affirmation of their opinions made them feel smarter, so they liked having her around. Or perhaps they were so convinced of their own ideas, so used to going unchallenged, that they imagined anyone who disagreed with them must be intellectually inferior.

Amir's secret jealousy made him feel like a spy or assassin who was obsessed with the mission of slipping a dagger into his enemy's side, even as he pretended to the world to be the same happy family man and respected ministry employee he'd always been. Even at home, cooing at his new daughter—whose long-awaited arrival delighted the whole family—Amir's thoughts would inevitably turn to his latest interactions with Ms. Musavi and whether he'd succeeded in making her look or feel just a little bit smaller.

The trick of it was in the subtlety of inflicting a wound without being noticed. Like waiting a few extra beats before acknowledging Ms. Musavi's entry into the conference room or quickly turning his attention to someone, anyone, who interrupted her. As colleagues followed Amir's lead, these little slights added up to a collective cold shoulder against the woman. One day, frustrated that she wasn't getting the room's attention, Ms. Musavi was reduced to pounding on the table with her fist, shouting like an impetuous child, "Listen to me! This is important." That was a proud moment.

Another scene that Amir savored for weeks was when he caught an actual error in a paper Ms. Musavi was presenting to the level III researchers. He was so excited, he actually hugged himself, and then, affecting a confused tone, asked, "Sorry, I don't quite understand. How did you account for the variability of seasonal rains?" The best part was how irritated she got, as if she couldn't believe he was asking something so stupid. And then, as he continued pretending that he was just confused, there was a beautiful, satisfying moment when she suddenly started, exactly as if someone had slammed the door behind her. "Forgive me for being such a dunce," Amir continued, twisting the knife with each word. "I'm surely missing something obvious, but could you explain one more time how you can assume even rainfall throughout the year?" Ms. Musavi, her flaming cheeks framed by her chador, stammered that she didn't want to waste any more of the group's time and that he should see her separately if he'd like to continue the discussion. The entire room understood what was happening, and it was all Amir could do to keep from revealing his hand with one last sarcastic comment or question about how grateful he'd be if Ms. Musavi could simply explain the brilliance of her thinking one last time.

The morning the envelope appeared, Amir had spent the cab ride to work thinking about how to use an upcoming division presentation to the assistant vice minister to good effect. It was one thing to cut Ms. Musavi down to size within their own division. It would be another thing entirely to do so in front of the big bosses.

The envelope was on Amir's desk when he arrived. It was one of those gold envelopes, about the size of a folded sheet of paper, with a flap that had a small hole for a metal clasp. Amir could tell immediately that the letter was from abroad, and he was pleased to see the return address from his alma mater. He sometimes got nostalgic about his years in Australia, where he and Seema had begun their married life, falling even more deeply in love and starting their little family. It was nice to know that someone at the university was thinking of him, even if it was just a form letter asking alumni for money.

But as soon as he picked up the envelope, Amir could tell it was too heavy to be a form letter. He tugged at the flap and ripped through the top seam, dumping the contents out on his desk—a pile of pictures plus a short, handwritten note on University of Melbourne stationery.

Surprise! I found these pictures of our last barbie. Fun times! Hope you're doing well back home. If I can ever finish this bloody dissertation, I'm going to visit. —K

Amir had no idea who K was. He picked up the first picture. It was a group shot of two women and two men huddled together beside a swimming pool. One of the men held long tongs that might be used to flip a steak.

Amir examined the men closely. He didn't recognize either of them. One had glossy skin, flat hair, and big eyes in a shade of brown or black that marked him as Indian or Bangladeshi. The other wore big wraparound sunglasses, so you could barely see the paper-white skin and shaggy blond strands of hair poking out from under a protective sun cap that someone with his complexion needed but that too few Australians actually used. Maybe he was a visiting Englishman or Norwegian.

Amir turned his attention to the women. One of them looked Chinese or Taiwanese, with shoulder-length hair and glasses. Amir had been surprised by how many Chinese there were in Australia—not just in a PhD program that attracted internationals, but folks who were born and raised there and spoke flawless English with thick Aussie accents.

The last woman had white skin with dark hair and eyes in an attractive combination that vaguely reminded Amir of Seema. But he didn't know her or any of these people. Which one was K? Which one had sent the letter?

Amir flipped through the rest of the photos. There were more people he didn't recognize, standing or sitting or posing for pictures at a typical Australian barbecue. The two women showed up in almost all the pictures, as if they were documenting their visit at a tourist attraction. He flipped back to the first picture, the one with the clearest view of the women's faces.

Recognition hit Amir like a slap across the face, like the slap that—more than a decade later—he was preparing to deliver to his own daughter's cheek, both of which caused his heart to race in confusion at the shocking position he had found himself in. Ms. Musavi unveiled, his daughter afraid of him—it was all wrong in some deep and fundamental way.

It was the eyebrows that confirmed it. Amir had seen those eyebrows swoop and lift and cluster with arrogance and irritation. He'd been obsessed for weeks and months with what he could do to flatten them in defeat. But he'd never imagined how they might look when not shrouded by the soft folds of a scarf and chador. He'd never guessed that those eyebrows could look so rounded and relaxed as they were tugged apart by smiles and laughter he'd never seen, or even imagined, on Ms. Musavi's face.

As he looked more closely at the photographs, he was surprised that it had taken him so long to recognize his nemesis. Despite the unfamiliar expression and missing chador, Ms. Musavi still exuded the same air of a serious and ambitious young woman. Her posture was strong, with an upward lift of her chin that communicated confidence and made it seem as if she was looking down her nose at the camera, even though she was the shortest person in the group. In one of the unposed pictures, she held her finger and thumb together in front of her body, clearly making a point that, Amir knew from experience, was likely brilliant. She wore no makeup and her clothes—a striped long-sleeved T-shirt and long pants—were quite conservative compared with the bikinis and swim shorts the other party attendees wore. Still . . .

Footsteps in the hallway reminded Amir where he was. In the Ministry of Reconstruction Jihad of the Islamic Republic of Iran, pictures like these were tantamount to pornography. He scrambled to shove them back into the torn envelope before anyone laid eyes on them, but the effort was unnecessary, as the footsteps receded down the hallway. Perhaps it was Ms. Musavi herself, headed to the private office she'd moved into when she was promoted.

Amir turned the envelope over and noticed that the "Dr."

portion of the "Dr. Musavi" in the address was underlined twice, as if someone—K?—was making a point of highlighting or celebrating the fact that the recipient was, in fact, a doctor. Clearly the letter had been meant for Ms. Musavi and was dumped on his desk by mistake.

It dawned on Amir that there might be severe consequences for Ms. Musavi if the photos were to get out.

Not that everyone working for the ministry, or other parts of the government, was as religious as they appeared. On road trips to the villages, when Amir and his colleagues had time to bond and reveal more about themselves, he'd been surprised to learn that some of the men he worked with never woke up for early morning *fajr* prayers. And when it came to ladies' hijab, well, everyone relaxed a bit while abroad. In Australia, even Seema—Amir's devoutly observant wife—traded in her heavy chador for a light, tunic-like manteau paired with cotton scarves that were tied, not pinned, under her chin.

But Ms. Musavi didn't even have a hat or bandanna on her head in a symbolic nod to Islamic coverings. And in some of the group pictures, she stood right up against male colleagues, everyone's arms draped around one another. Amir knew from experience that, in the Australian context, such proximity didn't mean anything sexual. But in Iran, a country where men and women didn't even shake hands, Ms. Musavi's behavior would be seen as unacceptable, unforgivable.

Really, how could she have been so stupid? Had no one taught her the consequences of letting down her guard? It would have been one thing if she'd wanted to emigrate and leave Iran altogether, but this was an ambitious woman who clearly wanted to succeed inside Iran. Her mother, her father, her brother, someone should have made sure she would be careful enough to keep some sort of covering, or at least make sure she was never photographed without it.

It dawned on Amir that he could get Ms. Musavi in trouble.

He could go straight to the deputy vice minister's office and hand over the envelope. Or he could just leave the pictures out casually, anonymously, in the break room, where their colleagues would eventually discover them, and the rumors would fly. How long would it take—hours? days?—before she was told to pack her bags and leave the building? How long would it be before Amir inherited her office and no longer had to tolerate the maddening sound of his colleagues' chewing and belching and loud-mouthed breathing at all hours of the day in their shared space?

Amir tried to savor the image of the proud woman's humiliation. He wondered how her eyebrows would react. But he couldn't muster much enthusiasm.

Was he really going to hand over these private pictures so they could be examined and passed around and pawed over by any number of men? Did Ms. Musavi, no matter how arrogant and rude, deserve that? She'd had a severe lapse in judgment in Australia, yes, but Amir was sure the woman had always been veiled in Iran. She wouldn't want her male colleagues to see her in such a state of undress, revealing everything that was hidden under her chador.

Amir sighed. He pushed his chair back from his desk and stood. Then he walked out into the hallway and toward Ms. Musavi's office.

"Yes?" she said when he knocked. Amir turned the handle and pushed open the heavy door. Ms. Musavi had her back to him, hunched over her computer. Amir waited and she eventually swiveled her chair toward him, her body first and then her head, and finally her eyes pulled reluctantly from her computer.

"Another mix-up," he said as he placed the envelope on a side table.

"You interrupted me for this?" she asked, clearly irritated.

"Well, I think you'll see that—"

"Where's the report on the Grameen Bank?" Ms. Musavi demanded. "It was supposed to be finished yesterday."

"Yes, well, it's not quite ready, but I should be able to have it to you by this aftern—"

"Unacceptable!" Ms. Musavi snapped. "Do you think I create deadlines for fun? Entire programs of research are based on these initial stages, and when you're late, it throws the whole schedule off."

Was she serious? An entire schedule of research thrown off because a report was one day late?

"If I can't depend on you to deliver," Ms. Musavi continued, "perhaps it doesn't make sense to keep you on the PRA account with Dr. Roberts. I worked hard to make sure the ministry would be taken seriously by an internationally renowned program. I'm not going to let you ruin that."

There was something about the set of her jaw and the tilt of her eyebrows, with one slightly higher than the other, that let Amir know she wasn't really worried about his report or Dr. Roberts. She was simply enjoying the power she had to scold him as he stood before her like a servant, unable to do anything but submit.

"You . . . ," he breathed.

Ms. Musavi smiled and raised her eyebrows as if she was quite satisfied to see that she'd rattled him.

Amir grabbed the envelope and pulled out the photos.

"You should be ashamed of yourself!" he sneered as he threw all the pictures on the desk. All of them except one, which he held up before her.

It was a gorgeous thing to watch Ms. Musavi's self-satisfied smile collapse on itself as she examined the picture in his hand, the pictures on the desk. Her entire face fell as if the interior infrastructure behind her forehead and cheeks had suddenly gone slack. Her jaw dropped and then closed, and her lips pressed together, tight as a razor blade. Her eyes flitted around the room, giving her the appearance of a trapped animal looking for escape, before coming to land on the photo still in Amir's hand.

"Please . . . ," she whispered, as she reached for it.

The sweetness of the moment was almost overwhelming, as if Amir's entire body was made of taste buds activated by a flood of sugar. Who was the powerful one now?

Amir lifted the photo triumphantly. It was the one in which Ms. Musavi, the Chinese woman, and the two men were bunched together. Ms. Musavi let out a sound that was halfway between a sigh and a whimper. She leaned forward, her arm outstretched, her fingers grasping. Amir backed away. Then he slipped the photo into his pocket and left the room, carrying with him the satisfying scene of his utterly vanquished foe.

A decade later, this was the scene that flashed before Amir's eyes as he raised his hand to his daughter—beautiful Fatimeh, so bold, so bright, so likely to one day inspire as much jealousy as Ms. Musavi.

"No, *azizam*. Not like that," Seema said softly.

Didn't she understand? It was his duty to hit their daughter, slap her hard enough to leave a mark, make sure she remembered this moment and never dared cross certain boundaries again. If word got out, if someone at the school had seen her talking to that boy or discovered the note he'd written, her reputation would be sullied, perhaps beyond repair. She might even be expelled. As she got older, the consequences for this sort of thing would only grow more fearsome. She might be taken to prison, flogged, have acid thrown in her face, her feet dipped into a vat of cockroaches. Amir had heard horrible things.

Amir ignored his wife and kept his focus on Fatimeh.

"How dare you?" he roared, reaching even higher so there was more space to cover, more opportunity to gain speed and maximize the pain he might inflict when his hand finally fell.

Fatimeh cowered before him, gaping at him from behind arms thrown up in self-defense. In his daughter's eyes, Amir could see confusion as she grappled with the question of who her father was and what he was capable of doing.

Amir's resolve faltered. Could she detect the fabricated nature of his anger? Could she see that it was all an act, that he didn't blame her at all, that he still wasn't sure he could actually bring his hand down to crash into the bones of her face? And for what? A scrawled note from a schoolboy? Amir had had his own childhood crushes. There was nothing more natural.

Now! Amir told himself. *Do it now!*

But he hesitated too long. Seema stepped between him and their daughter and gently pushed him back until Fatimeh was entirely out of reach.

"Fatimeh, go to your room until your father settles down," Seema instructed. Her voice was calm and assured. She knew him too well, knew that he didn't have it in him.

Panic took hold of Amir like a many-taloned creature sinking its claws into his chest as he remembered moving into Ms. Musavi's abandoned office. Amir screwed his eyes shut to block out the vision of his beautiful wife and daughter as he reached for the emotions he needed and found the anger and disgust that would serve him. Amir's pulse rose, along with a wave of repulsion until, eyes still closed, he spat, "I didn't raise my daughter to be a *jendeh* whore."

Seema gasped and Amir opened his eyes to see the effect of his pronouncement. *Jendeh* was a horrible word, an unspeakable word that conveyed the most dirty, depraved, and ugly aspects of human behavior. It was a shameful word that had never crossed Amir's lips, even when he had been a teenager and friends used it to show their daring. It was a word that had nothing to do with his radiant daughter, who was as pure and bright as the fields of poppies that greeted them every Nowruz on the way to Hamadan.

Fatimeh emitted a small cry. She hugged her arms across her belly and doubled over as if Amir had actually punched her, bruising the soft tissue under her rib cage. She backed into the corner and slid to the floor, her face crumpled into silent sobs.

Amir felt beads of sweat on his forehead. His legs were weak, as if he'd climbed the steep trails of Jamshidieh.

"How dare you?" Seema exploded. "She's your daughter. Your own flesh and blood!"

Looking at Fatimeh, crying as if her heart was breaking, Amir couldn't answer. The long muscles of his digestive system shifted, and he felt sick, like he might throw up or have a bowel movement. How much damage had he inflicted? Had he gone too far, saying words that might cause her to doubt her worth? All he wanted was to protect her.

If Ms. Musavi's father had done the same, she'd be running the ministry by now, Amir was sure of it. Instead, she'd resigned the very morning Amir had given her the pictures. Rumor was, she'd told the vice minister she was engaged, and her fiancé didn't want her working.

When he'd heard the news, Amir had run to Ms. Musavi's office, hoping to catch her and convince her to stay. He hadn't shown the photo to anyone and would be happy to return it. He'd just been momentarily angry—he'd never really intended to use it against her.

But Khanoom Doktor Azadeh Musavi had already left the building. She would never return again.

Daniel Saldaña París
Translated from the Spanish by Christina MacSweeney

Rosaura at Dawn

T>HE FENCE IS TOPPED with barbed wire and winds between the shrubs, climbs dry hillsides, zigzags capriciously, and extends into the ocean for about a hundred yards. It stands tall and threatening, rusting in the sunlight, the northernmost limit of a dream gone bad. People peer through it, projecting hopes and a new version of themselves beyond the ICE patrols. There is no escape from this place.

I came to Tijuana four years ago, after the accident. I remember that when I arrived, I'd just had the stitches removed from the wound on my leg, which looked a little like a bird's-eye view of that frontier line. For a time I'd tried to carry on as normal back in Mexico City. I went to work, said thanks when offered condolences. I smiled when people looked at me in pity, pretending I didn't know what they were saying behind my back: "That's the lady who killed her mother." But I didn't kill my mom. It was an accident, and there's no reason why I should smile if I damn well don't feel like it.

At night, my husband would turn on the TV and fall asleep in front of it. In the bedroom, I'd pretend to be asleep, and I did in fact sometimes doze for twenty minutes or half an hour before waking again as if I'd been shaken. In the early hours, my husband would come to bed and kiss my forehead, but we weren't really together, just sharing a refrigerator and, increasingly, profound silence.

I was given a lot of advice during the first weeks: meditate, see a therapist, find a lover, give up sugar. The only tip I followed was the one that took me by surprise: "Go to Tijuana." It was offered by a colleague who was a widow; by the way her eyes shone, I was immediately certain that she knew what she was talking about. The next day I packed a bag and, before leaving for the bus terminal, told my husband I was heading north and not to expect me back. He embraced me (I think it was the first time he'd done that without our having sex first) and gave me five thousand pesos from a cookie jar. He seemed relieved that I was leaving.

The first months weren't easy. I worked in a hotel, a pharmacy, and a party costume store whose only clients were prostitutes. Have you got a bee costume for adults? A Bigfoot costume? Zorro, but with a miniskirt? I found a small apartment in a noisy street, but as I didn't sleep much I'd spend the night looking out the window. All sorts of people passed by: tourists, drunks, drug dealers, Haitians, lone teenagers. That's how I met Severiano.

Through the window, I saw a man of around fifty standing under a streetlight on the corner near my building. He was wearing a hat and carrying a cardboard box tied up with a cord. I thought he must be a migrant, probably waiting for a *pollero* to take him to the other side, but after smoking in silence for a while, he untied the box and a huge, white, majestic bird appeared. Severiano grasped its legs, as though it were a chicken, and when no one was around, he launched it into the air. The bird initially flapped uncertainly but then found its balance and flew away, its wings extended like a white brushstroke in the Tijuana night sky. Severiano followed its progress until it was lost in the darkness above my building, and that's when he saw me in the open window. He smiled. It had been a long time since anyone had smiled at me.

"Hello," he said from below, raising his hat like someone in a Pedro Infante movie. We chatted awhile, making small talk, but some shady characters came by and were looking hard at him, so I invited him up to my apartment. I know you shouldn't do that sort of thing, especially not in Tijuana, but at that time I wasn't worried about being killed; I couldn't have cared less. I made chamomile tea, and we sat in the living room, which also held the dinner table and my wardrobe. I asked Severiano what kind of bird he'd freed, and he said he wasn't sure but thought she was some sort of giant cockatoo. Her name was Rosaura, but he hadn't freed her, he said: every so often, at night, he released Rosaura in different parts of the city, and she always found her way home. He went on to say that he had other birds, a lot of them, and one or two reptiles. When the police detained smugglers of exotic avian species, the wildlife department would contact Severiano and ask him to look after the birds until they found a biologist or a nature reserve to take them. They usually stayed with him for a month or two, but sometimes nobody came to collect them and Severiano ended up caring for the animals for years—or forever. He told me he had a farm in the hills near Tijuana with a view of the border, and as he said this I felt him turning to look at my legs, at the thick scar resulting from the accident. I asked if I could visit his farm. I wanted to see Rosaura close up, in daylight; something about her whiteness had me spellbound.

Instead of going to work the following day, I visited Severiano's farm. In the midmorning they called me from the store to tell me I was fired, but it didn't bother me because by then I knew that my destiny was to be with Rosaura, Pinocchio, Amarillo, and Rubeola. My fate was to help Severiano with the birds, learn to clean the aviary and to feed the hawk—it was kept apart from the others—with raw chicken and live mice, allow the zigzagging scar on my leg to fade slowly and the pure white of Rosaura flapping her wings in the borderland night to erase every trace of that fateful accident.

Severiano said I could stay in a small cabin some forty yards from his house. There was no bathroom, but that wasn't a problem. If I needed to piss during the night, I could do it outdoors, among the rocks and shrubs surrounding the cabin. I still hadn't recovered my fear of death, and thought that dying like that, squatting, bitten by a viper, was as good a way to go as any other.

The aviary was awesome: a palace, forty-five feet high and at least ninety in diameter, constructed from metal tubes, like the ones used in market stands, and completely covered in chicken wire. Severiano, who had been an engineer before buying the farm, had designed it single-handedly. Inside, there were areas of shade, fruit trees, a small pond, a scaled-down mountain of rocks with a gold mine, and even three smaller cages that housed the "punk birds," as Seve called them: the misfits, the unhappy or aggressive birds that attacked the others and had to be on their own. It was like a city inside there, and I very soon started to add my own ideas: I planted a nopal so the benteveo would peck the fruit; I designed a Jacuzzi with a fish tank motor for the pair of iguanas that roamed the ground.

On that basis, Severiano ceded me a section of the aviary, and that small kingdom, a tributary of his, became the center of my life. I bought sacks of corn and made a pyramid of cobs—it was a real success. Pinocchio, an oropendola, spent a lot of time in there making a little noise, and Severiano told me that before I came, he never spoke; he was a traumatized bird. I noticed that despite his usually undemonstrative nature, my teacher was proud of me.

Naturally, the animals didn't like all my ideas. I once managed to get ahold of one of those fat, red Buddhas and put it in my section, surrounded by a small stream, so it would look like a Chinese water feature, but after a few days, I realized that Amarillo—a pheasant who wouldn't fly and just hopped from one place to another—was afraid of the Buddha and would take long detours to avoid it. So I removed the Buddha to my cabin, where it stood facing the wall because I felt it watching me at night while I was undressing. (I don't want this to seem like a lack of respect: if a Christ figure had made me feel that way, I'd have done the same thing. We all have our beliefs, and that's okay by me.)

Severiano was a reserved, you could even say unsociable, man, and being around animals for so long had done nothing for his manners. But he became fond of me and, after a couple of years, offered to add a bathroom to my cabin. We completed the task together, and during those three weeks of heavy work under the hot-as-hell Tijuana sun, I got to know him much better than in the previous two and a half years, since he normally only spoke to ask me to buy birdseed, clean the cage, or take out Rubeola—the female iguana—to administer her eye drops. While we were building the bathroom, he told me that he'd once been married but had gotten divorced thirteen years before and hadn't fallen in love again. He told me he was from Zacatecas originally but had come to Tijuana as an adolescent with the dream of crossing over the border, just like everyone else.

And that dream had come true: he'd lived in San Diego and then Santa Monica; had been a gardener and dishwasher, and for nearly five years had driven a truck delivering fertilizer, but then he'd gotten mixed up in drugs, spent a few months in the can, and ended up being deported. After that, he had no desire to cross over again and preferred to view the line, that scar splitting the world in two, from up here. In return, I confided that I was married and had caused my mother's death. Severiano just nodded and, after a pause, asked me to fetch a shovel. For the first time, it seemed someone had offered me the condolences I'd hoped for, that someone had said something that made me feel a little better, or maybe it was simply that time had passed and I was now living in Tijuana and didn't have to listen to my husband watching TV at night, but the thing is that from then on, I finally began to think that my mother's death was going to be just one more event in my life.

When we'd completed the bathroom, Severiano told me he had to make a trip, had matters to settle in Zacatecas. I asked what sort of matters, but he skirted around the subject, and I understood that he didn't want to tell me; the moment for confidences had passed, and it would be best to return to our previous relationship, where he was something approaching my boss, or my mentor, my master in the art of caring for birds.

Before leaving, Severiano entrusted me with the last secret he'd kept during all that time working together: he taught me how to take Rosaura out and prepare her for one of her flights. He told me I had to feed her—just a little—and that before freeing her I must whisper some words in her ear, close to her beak. I can't repeat those words because Severiano made me promise not to share them.

On the third night after Severiano's departure, I got Rosaura ready, put her in her cardboard box, tied it with cord, and drove to the city in Seve's car. I chose a dangerous street near Calle Coahuila, where sex workers hang out to pick up clients. At around one in the morning, when my eyelids were drooping, I got out of the car with the box, untied the cord, and, following Severiano's instructions, spoke the secret words to Rosaura before launching her into the air. I was afraid that some idiot would take a potshot at her, but no one was looking. Rosaura took flight, and I experienced a strange sensation, like a weight of sadness in my chest, that stayed with me all the way back to the farm.

I sat outside the cabin all night. When I lit a fire, all the birds went crazy and began to sing and make a frightful racket. I think I dozed briefly or was maybe lost in my thoughts, but at first light I heard the flapping of wings, looked toward the border, and saw Rosaura, a white smudge gradually taking form, flying toward me over the horizon. I can't describe my feelings; it was as if she were an angel rather than a bird. Rosaura circled over the cage a few times, and the other birds seemed to be celebrating her arrival with chaotic screeches, and although I'd witnessed the spectacle before, when Severiano had released Rosaura, it had never felt so personal, as though the birds were celebrating me too, rejoicing that something inside me had also returned.

The one who never came back was Seve. Two months later a lawyer turned up to tell me that he'd left the farm to me.

Zak Salih
Three Niles

THE LAMB CAME WITH THEM to his grandfather's house. That would be the boy's first memory of those days in another life. The slight beast leaning against their luggage in the pickup truck's bed, ears flipping in the wind like the luggage tags, stamped FRA, tied to the suitcase shared by him and his father. The dusty white animal body rocking as they passed, uncomfortably, over the dirt roads leading from Khartoum International Airport to the residential areas north of the city. The closed eyes, the lips drawn back as if in a taut smile. The wedge of a face seeming to relish the breeze, unaware of the rough journey, the thick summer air, the man sitting across from it with his long leather satchel.

They would stay the night with them, his father had said amid the heat and noise of the livestock market. (Barely thirty minutes in this country that belonged to him and didn't, and already the thirteen-year-old boy was drowning in strange sights and sounds and smells.) They would sleep in the courtyard: the lamb tethered to a stake, the man on a cot assembled by his grandmother. In the morning, after coffee and biscuits, the man would say the necessary prayers in a language the boy couldn't speak but only parrot, then remove one of the knives from his satchel and run the blade across the lamb's throat. The butcher would be paid; the boy's uncle would drive him back to the livestock market just as he now drove them away from it; and that evening there would be a celebratory feast to honor the arrival of the boy and his father from America. There would be aunts and uncles and cousins from the surrounding villages. One uncle would drive eleven hours from Port Sudan. They would sit outside, in large circles around broad platters, and scoop hot flesh into their mouths with strips of bread pinched between the fingers of their right hands.

"All for us," his father had said while the sheep pushed against their legs. The boy fought the impulse to reach out to the animals, to run his fingers along the spray-painted prices on their snowy hides. "You don't have to eat much of the meat. A few bites."

"Won't there be vegetables?"

"There are always vegetables. This is about hospitality. Lamb isn't an everyday thing here, and they won't understand how you and your mother eat. Please."

Three days, the boy thought of this quick trip tacked on to his family's stay in Hamburg, where they'd been spending the last week of summer vacation visiting his mother's old college roommate. Three days. Three. Two. One. Until then, he was a hostage. Even though none of this was about him anyway. It was about his father.

And so, from that rough market of waiting flesh set up in a city square, from all those half-spent lives making the boy want to weep, to this, his grandfather's house. The home sat behind corrugated metal doors at the end of a sandy courtyard speckled with palms, built of the same bronze-colored brick as all the other houses on this street—as, it seemed, everything was here. It was the last week of August 1999, and the heat (as his father had warned him when they'd boarded at Frankfurt, leaving his mother and younger sister to fly back to Washington without them) would be fierce. Mercifully, though, much of the yard was shaded this late in the afternoon, and in this shade his grandfather waited for them to come in, with their suitcase, with his uncle's generous bulk, with the lamb hefted in the seasoned butcher's arms.

As if bracing for a test, the boy struggled to recall what his father had once told him about the old man. (He had little interest in his father's stories and refused to remember them.) Something about delivering mail down the Nile on British steamers, then becoming an imam in the village where his father had been born. Yes, that was it. Impossible for the boy not to think of his maternal grandfather teaching history at a community college in Arlington, while here, a universe away, this man on whom he'd never set eyes, aside from photographs, dealt out medicine in prayers and exorcisms and neat little cuts on fevered skin. Impossible still for the boy not to see something wizardlike in the short, slight man who came around his wife and raised his arms to them, the sleeves of his jalabiya unfurling like sails. He couldn't stop staring at the sharp nose, at the wispy goatee beneath lips that kissed his father all over his face, that whispered his father's name like a summoning from some misty afterlife.

Then it was the boy's turn. He gave his best smile and stepped into those white drapes. He felt his grandfather's sandalwood prayer beads against his back. Over the old man's shoulder, he watched the butcher lead the lamb to a corner of the courtyard.

His grandfather whispered, between furious kisses, a name the boy never thought of as his. When he finally finished, the boy looked to his father to translate.

"He says what a blessing it is for you to be here. He says Allah has favored him with such a strong grandson. You are dear and sweet to him, he says. You are a Muslim to make him proud."

If only the old man knew what a fraud he embraced! The boy suspected his father kept the truth a secret during the long phone conversations he had at the kitchen table, alone, while the boy's mother worked in the garden and his sister watched her Disney tapes and the boy stayed upstairs, alone as he preferred, with his comic books and his secret longings for neighborhood boys.

Those heavy voices on the phone, calling at dawn or deep into the evening, responding to the boy's "Hello" with a stream of Arabic so that he could only stand mute until the voices (sometimes his grandfather's, sometimes an uncle's) would simply say his father's name, drawing it out like a question, and the boy would yell for his father and hand over the phone. Then his father would become someone else, if only for the span of an hour, before his American life drew him back, and it would startle the boy to hear his father speak with such familiarity in a language that sounded, to him, like something crawling up a canyon. Now, in the courtyard, the boy's grandmother and cousins broke out in ululations, cheers, embraces, prayers in that same strange language. All that warm flesh and cool fabric, the sharp-white jalabiyas and floral-patterned hijabs, the jeans and sneakers and sandals. The photographs. The boy, his father, his grandfather—proud Muslims, shoulder to shoulder, posed like dignitaries, the moment charged with an air of solemnity that felt, to the boy, like the handoff of an empire.

His uncle brought out a video recorder, and the boy tried to dodge that sweeping arm for fear of any record of his presence here, where he'd never imagined setting foot until his father had announced the surprise trip over breakfast in their hotel. What adventure! What opportunity! They were never this close to Sudan! And what could the boy do? He was thirteen, and still at the mercy of his father. Now his mother and sister were on their way back to Washington, while he was here, broken Arabic dropping like rocks from his lips, broken English thrust valiantly before him, and his father translating for everyone.

"They are saying, 'Welcome to Sudan.'"

"I understand that much, Dad."

"Perhaps you don't need me then."

But damn it, the boy did. He was helpless, a delinquent student beholden to his only teacher, so he followed his father around the yard, embracing after his father embraced, waiting patiently for him to translate their words and his responses. The boy felt like a robot. He was afraid to touch anything, all of it ready to nip him for his years of shame. Repeatedly, he tried to tell each of his cousins his true name, not the name they used, but either they didn't understand him or they refused to acknowledge how anyone could go by a different name. And how would his father begin to explain it? What would he say? "Because my son has such little respect for me, for this land, I sent him to a private school so he could study our language, our faith, alongside brown boys like himself. I would have kept him there, even now, were it not for the money." And oh, how grateful the boy had felt for the financial strain that rescued him from that world of black blazers and tugged ears, that delivered him to public school, where his fourth-grade teacher asked her students if they had any nicknames, and he told her what he wanted to be called, the only name he swore to answer to for the rest of his life. That foreign final vowel, nicked off for good, neat as a circumcision.

Three days, he told himself. Three. Two. One. And already the sun was starting to set on the first. As they ate dinner in the courtyard, the boy watched the shade stretch and split the sand into brilliant lanes of yellow and gold. Along one wall of the house, under a wood awning, sat two clay pots of drinking water. The boy kept his eyes on the vessels throughout the small evening meal of salty cheese and bread and stewed vegetables. It was either that or stare at the resting lamb, to which everyone else, talking in joyous, incomprehensible Arabic, seemed oblivious. Those waterpots were the only things that made sense to him.

Occasionally the boy looked at his father. Never before had the serious man appeared so ebullient, so unlike the stranger he seemed back at home, absent without being absent, meeting his fatherly duties as well as anyone with his dark skin could in the white streets of his wife's childhood, where they still lived. The boy knew how satisfied his father was to have him here, to be here himself for the first time since he'd left for America, in 1975. Still, the words rushed from his father's mouth as if he, too, was aware of how swiftly time could move. Watching his father, the boy was struck with a sudden, terrible guilt at all the time his father had wasted on him—time fitting the boy for stories that clung like a tight wool sweater to his naked chest, an embarrassing family gift he was obliged to wear and give thanks for. He recalled his mother's parting words outside the terminal gates: "I need you to keep an eye on your father. This is his first time back since he left. Try to have some fun, and make sure he does too."

Dusk dropped into night. The front lamps snapped on and polished the courtyard with light, and then the boy noticed how serious his grandfather looked talking to his father. There was a pause, after which his father spoke, but the response didn't seem to please the old man. Their conversation intensified. His uncle joined in, appearing to come to his grandfather's defense, but it was too late. His grandfather struggled to his feet with help from the butcher (who'd been eating among them as their guest) and stalked across the courtyard to his room. The boy looked to his father for an explanation, but that lively face had settled back into seriousness. Conversation slowly resumed. His father picked up small clumps of rice, weighed them in his fingers, dropped them back onto his plate. He looked, to the boy, like a toddler pondering something serious in a sandbox while adults argued just out of earshot.

After a time, the women rose to take away the platters and plates, to transform the sitting room with its thick curtains and linoleum-covered floor into a bedroom for the boy and his father. They pushed narrow futons together, covered them in fresh white sheets. His grandmother kissed them both, said good night, and shut the sitting room door behind them. Next to him, his father lay with his eyes burning at the ceiling.

"Dad," the boy asked. "Did they ask why we bombed their country last year?"

The boy recalled words over dinner. *Clinton. Amrikiya.* His uncle miming a giant explosion and pointing over the courtyard wall. The boy wondered if more bombs would drop while they were here.

His father was silent for a time. Then he said, "Your grandfather is upset you don't speak Arabic. He's upset I didn't bring your mother and sister with us. He always had this idea I'd bring her back after we'd married, that I'd be gone only for a time."

"But you did come back."

"Three days."

Two now, the boy thought.

"Did you know your mother, before we married, wanted to come here?"

"No."

"She did."

"To live?"

The boy's father nodded.

"Wow," the boy said.

"Can you imagine?"

The boy couldn't. Her skin, so susceptible to sunburn? Impossible. Yet if he were as pale as that, he might have been spared this trip.

"It's you he wanted to see," his father said. "I think he expected someone else. But you are who you are. And I am who I am."

And that's as much as his father was willing to say. He wished the boy pleasant dreams, pulled the sheet up over his shoulders, and rolled away to face the wall. When the boy finally heard his father's delicate snores, he felt a profound sense of loneliness, as if his father's sleep had severed him from all familiarity here, and it was only he, on this bed, in this sitting room, in this house, in this country, in this universe. He begged for sleep, tried not to think of the lamb outside on the sand. The faster sleep came, the faster time would pass, and the faster they'd be back in his uncle's truck and headed to the airport. He'd memorized their flight details, saw them stretched out in front of him now, taut as a finish line:

Lufthansa flight 394, departing from Khartoum International Airport for Frankfurt Airport at 6:35 p.m., connecting with Lufthansa flight 202 to Dulles International Airport at 8:40 p.m. The next morning, after prayers, there was coffee, as promised: thick and black and sipped from small cups. There were biscuits, as promised: delicate shards dipped into the coffee and rushed to their mouths before crumbling in their fingers.

The boy and his father had traded their T-shirts and shorts for borrowed jalabiyas. Drinking and eating in the gentle breeze that slipped through the open sitting room door, wearing nothing underneath the loose garment but his briefs, the boy felt a curious sense of nudity. An illicit freedom, as if he were laid bare for all to see, and no one cared. He drank cup after cup of coffee, listened to the sounds of conversation. The boy had no idea what they said to one another, but the more they talked, the less he had to. He could sit here, drink his coffee, eat his biscuits, and wait it out. There it was, up ahead! Lufthansa flight 394!

The butcher wiped his fingers and stepped out into the courtyard. Soon the others followed. It was time. Through the open door, the boy saw the lamb, awake now and standing on its skinny legs. He trembled at the sight of that tender animal on the cusp of its own extinction. Or maybe it was the four cups of coffee circulating in a body unaccustomed to it at home. Whatever the reason, the boy couldn't rise. He couldn't follow the others into the courtyard.

The boy felt his father's hand on his shoulder. Such tenderness, so far from home! Was this the same hand that had once smacked the boy across the face for shaking his father during his evening prayer to say dinner was ready?

"Do you want to watch?"

"I'm not sure," the boy said.

"It's okay if you don't."

"I'll stay here."

His father went and took his grandfather by the arm. They left the boy in the sitting room with the half-finished cups of coffee and biscuit crumbs. Anxious, he began to pace. He kept his back to the open door, the open windows. He heard strips of prayer carried in on the breeze. Then a terrible silence. He waited for a scream, a high-pitched cry for mercy, but there was nothing. Or not nothing; merely a grunt, as of someone mildly frustrated. Then there were more prayers, and the sounds of his father and the others performing what the boy had been told was an old ritual from the village: hopping over the dying animal to celebrate its generosity.

Soon everyone came back inside. The talking resumed. The boy's grandmother cleared the plates. So effortless, the boy thought, this transition from conversation to slaughter and back to conversation again. From time to time, his grandfather looked at him. All the boy could see in the lines of that face was something of his father's when he'd say, to no effect, how much he didn't want to speak Arabic, to pray or fast when everyone around him—not his mother, and certainly not his younger sister—didn't have to.

The boy willed his body up and out into the courtyard to escape his grandfather's ancient judgment. The lamb lay in the darkening sand, still tethered to the stake. The boy leaned over and looked into its glassy eyes because he felt that's what his grandfather wanted. He stared at the neat red cut along the throat, the bib of blood underneath it, because that's what his grandfather wanted. The butcher stood at a remove, waiting. In time, he would carry the carcass into the kitchen and carve it into manageable pieces for the boy's grandmother and his aunt to season and cook. The boy's stomach lurched at the thought of all that meat searing, the pink giving way to gray. He ran to the clay water pitchers and drank down the urge to vomit.

After the noon prayers, which the boy mimed as he'd done during his private school years, as tender flesh was stripped from pale bone with kitchen knives, as it sat in oil and garlic and lemon juice, his father said they were going on a short trip.

"Where?"

"An oil refinery outside the city. Your uncle arranged it with a friend of the family. They want to impress us."

"But it's just oil," the boy said as they climbed into the cab of his uncle's truck.

"Not to them," his father said as the butcher climbed into the truck bed.

They dropped the butcher off at the livestock market, and the boy pretended to nap so he didn't have to see the lowing creatures, didn't have to wonder if any of them missed the lamb that had been carried off yesterday afternoon. Then they drove west along a road cut into the brilliant orange landscape, all that sandy earth the boy thought of whenever his father spoke of his boyhood spent in a small mud room with a roof of branches and leaves just ten feet from a generous curve of the Nile River. ("The White Nile," his father was always careful to note.) Could his father, then, have imagined where he was now? No, the boy thought. It would be as impossible to imagine as it was for the boy to see himself here and imagine not three days but an entire life. Like being stranded on the moon. And how could the boy weigh his own meager life against his father's? Crossing an ocean to study journalism and political science at Georgetown University, then off on assignments to places that, to the boy, were merely names on giant maps rolled down over chalkboards. Living with a mustache, then a beard, then an embarrassing Afro, and now the receding hairline he wore with pride. Living with the strangeness of that dark skin against the paleness of his wife's world, his own children's lighter shades of brown. All that time, all those lives, all that mixing with the world, converging in this man who jostled against him in the cab of a truck as they made their way into the desert. And what did that make the boy next to him? How could he be trusted with this landscape, with the people in it, who'd seemed, until just yesterday, as uncanny as characters in his comic books? He'd never admit this feeling to his father, and maybe he didn't need to. Maybe it was already perfectly obvious.

Up ahead, the refinery climbed like a gleaming spider from all that sand. His uncle stopped in front of a gate and waited for a security guard to approach. The boy stared at the automatic weapon in the guard's powerful hands.

His uncle rolled down his window and leaned out to speak to the guard in Arabic. After a minute, his tone deepened.

"Closed," his father said. "He's telling the guard we have a visit specially arranged. He's saying we came all this way."

Another minute of conversation passed. His uncle pointed directly at him.

"Now what's happening, Dad?"

"He's saying, 'Don't insult the Americans.'"

The security guard peered at the boy and his father. He smirked, made the sound of a bomb blast, and chuckled. The boy recalled a brief moment that previous spring, when they'd been on their way to the mall and his father had accidentally cut off a motorcyclist, and the man had rumbled up alongside them at the next stoplight, leaned into the open passenger-side window, and said, over the boy, to his father, "Nice driving, you stupid fucking nigger," before roaring off through the red light. His father had worn the same look he wore now: a blank, depersonalized stare, as if his brain, caught between anger and shame, couldn't figure out what to do next and so did nothing. Just as the boy had done nothing; had, in fact excused himself from the situation by thinking how unlike his father he was, by convincing himself that word, that agony, was his father's lot and not his.

Eventually his uncle conceded, or perhaps realized, with his American brother beside him, it wasn't worth a protracted argument or ridicule. His uncle and the guard smiled at each other as if this misunderstanding had been nothing but a game. His uncle backed the truck away from the refinery and turned east along the main road. The words between the boy's father and his uncle were sparse, hushed; their Arabic sounded wilted and in need of water. The boy searched the sky for planes: American bombers, German commercial carriers.

They returned to his grandfather's courtyard to find it already filled with arrivals for the evening feast. More faces, more introductions, more embraces, more photographs. Wide blankets and cots were brought into the courtyard, and the boy lay among his cousins and smiled and nodded and did the best he could with the little he had. For a time, he joined them in kicking a soccer ball back and forth, more to escape the thick smell of grilled meat coming from the kitchen than anything else. The finish line, he thought as he played. He could feel it already: the judder of wheels rising up into the plane's belly. He could hear it: the growing hum of their plane heading up and up and up, home and home and home.

When the lamb arrived, that breeze-loving face now just thick squares of blackened meat rimmed by rice, the boy looked to his father. He wanted his father to notice the effort he made to tear away a piece of bread, to grip the smallest possible piece of flesh, to slip it between his lips. The chewing—oh, how awful! But he was determined to make a show of gratitude, and when his father acknowledged what he'd endured, when the boy kissed his fingers like a chef to show his uncle's video recorder just how delicious the lamb was, he hated every single person in that courtyard for what they made him do, what they reminded him of.

After dinner he and his cousins resumed their soccer game. As they played in the dusk, the boy noticed his father and grandfather arguing once more. The boy took advantage of missed goals to chase the ball toward their argument. He caught those words, like a common refrain. *Clinton. Amrikiya.* His uncle looked aghast at what his father was saying. The boy's grandfather sat there between his sons, in silence. He gestured to the boy. The boy's father made a show of shifting his body, so that now he sat with his back to his kin.

After a moment, the boy left his cousins and dropped down next to his father.

"They think I'm responsible," his father said once he'd finished his mouthful of meat and rice. He laughed and shook his head in disbelief. "I didn't send those planes out here. They wanted to know how it makes me feel to raise you and your sister there, if I feel wrong about it. But I don't. I told them that given the chance, they'd want what I have. I chose to leave, they chose to stay. Now I feel like I've forgotten how to talk to them. I don't know what's happened."

There it was again: that gleam of tenderness, that breach in his father's armor. It was enough for the boy to whisper as if they were a conspiracy of two.

"Lufthansa flight three ninety-four," the boy said. "Lufthansa flight two-oh-two."

"I don't understand."

"One more day, and then we're going back home."

His father looked at him and considered this. The boy was prepared to fall into his father's arms, right there in front of everyone else, but one of the guests announced his departure. A family member? A friend? The boy had already forgotten, but it didn't matter. The gleam was gone, the breach closed. His father helped his grandfather to his feet, obediently. Together they led the guest to the courtyard doors.

That night, everyone who stayed slept outside on cots or blankets with their faces up to the cooling air. The boy lay alongside his cousins, and while they slept he projected himself into the next evening, when these three days would be behind him, and as he did, his father made repeated trips to the unventilated outhouse. The boy watched, through half-closed eyes, his father slink across the yard with one of the rolls of toilet paper they'd brought from their hotel in Hamburg to spare the boy from wiping with his hands. He imagined, with a fair share of glee, that intestinal distress, his father's exploding guts chiding him for being gone too many years, for having the audacity to come back, to act as if nothing had ever changed.

· · ·

Back now in his familiar khaki shorts. Back now in his familiar sneakers, the familiar dark blue T-shirt he'd worn the morning they left Hamburg. How ready he was, how happy! How he woke up with the dawn, performed the morning prayers with gusto! How he drank his grandmother's coffee and ate her bread and hard-boiled eggs with such relish—all while his father pulled himself along and waved away the invitation for the food his son happily accepted on his behalf.

And then they were back in his uncle's truck, not headed to the airport, not just yet, but for a morning excursion downtown, arranged by a friend of the family.

"The same one who planned yesterday?"

The boy's father was in no mood for such wit. He climbed into the truck bed with their suitcase and braced himself against the wheel wells.

"You can go inside," the boy said.

"I'm fine here. It's safer for you in there."

"Your stomach."

"There's nothing left to get rid of. You have your camera, yes?"

The boy pulled the palm-sized disposable out of his shorts pocket and held it up to his father's exhausted face.

His grandfather rode next to him in the cab. What could the boy, alone, say to the old man? They smiled at each other, both of them idiots for a time, then turned their attention to the passing landscape. His grandfather seemed morose, disdainful. The boy weighed his grandfather's joints and wrinkles, watched his fingers fumble with the strand of sandalwood prayer beads. When the truck bounced over an uncomfortable patch of road, they looked back to make sure the man dear and frustrating to them both in different ways was still there.

The family friend had made calls, many calls, and when the small caravan of overnight guests pulled up to the docks outside the National Museum of Sudan, there were nearly three dozen people milling around the wide stone steps with sacks and backpacks and picnic baskets. Behind them rested the double-decker diesel-engine ferry chartered for a three-hour trip along the river that ran through the city like the fat blue veins in the boy's brown feet.

His grandfather said something as they made their way up the gangplank.

"This is just like one of the British steamers he used to work on," his father said. "He can't remember the last time he was on a boat like this. Up and down the White Nile, delivering mail to the British and the Bedouins. Remember that story?"

"Yes," the boy said.

Slowly, so slowly the boy didn't even notice until everyone began to cheer and clap, the boat slipped away from the dock. The late morning was overcast, so the landscape appeared flat and gray in the disposable camera's viewfinder. He knew that when they returned and his father had the photos printed and the boy dutifully laid them out in a photo album he'd squirrel away high up on a shelf in his bedroom, all those shots would make shameful representations of the sweeping riverbanks, the trees leaning toward the river like crowds before a famous painting.

His father joined him at the gunwale, and for a time it was the two of them there, outcasts of a sort. The boy followed his father's finger with his camera, continued to take pictures. He felt like the worst kind of tourist: one who shoots where told, follows where led.

An ivory stalk and a dome poked over the tops of the palms.

"The Mosque of the Two Niles," his father said.

A stretch of pale brown building that looked, to the boy, like an egg crate.

"The University of Khartoum," his father said. "Where I went to school."

A white fort teeming with windows and terraces and soldiers.

"The Republican Palace," his father said.

The boy looked to the graying sky for the jigsaw shape of stealth bombers. He imagined these buildings, this landscape, obliterated from the face of the earth, as he'd worked so hard to obliterate this world from his life. He spied his grandfather sitting alone in a white plastic deck chair, watching the riverbank. He took a photograph.

The steamer churned alongside a stretch of land set like a comma between the cities of Khartoum North and Omdurman.

"Tuti Island," his father said, and pointed up ahead. He told the boy that was where the White Nile and the Blue Nile converged, becoming the single great river that wound north, as if dragged by a massive finger, all the way to the Mediterranean Sea. The boy looked to a spot where he saw, or thought he saw, a shifting band in the river where the two currents, one murky, one milky, met and intertwined. But there was no crash, no violence. No spectacle to suggest different currents fighting for dominance. The river ahead was complacent, the merging silent and unremarkable. Easy to overlook, were it not for his father's finger showing the way. The boy took a photograph, for all the good he thought it would do. What would the image be, back in America, but a four-by-six of river water, as innocuous as any stretch of water anywhere in the world?

Behind them, some of the women broke out in song: a popular tune, his father said, in praise of Sudanese fashion. Why dress in jeans, his aunts and cousins sang, why dress in a suit, when you can wear a jalabiya? How else will you feel the breeze kiss your body? The men danced in slow circles to the women's voices, kept time with their upraised right hands, goaded on the raucous singing and clapping and ululating. The boy watched his father's left foot tap to the rhythm of those voices. He waited for his father to leave him there, alone against the gunwale. He waited in fear for someone to come lead him into the dance, but when his uncle eventually came toward them, it was only to hand them two sandwiches wrapped in waxed paper.

"Cold cuts," his father said when he pulled apart the white bread.

The boy noticed the pained look on his father's face, wondered if they were now being teased. The Americans and their delicate stomachs. He knew all about taunts—one didn't make it through the world with his name, his skin color, and not encounter them. But to be taunted here? The river grew choppier, and as it did, the boy grew angry. He wanted to step into the center of all that dancing and singing, to silence it. He couldn't speak the language, no, but he could point at his digital watch. He could tell everyone aboard just how close to 6:25 P.M. they were. He could point to the sky, could mime the movement of Lufthansa flight 394 heading west. That, he knew, anyone could understand.

His father turned back to face the river.

"You want mine?"

"No," the boy said. "I'm not hungry either."

His father looked over his shoulder, then surreptitiously let the sandwich drop into the river. The boy did the same. It was the closest he'd felt to his father since they'd arrived here. Maybe ever.

Soon the steamer turned and began cruising down the opposite coast of Tuti Island. The current intensified, and now they had to hold on to the gunwale with both hands. There, the boy thought. The convergence. That's more like it. Then he noticed the clouds, the great paw of thunderheads creeping toward them, and frowned.

"They won't cancel our flight, right?"

"I hope not," his father said.

Everyone else, of course, ignored the skies, the approaching storm, until rain suddenly fell in sheets and wind rocked the boat more than any boat, the boy felt, had a right to be rocked. They joined the others huddled at the center of the boat. Their feet slipped on the deck; their clothes stuck to their bodies. Still, there was singing and eating, and the boy surged with anger. His grandfather sat patiently among them in a white plastic deck chair, another upended over him as a makeshift umbrella. There was something religious about the image. It struck the boy, in that moment, that had his father not left Sudan, this could very well have been him, wearing a wet jalabiya, caught in the mouth of two plastic chairs, sandalwood prayer beads dangling from his right wrist. That was his father's alter life, just as the cousins laughing around them were his.

Again, the boat heaved under their feet. Sandals and sneakers squealed. The laughter turned slightly uneasy. The land around them became a blur in the falling rain. Were they on the Blue Nile now? The White Nile? What did it matter, when the river tossed the steamer the way the boy would toss a tennis ball between his hands? Another dangerous lurch threw everyone about, sent them clutching for whatever was nearby: arms, tables, parts of the boat. The boy moved for his father's arm, grasped it with both hands, and it was then he saw, so swiftly that for a moment he wasn't sure he'd seen it, the starboard side of the steamer lift from the surface of the river and his grandfather, still seated in his plastic deck chair, tilt over and slide off the boat through a gap in the railing.

The laughter halted, abruptly, and when it turned to outright screaming, he knew he wasn't the only one who'd seen. His father let go of him, told him to stay put, and rushed out into the storm. His uncle followed. There were cries and signals for the boat captain to stop. But what could the captain do? What could any of them do in such a tempest but hold on while the steamer continued to pitch and yaw toward shore?

Even after the steamer finally jolted against the dock, that great paw continued to press down on them with thunder, with rain. Everyone stumbled and tiptoed and leapt down the gangplank. The boy's grandmother rushed along the dock to try to spot his grandfather somewhere out there in all that muddy churn. The boy's father and uncle scrambled up the wide stone steps toward the museum, cried out to onlookers for help. Dumbstruck, the boy realized he had no idea what the Arabic was for the word.

The steamer captain now blew the ship's horn, a deep bellow to summon the boy's grandfather back from the water with his plastic deck chairs, his sandalwood prayer beads. Back from the depths to watch his son and grandson with something that wasn't quite judgment, wasn't quite love. Caution, maybe. Concern. A slight frown and lowered eyes that said, Who are these sons, and what are they to me? The boy imagined he was the one who'd gone overboard into that mighty river. His was the corpse carried along beneath the surface, to be found, as he knew his grandfather would be, farther downstream. His was the body buried in a sandy cemetery, over which prayers were said. But found when? Buried when? How long would that take?

He broke away from the panic around him to find his father and his uncle and was halfway to the museum when they emerged. They nearly tripped descending the steps in the shattering rain. The boy's uncle pushed past him to where the rest of the family stood in a line along the dock.

"Dad," he said.

His father held fast to the boy, as if the boy were the only thing keeping the rain from washing him down the museum's stairs. The ship's horn boomed around them. The boy's grandmother, looking out at the river, began to wail. The boy's uncle yelled up at them; his father yelled back.

"Dad. Dad, what's happening?"

"They're sending police. They're going to search the river."

His father looked over the boy's head at the steamboat, the thrashing current beyond. The boy looked over his father's shoulder, at the still-dark sky, for any sight of Lufthansa flight 394.

"Dad, how long will it be?"

Had he said the words aloud? He must have, because his father looked down at him, aghast, as if the boy had suddenly appeared in front of him. He let go of the boy's arm and trembled as if fit to explode in one of the rages the boy knew so well. The boy waited for a slap. Instead, his father raised his hands to his wild face and began to screech.

"A'aba ja," he cried. "A'aba ja! A'aba ja!"

His father was a babe again, and these were his first words, the only words he could shape with his trembling mouth. The boy stood next to him on the steps, in the rain. A missing grandfather, a missed flight home. He wanted to cry alongside his father, but his eyes wouldn't cooperate. His father kept wailing, and the sound drew more cries from everyone on the dock, drew the attention of bystanders at the museum, seemed even to draw down on the boy the grim, unforgiving faces of the armless Nubian pharaohs alongside the museum entrance.

"Dad," the boy said.

He reached for his father, tried to pull the hands away from his face. His father resisted. There were only his knuckles and fingers, his cries.

"A'aba ja! A'aba ja!"

The boy had no idea how to arrange his father's noises into something coherent, something that could make sense to him. It sounded like something his father had been saying all his life, a primal cry dredged up from a time before the boy existed.

"I'm here," the boy said. "Dad, I'm right here!"

The boy shook and shook, but his father wouldn't remove his hands from his eyes, wouldn't stop wailing. He made to continue blindly down the steps to where the rest of the family was, but the boy held him back. He stood between his father and the rest of his family, an arid patch of land among all that unrelenting wet. *A'aba ja.* Was this some story his father had told him? If only he knew, they could weep and pray and rend their soaked clothes together, they could find something to fill the space between their miseries. But first he needed his father to stop wailing. He needed his father to translate.

Yah Yah Scholfield
Strange Fruit

Summer's the best time for picking. Though the fruit buds and ripens all year round, there's no better time than the height of summer, the heat radiating off the sidewalks and the car windows, people's radiators blowing out cool-hot air, the whirring sound of A/C mingling with blasting music, people laughing, people talking, cussing, the summer bugs. Feels like one big hum, your skin and scalp prickling with sweat, like you could wring yourself and hang yourself out to dry on the porch railing.

Mama's too sick to go with us this time, so me, Rochelle, Tito, and Kiki go by ourselves. Takes a while to get there if you don't got a car or a bike. Kiki and Tito—they're siblings, half—used to have bikes, but their daddy put them away after what happened to Ricky. Too close to home, he said, so now the four of us are walking down the street, some of us holding machetes, some of us holding black garbage bags, heading out to the field where all the fruits are. As we walk, people join us. It's some kids, some teenagers, some adults, but all of us have the same look, brown and Black skins carrying things, lugging wagons and strollers and shopping carts, holding knives and garden shears to make the cutting down easier, all going the same direction.

When I was little, Mama would hold the tools and I'd hold on to Tyrone. He was real big, even back then, but gentle as a butterfly. He'd let me sit on his shoulders if I asked, and I always asked because up there, you could see the whole block, all the houses and the curve of the hill, the subtle line where concrete became dirt and then field. Now that I'm big—not as big as him, nobody is big like him—I don't sit on Tyrone's shoulders. I just walk with a cramp in my side that I huff through. I'm the one holding the machete this time, and it feels serious in my hand. We usually use it for cutting open fruit, cutting the grass, and I guess it has the same purpose this year, only different because the shape of the fruit is different.

We're walking, and Rochelle is talking aloud, talking to anybody that'll listen to her. Kiki and Tito are like me, quiet and thinking. This is the fourth time they've been out to the field to pick the fruit, which is a lot but not as much as some people. One lady, Miss Johnson, she goes to the field just about every season, every year, and each time she goes, her shoulders sink lower and lower. She's somewhere near the back, folded over her son's shoulder, eyes red and mouth drawn tight like she got the dark, sour part of the plum right beneath the skin. Kiki and Tito are almost drawn in like that, 'cept that they're too young for it, and on them it looks like they're corpses, small and wrinkled.

It's real easy to lose yourself in a sea of people. The whole street is bodies carrying, bodies moving forward. I'm myself, then I'm just an arm and a leg, a neck, a head. Are those my box braids or hers? Whose brown hand is that? Whose dark eye and nose, whose lips, whose voice? I hold my machete close to my chest and think like an ant. March forward, march on, go with the line, you little black thing, don't get stepped on, don't get crushed, keep carrying things two times your weight and more.

Rochelle stops short. Bends down to scratch her ankle. People jostle her, push her around, but she doesn't seem to notice them. She bends down even farther, squatting, looking at something on the ground.

"Chel . . ." I tug the back of her shirt, ill fitting and splotched. Not hers. Her sister's, my cousin's. "Come on."

"Look!" And she shows me the hot asphalt, sparkling bits of broken glass on the street. Beer bottles, windows, whatever. Her mind is funny like that. Sometimes she can think plain and straight, narrow as a hall, and other times her mind goes wavy, circumventing the heavier stuff to pick up the lighter. Rochelle runs her hand along the street, picking up gravel and dirt and glass in her palm. I tug her along because I'm some of the only family she's got left, and if I leave her there on the street, touching broken bottles and sunlight, there'll be nobody from her family to pick this year. Usually somebody else, a friend or a play uncle, will take care of it, big folks from the neighborhood picking for somebody down and out, but Rochelle doesn't have much of anybody. Her daddy's gone and all four of her brothers, two of her sisters, and her mama is barely holding on, just scraps of meat stuck to the bone trying not to be blown away.

So, I make her come with me. I hold her hand with one of mine, and the machete in the other, and the three of us walk together, Rochelle in her sister's tie-dye shirt, and me thinking about my brother, Tyrone, who used to be her cousin as well.

When we get to the field—all of us, the whole damn neighborhood, practically—we see what we see every year. The trees heavy with fruit, the ground covered with the overripe ones, purple and oozing, blue and bursting with juice. The smell is unthinkable, the skin rotting and the pits turning sour. The newer fruits, still fresh enough to be recognizable as one person's or another's, aren't that bad, but they're stiff and banged up. These are wicked plants, fed by flesh and watered by blood. The roots are red; the fruits are strange. Still, every year, every season, every week, they're planted. Still, we return to the field and take our pick, filling our baskets and bags and wagons and carts so there's a little bit of peace and not so much of a smell.

This isn't my first time going to the field, but it is my first time picking. Usually, I'm at the edge of the field with all my cousins, doing kid stuff, kicking rocks and playing tag. We let the big kids and the adults handle the picking. Our hands were too new to be smeared with brown and red, the skins coming off like roach wings in our grasps. Sometimes, we'd look over and see them taking the fruit down or hauling it off the ground when it was overripe, and feel all shivery because it was a matter of when, not if, and just about everybody knew somebody in the field.

We spread out. Kiki and Tito go there, and Rochelle goes here, and everyone helps everybody else where they can. Some are weak in the limbs. Others are weak in the spirit, like their whole soul is doubled over. There's always crying on the harvest days, long and full of an unspeakable pain. For the thirteenth year in a row, Miss Johnson falls to her knees and beats her chest. I see grown men and women tearing their hair, face down on the ground wailing like children. My friends, people who I go to school with, stare blankly at the trees, swaying like saplings, too wrung out to cry. They pick their fruits. Their bodies grow weary, but they carry on—ants lifting, carrying, even when it hurts.

It used to be Tyrone would go into the field with Daddy, then the uncles, then finally by himself. He wouldn't let Mama do it alone. Didn't like the look on her face when she came back from it, like she'd been gutted and all her organs were on the outside of her, heart included, exposed to the air and raw. He was big, my brother Tyrone. He put the fruit over his shoulders and carried them home to replant them in a gentler garden. My brother was gentle, meeker than Jesus. Sweet, like a song, and all the old folks in the community remember him for taking the loads they couldn't, for being kind and nice and good.

I remember him the same way, nice and kind and good, big and gentle and sweet, but it doesn't seem fair. What if he was mean, like the Lewis girls? What if he was big and cold like Mr. Johnston, or big and unyielding like they say the others were? What if he was carrying a machete, like me, or a gun, like that boy? He didn't do nothing wrong, our Tyrone, but what if he was hungry like we all got hungry, needy like we all were needy?

No use wondering. I find the fruit low down in the poplar tree, blue and purple and bloodless. He's nothing like he used to be, just big and black and a little familiar around the mouth. He's tall, and the soles of his Nikes touch the top of my head. I feel like Miss Johnson, screaming, and like my friends, quiet and screaming too. On my own, I climb the tree and cut the branches. On my own, I untie the rope and gently lower him down to the ground, the rope burning my palms as it rushes through my hands. I cover his eyes with silver dollars, then cover his face.

We're through picking by sundown. There's still fruit in the trees and on the ground, some having been there for ages, unclaimed or unwanted. Maybe tomorrow people will come and pick again, or maybe they'll stay there, rotting on the vine, family too scared or too tired to take down another fruit, another neck, another leg. For now, we wrap our tools, our strange fruits, and we take them home where they belong, where they can be buried and known and remembered.

I'm not big like Tyrone was, but for the first time, I carry him on my shoulders. Let him see the whole block, where the field becomes the street, all the houses and the curve of the hill.

Chika Unigwe
Miracle in Lagos Traffic

THE DAY AFTER I ended my fasting for Ije, I was handed a miracle. With thinning hair and sunken cheeks, he'd rapped on the driver's side of the car window, begging for money. My driver, impatient with the slow-moving traffic, began to wave him away and I, for some reason, said not to do that. Maybe it was because praying and fasting had made me extra charitable. "Find some change for him," I told the driver. I always left money in the glove compartment of the 505 for incidentals. Never for the horde of beggars Lagos spawned. I agreed with Nze, my husband, that anyone resourceful enough found work to do, even in the present economy. Nze thought it was laziness and greed that drove able-bodied men and women to beg. Nze would know, he grew up poor. "And not once did it ever occur to my family to accost citizens and ask them for money."

The boy couldn't have heard me, but he glued himself to our car, and once he saw the driver open the glove compartment, he began to smile and raise his hands in thanks. He had a mouth full of small, surprisingly white teeth. The driver gave him a ₦1,000 note, muttering something he was wise enough not to let me hear. He likely didn't think I should be giving out money to someone who hadn't earned it, not when we hadn't raised his salary in the three years he had been with us. He asked about it once, after he learned that the driver of one of our friends earned ₦5,000 more than he did. Nze told him he could leave if he was no longer happy to work for us. "How many drivers earn forty thousand nairas?" Nze asked him.

The boy was effusive in his gratitude. He didn't move on to other cars. He sprinted beside ours like a wild animal, chanting, "God go bless you, madam. God go bless you plenty. God go give you anythin' wey you wan." I wasn't superstitious, but there was something about the prayer that made me feel that maybe I was really going to be blessed. Maybe this boy was the answer, the miracle that had necessitated the praying and the fasting in the first instance. So I wound my window down. Where did he live? Not far away. How old was he? Sixteen, he said. Same age as my twins, although he had the leathery look of an old man. Did he want to earn money? His head nodded manically, bobbing up and down so fast it made me dizzy to watch. He wanted to earn money. He could work hard. Wash cars. Cook. Whatever I wanted. "Yes, madam. Thank you, madam. God bless you, madam." I gave him my address and asked him to pass by on Sunday morning. Eleven A.M. Could he find the house? Yes, he could. "God bless you, madam."

Nze wasn't happy that I'd invited a street urchin—his words, not mine—to the house. I told him not to be such a snob. It was foolhardy, he said. He was going to tell the gateman to turn the boy back if he did turn up. Did I not know how dangerous that was? That he could be part of an armed robbery gang? Or kidnapping gang? "Really?" I said. "If he was part of a gang, would he be begging in traffic?" Nze had nothing to say to that. Armed robbers and kidnappers were raking in money. Only recently, a Protestant bishop was kidnapped on his way back to Onitsha from Lagos. His driver, killed on the spot. The kidnappers had asked for a ₦100 million ransom, which his congregation raised. The bishop had come on TV to talk about how his abductors had fed him only once a day. "Watery beans like shit, food you wouldn't even give to prisoners," as if the indignity of the terrible food was a worse crime than his abduction. "How much do you think a begging gig fetches?" I asked Nze. He grunted. He still didn't think it was a good idea that I had invited this stranger to our home. "And how do you know that he'll be a fit?" he asked. A sensible enough question, I admitted, but we wouldn't know if we didn't try, I said. Plus my intuition said it would work out. The idea to ask the boy to come had landed like a dove on my shoulders. My pastor would say it was my spirit. Nze rolled his eyes. He didn't put much stock in my instincts. Or my spirit. I had been praying for a miracle, I told him. Nze did not believe in miracles. He said something to me about chasing shadows. I said something caustic back. Our voices were dangerous and low because we didn't want the girls to know we were fighting. "A child his age shouldn't be begging in traffic. He should be in school," I said, trying again to convince my husband. It was thanks to a community scholarship that he had gone to a boarding school in Enugu and then on to Nsukka campus, which was where we met. He would never have met me otherwise, or if he had, he wouldn't have dared to talk to me. He was the son of a palm wine tapper. I was solidly middle-class, daughter of two college professors; our orbits would not have crossed. Unwilling to give up my advantage, I continued. We'd be killing two birds with one stone. We could change that boy's life, give him a chance at the kind of life the government couldn't give him, and help ourselves too, I said. "If it worked out," Nze said, already sounding resigned. It would work out, I said. But even if it didn't we wouldn't send him away empty-handed. We would still give him something. A bit of money, new clothes. I was relieved that we had averted a fight.

Nze and I had been fighting more than we used to. It felt as if in the last four months we'd fought more than we had in all of our twenty years together. The last thing our twins needed, with everything else going on, was for them to see their parents biting chunks off each other. But Nze and I agreed on little these days. Whatever I said, he countered. I spent my weekends in church. He spent his doing whatever. An illness like that, Violetta said when I complained to her, would put stress on any relationship. Don't take any rash decisions, she warned me. Violetta was my best friend, and the illness was Ije's, one half of the twins.

Ije's illness had started innocently enough. Four days of coughing that we hadn't thought much of. Lagos's dust in the harmattan was legendary, after all. Houses were coated in dust. Everyone coughed. That was why we always stocked up on cough syrup and ugolo. I gave Ije routine Benadryl to soothe the cough. And bitter kola to suck on, since she could not bring herself to bite into its bitterness. When she began to throw up, her stomach cramping, we didn't panic. Nze had made fish the night before, and there was something dodgy about the fish. Even I hadn't felt very well after eating it. I was sure he hadn't washed the fish properly but he was a man who cooked, and so I hadn't complained too much about how he ought to have washed the fish with alum first, soaking it in warm water. I made Ije a pot of chicken soup and told her to stay home from school. "Watch Nollywood movies. You'll be fine soon," I promised. On the seventh day, she asked if we hadn't noticed that her face was swelling: she looked as if she had been wrestling a stronger opponent. Nze took her then to see our family doctor because he could take the day off work. The doctor was concerned, Nze told me when I returned from teaching tedious teenagers mathematics at the high school. The doctor had ordered more tests and would call us when she had the results.

By the time the boy came on Sunday morning, accompanied by a man he said was his father, Nze had mellowed. My brain wave, he said, did not have to work the first time, but it made sense to try, and why hadn't we thought of it earlier? Lagos was full of people who would be willing to sell their organs for a bit of money, he said. He meant poor people. Only recently, a clip had gone viral on WhatsApp, of a woman who rented a house with no kitchen, no bathroom, and a living room that was always flooded in the rainy season. She slept on a couch because she had no bed. "Maybe we should be meeting these strangers elsewhere," Nze said. "In the future, maybe we should arrange to meet them at a restaurant, at least for the first meeting." I could have replied that our proposal wasn't something we should be discussing in restaurants full of people. Or that I was convinced we wouldn't need to find someone else, but I kept quiet. I was enjoying the fact that we were not arguing. The house seemed like a live thing, breathing and anxious, holding its breath to see how long our truce lasted. We hadn't told the twins what we were doing because what if, despite my spirit saying the boy would be a match, he wasn't? We mustn't raise their hopes, Nze cautioned, and I agreed with him on that. The girls had been begging to go to the beach at Landmark, so we sent them off with the driver. If they were suspicious at our suddenly giving in to this request, they did not say a word.

The boy said his name was Obike. His voice was hoarse and I couldn't remember if it had been like that two days ago, but he didn't speak much. His father did most of the talking. A small, wiry man, dressed completely in black, he looked like a bird of prey. He was a roadside mechanic, employed by a man who only paid him a commission. It killed him not to be able to fend for his family. He didn't want his son begging, but Obike insisted on earning money for the family as the eldest child. Sometimes Obike went to Balogun market and did odd jobs running errands for traders when they let him. I noticed then that the hands holding the bottle of Coke he was drinking were calloused. They did not look like the hands of a teenager. His grip on the bottle was so strong I feared the bottle would break. He smiled sheepishly at everything in our sitting room. The TV. The bookcase. The huge sculpture of a woman carrying a child on her back I bought at Elegushi market three years ago. "When my son told me someone offered him a job, I said let me come with him to make sure it's genuine. The city is full of ritualists," Obike's father cackled. He spoke Igbo. Comforted by the fact that we were Igbo too, he had quickly switched from pidgin English to our language. He'd come to Lagos as a young father ten years ago, lured by the stories of how easy it was to make money in the city. He'd left Udi, where his farming brought little in, and moved his family—his wife and three children—to the city, where he'd hoped to progress. Ten years and nothing to show for it. He was too ashamed to go back to Udi. With which mouth would he tell people that his son was a beggar? That his wife sometimes pretended to be deaf and dumb, walking around with a placard in traffic asking for alms? "We all do what we have to do," I said, wondering when to bring up the reason for our meeting. The job we hoped his son could do for us. Then Nze got right to it. He didn't believe in wasting time on small talk, buttering people up. He'd always say that he hadn't spent years running his own successful business to waffle around when there was business to be discussed. "So this is the proposal. If it works, your family will be set for life. One million nairas, a job in my business. Obike can go to school. We'll see to it. If your son isn't a right match, then shame."

Obike's father opened his mouth, shut it. He reminded me of a fish. He brought out a handkerchief and wiped his bald head as if he was sweating. Obike looked confused. He turned to his father. "Papa?" his voice squeaked. There was a silence and Nze spoke into it. I didn't know what exactly the doctor had said about the risks, but Nze said there weren't any. "Think about it," he said. Later, I would tell Nze that he should have told the truth. There was no surgery without risks, even if those risks were minimal, like the doctor had said. For both Ije and the donor. If it worked out, the boy would be better off after it than he was now. If I were in their shoes, I thought, I'd take the risk. Nze should have made that kind of case.

The doctor had called us in a few days after Ije's tests to discuss the results. He rattled off a diagnosis, introducing a whole new vocabulary into our home. Renal disease. Dialysis. Kidney transplant. The disease hung around like a monster sucking up air in our house. There was no cure, the doctor said. She either went on dialysis for life or had to get a transplant. But for the transplant, there was a long list and very few options for donors. Perhaps her twin could donate one? "People don't really need two kidneys," the doctor said as nonchalantly as if he were discussing Amaka, Ije's twin, deciding to get a haircut to chop off her hair. If she was compatible, that'd be the best, he said. I wanted to gouge out his eyes. God forbid, I said. There must be some other way. How could I ask a healthy sixteen-year-old to give up a kidney for her sister? I would sacrifice for my daughter, but it wasn't her sister's place to do that. I tested but was no match. Something about HLA compatibility or whatever. Nze was an AB blood type to Ije's A, which ruled him out too. There was no need to ask Amaka to test because we were never going to allow her to donate her kidney. She was still young, had her whole life ahead of her. Besides, if something went wrong, we could lose both children. It was Violetta who told me about the black market. She introduced us to some man who said he could get us a donor but "it go cost ooo." He wanted ₦100,000 for every person he brought to us that was tested. And if there was a match, we'd pay ₦20 million before the surgery and half of that after. Where were we supposed to get ₦30 million from? And how many people would we have to go through to find a match?

Plucking Obike from traffic had not been planned. That he would match was an unexpected bonus, never mind what my spirit told me. My intuition, my spirit, did not always get it right. When I was pregnant with the girls, I was sure I was having boys. I had bought boy clothes and held boy names under my tongue. When Ije started coughing, my spirit hadn't been able to detect that something was seriously wrong with her. So who was to say that it wouldn't have led me astray this time? But it had been right enough times in the past for me to trust it. In the most notable example, I had planned to travel to Enugu by bus for a wedding. I woke up that morning with a heaviness in my chest that I knew was my spirit's way of forcing me to listen to it. The bus I would have been on was attacked later that day by unknown gunmen, just after the Niger Bridge. The papers said no one survived. Now, with Obike, my spirit whispered to me that everything would be all right, the same way it did the day I met Nze after a series of really terrible boyfriends. Besides, Obike was perfect. His father had asked for some of the money up front so that Obike didn't have to beg. So he could stay home and eat well and sleep well. We gave him ₦250,000, more money than the family had ever seen at once, the father said. And we went further, thinking up new ways to help the family because the fire had been lit inside us. We sent the driver to their house with bags of rice and tubers of yam, crates of soft drinks and cartons of juice. It was as if we were marrying Obike, fattening him up before the wedding. The driver brought back their thanks. I didn't tell him what our business was, but I saw a look creep into his eyes the first time we sent him over with foodstuff, a look both sly and judgmental. Whatever it was, he knew better than to speak his mind. Nze said it was jealousy.

The last time I saw Obike, his skin shone as if he'd shed his previous skin. He looked like a church hymn. All glorious and pure. His eyes gleamed like something new. He'd grown supple on our food. He'd come to say thank you before going into hospital the next day to begin the procedure. I was surprised that he'd come to the house, as that hadn't been the plan. But I was touched. If I were in his shoes, I might have been overcome with gratitude too and visited my benefactors. Nze wasn't home when Obike came, but the girls and I were. The twins were awkward around him, as if they didn't know how to behave with this boy who was giving a part of him to save one of them, but they talked a lot about him when the family was alone. Ije offered him a drink, and when she brought it, she and Amaka sat at either side of him. They didn't ask him any of the questions they wondered about, like what his hobbies were or what his favorite food was, and he appeared to be intimidated into quietness, the way boys of his age often were in the presence of girls. After a short while, my daughters disappeared into their bedroom. Obike did not seem to mind. He smiled at me, white teeth flashing. His family was going from zero to one million because of him, he said. And all for a small, noninvasive surgery to remove something he didn't need anyway. He sounded like Nze talking to his father, using the same words my husband had used—*noninvasive, small surgery, in and out*—as if he were mocking him, but that couldn't have been it, I thought. "God bless you, Ma," he said over and over again. His nails were clean. He looked like the kind of teenager I was used to seeing in our neighborhood. He could have been any of my neighbors' children. What a difference, I thought, ₦250,000, good food, and a few months could make. Once Ije came out of hospital with her new kidney, we were going to go on holiday. Somewhere fun we had never been to, like Ghana or Senegal. We talked of maybe even bringing Obike with us. He'd never been on a plane before. "Imagine taking him on an airplane," I told Nze, giggling like a child, high on our munificence. The girls couldn't stop talking about it: what they would do on holiday, how nice it would be to have a brother (what else to call someone who was giving you a kidney?). The house bubbled with our happiness, the walls glimmering in ways I hadn't noticed before. The monster that had been sucking up air disappeared, disintegrated into nothing.

The day of the procedure, the sun shone with a stunning brightness. The plan was for the driver to pick up Obike and drive him to the hospital while Nze and I drove with Ije. That morning, even Nze joined me when I knelt to offer a prayer of thanksgiving. "My heart is full, full, Lord," I said, unable to articulate my joy. Underneath that joy was an anxiety that Nze dismissed when I mentioned it to him. Ije would be fine, he said. There was very little risk to her. "But every surgery carries some risk," I said, repeating the doctor's words. "Not for Ije. What does your spirit tell you? Listen to it." I closed my eyes and an assuring calmness washed over me. This time, I was certain, my spirit would not deceive me. Nothing could go wrong. We had Obike, grateful for the life we were giving him, and his compatible kidney, a competent doctor. "It's all up from here, isn't it?" I asked Nze.

We had just arrived at the parking lot of the hospital when the driver called me. Obike was nowhere to be found. "In fact, madam," the driver said. "In fact, de house no even dey again." It was as if Obike's house, a wood and zinc shack, had never existed, he said. "E don disappear like ghost." Something in his voice sounded like he might have been laughing.

The O. Henry Prize Winners 2025

The Writers on Their Work

Wendell Berry, "The Stackpole Legend"
What details or characters did you cut on the editing floor?

I don't have an "editing floor." I believe strongly in cutting, but even more in not wasting words. I was young long enough ago to have inherited the storytelling tradition of my people who have lived here more than two hundred years. Everything has changed by now, but the people I grew up among talked all the time, but mostly they were not long-winded. Mostly they talked to the point and did not waste words.

Wendell Berry has lived with his wife, Tanya Amyx Berry, at Lanes Landing on the Kentucky River since 1965. He has written fairly steadily, and from time to time taught and lectured. Their living has come partly from subsistence farming and subsidence housekeeping. They have two children, five grandchildren, and four great-granddaughters, all of whom live nearby.

Gina Chung, "The Arrow"
What inspired your story?

Often what comes to me first when starting a story is a particular voice or image. In writing "The Arrow," the first image that came to my mind was that of two women walking together in the cold in New York City, amid a festive holiday backdrop, not talking to or looking at one another at all. I wondered who these women were, who they were to each other, and why they were there together but still so alone. Separately, I had also started working on a story about a single woman who learns that she is pregnant but isn't sure who the father is, and decides to keep the baby. This story was originally intended to be more comic in nature, but the situation became much more bittersweet and complicated once my main character's mother entered the picture. Once that happened, the rest of the story clicked into place, and that first image of the two women walking together in the cold came back to me, and I realized that they were my protagonist and her mother.

A lot of my work deals with the complications of family. I'm interested in characters who are compelled in some way to seek out a vastly different way of living than what they might have learned within their family of origin. While all of us must eventually decide what lessons to discard or keep from our childhoods, there are, of course, limitations to how far we can get away from those origins—particularly when they may have been painful or challenging. I'm especially interested in what those decisions look like when the possibility of creating a new family becomes part of the equation. "The Arrow" was my attempt at unpacking some of these ideas.

Gina Chung is a Korean American writer from New Jersey currently living in New York City. She is the author of the short-story collection *Green Frog,* which was a Good Morning America Book Club Buzz Pick and long-listed for the 2024 New American Voices Award, and the novel *Sea Change,* which was long-listed for the Center for Fiction First Novel Prize, a 2023 B&N Discover Pick, an APALA Adult Fiction Honor book, and a *New York Times* Most Anticipated Book. A recipient of the Pushcart Prize, she is a 2021–22 Center for Fiction/Susan Kamil Emerging Writer Fellow and holds an MFA in fiction from the New School.

Addie Citchens, "That Girl"
What made you want to re-create this particular world/reality in fiction?

So many reasons for this story! Primarily, the languid, silky aesthetic is what drew me to re-creating this world in fiction. I can see, feel, and taste it, and it's simply good shit. The star-crossed lovers in "That Girl" lived in a world that wasn't ready for them, and to be honest, they weren't ready for each other. They were just too young, naïve, hopeful, and all those other things that make one ripe for heartbreak. The story represents the unchaseable high of a first love but also the fact that we come to ourselves already knowing who we are. That was part of the heartbreak—which is common I think—when a "well-meaning" adult tries to wrench you out of your self-awareness. I wanted to use a particular rhythm and vernacular for this story because of the surprisingly large and diverse group of people who staunchly adhere to notions of what's canonically "correct," who need to be intellectually knocked around a bit. In that vein, I wrote this work, not just for the sake of the word, but to underscore how the Black female body is treated and the broader geographic, cultural, and environmental implications of that.

Addie Citchens is a Mississippi Delta–born writer of the blues. Her work has been featured in *Callaloo, Oxford American, The Paris Review,* and *The New Yorker,* among others. She was Farrar, Straus and Giroux's inaugural Writing Fellow, and her forthcoming novel, *Dominion,* is slated for release in August 2025. Her blues history work features prominently in *Mississippi Folklife* magazine.

Michael Deagler, "The Pleasure of a Working Life"
What inspired your story?

This story was loosely inspired by the experiences of my father, Dan Deagler, while he was working for the post office, which always struck me as a fertile setting for fiction. He worked there for forty years, as a letter carrier and then a postmaster, and I heard a lot about the characters and petty dramas he dealt with over the decades. I've reached the age now where I'm starting to think back on my own career and the opportunities I might have had to do something else with it. My working life has been so different from my father's. I'm a "writer," which really just means I'm kind of an academic, kind of a freelancer, kind of a loafer (different amounts of each at different times). I certainly do less work than he did, and I can't help but think sometimes, *When my dad was my age, he'd already been at the post office for fourteen years.* I suppose this story is my attempt to think about his career, my career, a little bit about the career of my grandfather Bill Deagler (who also worked at the post office), and the extent to which your job becomes your life; how you have to figure out how to live inside it.

Michael Deagler was raised in Bucks County, Pennsylvania. His first novel, *Early Sobrieties,* was published by Astra Publishing House in 2024. He lives in Los Angeles, where he is pursuing a PhD in creative writing and literature at the University of Southern California.

Lindsey Drager, "Blackbirds"
What inspired your story?

I was thinking a lot about time when writing this story. Time and distance. I was thinking about the way time elongates and folds when one is having an asthma attack. That omniscient third-person narrator—who is so closely focalized through the young girl but who becomes a bit more overt and objective at points in the story—I was imagining that narrator as an older version of the young girl. I was aiming for a dual sense of distance and intimacy by having the third-person-omniscient narrator occupy the position of both the girl in the moment and also, simultaneously, the adult she might become. As I was drafting, I didn't know the story was operating in the mode of the uncanny until I reached the end of the telephone scene when the young girl stays on the line listening and imagines an older version of herself on the other end. In a way, the story's telling corrupts the girl's wish to speak to her older self by reversing the roles; if you read the narrator as an older version of the girl, that woman is indeed speaking but the girl can't hear her. Perhaps the narrator is doing the gentle work of letting the reader know the girl gets out of this or perhaps she's an adult reviewing these events and finally coming to terms with what they might mean in the context of her life now. I wanted to play with those possibilities—or rather, the story wanted me to play with them and kind of conveyed that to me. The story kept requesting imagery that evoked the overview effect. The Ferris wheel or the pterodactyl, for example. I love the idea of the overview effect: that sense that when you're far enough away, above, beyond, you are estranged from what might seem so ubiquitous in your everyday life and so you see it through a new, awe-inducing lens. I have found in my life it is hard to gain that distance. But fiction permits us this. It affords us the opportunity to gain access to the interiority of another in a way that possibly no other medium can. A reader is more inside another's mind in third-person omniscient than they can ever be inside another's mind in the world off the page. In free indirect, a reader can know more about what a character is thinking than the character knows themselves. And while this might feel to the reader like intimacy, it can just as easily feel distancing and estranging, inducing something like the overview effect. For me, being inside another's consciousness is one of the most exquisite and unsettling places to be. That fiction allows us this access strikes me as at minimum a magic trick and at most a miracle.

Lindsey Drager's novels have won a Shirley Jackson Award, been finalists for two Lambda Literary Awards, and have variously been translated into Spanish and Italian. A 2020 NEA fellowship recipient in prose and winner of the 2022 Bard Fiction Prize, she is an assistant professor at the University of Utah. Her latest novel, *The Avian Hourglass,* is a failed retelling of *Pinocchio* concerning twenty-first-century states of precarity.

Clyde Edgerton, "Hearing Aids"
What inspired your story?

During a forty-five-minute (or so) MRI I heard many odd, loud sounds coming from the MRI machine. As many of you know, during an MRI you are cocooned into a large machine. During my session, to help pass time, I made the sounds into words . . . one after the other. Sometimes I made one repeating sound into several different words. Later that day, the same thing happened when I heard my stream of urine landing in water. I found myself translating the sounds into random words. I thought: This has happened to me before and has probably happened to other people, but rather than going about saying to people, "Do you think up random words during an MRI or when you urinate?" I thought up the beginning to my story, and all else followed.

As I wrote, I realized that the perspective of an older, white male—likely to be considered dull by some readers—would help me finish the story. And in the end, I was happy to be unsure if the story was finished.

Clyde Edgerton is a writer from North Carolina. He has published ten novels and two nonfiction books. His most recent publisher is Tenpenny Books in Chattanooga, Tennessee.

Dave Eggers, "Sanrevelle"
What inspired your story?

The settings, at least, are based on some real places and phenomena in the Bay Area. About twenty years ago I went to my first lighted boat parade one Christmas out here, and I was floored by the otherworldly beauty of these bright and madly decorated boats against the inky-black water. I thought it would be a surreal setting for someone in love to be searching for their mate. As a contrast, I wanted my hero to be living in a constricted, dank place, full of failure and confusion. I chose the Millennium Tower in San Francisco, a real high-rise that's actually sinking, a little bit every year, into the clay deep beneath the city. For a long time now, I've been fascinated by the dichotomy here in San Francisco, between the landlocked neighborhoods of the city, which have gotten a very bad rap over the last few years, and this vast gorgeous body of water surrounding us on three sides, full of sailboats and seals and whales and things like the lighted boat parade. In a way, towers like the Millennium try to give people a bit of both—the views of the water but also the energy of the city—but in the case of this particular building, it didn't work. There's nothing quite like a found metaphor.

Dave Eggers is the founder of *McSweeney's* and the author of *The Eyes and the Impossible*, *The Circle*, and *A Hologram for the King*, among other books.

Madeline ffitch, "Stump of the World"
Why was the short-story format the best vehicle for your ideas?

"Stump of the World" features characters from my current novel. I wrote it while I was deep in the middle of writing that novel, yet the tone, language, circumstances, and timing of the story could not be more different from the novel these people also live in, so much so that in some ways it's more like an exercise in multiverse imagining (which Emma would object to but Teddy would love). When I am working on a writing project, I find it companionable and helpful to have writing or art from another medium or genre nearby to refer to and be in conversation with. I think that dipping into other modes can be an important way for me to hold on to the life of storytelling and the relentless possibilities of words and the world.

Madeline ffitch is the author of the story collection *Valparaiso, Round the Horn* and the novel *Stay and Fight,* which was a finalist for the PEN/Hemingway Award, the Lambda Literary Award for lesbian fiction, the Washington State Book Award, and the Los Angeles Times Book Prize, and was the 2023 Ohio Center for the Book pick for the National Book Festival. She is the recipient of a 2024 O. Henry Prize and was included in the 2024 *Best American Short Stories* anthology. Her writing has appeared in *Harper's Magazine, The Paris Review, Granta, Tin House,* and elsewhere. Her second novel, about kitchen-table antifascism in Appalachia, is forthcoming from Farrar, Straus and Giroux. She writes and organizes in Appalachian Ohio.

Indya Finch, "Shotgun Calypso"
Did you know how your story would end at its inception?

The ending of "Shotgun Calypso" is the part of the story that underwent the most transformation the most amount of times. It's my oldest story, I wrote it many years ago when I was in an undergraduate fiction writing class. Even then, the ending didn't work. It's hard to remember now, but I think, in that first very early draft, Calypso and Clio look over the fence and find a "dim bulb" of a boy named Wes, whom they immediately take turns kissing. I didn't always know what the story wanted to say. Ideas for my work often come from dreams, as this story did, so sometimes the work of deciphering what it all means comes after I've already written a draft that is in effect pure transcription from my subconscious. The initial ending was a deviation from my dream, in that Lonnie beat Valentina viciously with a bowling trophy. I couldn't see the point or value in writing that.

So when I realized this story was about sexuality in part, I figured out what I wanted to say. The action of Lonnie's finger in Calypso's mouth has set off so many ripples for the girls that they will feel their entire lives. And whether they know it or not, all sexual affairs can find their beginnings here, for better or for worse. But Wes didn't bear that out so I cut Wes out. I had them drive back home and encounter a different boy named Cameron; eventually he got cut too. Then the story ended as soon as the finger entered the mouth and then later Wes came back! He got a little more dialogue and a little more to do, he disgusted one sister and entranced the other, but nope, that didn't last either. My thesis adviser Alexia Arthurs gave some great advice that made me think yes, the ending is not on Wes, but it's somewhere near the trampoline. So on the bounces it ended. Eventually, I felt in all other ways the story had crystallized into its final form, except the ending, and maybe this was just destined to be one of those stories whose ending didn't work. So I left it alone, for years. I left it alone for so long that I struggled to reach back to Calypso's voice.

I told this much to Megan Cummings, whom I worked with on the story at *A Public Space,* along with my constant struggle to find a proper ending. We talked on the phone and I remember being barely moved into my new apartment when we chatted. Those conversations led me to an epiphany or two, which let me finally, after so much fanfare, write the ending that fit. So, it took a long time and great readers and editors to show me all the pieces were there but not in the right configuration.

Indya Finch is a writer from rural East Texas. They received a BA in film from Sam Houston State University and an MFA from the Iowa Writers' Workshop, where they received the Truman Capote

Fellowship. Their work can be found in the *Oxford American* and *A Public Space*. They live in Iowa City.

Alice Hoffman, "City Girl"
What inspired your story?

"City Girl" was inspired by the neighborhood of Chelsea in Manhattan, where I have lived on and off for most of my life. I've seen huge changes in the neighborhood over the decades and every time I think I'm ready to leave New York I fall in love with Chelsea all over again. So here's my love song to my neighborhood, written about the worst of times, when anything was possible.

Alice Hoffman is the author of more than thirty works of fiction, including *The World That We Knew; The Marriage of Opposites; The Red Garden; The Museum of Extraordinary Things; The Dovekeepers; Here on Earth,* an Oprah's Book Club selection; and the *Practical Magic* series, including *Practical Magic; Magic Lessons; The Rules of Magic,* a selection of Reese's Book Club; and *The Book of Magic*. She lives near Boston.

Jane Kalu, "Sickled"
What details or characters did you cut on the editing floor?

It took four years and many drafts to arrive at this version. Though I always understood the story between the sisters, it took me a while to figure out the characters around them. They always had parents but I struggled to see who these parents were and what roles they played. I knew that Dad was always absent and Mom was always home, so in many drafts Dad had a job and Mom was a housewife. What eventually helped me arrive here was looking from the outside in—the country's political state during the year in which I set the story finally solved the problem. And as soon as I figured out that Mom's job had been affected by the political reforms going on across the country, the tension between the characters naturally emerged.

Building the immediate world around the family was also a challenge. In the first draft, I had Mom fighting with neighbors, and Bube, the girls' love interest, appeared in more scenes. In another draft, there were additional scenes of the girls at school and with friends. Ultimately, these choices felt distracting and took away from the closing-in effect I wanted for the story. I wanted to create a sense that the women were all trapped in the house and couldn't leave unless someone was dying. In the end, even though these threads didn't make it into the final draft, they helped me understand the world and the characters well enough to arrive where I did.

Jane Kalu is studying for a PhD in creative writing and literature at the University of Southern California. Her short fiction has been featured in *American Short Fiction, Narrative Magazine, Boston Review, The Hopkins Review, Isele Magazine,* and elsewhere. Jane's writing has received support from Vermont Studio Center, the Storyknife residency, and *American Short Fiction*. She's at work on a novel and a collection of short stories.

Thomas Korsgaard, "The Spit of Him"
What inspired your story?

I was sitting at my desk and was just about to shut my computer down after a long day working on a quite different story when an image appeared to me like a bolt out of the blue. A boy, about ten years old, walking along a road in the rain—unsuitably clad in a pair of baggy pajamas, no raincoat, a laptop bag slung across his shoulder. But despite the rain this boy was in some way indomitable. That was what came to me—nothing else—but I wanted to know what was going to happen to him.

Thomas Korsgaard (born 1995) made his debut at the age of twenty-one in 2017 with the autobiographical novel *If Anyone Should Happen By,* which became a runaway bestseller both in Denmark and abroad. In 2018, the sequel *One Day We'll Laugh About It* followed, and in 2021, *You Probably Had to Be There* concluded the so-called Trilogy About Tue. The last volume earned Korsgaard the prestigious, once-in-a-lifetime Golden Laurels, making him the youngest recipient of the prize.

Martin Aitken's translations of contemporary Scandinavian literature are widely published. His work has been short-listed for the major international literary awards. Among other prizes, he received the PEN Translation Prize in 2019 and the National Translation Award in Prose in 2022.

Ling Ma, "Winner"
What inspired your story?

Walking to the liquor store one night, I passed this run-down apartment building that I've seen a million times before. For some reason, it stood out to me then. I felt familiar with this building—its dustiness, the faded exterior paint, and the cracking of the wooden door frames and windows. I have lived in places like this, I have visited friends in homes like this. The building was situated near a major intersection; there was a sense that it was not well protected from outside elements—the traffic lights, the emergency vehicles that blare down the street at all hours. I had this initial idea about a woman, a lottery winner, who is compelled to return to her former apartment. Every time I walked by that building, I would think about her.

At the time when I noticed this building, I had returned to Chicago after grad school, and had actually moved back into the same apartment I had occupied five years earlier. I probably had the vague idea of resuming my life as before. But during the five years I had been gone, my circumstances had changed, the neighborhood had changed, and I was on the verge of still more changes, ones I could barely glean at that point.

More recently, I was asked to contribute an original work of fiction to *The Yale Review*. This was a stipulation of winning a prize that had been administered by Yale University. I decided to write out this idea. To be honest, I don't think it's a finished story yet. I wrote it quickly, within a few months. Winning the prize changed my life (I was able to quit a job), but there is no way to understand it other than as a random lightning strike. That inability to make sense of luck . . . I think it made its way into this piece.

Ling Ma is author of the novel *Severance* and the story collection *Bliss Montage*. She is a recipient of a MacArthur Fellowship, a Windham Campbell Prize in Literature, and a National Book Critics Circle Award. Her fiction has appeared in *The New Yorker, The Atlantic, Granta,* and *VQR*. She lives in Chicago.

Anthony Marra, "Countdown"
What inspired your story?

In 2015, I published *The Tsar of Love and Techno*, a book that used the linked-story form to explore historical erasure and recovery across twentieth-century Russia. Several stories revolved around a veteran of the Russian-Chechen conflict who succeeds in obtaining a draft deferment for his younger brother, albeit at a tragic cost. I had no plans to return to *Tsar*'s characters until the Russian invasion of Ukraine in 2022, when I found myself thinking of the veteran's younger brother, Alexei. What would his life look like?

How had two decades of Putinism warped his politics, morality, relationships? How had the passage of time changed him? Would I still recognize him? Stories, for me, begin with a series of generalized questions like these that become increasingly granular as I work. Questions become curiosity and curiosity becomes fiction.

Anthony Marra is the *New York Times* bestselling author of *Mercury Pictures Presents, The Tsar of Love and Techno,* and *A Constellation of Vital Phenomena.* His work has been translated into more than twenty languages.

Lori Ostlund, "Just Another Family"
What did you have to figure out or learn in order to be able to write or finish this story?

I have become increasingly suspicious of cynicism. I turned sixty this year, so whether this rejection of cynicism is a function of age or a response to an increasingly fraught world, I do not know. I do know that I set this story aside for many years; the old version was much shorter and, I realize now, more cynical, and when I came back to it after a fallow writing period, the story grew longer, the ending more hopeful, which, for me, is reflected in the drawing that Petra—Rachel and Sybil's niece—makes of the two of them: the Bubble Family. Years ago, in the nineties, I made a note about something that a friend's child asked one night when the family was over for dinner. She turned to her parents and asked, of my now wife and me, "Were Lori and Anne born in a bubble together?" It was a sweet question, a question that seemed to us oddly perceptive for a three-year-old, as though she sensed not only our connection to each other but the fact that it set us slightly apart from the rest of the world in those more intolerant times. When I first incorporated her question into that early draft, it was in service only of reflecting the latter, the sense of not belonging, but when I returned to this story in late 2022, I wrote into Petra's question, and it began to change, to accrete meaning, so that by the end, it had dovetailed with the title in a way that brought certain threads together but, more important, reflected hope.

Thank you to *New England Review* for giving this very long story a home, especially Carolyn Kuebler and Ernest McLeod, and to Edward P. Jones and Jenny Minton Quigley for giving it this wonderful additional home.

Lori Ostlund is the author of the novel *After the Parade*, a B&N Discover pick and a finalist for the Center for Fiction First Novel Prize, and the story collection *The Bigness of the World*, which received the 2008 Flannery O'Connor Award for Short Fiction, a California Book Award, and the Edmund White Award for Debut Fiction. Her third book, a story collection entitled *Are You Happy?*, which includes "Just Another Family," was published by Astra Publishing House in May 2025. Lori is the series editor of the Flannery O'Connor Award for Short Fiction. She lives in San Francisco.

Ehsaneh Sadr, "Mornings at the Ministry"
What inspired your story?

"Mornings at the Ministry" was inspired by the death of Mahsa Amini and Iran's Women, Life, Freedom movement. Remembering my own experiences at the hands of Iran's morality police, I felt retraumatized, heartbroken, and deeply angry about the loss of Mahsa and other beautiful young women who have so much to contribute.

Mahsa's death also made me think about the ways in which women's voices and contributions are silenced or otherwise lost in less dramatic ways. At the time, my cohort of California moms—

PhDs and former C-suite executives who'd invested years in our children's schools and upbringing—were grappling with a realization of what they'd lost in a society that does not value this sort of work or provide easy on-ramps back into fulfilling careers. In this experience, many of our men were not so different from Amir: well-intentioned but entirely clueless about the challenges we faced.

The setting of the ministry was inspired by my work at the Ministry of Reconstruction Jihad in Tehran with generous colleagues and mentors who gave me more opportunities than my seniority or experience deserved. For the workplace drama between Amir and Ms. Musavi, I pulled from a petty episode back home in the United States when I was disappointed by a colleague's promotion for what I perceived to be a lot of kissing up while kicking down. And for Amir's central parenting dilemma, I drew from the fear-based temptations I've felt to push my own children to conform in ways that might maximize their chances of future success but might also inflict real harm.

Ehsaneh Sadr's debut novel, *A Door Between Us,* is the only work of fiction to explore the 2009 Iranian Green Wave from the perspective of both regime opponents and regime supporters. While she has lived in Tehran, Salt Lake City, and the Washington, D.C., area, Ehsaneh currently resides in the Bay Area of Northern California.

Daniel Saldaña París, "Rosaura at Dawn"
Do you consider your story to be personal or political?

My story is both personal and political. As in much of what I write, space is one of the triggers for the fiction. In this case, the space is Tijuana, the city where my mother has lived for twenty years. It's a city that has always fascinated me because it attracts people from all over the world, but most people arrive intending to cross into the United States. It was interesting to imagine a character who doesn't see Tijuana as a point of passage to somewhere else but as a final destination, arrived at after a traumatic event in their life.

Another aspect that interested me was the situation of animals in a place like Tijuana. The same circumstances of trafficking, exploitation, and precariousness that affect human beings also impact other species, and in the story, I set out to explore the relationship that forms between rescued animals and a character who, in some way, is rescued in turn by contact with the animals.

Daniel Saldaña París is a writer. He is the author of *Ramifications, Planes Flying over a Monster,* and *The Dance and the Fire*. He was a 2022–23 Cullman Center Fellow at the New York Public Library, an Eccles Centre & Hay Festival Global Writer's Award winner in 2020, and a finalist for the Herralde Prize in 2021. He currently splits his time between Mexico City and New York.

Christina MacSweeney is an award-winning literary translator, working mainly in the areas of Latin American fiction, essays, poetry, and hybrid texts. She has translated works by such authors as Valeria Luiselli, Verónica Gerber Bicecci, Julián Herbert, Jazmina Barrera, Karla Suárez, and Elvira Navarro. She has also contributed to anthologies of Latin American literature and published shorter translations, articles, interviews, and collaborations on a wide variety of platforms. Her most recent translations are Jazmina Barrera's *Cross Stitch* (currently short-listed for the Queen Sofía Institute Translation Prize) and Clyo Mendoza's *Fury*. In 2024, she was granted a Sundial House Literary Translation Award for her translation of Verónica Gerber Bicecci's *The Company*.

Zak Salih, "Three Niles"
What inspired your story?

With "Three Niles," truth was a gateway to fiction—then a gateway back to truth. The story began as a personal essay about my experience visiting Sudan at seventeen with my father, and about the persistent disconnection a first-generation immigrant can feel from the country and people that are part of their blood. The visit itself was innocuous and, in hindsight, rewarding. As a fiction writer, however, this didn't excite me. I found myself pondering revisionist histories. Histories where events from that trip turned out quite differently. Histories that better captured the complex ideas and emotions I wanted from my essay. So, to put it bluntly, I made a bunch of stuff up, and the result is more honest and real than what actually happened.

Zak Salih is the author of the novel *Let's Get Back to the Party,* published in 2021 by Algonquin Books. His fiction and nonfiction have appeared in *The Kenyon Review, Fairy Tale Review, Foglifter, Epiphany, The Florida Review, The Millions,* the *Los Angeles Review of Books,* and other publications. He lives in Washington, D.C.

Yah Yah Scholfield, "Strange Fruit"
Do you consider your work to be personal or political?

As a Black person living in America, everything I do is political. My most private, personal actions and tastes, the stories I dare to tell, are political, rooted in centuries of discrimination and prejudices. "Strange Fruit" is political, yes—the extrajudicial executions of Black Americans can't help but be—but it's deeply personal as well. I wrote it grieving for those who've been killed before, for those whose names we know and those whom we'll never have the chance to grieve. I wrote it for Breonna, for Sonya, for Hind, for

Refaat, and I wrote it for myself. God willing, my body will rest easy when my time comes, and not in that strange orchard.

Yah Yah Scholfield's work has been featured in *Fiyah*, *Stillpoint Magazine*, *Death in the Mouth* volume 1, *Unspeakable Horror 3: Dark Rainbow Rising*, *Readers Beware*, *Peach Pit*, and *Southern Humanities Review*. They have also published a short-story collection, *Just a Little Snack*. When they're not terrifying innocents, Yah Yah is a professional stay-at-home daughter in Atlanta with their cats, Sophie and Chihiro.

Chika Unigwe, "Miracle in Lagos Traffic"
What inspired your story?

In May 2023, a Nigerian senator, his wife, and a physician were jailed in the UK for trafficking a poor street trader into the country to harvest his kidney for the senator's sick daughter. The plot was foiled when a suspicious medical consultant discovered that the young donor apparently had no idea what he was giving up. The victim, likely fearing repatriation to Nigeria, fled and reported the scheme to the British police. Nigerians were divided on whether the young man had intended to outsmart the senator all along—seizing a life-changing opportunity to move to the UK—or whether he truly hadn't known what he had been paid to sacrifice. From the start, I knew I wanted to explore all the questions this incident raised in fiction. However, I wasn't sure until I began that it would become a short story.

Chika Unigwe was born and raised in Enugu, Nigeria. Her novels include *On Black Sisters Street* and *The Middle Daughter*. She shuttles between Atlanta, Georgia, and Milledgeville, Georgia, where she is a professor of creative writing at Georgia College. Widely translated, Unigwe has won numerous awards for her writing.

Publisher's Note
A Brief History of the O. Henry Prize

Many readers have come to love the short story through the simple characters, the humor and easy narrative voice, and the compelling plotting in the work of William Sydney Porter (1862–1910), best known as O. Henry. His surprise endings entertain readers, including those back for a second, third, or fourth look. Even now one can say "Gift of the Magi" in conversation about a friendship or marriage, and many people around the world will know they are referring to the generosity and selflessness of love.

O. Henry was a newspaperman, skilled at hiding from his editors at deadline. He spent his childhood in Greensboro, North Carolina; his adolescence in Texas; and his later years in New York City. In between Texas and New York, he was caught embezzling and hid from the law in Honduras, where he coined the phrase "banana republic." On learning his wife was dying, he returned home to her and to their daughter, and subsequently served a three-year prison sentence for bank fraud in Columbus, Ohio. Accounts of the origin of his pen name vary: one story dates from his days in Austin, where he was said to call to the wandering family cat, "Oh! Henry!"; another states that the name was inspired by the captain of the guard at the Ohio State Penitentiary, Orrin

Henry. In 1909, Porter told *The New York Times,* "[A friend] suggested that we get a newspaper and pick a name from the first list of notables that we found in it. In the society columns we found the account of a fashionable ball. . . . We looked down the list and my eye lighted on the name Henry. 'That'll do for a last name,' said I. 'Now for a first name. I want something short.' 'Why don't you use a plain initial letter, then?' asked my friend. 'Good,' said I, 'O is about the easiest letter written, and O it is.' "

Porter had devoted friends, and it's not hard to see why. He was charming and had an attractively gallant attitude. He drank too much and neglected his health, which caused his friends concern. He was often short of money; in a letter to a friend asking for a loan of $15 (his banker was out of town, he wrote), Porter added a postscript: "If it isn't convenient, I'll love you just the same." His banker was unavailable most of Porter's life. His sense of humor was always with him.

Reportedly, Porter's last words were from a popular song: "Turn up the light, for I don't want to go home in the dark."

After his death, O. Henry's stories continued to penetrate twentieth-century popular culture. Marilyn Monroe starred in a film adaptation of "The Cop and the Anthem." The popular western TV series *The Cisco Kid* grew out of "The Caballero's Way." Postage stamps were issued by the Soviets to commemorate O. Henry's one hundredth birthday in 1962 and by the United States in 2012 for his one hundred fiftieth. The most lasting legacy began just eight years after O. Henry's death, in April 1918, when the Twilight Club (founded in 1883 and later known as the Society of Arts and Sciences) held a dinner in his honor at the Hotel McAlpin in New York City. His friends remembered him so enthusiastically that a group of them met at the Biltmore Hotel in December of that year to establish some kind of memorial to him. They decided to award annual prizes in his name for short-story writers, and they formed a committee to read the short stories published in a year and a smaller group to pick the winners. In the words of the first series editor, Blanche Colton Williams (1879–1944), the memorial was intended to "strengthen the art of the short story and to stimulate younger authors."

Doubleday, Page & Company was chosen to publish the first volume, *O. Henry Memorial Award Prize Stories 1919.* In 1927, the society sold all rights to the annual collection to Doubleday, Doran & Company. Doubleday published *The O. Henry Prize Stories,* as it came to be known, in hardcover, and from 1984 to 1996 its subsidiary, Anchor Books, published it simultaneously in paperback. Beginning in 1997, *The O. Henry Prize Stories* was published annually as an Anchor Books paperback. It is now published by Vintage Books as *The Best Short Stories: The O. Henry Prize Winners.*

How the Stories Are Chosen

The guest editor chooses the twenty O. Henry Prize winners from a large pool of stories passed to him by the series editor. Stories published in magazines and online are eligible for inclusion in *The Best Short Stories: The O. Henry Prize Winners*. Stories may be written in English or translated into English. Sections of novels are not considered. Editors are asked to send all fiction they publish and not to nominate individual stories. Stories should not be submitted by agents or writers. All stories must be the product of human creativity.

The goal of *The Best Short Stories: The O. Henry Prize Winners* remains to strengthen and add visibility to the art of the short story.

The stories selected were originally published between September 2023 and September 2024.

Acknowledgments

Thank you, Marion Minton. Thank you, Diana Secker Tesdell, Julia Harrison, Ruthie Wood, Clara Pakman, Heather Clay, Anna Noone, Jordan Rodman, Jen Marshall, Aja Pollock, Eddie Allen, Jennifer Brennan and Drew Richardson at Symphony Space, and Emily Firetog at Literary Hub. Thank you, Edward P. Jones, O. Henry Prize Winners, and brilliant magazine and journal editors. And as always, love to Dan, Sam, Gus, and Leo Quigley.

Publications Submitted

Stories published in magazines and online are eligible for inclusion.

For fiction published online, the publication's contact information and the date of each story's publication should accompany the submission.

Stories will be considered from September 1 to August 31 the following year. Publications received after August 31 will automatically be considered for the next volume of *The Best Short Stories: The O. Henry Prize Winners*.

Please submit PDF files of submissions to jenny@ohenryprizewinners.com or send hard copies to Jenny Minton Quigley, c/o The O. Henry Prize Winners, 70 Mohawk Drive, West Hartford, CT 06117.

Able Muse
www.ablemuse.com
www.ablemuse.com/submit-what
 -online
Editor: Alexander Pepple
Quarterly

After Dinner Conversation
www.afterdinnerconversation.com
info@afterdinnerconversation.com
Editor in Chief: Kolby Granville
Monthly

AGNI
www.agnionline.bu.edu
www.bu.edu/dbin/agni/
Editors: Sven Birkerts and William Pierce
Biannual (print)

Alaska Quarterly Review
www.aqreview.org
alaskaquarterlyreview.submittable.com/submit
Editor: Ronald Spatz
Biannual

Amazon Original Stories
www.amazon.com
Submission by invitation only
Editorial Director: Kjersti Egerdahl
Twelve annually

American Short Fiction
www.americanshortfiction.org
americanshortfiction.submittable.com/submit
Editors: Rebecca Markovits and Adeena Reitberger
Triannual

Antipodes
www.wsupress.wayne.edu/journals/detail/antipodes-0
digitalcommons.wayne.edu/antipodes/submission_guidelines.html
Editor: Brenda Machosky
Biannual

Apalachee Review
www.apalacheereview.org
apalacheereview.org/submissions/
Editor in Chief: Rafael Gamero
Annual

Apogee Journal
www.apogeejournal.org
docs.google.com/forms/d/e/1FAIpQLSe1abTIw7xgxMoI5W5JMQDQdyXDNXibAPy3cXBNRxb_WH6ksg/viewform
Executive Editor: Alexandra Watson
Biannual

The Arkansas International
www.arkint.org
acwlp.submittable.com/submit
Editor in Chief: Rebecca Gayle Howell
Biannual

Arkansas Review
www.arkreview.org
mtribbet@astate.edu
Editor: Marcus Tribbett
Triannual

ArLiJo
www.arlijo.com
ArLiJo@myyahoo.com
Editor in Chief: Robert L. Giron
Twelve to twenty issues a year

Ascent
www.readthebestwriting.com
ascent@cord.edu
Editor: Vincent Reusch

The Asian American Literary Review
www.aalrmag.org
editors@aalrmag.org
Editors in Chief: Lawrence-Minh Bùi Davis and Gerald Maa
Biannual

Aster(ix)
www.asterixjournal.com
Solicited submissions only
Editor in Chief: Angie Cruz
Two or three times per year

The Atlantic
www.theatlantic.com
fiction@theatlantic.com
Editor in Chief: Jeffrey Goldberg
Monthly

Baltimore Review
www.baltimorereview.org
baltimorereview.submittable.com/submit
Senior Editor: Barbara Westwood Diehl
Quarterly

Bat City Review
www.batcityreview.org
batcityreview.submittable.com/submit
Managing Editor: Sarah Matthes
Annual

Bellevue Literary Review
www.blreview.org
blreview.org/general-submissions/
Editor in Chief: Danielle Ofri
Biannual

Bennington Review
www.benningtonreview.org
benningtonreview.submittable.com/submit
Editor: Michael Dumanis
Biannual

Black Warrior Review
bwr.ua.edu
bwr.submittable.com/submit
Editor: Samantha Bolf
Biannual

BOMB
www.bombmagazine.org
bombmagazine.submittable.com/submit
Editor in Chief: Betsy Sussler
Quarterly

Booth
booth.butler.edu
booth.submittable.com/submit
Editor: Robert Stapleton
Biannual

Boulevard
www.boulevardmagazine.org
boulevard.submittable.com/submit
Editor: Dusty Freund
Triannual

Cagibi
www.cagibilit.com
cagibilit.submittable.com/submit
Editors: Sylvie Bertrand and Christopher X. Shade
Quarterly

CALYX
www.calyxpress.org
www.calyxpress.org/general-submissions/
Editors: Elizabeth Brookbank, Marjorie Coffey, Emerson Craig, Judith Edelstein, Emily Elbom, Carole Kalk, Karah Kemmerly, Christine Rhea
Biannual

The Carolina Quarterly
www.thecarolinaquarterly.com
thecarolinaquarterly.submittable.com/submit
Editor in Chief: Ellie Rambo
Biannual

Carve
www.carvezine.com
Not currently accepting submissions
Publisher: Matthew Limpede
Quarterly

Catamaran
www.catamaranliteraryreader.com
catamaranliteraryreader.submittable.com/submit
Editor in Chief: Catherine Segurson
Quarterly

Cherry Tree
www.washcoll.edu/learn-by-doing/lit-house/cherry-tree/
cherrytree.submittable.com/submit
Editor in Chief: James Allen Hall
Annual

Chestnut Review
chestnutreview.com
chestnutreview.submittable.com/submit
Editor in Chief: James Rawlings
Quarterly

Chicago Quarterly Review
www.chicagoquarterlyreview.com
chicagoquarterlyreview.submittable.com/submit
Senior Editors: S. Afzal Haider and Elizabeth McKenzie
Quarterly

Chicago Review
www.chicagoreview.org
chicagoreview.submittable.com/submit
Editors: James Garwood-Cole and Clara Nizard
Triannual

Cimarron Review
www.cimarronreview.com
cimarronreview.okstate.edu/submission/
Editor: Lisa Lewis
Quarterly

The Cincinnati Review
www.cincinnatireview.com
cincinnatireview.com/submissions/
Managing Editor: Lisa Ampleman
Biannual

Cola Literary Review
www.colaliteraryreview.com
colaliteraryreview.submittable.com
    /submit
Senior Editors: G. E. Butler and
    Jacob Walhout
Annual

Colorado Review
coloradoreview.colostate.edu
    /colorado-review
coloradoreview.submittable.com
    /submit
Editor in Chief: Stephanie
    G'Schwind
Triannual

The Common
www.thecommononline.org
thecommon.submittable.com
    /submit
Editor in Chief: Jennifer Acker
Biannual

Confrontation
www.confrontationmagazine.org
English Department
LIU Post
720 Northern Blvd.
Brookville, NY 11548
Editor in Chief: Jonna G. Semeiks
Biannual

Conjunctions
www.conjunctions.com
conjunctions.submittable.com
    /submit
Editor: Bradford Morrow
Biannual

Copper Nickel
www.copper-nickel.org
coppernickel.submittable.com
    /submit
Editor: Wayne Miller
Biannual

Cream City Review
uwm.edu/creamcityreview
creamcityreview.submittable.com
    /submit
Editor in Chief: Camilla Jiyun
    Nam Lee
Biannual

CutBank
www.cutbankonline.org
cutbank.submittable.com/submit
Editor in Chief: Jenny Rowe
Biannual

The Dalhousie Review
ojs.library.dal.ca/dalhousiereview
Dalhousie.Review@dal.ca
Editor: Anthony Enns
Triannual

Dappled Things
www.dappledthings.org
dappledthings.submittable.com
/submit
Editor in Chief: Katy Carl
Quarterly

december
decembermag.org
december.submittable.com/submit
Editor/Publisher: Gianna Jacobson
Biannual

Denver Quarterly
www.du.edu/denverquarterly
denverquarterly.submittable.com
/submit
Editor: W. Scott Howard
Quarterly

Descant
descant.tcu.edu
descant.submittable.com/submit
Editor in Chief: Matt Pitt
Annual

Dracula Beyond Stoker Magazine
www.draculabeyondstoker.com/
submissions@draculabeyondstoker
.com
Editor: Tucker Christine
Biannual

The Drift
www.thedriftmag.com
fiction@thedriftmag.com
Editors: Kiara Barrow and Rebecca
    Panovka
Triannual

Driftwood Press
www.driftwoodpress.net
driftwoodpress.submittable.com
/submit
Editors: James McNulty and Jerrod
    Schwarz
Annual

The Dublin Review
thedublinreview.com
enquiry@thedublinreview.com
Editor: Brendan Barrington
Quarterly

Ecotone
ecotonemagazine.org
ecotone.submittable.com/submit
Editor in Chief: David Gessner
Biannual

Electric Literature
electricliterature.com
editors@electricliterature.com
Executive Director: Halimah
    Marcus; Editor in Chief: Denne
    Michele Norris

Epiphany
epiphanyzine.com
epiphanymagazine.submittable.com
Editor in Chief: Noreen Tomassi
Biannual

Epoch
www.epochliterary.com
epoch.submittable.com/submit
Editor: J. Robert Lennon
Biannual

Event
www.eventmagazine.ca
eventmagazine.submittable.com/submit
Editor: Shashi Bhat
Triannual

Exile Quarterly
www.exilequarterly.com
exilepublishing.submittable.com/submit
Editor in Chief: Barry Callaghan
Quarterly

Fairy Tale Review
www.fairytalereview.com
fairytalereview.submittable.com/submit/
Editor: Kate Bernheimer
Annual

Fantasy & Science Fiction
www.sfsite.com/fsf/
fandsf.moksha.io/publication/fsf
Editor: Sheree Renée Thomas
Bimonthly

Fence
fenceportal.org
fence.submittable.com/submit
Editorial Co-directors: Emily Wallis Hughes and Jason Zuzga
Biannual

Fiction
www.fictioninc.com
submissions.fictioninc.com/
Editor: Mark Jay Mirsky

Fiction River
fictionriver.com
Not currently accepting submissions
Editors: Kristine Kathryn Rusch and Dean Wesley Smith
Six times a year

The Fiddlehead
thefiddlehead.ca
thefiddlehead.submittable.com/submit
Editor: Sue Sinclair
Quarterly

Five Points
fivepoints.gsu.edu
fivepoints.submittable.com/submit
Editor: Megan Sexton
Biannual

The Florida Review
floridareview.cah.ucf.edu
floridareview.submittable.com
   /submit
Editor and Director: David James
   Poissant
Biannual

Foglifter
foglifterjournal.com
foglifter.submittable.com/submit
Editor in Chief: Michal "MJ"
   Jones
Biannual

Fourteen Hills: The SFSU Review
www.14hills.net
fourteenhills.submittable.com
   /submit
Co-editors in Chief: Michaela
   Chairez and Christopher Jones
Annual

f(r)iction
frictionlit.org
frictionlit.submittable.com/submit
Editor in Chief: Dani Hedlund
Triannual

Gemini Magazine
gemini-magazine.com
submit@gemini-magazine.com
Editor: David Bright
Four to six issues per year

The Georgia Review
www.thegeorgiareview.com
thegeorgiareview.submittable.com
   /submit
Director and Editor: Gerald Maa
Quarterly

Gold Man Review
www.goldmanreview.org
goldmanpublishing.submittable
   .com/submit
Editor in Chief: Heather
   Cuthbertson
Annual

Grain
grainmagazine.ca
grainmagazine.submittable.com
   /submit
Interim Editor: Elena Bentley
Quarterly

Granta
granta.com
granta.submittable.com/submit
Editor: Sigrid Rausing
Quarterly (print)

The Greensboro Review
greensbororeview.org
greensbororeview.submittable.com
   /submit
Editor: Terry L. Kennedy
Biannual

Guernica
www.guernicamag.com
guernicamagazine.submittable
.com/submit
Publisher: Magogodi aoMphela Makhene

Gulf Coast: A Journal of Literature and Fine Arts
www.gulfcoastmag.org
oastajournalofliteratureandfinearts
.submittable.com/submit
Editor: Rosa Boshier González
Biannual

Harper's Magazine
harpers.org
666 Broadway, 11th Floor
New York, NY 10012
Editor: Christopher Carroll
Monthly

Harpur Palate
harpurpalate.binghamton.edu
harpurpalate.submittable.com
/submit
Editor in Chief: Hannah Carr-Murphy
Biannual

Harvard Review
www.harvardreview.org
harvardreview.submittable.com
/submit
Editor: Christina Thompson
Biannual

Hayden's Ferry Review
haydensferryreview.com
hfr.submittable.com/submit
Editor: Susan Nguyen
Biannual

Hobart
www.hobartpulp.com
hobartsubmissions@gmail.com
Founding Editor: Aaron Burch;
Publisher: Elizabeth Ellen

The Hopkins Review
hopkinsreview.com
thehopkinsreview.submittable.com
/submit
Editor in Chief: Dora Malech
Quarterly

Hotel Amerika
www.hotelamerika.net
hotelamerika.submittable.com
/submit
Editor: David Lazar
Annual

The Hudson Review
hudsonreview.com
www.hudsonreview.com
/submissions/
Editor: Paula Deitz
Quarterly

Hunger Mountain
hungermtn.org
hungermtn.submittable.com
　/submit
Editor in Chief: Adam McOmber
Triannual

The Idaho Review
www.idahoreview.org
theidahoreview.submittable.com
　/submit
Editor in Chief: Anna Caritj
Annual

Image
imagejournal.org
Not currently accepting
　submissions
Editor in Chief: James K. A. Smith
Quarterly

Indiana Review
indianareview.org
indianareview.submittable.com
　/submit
Editor in Chief: Yaerim Gen Kwon
Biannual

Into the Void
intothevoidmagazine.com
intothevoidmagazine.submittable
　.com/submit
Editor: Philip Elliot
Quarterly

The Iowa Review
www.iowareview.org
iowareview.submittable.com
　/submit
Editor: Lynne Nugent
Triannual

Iron Horse Literary Review
www.ironhorsereview.com
ironhorse.submittable.com/submit
Editor: Leslie Jill Patterson
Triannual

Jabberwock Review
www.jabberwock.org.msstate.edu
jabberwockreview.submittable.com
　/submit
Editor: Becky Hagenston
Biannual

The Journal
thejournalmag.org
thejournal.submittable.com/submit
Managing Editor: Isaiah Back-
　Gaal
Four times a year

Joyland
joylandmagazine.com
joylandmagazine.submittable
　.com/submit/89567/joyland
　-submissions
Editor in Chief: Michelle Lyn
　King

The Kenyon Review
kenyonreview.org
thekenyonreview.submittable.com
 /submit
Editor: Nicole Terez Dutton
Four times a year

**Lady Churchill's Rosebud
 Wristlet**
www.smallbeerpress.com/lcrw
150 Pleasant Street, #306
Easthampton, MA 01027
Editors: Gavin J. Grant and Kelly
 Link
Biannual

Lake Effect
behrend.psu.edu/school-of
 -humanities-social-sciences/lake
 -effectlakeeffectaninternational
 literaryjournal.submittable.com
 /submit
Editors: George Looney and Aimee
 Pogson
Annual

Lalitamba
lalitamba.com
lalitamba_magazine@yahoo.com
Editor: Shyam Mukanda
Annual

Literary Hub
www.lithub.com
Not accepting fiction submissions
Editor in Chief: Jonny Diamond

LitMag
litmag.com
litmag.submittable.com/submit
Editor: Marc Berley
Annual

Little Patuxent Review
littlepatuxentreview.org
littlepatuxentreview.submittable
 .com/submit
Editor: Chelsea Lemon Fetzer
Biannual

The Louisville Review
www.louisvillereview.org
thelouisvillereviewfleur-de-lispress
 .submittable.com/submit
Managing Editor: Amy Foos
 Kapoor
Biannual

MAKE: A Literary Magazine
www.makemag.com
Not currently accepting
 submissions
Managing Editor: Chamandeep
 Bains
Annual

The Malahat Review
www.malahatreview.ca
malahatreview.submittable.com
 /submit
Editor: Iain Higgins
Quarterly

The Massachusetts Review
massreview.org
www.massreviewsubmissions.org/
Executive Editor: Jim Hicks
Quarterly

The Masters Review
mastersreview.com
themastersreview.submittable.com
    /submit
Editor in Chief: Cole Meyer
Annual (print)

McSweeney's Quarterly Concern
www.mcsweeneys.net
Letters@mcseweenys.net
Founding Editor: Dave Eggers
Editor: Rita Bulwinkel
Quarterly

Meridian
readmeridian.org
meridian.submittable.com/submit
Editor in Chief: Coby-Dillon
    English
Annual

Michigan Quarterly Review
michiganquarterlyreview.com
mqr.submittable.com/submit
Editor: Khaled Mattawa
Quarterly

Mid-American Review
casit.bgsu.edu/midamericanreview/
marsubmissions.bgsu.edu
Editor in Chief: Abigail Cloud
Semiannual

Mississippi Review
www.mississippi-review.com
mississippireview.submittable.com
    /submit
Editor in Chief: Adam Clay
Biannual

The Missouri Review
missourireview.com
submissions.missourireview.com
Editor: Speer Morgan
Quarterly

Mizna
mizna.org/articles/journal
mizna.org/journal/submissions/
Executive and Artistic Director:
    Lana Barkawi
Biannual

Mount Hope
www.mounthopemagazine.com
mounthopemagazine.submittable
    .com/submit
Editor: Edward J. Delaney
Annual (print)

n+1
www.nplusonemag.com
submissions@nplusonemag.com
Senior Editors: Lisa Borst, Tess
    Edmonson, Chad Harbach,
    Charles Petersen, and Sarah
    Resnick
Triannual

Narrative
www.narrativemagazine.com
www.narrativemagazine.com
 /submission
Editors: Carol Edgarian and Tom Jenks
Online content published continually; print edition published occasionally

NELLE
www.uab.edu/cas/english publications/nelle
nelle.submittable.com/submit
Editor: Lauren Goodwin Slaughter
Annual

New England Review
www.nereview.com
newenglandreview.submittable.com/submit
Editor: Carolyn Kuebler
Quarterly

New Letters
www.newletters.org
newlettersmagazine.submittable.com/submit
Editor in Chief: Christie Hodgen
Biannual

New Ohio Review
newohioreview.org
newohioreview.submittable.com/submit
Editor: David Wanczyk
Biannual

New Orleans Review
www.neworleansreview.org
neworleansreview.submittable.com/submit/19686/fiction-ongoing-submissions
Editor: Lindsay Sproul
Biannual

New Pop Lit
newpoplit.com
newpoplit@gmail.com
Editor in Chief: Karl Wenclas

New South
newsouthjournal.wordpress.com
newsouth.submittable.com/submit
Biannual

The New Yorker
www.newyorker.com
fiction@newyorker.com
Editor: David Remnick
Weekly

Nimrod International Journal
nimrod.utulsa.edu
nimrodjournal.submittable.com/submit
Editor: Eilis O'Neal
Biannual

Ninth Letter
ninthletter.com
ninthletteronline.submittable.com/submit
Managing Editor: Liz Harms
Biannual

Noon
noonannual.com
c/o Diane Williams
1392 Madison Avenue, PMB 298
New York, NY 10029
Editor: Diane Williams
Annual

The Normal School
www.thenormalschool.com
normalschooleditors@gmail.com
Editor in Chief: Steven Church
Biannual

North American Review
northamericanreview.org
northamericanreview.submittable.com/submit
Fiction Editor: Grant Tracey
Triannual

North Carolina Literary Review
nclr.ecu.edu
nclr.submittable.com/submit
Editor: Margaret D. Bauer
Triannual

North Dakota Quarterly
ndquarterly.org
ndquarterly.submittable.com/submit
Editor: William Caraher
Quarterly

Northern New England Review
franklinpierce.edu/nner
northernnewenglandreview.submittable.com/submit
Editor: Margot Douaihy
Annual

Notre Dame Review
ndreview.nd.edu
notredamereview.submittable.com/submit
Fiction Editor: Dionne Bremeyer
Biannual

The Ocean State Review
oceanstatereview.org
oceanstatereview.submittable.com/submit
Senior Editor: Charles Kell
Annual

The Offing
theoffingmag.com
theoffingmag.submittable.com/submit
Editor in Chief: Mimi Wong
Ongoing

One Story
one-story.com
one-story.submittable.com
Executive Editor: Hannah Tinti;
    Editor in Chief: Patrick Ryan
Monthly

Orca
orcalit.com
orcaaliteraryjournal.submittable.com/submit
Publishers/Senior Editors: Joe Ponepinto and Zachary Kellian
Triannual

Orion
orionmagazine.org
Not currently accepting fiction submissions
Editor in Chief: Sumanth Prabhaker
Bimonthly

Outlook Springs
outlooksprings.com
outlooksprings.submittable.com/submit
Editor in Chief: Jeremy John Parker
Triannual

Overtime
www.workerswritejournal.com/overtime.htm
overtime@workerswritejournal.com
Editor: David LaBounty
Triannual

Oxford American
www.oxfordamerican.org
oxfordamerican.submittable.com/submit
Editor: Danielle Amir Jackson
Quarterly

The Paris Review
www.theparisreview.org
theparisreview.submittable.com/submit
Editor: Emily Stokes
Quarterly

Passages North
www.passagesnorth.com
passagesnorth.submittable.com/submit
Editor in Chief: Jennifer A. Howard
Annual

Pembroke Magazine
pembrokemagazine.com
pembrokemagazine.submittable.com/submit
Editor: Peter Grimes
Annual

The Pinch
www.pinchjournal.com
pinchjournal.submittable.com/submit
Editor in Chief: Courtney Miller Santo
Biannual

Pleiades
pleiadesmag.com
www.pleiadessubmissions.com
Editor: Jenny Molberg
Biannual

Ploughshares
pshares.org
Emerson College
120 Boylston St.
Boston, MA 02116-4624
Editor in Chief: Ladette Randolph
Triannual

Post Road
www.postroadmag.com
postroadmagazine.submittable
.com/submit
Managing Editor: Chris Boucher
Biannual

Potomac Review
mcblogs.montgomerycollege.edu
/potomacreview/
potomacreview.submittable.com
/submit
Editor: Albert Kapikian
Biannual

Prairie Fire
www.prairiefire.ca
Prairie Fire Press Inc.
423-100 Arthur Street
Winnipeg, Manitoba R3B 1H3
Editor: Carolyn Gray
Quarterly

Prairie Schooner
prairieschooner.unl.edu
prairieschooner.submittable.com
/submit
Editor in Chief: Kwame Dawes
Quarterly

PRISM international
prismmagazine.ca
prisminternational.submittable
.com/submit
Prose Editor: Natasha Gauthier
Quarterly

A Public Space
apublicspace.org
apublicspacedemo.submittable
.com/submit
Editor: Brigid Hughes
Quarterly

PULP Literature
pulpliterature.com
docs.google.com/forms/d/e/1FAIp
    QLScGor2WqAXCA1FwKUu2
    gKGcsV88ubFbFyxtx9zsOsecw
    uQnUw/closedform
Editor in Chief: Jennifer Landels
Quarterly

Raritan
raritanquarterly.rutgers.edu
rqr@sas.rutgers.edu
Editor in Chief: Jackson Lears
Quarterly

Redivider
redivider.emerson.edu
redivider.submittable.com/submit
Editor in Chief: Katie Mihalek
Biannual

River Styx
www.riverstyx.org
www.riverstyx.org/submit
Managing Editor: Bryan Castille
Three or four times per year

Room
roommagazine.com
room.submittable.com/submit
Managing Editor: Shristi Uprety
Quarterly

The Rumpus
therumpus.net
therumpus.submittable.com
    /submit
Editor in Chief: Aram Mrjoian

Salamander
salamandermag.org
salamandermag.org/submit/
Editor in Chief: José Angel Araguz
Biannual

Salmagundi
salmagundi.skidmore.edu
Skidmore College
815 N Broadway
Saratoga Springs, NY 12866
Editor in Chief: Robert Boyers
Quarterly

Saranac Review
saranacreview.org
saranacreview.submittable.com
    /submit
Executive Editor: Sara Schaff
Annual

The Saturday Evening Post
www.saturdayeveningpost.com
editors@saturdayeveningpost.com
Editor: Patrick Perry
Six times a year

Short Story Day Africa
shortstorydayafrica.org
info@shortstorydayafrica.org
Executive Editor: Rachel Zadok

The Southampton Review
www.thesouthamptonreview.com
thesouthamptonreview
    .submittable.com/submit
Executive Editor: Lou Ann Walker
Biannual

The South Carolina Review
www.clemson.edu/caah/sites/south
    -carolina-review/index.html
thesouthcarolinareview
    .submittable.com/submit
Editor: Keith Morris
Biannual

South Dakota Review
southdakotareview.com
southdakotareview.submittable
    .com/Submit
Editor in Chief: Lee Ann
    Roripaugh
Quarterly

The Southeast Review
www.southeastreview.org
southeastreview.submittable.com
   /submit
Editor in Chief: Laura Biagi
Biannual

Southern Humanities Review
www.southernhumanitiesreview
   .com
southernhumanitiesreview
   .submittable.com/submit
Editors in Chief: Anton DiSclafani
   and Rose McLarney
Quarterly

Southern Indiana Review
www.usi.edu/sir
southernindianareview.submittable
   .com/submit
Editor: Ron Mitchell
Biannual

The Southern Review
thesouthernreview.org
submissions.thesouthernreview.org
Editors: Jessica Faust and Sacha
   Idell
Quarterly

Southwest Review
southwestreview.com
southwestreview.submittable.com
   /submit
Editor: Greg Brownderville
Quarterly

St. Anthony Messenger
www.franciscanmedia.org/st
   -anthony-messenger/
MagazineEditors@
   FranciscanMedia.org
Executive Editors: Christopher
   Heffron and Susan Hines-
   Brigger
Monthly

The Stinging Fly
stingingfly.org
stingingfly.submittable.com/submit
Publisher: Declan Meade
Biannual

Story
www.storymagazine.org
www.storymagazine.org
   /submissions/
Editor: Michael Nye
Triannual

StoryQuarterly
storyquarterly.camden.rutgers.edu
storyquarterly.submittable.com
   /submit
Editor: Paul Lisicky
Quarterly

subTerrain
www.subterrain.ca
subterrain.submittable.com/submit
Editor: Brian Kaufman
Triannual

Subtropics
subtropics.english.ufl.edu
subtropics.submittable.com/submit
Editor: David Leavitt
Biannual

The Sun
www.thesunmagazine.org
thesunmagazine.submittable.com
Editor and Publisher: Rob Bowers
Monthly

Swamp Pink
swamp-pink.cofc.edu
swamppink.submittable.com
 /submit
Fiction Editor: Anthony Varallo
Semimonthly

Taco Bell Quarterly
tacobellquarterly.org
tacobellquarterly.submittable.com
 /submit
Editor in Chief: M. M. Carrigan
It comes out when we feel like it

Tahoma Literary Review
tahomaliteraryreview.com
tahomaliteraryreview.submittable
 .com/submit
Fiction Editor: Leanne Dunic
Biannual

Third Coast
thirdcoastmagazine.com
thirdcoastmagazine.submittable
 .com/submit
Editor in Chief: Amanda Scott
Biannual

The Threepenny Review
www.threepennyreview.com
www.threepennyreview.com
 /online_submissions/
Editor: Wendy Lesser
Quarterly

Virginia Quarterly Review
www.vqronline.org
virginiaquarterlyreview.submittable
 .com/submit
Editor: Paul Reyes
Quarterly

Washington Square Review
www.washingtonsquarereview.com
washingtonsquare.submittable
 .com/submit
Editor in Chief: Joanna Yas
Biannual

Water-Stone Review
waterstonereview.com
waterstonereview.com/submissions/
Editor: Meghan Maloney-Vinz
Annual

Weber
www.weber.edu/weberjournal
weberjournal@weber.edu
Editor: Michael Wutz
Biannual

West Branch
westbranch.blogs.bucknell.edu
westbranchsubmissions.bucknell
　.edu/
Editor: Joe Scapellato
Triannual

Western Humanities Review
www.westernhumanitiesreview
　.com
whr.submittable.com/submit
Editor: Michael Mejia
Triannual

The White Review
www.thewhitereview.org
www.thewhitereview.org
　/submissions/
Editors: Rosanna Mclaughlin,
　Izabella Scott, Skye Arundhati
　Thomas
Triannual

Willow Springs
www.willowspringsmagazine.org
willowsprings.submittable.com
　/submit
Editor: Polly Buckingham
Biannual

Witness
witness.blackmountaininstitute.org
witnessmagazine.submittable.com
　/submit
Editor in Chief: Xueyi Zhou
Biannual

The Worcester Review
www.theworcesterreview.org
theworcesterreview.submittable
　.com/submit
Editor: Carolyn Oliver
Annual

Workers Write!
www.workerswritejournal.com
info@workerswritejournal.com
Editor: David LaBounty
Annual

World Literature Today
www.worldliteraturetoday.org
worldliteraturetoday.submittable
　.com/submit
Editor in Chief: Daniel Simon
Bimonthly

X-R-A-Y
xraylitmag.com
xray.submittable.com/submit
Editor: Jennifer Greidus

The Yale Review
yalereview.org
theyalereview.submittable.com
　/submit
Editor: Meghan O'Rourke
Quarterly

Yellow Medicine Review
www.yellowmedicinereview.com
editor@yellowmedicinereview.com
Executive Editor: Judy Wilson
Semiannual

Zoetrope: All-Story
www.all-story.com
Not currently accepting
 submissions
Editor: Michael Ray
Quarterly

Zone 3
zone3press.com
ceca.submittable.com/submit
Fiction Editor: R. S. Deeren
Biannual

ZYZZYVA
www.zyzzyva.org
57 Post Street, Suite 708
San Francisco, CA 94104
Editor: Oscar Villalon
Triannual

Permissions

Grateful acknowledgment is made to the following for permission to reprint previously published materials:

"The Stackpole Legend" first appeared in *The Threepenny Review*. Copyright © 2024 by Wendell Berry. Reprinted by permission of the author.

"The Arrow" first appeared in *One Story* and subsequently published in *Green Frog: Stories*. Copyright © 2024 by Gina Chung. Used by permission of Vintage Books, an imprint of the Knopf Doubleday Publishing Group, a division of Penguin Random House LLC, and the author. All rights reserved.

"That Girl" first appeared in *The New Yorker*. Copyright © 2024 by Addie Citchens. Reprinted by permission of the author.

"The Pleasure of a Working Life" first appeared in *Harper's Magazine*. Copyright © 2024 by Michael Deagler. Reprinted by permission of the author.

"Blackbirds" first appeared in *Colorado Review*. Copyright © 2023 by Lindsey Drager. Reprinted by permission of the author.

"Hearing Aids" first appeared in *Oxford American*. Copyright © 2023 by Clyde Edgerton. Reprinted by permission of the author.

"Sanrevelle" first appeared in *The Georgia Review*. Copyright © 2024 by Dave Eggers. Reprinted by permission of the author.

"Stump of the World" first appeared in *The Paris Review*. Copyright © 2023 by Madeline ffitch. Reprinted by permission of the author.

"Shotgun Calypso" first appeared in *A Public Space*. Copyright © 2023 by Indya Finch. Reprinted by permission of the author.

"City Girl" first appeared in *Harvard Review*. Copyright © 2024 by Alice Hoffman. Reprinted by permission of the author.

"Sickled" first appeared in *American Short Fiction*. Copyright © 2024 by Jane Kalu. Reprinted by permission of the author.

"The Spit of Him" first appeared in *The New Yorker*. Copyright © 2024 by Thomas Korsgaard. Reprinted by permission of the author and the translator. Translated by Martin Aitken.

"Winner" first appeared in *The Yale Review*'s December 2023 issue. Copyright © 2023 by Ling Ma. Reprinted by permission of the author.

"Countdown" first appeared in *Zoetrope*. Copyright © 2024 by Anthony Marra. Reprinted by permission of the author.

"Just Another Family" first appeared in *New England Review* (2023) and subsequently published in *Are You Happy?* (2025).

Copyright © 2023 by Lori Ostlund. Used by permission of Astra Publishing House and the author. All rights reserved.

"Mornings at the Ministry" first appeared in *Ploughshares*. Copyright © 2024 by Ehsaneh Sadr. Reprinted by permission of the author.

"Rosaura at Dawn" first appeared in *The Yale Review*. Copyright © 2024 by Daniel Saldaña París. Reprinted by permission of the author and the translator. Translated by Christina MacSweeney.

"Three Niles" first appeared in *The Kenyon Review*. Copyright © 2023 by Zak Salih. Reprinted by permission of the author.

"Strange Fruit" first appeared in *Southern Humanities Review*. Copyright © 2024 by Yah Yah Scholfield. Reprinted by permission of the author.

"Miracle in Lagos Traffic" first appeared in *Michigan Quarterly Review*. Copyright © 2024 by Chika Unigwe. Reprinted by permission of the author.